Nabile Fares

Discovery of the New World

The Olive Grove
Memory and the Missing
Exile and Helplessness

Translated and Annotated by
Peter Thompson

Preface by
Pierre Joris

DIÁLOGOS
NEW ORLEANS

Discovery of the New World:
The Olive Grove
Memory of the Missing
Exile and Helplessness
Nabile Farès
Translated by Peter Thompson

Cover art: The calligramme on the cover is a facsmile of the
original typewriter art by the author. The image originally
appeared on the cover of *L'Exil et le désarroi* (François Maspero: Paris. 1976).
A translation of the calligramme appears on page iv.

Printed in the U.S.A.
First Printing
10 9 8 7 6 5 4 3 2 1   20 21 22 23 24 25

Library of Congress Control Number: 2020950479
Farès, Nabile
Discovery of the New World / Nabile Farès;
with Peter Thompson (translator; introduction)
and Pierre Joris (preface)

p. cm.
ISBN: 978-1-944884-90-1

DIÁLOGOS
dialogosbooks.com

ACKNOWLEDGMENTS

Discovery of the New World is a translation and collection of a trilogy of novels, originally published in France as follows:

La Découverte du nouveau monde:
Vol. I, *Le Champ des oliviers*, Editions du Seuil, 1972
Vol. II, *Mémoire de l'Absent*, Editions du Seuil, 1974
Vol. III, *L'Exil et le désarroi*, Librairie François Maspero, 1976

Peter Thompson's translation of *L'Exil et le désarroi* was previously published by Diálogos as *Exile and Helplessness* in 2012. The other two volumes appear here for the first time in English. Diálogos is grateful to Editions du Seuil, Librairie François Maspero, and the heirs of Nabile Farès for permission to publish this collection.

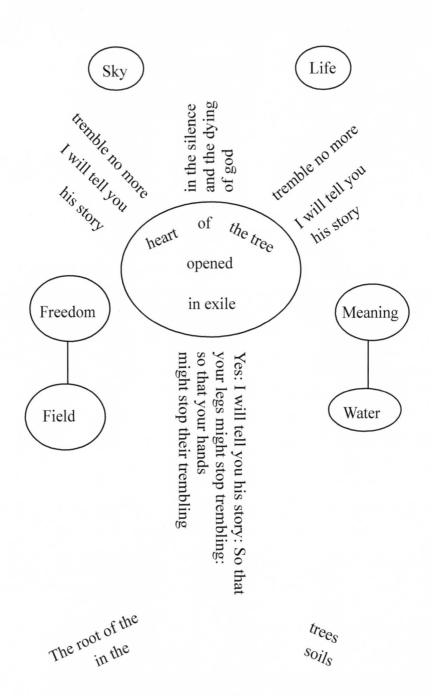

Sky

Life

tremble no more
I will tell you
his story

in the silence
and the dying
of god

tremble no more
I will tell you
his story

heart   of   the tree
opened

in exile

Freedom

Meaning

Field

Water

Yes: I will tell you his story: So that
your legs might stop trembling:
so that your hands
might stop their trembling

The root of the
in the

trees
soils

DISCOVERY OF THE NEW WORLD

The Olive Grove

Memory and the Missing

Exile and Helplessness

TRANSLATOR'S NOTE

Peter Thompson

Nabile Farès was a Kabyle, a Berber, and one who spoke Berber before he spoke Arabic or French—one who wrote throughout his life about Kabylia and its Berber stronghold. In fact his doctoral thesis centered on the figure of the Ogress in Berber folklore. It is worth noting that Kabylia is one part of Algeria never fully subdued by Arab or French invaders.

This ethnologist, philosopher, dramaturge, poet, novelist and psychoanalyst was born in Collo (Kabylia peninsula) in 1940. Thus he was a teenager at the time of the student demonstrations and the reciprocal massacres (French forces and settlers versus the Algerians) which began the Algerian War (the war of independence, 1954-62).

Farès's father, Abderrahmane Farès (an administrator who became head of the provisional government after independence), sent him to France to study—and to be safe. Towards the end of the war, Nabile was one of the few Algerian students in Paris to choose to return to the struggle. He was on the east side of the Tunisian border—where FLN (National Liberation Front and their army) camps operated—when the war ended. A rich footnote to this era is that Farès carried the manuscript of *Yahia, Pas de chance*, his first novel, through France and North Africa in his back pack. *Yahia* was published in 1970.

Many Algerian writers saw the next years—eventually spanning decades—as a disappointment, then a betrayal. The victorious FLN became a one-party government, and a repressive one at that. The silencing of voices, an "Arabization" policy (Berbers are not Arabs), the discouragement of the French language, corruption, cronyism, authoritative Islam, and the receding of traditional (Berber) feminine roles are among the exactions that drove Mohammed Dib, Assia Djebar, Rachid Boudjedra, Farès and Kateb Yacine—among others—into exile. Worst was a collusion with neocolonial business interests (sharply outlined in Farès's *Un Passager de L'Occident*, translated as *A Passenger From the West*), and, as a dark corner within the arch of this French shadow, the adoption of French torture techniques against insurgents. All this kept most writers—some of whom, like Farès, could no longer publish in Algeria—in France. Most of this group died in the exile that became an indelible mark of their work (particularly Farès's novels and poetry). Farès died in Paris in August, 2016—recently married, having taught in Grenoble, founded a theater in Aix, received the Kateb Yacine Prize for lifetime achievement (1994), and provided psychoanalysis for years—often helping immigrants with their trauma.

During his student years he switched his "second" language (a diploma requirement, and really the third, after Berber and French) from Arabic to English. This is significant in two ways. First, it perhaps asserted the resentment many Berbers feel about the Arab invasions and dominance in North Africa. Secondly, novels in English—specifically American ones—were an element in his artistic development. [We add, here, that Farès's English ability made him a lively and involved partner in the translation of his work.] Erskine Caldwell and Faulkner were especially influential. This influence was also felt by Farès's contemporaries, including the (somewhat earlier) foundational group of Djebar, Dib, Kateb, Mouloud Feraoun and Mouloud Mammeri. Emmanuel Levinas, whom Farès met in his student years, was important to him, as was the novelist Witold Gombrowicz.

Another influence was the Moroccan, Abdelkébir Khatibi, Farès's contemporary and a friend. Khatibi's experiment with his "*bi-langue*," a permanent tension between languages (as a result of colonialism), was the model for a creative, non-dogmatic, ontological sense of possibilities for the writer in the postcolonial age. What Farès did with this shows less tension in every line (in the novels), but adopts a similar sense of fragmentation in both poetic image and plot: a personal identity in flux, a language and identity always self-defining in terms of an Other, yet not an identity in crisis or political revolt. The constant influence of the Other is the alterity ("*altérité*") central to many studies of Farès, including Mohammed-Saâd Zemmouri's extended work, *La Dialectique de l'identité* and his article "La Passsion de l'altérité chez l'écrivain Nabile Farès." As a literary preoccupation it also derives from phenomenology, from Heidegger, Merleau-Ponty and Sartre, and from their influence on many writers of the 1950s and 1960s, including the French *Nouveau Roman* (New Novel) group. In the latter group Claude Ollier made a profound impression on Farès. His *La Mise en scène* is set in Morocco, and his *Le Maintien de l'ordre* has a nameless setting but is based on French repression in Algeria.

As with much of modern poetry—as with the Hegelian dialectic that the Surrealists invoked in their definition of poetic image—Farès developed (in his protagonists) a dialectical approach to identity. Beyond that, and before examining it further, we note that he "deterritorialized" his protagonists, in the Deleuzian sense (*Yahia, A Passenger From the West, L'Exil et le désarroi*—the latter translated as *Exile and Helplessness,* the present Volume III). Their complex identities evolve as a function (with positive and creative quantities in the mix) of separation from homeland and mother tongue. The "New World" in his trilogy *La Découverte du nouveau monde,* and James Baldwin's coming to Paris "from the West" (*Passenger*), structurally serve this purpose in the novels. With the topic of exile so prominent, it is remarkable—and constantly rewarding for the reader—that we learn so much in addition about Algeria and its history (*The Olive Grove, Exile and Helplessness*).

The complex issues of identity in the modern world—but also in the exile of the postcolonial context—have been given special emphasis by Deleuze and Guattari (in *Mille Plateaux, A Thousand Plateaus*). Their sense of identity (an exiled Algerian would be an example) as a "minoritarian" identity, as a project of *becoming*, is a broad avenue for understanding Farès's poetry (particularly *Escuchando tu historia*, translated as *Hearing Your Story,* and *L'Exil au féminin*, translated as *Exile: Women's Turn*), along with the characters in the novels (the trilogy, *Passenger, Yahia, Exile and Helplessness*). Réda Bensmaïa's chapter in *Experimental Nations* is particularly helpful on exile and "minoritarian" identity. Valérie Orlando's chapter in *The Algerian New Novel* is the other extensive scholarly piece available in English. The prefaces to all the English translations are useful (the very recent work, published to acclaim in Algeria, is not translated)—especially Bensmaïa's introduction in *Hearing Your Story* and Pierre Joris's in *A Passenger From the West.*

Concerning the Translation

My original note for Volume III, published in 2012, was brief:

This is the third volume of Farès's moving trilogy, *La Découverte du nouveau monde*. The road to its publication and translation was not without adventure. It has a different shape, in several ways, from that of *Le Champ des oliviers* and *La Mémoire de l'absent.* More singularly, it is one of the (few) great feminist texts to arise from the Arab world. Its feminism is on a level with the courage and respect developed in Abdelkébir Khatibi's and Rita El Khayat's letters, in their great epistolary work *Open Correspondence.*

One of the bridges this volume crossed was the question of the next book—after *Hearing Your Story* and *A Passenger from The West*—to bring into the English-speaking world. Farès and I discussed this over a period of three years. I am very grateful for these conversations, for Corsican wine, for his blessing, and for his patience in many, many things. Of course, I am most grateful for the anguish and poetry of this unusual text.

To this I should add that Farès and I struggled over the title for this volume. Nothing elegant arose in the English, until he drew on his psychoanalytic training and suggested the term "hilflosigkeit,"—helplessness. A profound element of his own exile and of his therapeutic work with immigrants.

The preface by my distinguished colleague is an essential insight into Farès and this great work. My thoughts about his writing have, in any case, appeared in the other translated volumes of his poetry and prose. For those interested in the translation itself, my ideas about that process appear in the issue of *Expressions Maghrébines* ("Translation and Alterity," in volume 17, number 2) dedicated to Farès, and in the book of homage published in Algeria in 2019, *Nabile Farès—Un Passager entre la lettre et la parole* (article, "Une Traduction"). My interview with Farès (*Crisolenguas,*

2008) begins the acquaintance that became a friendship, and initiates our collaboration on translation.

The title of the second volume is adventurous but in keeping with the several types of absence and memory that are the subject matter and medium of the book. The neologisms, inconsistencies, indentations and spacing belong—as does the joyful generosity of translation itself—to the author.

It remains to thank Bensmaïa and Orlando for encouragement. Also instrumental were Roger Williams University, the epochal vision of William Lavender and Diálogos Books, the profound Pierre Joris, and the elegant editorial touch of Anna Bliss.

Kateb Yacine is the chronological and esthetic preface to most of North African writing in French. I think Farès, who won the Kateb Yacine Prize in 1994, would be glad of this further introduction (from *Le Polygone étoilé*) not only to the weave of his themes but to the modern Algeria of his exile years:

> *Toute guerre est un héritage*
> *Et seuls nos pères décapités*
> *Se disputent le ciel*
> *Tandis que leurs lignées*
> *Pour les voir se confondent*
> *Jusqu'à ne plus connaître leur emblème*

> Every war is heritage
> And only our decapitated forbears
> Argue over heaven
> While their descendants,
> To make them out, mix
> Till they know not their heraldry

—Peter Thompson

PREFACE

Pierre Joris

Being is not given in midstream. Man is a migration.
—Nabile Farès

The first thing that hits me every time I open or reopen one of Nabile Farès' books is the immediacy of the intense struggle— simultaneously, the glorious success— of a text that stays at white heat by bending/bedding itself between what some would call the "genres" of poetry & prose. But that concept of "genre" can come only for such a text *after* the fact of the writing and is thus as an imposition (often by the publisher who thinks that a book categorized as "roman / novel" will automatically sell more than one called "poésie / poetry.") In this case a more interesting distinction is the one Mohammed Dib, Nabile Farès's elder by twenty years, once provided by dividing North African literature into two camps: the *imperial-classical* and the *anarchic-romantic,* the latter the product of what he called cryptostasis, or "history's shadow." The imperial-classical would be the one into which most authors fell who wrote in Arabic, the supposedly traditional language of North African islamo-arabic culture, which the victorious post-independence governments exerted much effort to impose on the newly liberated country. The literature thus produced is in the main stilted & not memorable. Those in Dib's anarcho-romantic camp are those writers who decided to keep using the old colonial language, French, while bending it to their anarchic needs (language-wise, at least, even if the powers that be would often also designate them as such, politically speaking). Farès is clearly central to this tradition— a tradition that further often arises from or is at least culturally and politically conscious of the fact that Arabic, as Kateb Yacine pointed out, was just another colonial imposition that had been suppressing the autochthonous Amazigh cultures and languages for a millennium and more. And that as Kateb also pointed out, the Algerians had won their War of Independence against the France and thus French was rightfully theirs— as the spoils of war.

Nabile Farès' trajectory shows how it could not be otherwise: born in 1940 in Collo, Little Kabylia, to a prominent family of Berber origins (grandfather was a notary, father an important political figure) he took part in high school strikes in 1956, then joined the FLN— the National Liberation Front— and the ALN— the National Liberation Army. In 1962, after Algeria had won its independence, he moved to France, the manuscript toward his first novel in his satchel, to do graduate work in philosophy, literature, & ethnology. He taught literature in Paris, Algiers & was Professor for Comparative Literature at the University of Grenoble before starting a career as a psychoanalyst in Paris where he died in 2016.

Still, writing had always been the center and what I keep hearing as I read his books is a fierce request to witness: to witness history in the making, specifically the history of Algeria as he lived it as both actor and witness from the colonial days of his childhood through the struggle for liberation and on to the tragic *rigor morti*s the once revolutionary political power group fell into over time. But the work can in no way be reduced to "historical" novels or fiction, in that the implication of the writer is total, as actor, human & historian. Farès, to me, represents the writer-as-historian much as the American poet Charles Olson had tried to define and emulate him: not as post-fact outside observer-scholar or fictioneer, often in the pay (actual or symbolic) of the victorious party, but as one who, following the Greek etymology of the term "istorin," acts to *find out for oneself*. Quoting Bertolt Brecht in *The Olive Orchard* to the effect that "history is written *after* the catastrophes," Farès is aware that he is and has to remain implicated at every level in the events— and that this also includes shouldering the responsibility (qua "ability to respond") of being critical, of not allowing himself to act as a supposedly "objective *post facto* bystander." The revolution does not end with the victory of independence, but has to continue in(to) the daily life of both society and self. (If he were still with us, Farès would love the current popular uprisings and demonstrations against the tottering regime of an alzheimerian FLN). This is evident from his earliest books on, with their core-themes of rebellion against the established or re-imposed religious traditions and the newly formed conventions of Algeria since independence. His first novel, *Yahia, pas de chance* (published in 1970; "Yahia, No Chance") introduced a quest that was to haunt his later works, including *La D*écouverte du nouveau monde ("The Discovery of the New World"), the trilogy underhand: the search for the self takes him back to his childhood, and further still, to the pre-Islamic voices of inspiration tied to the earth and the Amazigh cultures that arose from this earth.

I have written elsewhere about the linguistic complexities that haunt the work of the post-independence generations of Maghrebi writers, showing— in the work of Abdelwahab Meddeb, Habib Tengour, Driss Chraïbi or Abdelkebir Khatibi—how their French is haunted, or better, ghosted by the spoken mother-tongue, Arabic, and in the case of the Amazigh among them, also by their Berber language. These nomadic moves, through these various layers of spoken and written language, make for a writerly consciousness that is both playful and deeply aware of the elasticity and limits of its medium. Farès, maybe more than most, is able to play with— dismantle and reassemble, twist and reorder, mirror and disfigure— the various elements, modes and levels of language, from word-etymologies to puns, from syntax to punctuation. Permit me to quote a piece I wrote some years ago, for no other reason than that the pleasure of reading Farès had, as it does so often, made me pull out a notebook and start writing. It may help not only to explicate the difficulties the translator of Farès comes up against—brilliantly handled, I believe, by Peter Thompson in the book at hand—, but also to illustrate this lushness of the writing as well as the sardonically comic play that may be all too easily missed in the language's layered or in-folded complexities. I am rereading *Le Champ des Oliviers / The Olive Orchard* sitting in a café in Paris years before it was translated:

When I read I translate (we all do this, though mainly into "sense," our sense, taking it away from language) but I am afflicted: I (also) translate as I read into other languages, into English in this case as the original text is in French (well, at least on the surface: it is traversed by Kabyle Berber and Arabic, or those are its basement vaults, its subterranean blood circulation systems, waterways, canalizations, rhizomatic networks— like the ancient irrigation systems spreading the water welling up from a deep source in the desert into a network that becomes oasis lushness, which is how I see Maghrebian literature as the lushness of writing in the contemporary desert of French literature— as both necessary irrigation and irritation).

And this French text is exhilarating again this morning, translating immediately (well, no, I stop & search for the English words, but I'm not "really" translating yet, I am not writing it down, it is only a part of my "reading" of Farès' text) thus immediately haltingly or haltingly immediately into some sort of English that I may or may not ever write down as a translation.—Interjection: no more need to even think of doing that: what you are holding in your hands, dear reader, is the excellent translation of these novels by Peter Thompson, done since that rereading some years ago—. I order another coffee ("an elongated coffee," un café allongé, i.e. the waiter will bring the little espresso / harsh, over-roasted, certainly not the "pure Arabica" it would claim to be if I had the folly of asking after its origins / in a larger cup accompanied by a little silver pitcher of hot water with which I'll "elongate" the beverage)— an excuse, somewhere, somehow, subconsciously, to be able to lay the book down a minute, take off my glasses, eyes smart, rub them, look across the street, at the sky, still blue, but not a Mediterranean blue here in the pays d'oïl, relax the sight, but the translation machine keeps churning, I am thinking of the paragraph just read, it has the word bikini in it twice, & it should be easy to translate—but I'm not sure that it is in fact, there must be more going on here for Farès to insist on the word, putting it into caps the second time around: BIKINI. The coffee comes, I irrigate the stingy espresso with a flow of hot water, now no more need to add sugar, sip some, return to the book. Here are the sentences I've been thinking about:

Siamois II remet ses frusques. Un bikini grandeur majuscules: BIKINI. Un tricot de peau assorti aux sourcils: brousailleux.

Which, fairly straightforwardly translates as:

Siamese II puts his gear back on. A bikini of capital size: BIKINI. An undershirt matching the eyebrows: bushy, tousled.

But why, why would this weird & hilarious character (who of course has a double in the book, called Siamese I) wear a bikini. I cannot figure it out either in French or in English. What can he mean? Could it be a reference of some sort to the Bikini Islands? Nope. Just a sort of fun play on making the smallest piece of vestment women wear large, larger? A capital tiny bikini? There is nothing so far in the text that would make the "Siamese II" character a woman anyway. A transvestite? A cultural travesty of some order? All I can hear is the "bik" which could possibly go to ballpoint, in French "un bic," the writer's instrument.

Can't find it. Finish coffee, go home. Locate texts on Farès—my luck, the first one I come to cites an interview with Farès speaking about exactly these lines, this word. Farès explains to a bemused interviewer (who had also thought of the ballpoint pen!):

Take for example what I write there in caps I AM A BIKINI There it is, written in large letters. Why do you laugh? It is one of the most important things in the book, this word BIKINI that makes you laugh!

Go further: the French call us "bicots," "bics" [~ "dirty Arabs", contemp. US "towelheads", maybe closer to the n-word] I am "un bic qui nie..." / a "bic" who says no. I refuse to be a "bic"! I refuse to be subjected to the racism of the language of the French...

Untranslatable. Of course. But also, I submit, untranslatable for the French reader. Who, I am sure, will not be able to read the pun in this word any better than an English speaker. So it will be translated as bikini. A funny, startling but incomprehensible island in the language sea of Farès' narrative.

Peter Thompson also left it as BIKINI, but that is the fate of the translator: to know that some things you see or can uncover in the text you cannot get over when the original has the complexities of the enriched "French" of the great Maghrebian authors. Another Algerian, the poet and novelist Habib Tengour, wondered about this North African complex identity in one of his essays, thus:

Who is this Maghrebian? How to define him?

"The woods are white or black despite the hidden presence of nuances.

Today definition fascinates because of its implications. A domain that misleads. Political jealousy far from the exploded sense of the real.

Indeed there exists a divided space called the Maghreb but the Maghrebian is always elsewhere. And that's where he makes himself come true.

Jugurtha lacked money to buy Rome.

Tariq gave his name to a Spanish mountain.

Ibn Khaldûn found himself obliged to give his steed to Tamerlane.

Abd El Krim corresponded with the Third International....

And Nabile Farès tried—& I believe, succeeded—in getting all those complexities into his oeuvre. Now read this book.

—Pierre Joris
Bay Ridge, Brooklyn
June 2020

THE OLIVE GROVE

VOLUME I OF THE TRILOGY

DISCOVERY OF THE NEW WORLD

TRANSLATION OF *LE CHAMP DES OLIVIERS*

VOL. I, *LA DÉCOUVERTE DU NOUVEAU MONDE*

BY NABILE FARÈS, SEUIL, 1972

TRANSLATED AND ANNOTATED BY
PETER THOMPSON

To Pierre Kaufman
and François Bott,
this dedication and this book.

PART ONE

The Ogress Whose Name Is Obscure

When the time came for her to deliver, she withdrew to the most hidden room and surrounded herself with doctors and diviners. And they began to whisper. Important men entered the home with sober expressions and came back out pale, with an air of worry. And the price of fine white face powder doubled in the beauty shops. In the streets the people gathered, and waited from morning till night, their stomachs hollowed.

The first sound to come forth was that of a tremendous fart shaking the timbers of the house, followed by a great shout, '*Peace*,' followed in turn by a growing stench. Immediately, blood sprang forth in a watery trickle. And then came an interminable series of other noises, each more frightening than the last.

Great Babylon vomited and they thought they heard '*Liberty*,' she coughed, and they thought it was '*Justice*.' She farted once again, and they took it for '*Prosperity*.' Then, wrapped in a bloody sheet, carried out to the balcony and shown to the masses as bells tolled—a kid whose squalling was *War*.

And a thousand were its fathers.

From *Unpublished Stories*
Bertolt Brecht (L'Arche Editions)

"Being is not simply granted, as you walk your road," Amin, the Old Teacher, used to say. *"Man is an arrangement. A migration, in this world."*

I

Origins

I...... 8:57 at night. February 8, 1971. Track 10. A train leaves Paris, headed for Barcelona. My garnet-colored suitcase (Brandy Fax speaking, also writing, reading, staring, living, weeping, longing, puking, also…) carries within it some red wool pants, a shirt, five pounds of oranges, a carton of cigarettes, briefs, a pair of shoes. A chunk of Paris, Three Books. One of these treats primitive societies. The suburban trains (Brandy Fax observing) (Brandy Fax is the name I've given myself in order to fully sketch out (me, a primitive from the Old World) the framed panorama of Westernness: that edge between two worlds) sport strange, glowing signals as, switching tracks, they branch off from the Main Lines and veer toward the tenements you see (Brandy Fax here) all lighted up like radios. His right hand (Brandy Fax is writing this) rests on the cover of a paperback. Entitled *The Steppes*. Followed by other accounts. He gazes through windows above the tracks (Brandy Fax doing the looking) and his image trembles, his forehead furrowed like autumn land waiting to be plowed. He's not on the platform. But on the train, on a train that doubles his body with a rail reality, a real reality. He's alone. The compartment is Deluxe Second Class. Where he can read or write under a white fluorescent light. The SNCF blankets are merely part of a universe run through with power lines that bring the night right up to your eye. The impossible winter nights are beginning their hellish rounds (Brandy Fax thinks about the two freezing months he's just spent in Paris with the most astounding person[1] it had ever been his fate to encounter) while the SNCF conductors fret over this passenger who fills a solitary compartment with pen, notebook, volume. "Yes." "That will take you a while?" is asked. Who's asking? Who asks? "A while of what?" One could say? A long time of what? Of launching words into the air? (Brandy

---

1   It is possible this is James Baldwin; their acquaintance lasted a few months, and had just happened. Farès's adjective, "*terrible*," can be both positive and negative. This episode occurs in *A Passenger from the West* (1971).

Fax's own culture is one of orality.) But he says. Brandy Fax. He says. To keep on being what in fact he is. He says. "No, I don't have much more to do. An hour or two. I don't know. Maybe I'll stay all night. My night." "OK. OK. We'll decide later. You have a berth?" "Yes. And more... my couchette is number 45." The conductors leave. Night waxes around the train while the billboards retreat from the tracks, toward the roads, lobbing flashes (sharp) of white light across my eyes. This is his third trip to Barcelona and he, Brandy Fax the Fifth ( ) ( ) has put aside what he wanted to write[2] about one of the most central figures North Africa had ever known. The O... A doubt persists. This dissertation on the meaning of a rare Ogress, little known in Europe, will never get anywhere (where) (see the light of day) (night) (perhaps not) (?) (Who knows?) Obsession? The slow task of remorse, as the poet said (You'll devote the bulk of your time to obsession) Obsession! The quality of the works that arise from it. May obsession go fuck itself along with all its creations. "That'll take you a while?" I've seen it all. An hour or two. I've seen it all. And I'm leaving. Me. Brandy Fax ( ) ( ) For Barcelona. As I'm leaving I think "*I must have been a victim (I am a victim) of a global thought. Not mine. But one belonging to everyone else. Everyone who wanted to keep me under the ground. Down in the barely reachable loci of mystery. (rarely visited). (of mystery) The mystery of my eloquence. This eloquence that has (already) run me through a good many wars.*" Yes. Who can speak about an Ogress without having one. On top of the ability (that faculty!) to avoid the all-consuming work on the Ogress. Certain artistic gifts. Utterly artistic. Scientific, even. Because I'm a scientist. Me. Brandy Fax ( ) ( ). I'm sewn together from all the cloaks of science, scientificness. And the audience was huge. Hardly smaller than a movie's. They wanted the movie version. Probably. Thought they were going to see a movie. I stepped forth. But not at all as they had wished. And such is, was, the Truth the Irony of this question "*What do I signify? Me? The Ogress of Obscure Name...*" since I've spoken of a being whose reality everyone knows or suspects and yet who doesn't exist. Enigma! Yes. Enigma. The Ogress doesn't exist. She

---

2   Farès's Sorbonne dissertation, the doctorate referred to here, had the Ogress as a focus: *L'Ogresse dans la littérature orale berbère*. As with the subject of the previous note, many of Brandy Fax's data refer inarguably to Farès's life. His creation of the particular pseudonym has been treated by several researchers.

doesn't exist. *"Like a railroad A house A tree Power lines A traveler A fluorescent light A tangerine A cigarette A cigarette butt A glance A star A thought A book A conductor An Austerlitz Station A month A day A February An omelet A winter Paris A nice hot shower Peanuts A typewriter A night of love A doctorate A backyard A Monsieur-le-Prince Street*[3] *A Metro ticket A bus An espresso A few bad days A meal at Claude's A brawl Private lessons An OK Bar A pimp's life Pastis drinks Pastis drinks triple strength Brown hands Potatoes Ragouts Potato ragouts A manuscript A railroad crossing"* Yes. The Ogress exists. *"Not so. Like this phone booth This phone Where this Call comes from."* Yes. My love. From so far away. From that space you grew up in. Mine. Independently of this world. There where you were led before coming into this world. *"Not so. Like a slice of brie. A desire to wolf food A cold night An explosion A brain blowing up A bomb..."* The instant you were coming into the world. Into the world's war. The war of all worlds. In all the world's streets. *"Not so. Like ID cards Visas Registration cards Passports Piles of passports Customs booths Groceries Grocery accounts Bogus jobs Gas stations University research Empty stomachs..."* Yes. The Ogress exists for those who. *"Not at all. Like a skirt. A glass of wine A glass of nothing An odor of... A scent of breast A scent of wheat A scent of sperm A scent of bread A scent of cream A scent of milk A scent of leg A scent of neck A scent of legs around my neck A scent of ocean A scent of piss A scent of white A scent of..."* Yes. Over and above the murders I might have committed. In the back and forth of different eras. While. Here. In the negligent word reading writing of your moment. I progress. Underpinning. In this youthful industry where your time and its creation burgeons. Thus it's called. Dawn's ensemble. Thus it is named. Where there came. With a savor of seaweed and furtive moray eels. Like any greeting you might give. That you thought you could give to your other self. Who. In a first unknowing move might invite you. You. Bruised by the first day. *"A man who runs A bullet seeking A town crumbling A man dying A train fleeing A town dying A calf at teat A woman on her deathbed."* "No. Leave it. I don't sleep that much at night." The compartment is off now. A black light inside. While. Beyond the windows. There flows. Shivering. A sweet and slumbering land. A countryside where

---

3   This was the address of Farès's principal apartment at the time—Paris.

seeps a dream of a place where the man… Light clouds. Milky. Where darker sky pokes through here and there. While before the fields. Towards the hedgerows. And the groves. Near the farms where no light wanders. I divine. Me. Brandy Fax ( ) ( ). The presence of several characters from old tales. Yes. The Ogress exists. Sweet land where man learns the fullness of gesture. Of his place. Of his displacement. Where life is a law of presence. Where the reaches once they're surveyed push fear away. Intimate. The fear of oneself. The fear of the utter abandonment of self. Fear of dereliction of the self. Fear of being duped. And, at the same time. Joy of a world eluding itself. With play of universal limbs. Yes. The Ogress exists. And yet she lacks the reality of a wooden match a cigarette a bike a Citroen a barbecue a tire chain a highway a caravel a jar of mustard a parking lot a hairdresser a supermarket a pipeline a steamboat a tractor a church a cathedral a Boeing a presbytery an Inox an ocean liner a cigarette lighter a museum a van full of cops a moped a Renault Dauphine an airport a microphone a runway a safari a carbine a Mauser a bazooka a tank a blockhaus a machine gun mad genitals mad bullets streaming toward mad bodies bodies falling hands burning skin burning faces burning : "*Napalm, Lahyachi shouted. Napalm. The refugees will be here any minute.*" Those who yell And ask And speechify And pant And swear And Insult And yell And who die *Why? Why?* Yes. The Ogress exists. The town of Limoges. At midnight. Nobody on the station platforms. Only the cold. A cold that makes your fingernails stand out. (I'm eating a French loaf that costs 15 cents and an orange.) The sign for Millevaches. A seven-minute stop. Deep inside. Light veiled by fog. The signs for a bar-buffet that's empty. I'm alone. Notebook and pen in my pocket. Brandy Fax is wearing a tie and his border-crossing jacket. His stomach is cramping. There are times when his stomach cramps up. Border crossings have always given him stomach cramps. He recalls. How it was. In the year 1c-1.[4] As he was coming back from Morocco. And was stopped at the Bourg-Madame crossing by a border guard. And was taken. Well after the *national liberty of his country*, to the back room of a police station. There where they registered. Still register. The identities of all who will cross the border. Have crossed. Must

---

4   1963 or 1964. Farèsian obscurity of an unusual type. It is possible that he designates the first year of Independence this way.

cross. A frontier post. Yes. Not more than two years after the independence of his country. But he had to believe. Accept it as true. That the news of this independence of his country had not reached the frontier post of Bourg-Madame. Because he was led away. Machine gun bouncing on a stomach. A fee demanded just to really cramp up the stomach. Then his back. At the back of the identity card room. They told him to respond. Yes. To respond. If he was in fact the son of a father, Ab...[5] and a mother A... And he had to reply. To say. "Yes. They've already come through here? To Bourg-Madame?" And they told him to keep quiet. Keep quiet. Because. It seems. With identity papers in hand. I mean. That he was a deserter. It would seem. These identity papers somewhat washed out. I mean to say. And dating from. Clearly. From two years before the independence of his country. An identity card he was astonished to see there. In a frontier post. Where he'd shown up. For the first time. The very first time. In those days. He never went through border crossings. He was living in Paris. Yes. In those days. And went all through the streets. Boulevards. Avenues. In search of his real identity. His real identities. They'd told him his real identity was in the process of being created. Across there.[6] In the mountains of his country. And then. Also. Here. In the streets of Germany. In the streets of Italy. The streets of Europe. Lovely Europe. Whose Metros he knew so well. Whose waiting rooms. Suburban trains. Hotels. So then he had accepted the creation of his identity. Because *"it's so comforting to believe; to be able to believe; in a weak moment; or a strong one; that you might be; that you have the right to be; yes; the very author of your birth. That your birth is not meaningless. That it counts for something in people's lives. In the life of the world. In the life of the stars. In the Earth's life. The clouds' life. The sand's life. In life yes IN life. That your birth is not in the least a mystery, nor misfortune. No. It is birth. Birth pure and simple. And that it's there. In you. All through you. In your bed. In your sheets. In your limbs. In your thoughts. Your underwear. Your writing. Your sink. In your vertebrae. In your toes. In your hands. In your nerves. In your gums. In your teeth. In your piss. In your happiness. In everything. All through you. It was so comforting to think. To be able thus to think. To be the author of*

5   In Farès's case, Abderrahmane—at that moment the provisional head of the Algerian government.

6   Algeria; the assertion, as often with Farès, is an attack on state pronouncements.

your birth." That's what they had told me. And I had accepted it, believed that I could be the author of my birth. And the customs officer had approached to announce. Just like that. From the depths of an ID office. That I had no nationality. But that, even so, I was a Deserter. Yes. A Deserter. Me. Brandy Fax. ( ) ( ). Deserter in the year 1960. I knew well, that, back home. At the very moment that everyone aspired to a nationality. Nobody had understood you can belong to a history. That you could be a deserter from something. From some law. Some life. No. They held us suspended. We've always been suspended among several histories and several lives. Without any *true* belonging. And now I was a deserter. "By what order. I'm asking you. Since when. Would I be a deserter. Have you ever recognized. Or said to me. A single time? A single time, who I was? Where I came from? Who I came from? Among all your drafts of history? And now, I'm a deserter? By what law? A law that might have actually recognized me? Me? The child of the waysides. The one they gave a name to, without naming his name. Ill-timed, any asshole who might try to tell me who I'm *really* from. "You should have done your military service" the border guard said. And me, not really a speaker of border guard language. "But, tell me, *news*? News? It doesn't get as far as Bourg-Madame? It never gets here?" "This card of yours is really old. I mean really old." In two years. I. Brandy Fax ( ) ( ) have changed nationality three times. So this ID card you insist on. Which dates back four years. Me. Brandy Fax. I say. Very simply. It's false. It's a completely false one. As to this military service. You understand. This depends on where you were born. And I. I just don't care about the service. It's meaningless for me. I was born far across from Lovely Europe.[7] By the sea. I love it there. Although. Ever since my cousins started to emigrate. I've been a bit sad. As if they'd scraped the sand clean. There. Yes there. Right under my feet. That's why it's so hard to believe *Really Believe* in a single identity card. So you'll easily understand that… The border guard and his machine gun, minus safety catch. They could just go fuck themselves over these four years. I was worried. But also at ease. All those four years. "I'm going to go check at the government office in Perpignan." Right. "Go check. Me. I'm having

---

7   This scene prefigures, more than anything in Farès's first two novels, his life-long formulations of "identity." It is a distinct source for a similar scene in Réda Bensmaïa's *L'Année des passages* (1997; translated as *The Year of Passages*).

lunch." A border guard lunch. And I'll devour them all someday. All these border guards. Yes. At the very moment. The moment they decide they can legislate the whole Earth. I'll swallow them whole. This was on a return from Morocco. While he was dining off a border guard. And it was three o'clock. It was three when he learned he was free. He could once again travel through France. Go off to the Jura Mountains. They were going to tear up that old ID. That rather pale card (pale green). They were giving him another one. Sharper. Much clearer. So ever since. I. Brandy Fax. I flee before these overly clear ID cards. With a smile to make you wave your shirt at the passing train. And a voice to smother horizons under American scalps. Yes. I. Brandy Fax. I hate America. For all those it has killed. For almost thirty-one years. Yes. Just like that. As naturally as anything. Because ever since meeting America. I've lost my former name. Yes. Mine. The one they gave me back home (?) Back home? Mquides.[8] Yes. He who neither sleeps nor feels sleepy. Mquides. Father of woe. Who sleeps not nor feels sleepy. And so I watch. I stay up and watch. *"For a denunciation of this world I am supposed to get to know. I wait for a condemnation of the world that gave birth to me. I watch."* Yes. Me. Mquides. And it was eleven-thirty at night when I found myself in direct contact with the being. That being. The most devouring one there is. In this world… What is there to say of my earliest origins? Not much. In modern parlance. Because I belong to one of the world's origins. A mythic one. Because. For me. With complete certainty. The world was given birth. Given birth. By a prodigious and ENORMOUS being. Who then engendered most of the PRODIGIOUS ENORMOUS beings. That the earth (The World) has (have) borne in this orb. *Chronos. Gargantua. Blue-Beard. Hanga-Hanga. Awarzeniu…*[9] And many more. Owe their origin to this first prodigy of the world's origin. This simple game. Between me. Mquides. And that prodigious Enormous being. Mquides. Who sleeps not nor feels sleep. The Ogress. Yes. The Ogress. I have had her. With me. In

---

8   The following text is Farès's usual explanation of Mquides (which appears in other works). The reader will readily find internet references for most elements of Berber folklore, Berber and Arabic words, and proper nouns that recur in the trilogy.

9   The list of prodigies, here in the sense of giants, includes Awarzeniu, a Berber variation of "ogre."

me. There. All through me. In the prodigious Enormous origin of the world.

Discovery of the New World

II

Discovery

II......The Ogress? Yes... I'm here... Right near... Very near... Below and also above the world... I... Travel. With success... For how long?... Yes... A long time... A very long time... Several centuries... Goes without saying... Three or four millennia... Yes... Just above... Or just below... In the thawing... Yes... The thawing of this world... The one you live in (used to live in) in all ignorance of your world... After the ice ages... At this place of springing forth... In the rising of worlds... Near a creation... That creation similar to the moment you suddenly appeared Alive. In the towns of the rich desert... The moment that the doe[10] could slake her thirst. at the moment the man / woman could go on beyond the dunes without fearing thirst / ... at the moment when milk flowed more freely than sand / ... at the moment the jackal / yes, the jackal / war's ignoble being / could drink / drank / the whole world's milk ... / ...Yes. I'm here... Right near... Well underneath the world... / And the desires of the world... / ...at the root of all the obsessions of the world... / ...Thus. Yes. / ... of all that constitutes the haunting of the world. : ... envy... / ...glory... / ...blasphemy... / ...hatred... / ...hatred of self... / ...Or of others ...precious happiness... / ...misery.... / ...undeniable misery... / ...all bragging... / ...boasting... / ...pretension... / ...stupidity... / ...yes stupidity... / ...the unnumbered stupidity... / ...numbering stupidity... / ...stupefying stupidity... / ...decay... / ...dejection... / ...impotence... / ...naming... / ...incredible issuing of names... / ...delinquency... / ... credulity... / ...honor... / ...lying... / ...identity... / ...lying... / ... penury... / ...power... / ...imperial power... / ...deafness... / ...impotent imperialism... / ...precious ways... / ...abundance... / ...the unsayable... / ...the unforeseeable... / ...unbelieving... / ...bastardy... / ...primacy... / ...pride... / ...imbecilic pride... / ...murderous pride... / ...impotent pride... / ...faith... / ...presumption... / ...raving presumption... / ...the

10   A figure in *A Passenger from the West* and other works.

36

venerable... / ...the respectable... / ...camembert... / ...degeneration... / ...courage... / ...lovely courage... / ...enjambment... / ...crossing over... / ...detouring... / ...diverting the laws... / ...fruition... / ...the law... / ...intelligence... / ...shining intelligence... / ...sparkling... / ...plays on words... / ...the life of words... / ...usurping... / ...rigor... / ...giving birth... / ...lightness... / ...enjambment... / ...difference... / ...injustice... / ...cruelty... / ...insatiable cruelty... / ...fury... / ...legitimate fury... / ...Yes... I'm here[11]... / ...at the origin of words... / ...at the origin of the formulation of words... / ...the origin of the meaning of words... / ...the tension of words... / ...the nerves of words... / ...the electricity of words... / ...the palpitation of words... / ...the pain of words... / ...the thirst that words have... / ...their color... / ...the warring of words... / ...the mush of words... / ...the spurting forth of words... / ...the flaming up of words... / ...the soil of words... / ...the sky of words... / ...the universe of words... / ...the roundness of words... / ...the spacing of words... / ...the fog of words... / ...the mask worn by words... / ...the speech of words... / ...the scripture of words... / ...the enthusiasm of words... / ...the liveliness of words... / ...the functioning of words... / ...the wordiness of words (hah! indeed: the wordiness of words)... / ...the mountain of words... / ...the cavern of words... / ...the philosophy of words... / ...the images of words... / ...the representations of words... / ...the ideas words have... / ...the symbolism of words... / ...the gesture of words... / ...the reunions of words... / ...the disputes of words... / ...the jurisdictions of words... / ...the defense arguments of words... / ...the trials of words... / ...the chambers of words... / ...the plains of words... / ...the trains of words... / ...the ships of words... / ...the ocean liners of words... / ...the cargos of words... / ...the freighters of words... / ...the ports of words... / ...the seas of words... / ...the continents of words... / ...the talwegs of words... / ...machineguns of words... / ...bombs of words... / ...swimming pools of words... / ...bottles of words... / ...rivers of words... / ...shores of words... / ...roadblocks of words... / ...

---

11 The following section lays out the heart of Farès's understanding of a writer's humble function vis-à-vis the language. He suggests, as he did in conversations and interviews, the tentativeness and receptivity of the writer, the mutability of the initial artistic impulse. He is trying to invoke a pre-verbal state, the Surrealists' "zone," Pound's "antennae," Eliot's "catalyst," the Language Poets' and Lettrists' abdications.

careers of words... / ...mineshafts of words... / ...cities of words... / ...
catastrophes of words... / ...collapses of words... / ...losses of words... /
...shrewdness of words... / ...wittiness of words... / ...pen-holders of
words... / ...boxes of words... / ...pillows of words... / ...showers of
words... / ...willpower of words... / ...decisions of words... / ...steps of
words... / ...stairwells of words... / ...seaweeds of words... / ...flotsam
of words... / ...seasides of words... / ...fishschools of words... / ...sirens
of words... / ...conflagrations of words... / ...seizings of words... / ...
thefts of words... / ...prisons of words... / ...flowerbeds of words... / ...
bouquets of words... / ...cemeteries of words... / ...histories of words... /
...narrations of words... / ...plagiarisms of words... / ...inscriptions of
words... / ...cards full of words... / ...embryos of words... / ...lacks
of words... / ...penuries of words... / ...slurrings of words... / ...four-
word words... / ...fivewords... / ...avalanches of words... / ...volumes
of words... / ...circumference of words... / ...ellipses of words... / ...
craters of words... / ...obelisks of words... / ...mosques of words... / ...
cathedrals of words... / ...saunas of words... / ...babouches of words... /
...headscarves of words... / ...caps of words... / ...vestments of words... /
...cinemas of words... / ...pants of words... / ...bathtubs of words... / ...
torturings of words... / ...soldiers of words... / ...murders of words... /
...gunshots of words... / ...bullets of words... / ...brothels of words... /
...fiestas of words... / ...living rooms of words... / ...encyclopedias of
words... / ...streets of words... / ...light-rays of words... / ...landscapes of
words... / ...fountain-words... / ...grasslandwords... / ...aroma-words... /
...explosions of words... / ...rock-words... / ...village-words... / ...
beacons of words... / ...time-and-place words... / ...emplacement-
words... / ...shadow-words... / ...tree-words... / ...leaf-words... / ...root-
words... / ...of vegetable-word... / ...of mineral-word... / ...pentothal-
word... / ...animal-word... / ...lizard-word... / ...serpent-word... / ...
elephant-word... / ...hedgehog-word[12] ... / ...turtledove-word... / ...
thrush-word... / ...olive-word... / ...pomegranate-word... / ...milk-
word... / ...biscuit-word... / ...child-word... / ...blueberry-word... /
...autumn-crocus-word... / ...thistle-word... / ...belief-word... / ...
mercy-word... / ...vestige-word... / ...belonging-word... / ...delirium-

---

12   The hedgehog is a figure in Berber folklore.

word... / ...verb-word... / ...plural-word... / ...justice-word... / ...circle-word... / ...power-word... / ...law-word... / ...complaint-word... / ...quail-word... / ...partridge-word... / ...hare-word... / ...Yes... / ...at the origins of language creation... / ...Yes... / ...at the origin of the people's creativity... / ...at the origin of popular imagination... / ...of popular semantics... / ...of the universe of popular forms... / ...Yes... / ...Me... / ...ENORMOUS... / ...AND... / ...ABUNDANT... / ...YES... / ...ME... / ...INFALLIBLE OGRESS... / ...PERNICIOUS OGRESS... / ...YES... / ...ME... / ...HUMAN OGRESS... / ...INDUSTRIOUS OGRESS... / ...NUPTIAL OGRESS... / ...PRIMEVAL OGRESS... ANTECEDENT... AND... YES... LOVING... / *in love with the days / nights / with the ploughings / the fields / the olive groves / the palm groves / the oases protecting my friend the camel driver from his long hauls / with my friend the dark star / the orchards / fig trees / pomegranate trees / silos / hedgehogs / the woods they make their way in (the hedgehogs) / the wild scents / of the spring's first heat / of carob trees / donkeys / falcons / falcons and greyhounds / rain / the speech of the rain / speech of life / speech of love / speech of joy / of drunkenness / of the people's giddy drink / of rites / of seasons / of change / of war /* ...YES...I... The Original Ogress... She who devours all prohibitions... / ...She who exacts all permissions... / ...Who condemns fear... / ...Who annihilates trembling... / ...Who kindles intelligence... / ...(popular intelligence)... / ...Who breathes life into intelligence... (popular intelligence)... / ...Who multiplies intelligence (popular intelligence)... / ...Who creates popular intelligence... / ...Yes. Me... The Original Ogress...The Ogress with multiple names... / ...multiple games... / ...multiple appearances... / ...multiple breasts... / ...multiple lips... / ...multiple eyes... / ...Yes It's really Me / Come for You / The Ogress / Mquides / Brandy Fax / It's me who /

/ 7:20 a.m. A gray day that lays out the earth on a background of rain. Breakfast is just coffee. Black. A Toulouse croissant. Soon the sea will appear from the Perpignan station and beyond

The sea.

This night spent in the Ogress's company has blanched my eyes and grown some stubble. I've become a somewhat compressed gentleman. Who might shower (so to speak) in a basin the size of an ashtray.

I'm afraid.

Port-Vendres. Soon. Out there. Very near. Extremely near. Within me. Gray. But close.

There. Bumping on the sand. Far off. But Blue-and-green.

There. Far off. But transparent. Far off. But full-on and daily /

speak:

III

Elements

III...... The scene takes place as a dialogue between mutes wherein each listener, abruptly finding himself a bit close, decides to travel. One of them, clever enough to have grasped the situation both of them had been condemned to—dozens of years before, by children in a rush to become Grown-up Parents—plans to offer his companion in misadventure the strange story of a man no bigger than a cigarette lighter's flame, a man who had tried to settle the issue of traveling by staying awake and ready to depart at the slightest sound, having failed to cross a wide public pool and there having pondered the connections there might be—at such a moment in language (20th century)—between those two great mysteries handed down from all the medieval seminaries: *The Eye* and *The Mind*. But, as was so delightfully recounted, in the narrative that Siamese I gave Siamese II about certain exchanges that happened between these two spontaneous human tendencies, one towards spiritualism, the other toward voyeurism, there were surprises, surprises, surprises......This is what we want to get down, and here is how the bigger of the (mute?) Siamese twins spoke to the other, as negligently as you can imagine, without turning toward him or looking at him:

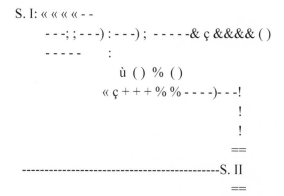

S. I: « « « « --

     - - -; ; - - -) : - - -) ; - - - - -& ç &&&& ( )

     - - - - -   :

         ù ( ) % ( )

        « ç + + + % % - - - -)- - -!

                !

                !

               ==

---S. II

               ==

Translation:

S. I à S. II: "taking some kind of trip in times like these? To go where? Really, to go where?"

S. II à S. I: "?"

S. I à S. II: "today, ten years after the fiftieth of this century (the XXth) and eight years after its disappearance, we can say—only spectral-agents[13] travel, and heads of state."

Siamese twin II, all alone in his corner: "and + + + + + + + ..."

Siamese twin I to Siamese twin II: "for world peace, as they say? They're all the same, only the names change."

(Siamese twin II's knees are shaking and his legs fly into his brother's, causing him to topple over and preventing him from speaking. Not true, they both fall over. They pick themselves up, sort their arms and legs, two by two, get back the way they had been, standing back to back, and exchange signs.)

Siamese twin I is not happy. He shoulders his brother, readjusts his joints.

Siamese twin I to Siamese twin II: "I know a guy who tried, over a period of about six years—these last six years—to learn and retain the names of all the heads of state that have come marching through during this time. He only remembered three: Mao Tse-Tung, Ho Chi Minh and Fidel Castro. The rest, you saw them around everywhere. So anyway this guy that tried to remember them all, I think he went crazy... / ...Hold that thought.

: Siamese twin II, having imagined, who knows why, that he could, without any effect on his hip-baggage, sit down and get undressed (the flight of these syllables offering the body the same poetic soaring as caresses offered by a singularly gifted girl—for whom the art of bedding gentlemen is as powerful as that of any modern, recent, Egyptian you'd

---

13 This is a word Farès created, unless it is a typo—and it would be a rare typo in the well copy-edited original. It appears to combine fantasme, fantassin, fantasque (adj.), fantoche and fantôme. Several guesses have been made, and Valérie Orlando's (The Algerian New Novel, 2017) "pain-in-the-ass" is quite likely correct, with its reference to fantoche (puppet). The present choice emphasizes shadowy agents or fixers behind the government.

find before a pyramid) draws his brother into a mishmash that makes clear simultaneously to both of them (one always being alongside the other) that the garbling of phrases, their loss of balance… An exchange took place:

"Give me yours. I'll give you mine. The two of us make a pair. That's all there is to it."

A few sounds. Laughs. Minor suffocations. Shudderings. Bumpings. Right. Now Siamese twin II turns back to Siamese twin I who's ready to pick up his narration. Siamese twin II gets all his gear in order. Bathing suit, extra-large: BIKINI.[14] A vest of various skins: bristly as eyebrows. A sharkskin watch (for nibbling at the seconds and hearing them snicker among the minutes)

some kind of stocking, old-fashioned, moth-eaten, full of holes, streaming shreds

of wool in muddled colors, an Argyle Stocking,

that's all you need to set off,

a great cape to roll up

his brother in

and never let him go.

Siamese twin I, as you've guessed, had seen nothing of all this, had kept right on talking, and was saying:

"At first, that worked OK. This guy, in order to learn and retain all the names of the heads of state that travel all over for world peace, here's what he did. And a clever bastard!… On each wall of his room, 4 Miros Street, seventh landing, in total blackness, the light switch missing and the bulbs broken, he had left enough room, with the help of thumbtacks, to fit the clippings he cut out of the living flesh of the newspapers. Not all that pretty to look at… Each photo had a film of hypocrisy over it, in which swam—oh with such aplomb and serenity—the faces of several of these blessings to humanity.

Stars? Personalities? Talking Heads on the Cock-it-Up sets? You wouldn't want to bet on nor risk mentioning the names of those whom we daily have the right—enjoying our breakfast of croissants in the warm, flaky-crust aroma of a café—to swallow.

---

14 A "bic qui nie," an Algerian who denies or refuses—see Pierre Joris in the Preface.

The experience is mundane, and no one can be deprived of it. So we won't mention the names of these Talking Heads on the Cock-it-Up sets, and we'll go on with the tale of Tiny Lighter Flame.

Travel? To go where, exactly? That was the question, and we won't avoid it: no: no: and no again.

Your turn, Siamese twin I."

And Siamese twin I continues:

"So, this guy, beneath each photo, had glued the mouthings that all these celebrities (and they must have been slightly higher in number than the pacifying mechanisms you can fit in a crate of grenades) had issued during their stop overs, to various ignorant-of-reality journalists (Twentieth, in the scheme of the centuries) who, from the bottom of the steps rolled against the fat belly of the cockpits, in the silence of the planes' engines and lighted by their metallic glint, hastened, jabbing with their Bics, to gather every syllable that our illustrious personalities might let fall, and who, in the course of their jottings, would create—not without some kind of assemblage and sequence, later—the equivalent in speech (and in importance) of what is (and must necessarily be) a cooking recipe addressed, in a code unknown to the initiates of these types of Cock-it-Up presentations, to some animal as unfamiliar with sauces and spices as a wounded tiger or panther (it's the Ogress speaking). It's enough to make you devour down to the bone whatever messenger brings it to you; enough for you to find yourself again, all in the same movement, in the first blush of that wisdom, after so much wandering in the attempt to understand similar writings—a wisdom requiring: that after reading, all of them (all) were entirely consumed."

Parentheses: (These digressions we're undertaking in the speech attempts of Siamese twin I must not (above all not) be considered of no use to the overall flow of the narrative. Far from it because, owing to the purely gestural intercourse of the mute Siamese twins, these digressions have (essential, for them) the aim to make clear to the reader (if only, however, he has been visited, perhaps one night in his life, by that which in theology bears the lovely name Grace. Thanks to which we ourselves have been made more aware, and which helps us to put up with—despite a few detours into twenty-dollar hotels and love-motels—this condition of limited humanity.) all that this unpronounced dialogue can be. Inasmuch as these digressions might strongly resemble some by-path, one we might have embarked on without first assessing all the perils it would lead to, and without (however) our forgetting for a second that we're talking about Little Cricket Flame.[15] And so it behooves us to repeat our question, and to leave a little white space gaping between the words so as to allow anyone who might have not only the spare time but the intelligence and the goodness to clarify for us this place toward which we've posed the question: Traveling? To go where? :

         :   :   .

As for us (always in parentheses) and as for our Siamese twins, this question was only slightly relevant to broaching the character named earlier, Little Cricket Flame, whose flamboyant liveliness, sometimes the color of C, swimming pool-blue, sometimes trash-barrel-green with compressed vitascorbol-yellow, sometimes fire red or "sublimated" anger (this last term, borrowed from a wise contemporary "Psychoanalysis" observation (so be it), requires some explanation about the origins of the meaning of "anger" and its splitting off as fire, fire of therapeutic value), because (and you were probably just on the verge of grasping this chaotic train of thought) Little Cricket Flame is not a poetic way of naming a phenomenon or a person we might run into, but a way of pointing out an awareness of a certain number of contemporary realities (so be it for them too), and, to be more precise about the attention we're paying Little Cricket Flame in her anger-red moments, it's also to confirm a temptation to destroy what is nowadays everywhere designated as our primary essence, or, as the linguists assert, the vehicle for our essence, that is: that fleshy layer, that inexhaustible, pyrobolant, guava-like, hard, sometimes cracked-and-died-out-hollow and sometimes lawn-tender or apostle's special preserves layer (Nobility new-style), and which is none other than language-beauty (so they say) (and so be it!), speech and not writing, but instead this telling-

15 Bic lighters (the company is French) were new at about this time, and an early competitor was "Cricket." There is an extensive paean to a prototype near the beginning of *A Passenger from the West.*

of-the-telling that is meaning, this warped present surface where there is hidden the spoken—manifested in the manifestation of speech—the blinding dialectic of absence wherein he who speaks is hidden in the silt of words, the labile and deceitful space like the dangling shape of the moon that's fallen in a well, a declension rather like the strip tease of various lives on the couch of Doctor-All-Desires, well suited, according to the customs and level of exaltation of the patients and all those strung out on instant revelations, for detecting the relation of the evils in the constellation Oedipus, that star-shape of ancient destinies, first apparition of Common Reason and the Seminal Virtues belonging to Stoicism, certainly present in all our most fabular dreams, the Mother satisfied by her son's desire, gentle election of kings in the abyssal reign of secluded joy, sidereal perfection (I feel there's no doubt about this) that unpacks consciousness and spits it forth amid the light of the stars, which fly which fly which fly What idiocy the father and the glory of the father and the fatherland and the father's name and the father's old face and the father's hand and the father's house and the father's sadness (Old Kierkegaard and the son's despair) (I will soon die) and his truth, the truth of father's-truth, let him keep it close it's for him alone: Once (here begins a story) there was a king who was given to stealing skulls, the dangerous prayers that might arise in skulls, the skulls of his subjects who had languished in prison since the age of shaving cream and the licorice of storms. So (the story goes on) no one could say if, with such instruments, they could (his subjects) heave themselves up onto the throne of this king of the suds-storm and MAKE OFF WITH HIS BEARD. Not that they were fevered with majesty like him (when still bearded). Among the subjects of this (bad) (good) (?) (doesn't matter) king. There was one prisoner among the prisoners. Clever with all the ruses of language and who. Notwithstanding certain political qualities. Had always preferred to live apart from all the true temptations of this world. And. Through efforts worthy of praise. Was trying to stay at the surface of the water they had pulled him from. Just as winter threatened. And the air became asphyxiating. And his sight could fail him.

They conceived. For him. This movement. Which. Coming out of the roughest prison. Shed light on the plainest of gesticulations. Thus

The saltwater fish   has
no more   water
           he
      is   abandoned
        to   the seaweed
  and
   quivers
     to his death.

"mom is a fish."
        William   says   . Where's that?
     "Meanwhile I'm dying."
"mom is a cemetery beneath the waves"
Who says

that? And where?

"The ballad of the Prisoner."

The Prisoner

III'......

"I

       possess
    more lands
       (rich ones)   to that extent
     (or) (fallow)   there   than
        (thus) (I would see)
   with a hand in the water. Caught in the water.
     See. Live. Live. And see."

"Stay This Way. (being young). Myself. There. At
the rim of my eyes. My tongue. And your law."

"Orange
Marine   the age
  where   the cradling   of
          your body
   Young Seaweed   Loving
    its being
      in body
    and   shipwreck."

<u>The Prisoner invents a Panorama. There where my Earlier life dwells.</u>
<u>From before the birth of my prison. There where my present life is stirring.</u>
<u>If my Mom now sleeps in the cemetery of fishes, it's that she has returned</u>
<u>to the place she came from, where she brought me from. That's why I can't</u>
<u>be "free" in the open air. Here nothing sustains me: not air, not "free" air.</u>
<u>Water alone holds me up. Or wine. I see clearly now:</u>
     ... ...when the stars finally mix with wine

And in……..

I need to be able to see even more clearly. To invent a fabulous color. I need to believe in the discovery of a color of fable. A color that gives birth. That engenders my color. Like open air. Abundant. That I'm breathing. Mother is an Ogress. A fishy Ogress. I've got to advance, through this morning. The dawn. The beginnings of a day.

……and in the mouth tears flow….

Thus. My mother's freedom. From the sea. That rises up in me. From the depths of a prayer. Suitably. Which I'm living. The first joy of my aquatic reign.

…….and then is heard the echo……..

Nearby. Like that memory from before my birth. That repeats itself. Like the rehearsal of a sub-marine memory. That sings in me. That dwells in me. Unjustly present. With no escape. That repeats me. Tirelessly. This despair in the infinite.

…..of my native land…..

. Yes. Nativity of the wave where I was so preciously folded in with the other.

. So preciously.

…..and I'm listening…..

. From a very precocious birth. Like a shield. That the sea held out around me. Dying to see me so preciously melded with another.

…..frozen in place…..

. And impregnated me with its phosphorescent vitality.

…the morning's thrush signing…..

Yes. An affirmation I dwell within. Thirst makes me rave and my hands are coming off. Like two severed wings at shore's edge. And my mouth stutters. Staggers. And condemns itself to drink of beauty. That heady wine of beggars.

:   I love
        this warmth
        creeping down
        my throat.

———

That pulls at my throat

knots it
hammers it
lives it.

———————

Drowns it
maddens it
shatters it
ruins it.

———————

:

———————

"I drink, starting in the morning, a stew-like white wine with a few
Parisian friends from all the craziest countries: Brazil, Argentina, Mexico;
Egypt, Afghanistan, Algeria, Morocco, Chad and Arab Oil.....
      ......and all of us, in a bistro
        on Rue Casimir,
        read through,
        on the bar's zinc,
        our defectors'
        memoirs......
            … … … …

Then	*and,*
the echo	*I listen*
of	*transfixed*
my native	*to the*
land	*morning*
rings out	*thrush"*

           … … … …

"My Mom is such a lovely fish."

"the prisoner is a malcontent."

the prisoner's words:

"I'll use another language so that I'm really understood. So that they know. That what makes me able to act in the straits of my prison. Is this Sublime hope of seeing. One day. Soon. The world crumbling after He resigns. A resignation that He is ready to turn in. Despite what I can still recount of my surroundings. Which still charm me."

"Qu'est-ce que j'oy! Ce suis-je?
Qui ? Ton cuer qui ne tient mais
qu'à ung petit filet : Force n'ay
plus, substance ni liqueur, Quand
je te vois retraict ainsi seulet,
com povre chien tapy en reculet.
Pourquoi est ce ? Pour ta folle
plaisance."[16]

"Yes. I can always promise what I can only hold onto. Sum total. There. At this moment in space where I am. Prisoner of time and place/ Though living in this world where

"Filth we love, filth flees."

Without being able, the slightest bit, to escape

"We flee honor, it flees from us."

FOR a pleasure distinctly other The one we believe to have sprung from us While it comes to us from that time when

"Yet pray God that He absolve all things."

---

16 Surprisingly, this François Villon (from "The Debate Between the Heart and the Body"—the following italics are from a ballad, "La Grosse Margot") is not one of his many poems explicitly about prison, punishment or death:
Who is it that I hear?—It is I./Who?—Your heart, who holds on by a mere/thread. My strength/is gone, substance and fluid, too, when/I see you withdrawn and lonely/like a poor cur huddled in a corner./And why are you thus? Through your crazy/indulgences.

- I will need to be able to see more clearly. To invent a fabulous color. To believe in the
  - discovery of a fable color.
  - Yes. A color that fathers. Yes. That fathers my color.
- Like a movement on the ocean. In the mother-sea. Equal to the day. That day in the world
  - when
  - You'd have to invent a fabulous color.
- That of the lips in which I used to bite my name. Where I took my name. Intimately.
  - Your lips.
  - My name.
  - The first Day.
- I need to be able to say this name. Yes. This name. Without coming up with another. Mine. The one you gave me in the birth of the world. This new world's name. Inches from the mother, sand from the sea.

Between the two hills of the Day. And your hand. Resting. Yes. Resting there. In your birth. Yes.

Birth.

(Of the valley)

Beneath the world. At that place Where I discover so many scattered elements in languages That I no longer know which language to trust. Mine. The language of others. That of all the others.

Are you the author of your own language? It's like a question I pose against the impact of that

Yes. Is one the author of his own language?

I know several languages and several languages The Vowel "A" opened upon me Like your " 👁 " upon the Valley The Vowel "i" rising toward You Like the old "Ω" of Old Akbou's And the ring "h" stalking toward Them and every part of their bodies *I might invent other languages* "As a question that I pose Against this impact of the World and the Murder *The Day* the Name is never again similar after *The Identical or the Murderous* That which delivers to the World barely clothed children

I'm familiar with several beings of language scattered Vowels by so many names"

"The prisoner"

III.'

IV

The Prisons

IV...... Here. After the third Prime number. Here it reached the limit of meditation. And it constructed. In such a clever way. Yet so perilously for me. Its abyss. Well beneath the foam of the world. Or else. So far above. That I had to. Repeatedly. Reassure myself through the streets. The cinemas. The price slates at the groceries. That I was still part of this world. The one in which I work. So hard. By the miracle and splendor of a *Little Cricket Flame* whose beams, as incisive as they were real, were at the origin of the one creation. Of a collaboration. Whose effect. And whose love. Produced. After the prisoner's ballad. A kind of compensatory "*ballad*e." Wherein came to be expressed. One by one. Several of the creatures of *Theater* and of *Literature.*

This is how there unfolded. In the confines of a café. A thoroughly modern play. Which this café owner. One of the great pursuers of losing propositions. Had imagined. And which he rehearsed with his bottles of Bordeaux. Of Casanis. Of Pastis. Of Anis. Morgon wine. Gin-Fillies. Whiskey-Tarts. And Strawberry-Macao.

His name was Kalymnos. And nominally his title was Sponge Fisher. Because of the dives he took. The way he did. Once a year. In one of the inlets of the same name. A few thousand miles from Athens. A few years before the Military of that other country became the putative. Champions of a new era of political democracy. It was then that he received. Yes. After giving up sponge fishing. His theater. His repeating-rehearsal theater. Sort of a fully automatic theater. Whose first shows had the title *"The Scene Begins."* Then. After several days of getting ready and raising the curtain. This other very elegant title. Long. But. Elegant. *"The Action Begins or God's Raving In The Sudden and Princely Encounter Between Don Juan and Harlequin Rough Draft of The Universe."* And. These were. The first scenes as the curtain rose.

Curtains rising:

"The customers are going crazy; the walls creak, crack open, behold, blush, while the TVs explode on the counters, while the fuses expel the singing actor-puppets on jet-propelled suppositories.

Movie houses undress, and we see, behind the crazed screens, film directors chewing reels of film under a drum roll sun. Two cannibals appear, an Ogress at their side.

The script-girls shake like jack hammers and disappear, shrieking, into the earth's whirlwinds.

The sky is red. RED. Violently red. Red. Very blue, in fact. And below, the workers of all the poor countries climb the barriers of their work and reach (Wondrously) the Pullman car of the Sky.

A cry rises with them: BOUNDLESS.
Their voices reach out full-throated
They sing out
"It's the l.....
     It's the beginning of the scene."

The café owner's presentation:

(the owner is seated like a cocktail-hour customer, a double Ricard on hand, his butt on a wooden stool, behind the beer tap. He has an El Guajiro cigar in the corner of his mouth. He moistens the cigar every now and then and spits some tobacco on the bar, like chewing plug. There's nobody there, just the owner and his cigar. Suddenly he starts talking, all alone, just like that, and the world opens, opens up before him like the birthing of a universe. Here's what he says):
          "They're up in the vast ether
             next to God and St. Peter."
(don't lose sight of that encounter. The Princely one, you understand. Of Don Juan and Harlequin. Try not to swallow my cigar. "El Guajiro."

The name of a Brazilian Indian. One of the ones we assassinate. We've been assassinating for a long time. A primitive type, of course. Like all these primitives that drop in here, to have their glass of petroleum. Straight and dry.)

> *"Harlequin sits*
> *on the stepladder*
> *of the moon...*

(Harlequin's approach is born out of the fabular reach of my cigar. No one can prevent the smoke of my cigar from invading the earth and the galaxies that protect it. I take a sip of Ricard. My new border guard. My God. What do I see?)

> *...and*
>
> *he eats the clouds*
> *that pass below*
> *his feet looking*
> *like cotton candy."*

(My God what's this I see?)

> *"Harlequin is filthy*
> *and*
> *above all*
> *pale."*

(I've absolutely got to wake Harlequin up. My approach. And my vocabulary. Hard to manage, because of my cigar which now begins to stutter. Better drink. A sip. Two sips of Ricard. Then drink. Drink some more.)

> *"Don Juan*
> *and his series of skirts*
> *they all try to move*
> *to the tune of Time*
> *while humming*
> *a gypsy romance."*

The café guy takes two more drinks, big ones. He snickers, poor bastard. All alone. Then, as if an alcohol tear has fallen on his eyes, he gives his lips a swipe with his cigar. Which has gone out. He takes Tiny Bic Flame out of his pocket, looks at it. Good. And lights his cigar.

> *"Don Juan*
> *is still*
> *far off in the sky*
> *But*
> *between winks*
> *an event*
> *is announced."*

(Just in time. There occurs. The event. It blows my mind. From my fingers on up. I see the sky. I see the sky, oh my God. Like a bottle held in my fingers. I see the sky. As if a grenade, pinched in my fingers.)

(The café owner is seized with a Molotov urge. He spits lavishly, cigar juice, and gazes at Little Cricket Flame who, always alert, lights his fingers like birthday wicks. Candles. Yes. Little Cricket Flame seems to be celebrating the announcement of some event.)

> *"A single color*
> *edges*
> *Earth and the world*
> *Earth*
> *spinning on its*
> *spike*
> *as in the Geography*
> *books."*

> *"Silence.*
> *A period (.)*
>   *luminous*
> *moves about (.) with (.)*
>   *the speed*
> *of (.) blas (.) phemy."*

(It is here the event takes place. Took place. In my bistro on Casimir de La Vigne Street. In Paris. In the 6th arrrondissment.[17] Here where, in between customers, I can intensely live this event. Most intensely. Sometimes I imagine, from the vantage point of the stunning spectacle of my beer tap, that this event might take shape somewhere else. Out there, where its true place is. In the world. Out beyond my bistrot's door and my beer tap. In front of. Yes. Right in front of certain customers of mine. Those who come to eat here after crossing Paris in their Alfa Romeo. For them, I always whip up something instant to stuff them with. Yes. Instant. And which, on my snazziest menu, I give the name Pastoura Kalymna. A mixture ... of... marinade with salty sponge juice. Oh they like it. Just like that. Then, other days. Other nights. I don't see any. There are no more customers. I'm alone. Or. At least. I'm waiting for my companion Arezqi. Arezqi, who works at Orly Airport. "Three Suns" at Orly. He serves coffee there. Moorish coffee. Wearing a blue uniform. With a red burnous over it. As red as the burnous the spahis wore. The Spahis of Algiers. Now the Spahis of Algiers have green shirts and pants, green like spring grass. So this Arezqi. Arezqi who has always had a thing for red burnouses left the spahi corps to serve Moorish coffee at Orly. So there he is, Arezqi the spahi. Poem for Arezqi.)

" (.) *to*

(.)

... (.) ...*speed.* ....(.).....(.)..... *blas*.... *5* .... *Mach*......*20* ..... *Mach*.... *o*.... (.) .....*ne*... (.) .... *spee* ... *40*... .... *Mach* ..... *60*..... *M*.... *More Machs*........ *Than* .....*spee,,,d...d..d than*....

(.)...*o..ne*...(.) .... *spee..d..d*......... (.) ...*than*.... (.) ... *blasphemy*....... *Yes.*

"*It's God*
(*the Father*)
who shows up
and
who

_____

17 This is the neighborhood ("arrondissement") Farès knew best in the early 1970s, where a number of nondescript scenes take place, along with the nightclub scene and the Smadja's bookstore scene in *Passenger*.

58

> *gets down*   (yes)
>   *from*   *his*
>   *bicycle."*

(The café owner's fingers are in flames. Incandescent. As incandescent and flaming as a Little Cricket Flame.)

(I'm burning to arrive at the same moment as God the Father.) (Yes. I'm on fire. My ten fingers are ablaze. My so so lovely ten fingers. God. This heat is terrific. As terrific as my ten fingers. Aflame.)

> *"God, the Father*
> *scratches at*
> *a star*
> *and hangs*
> *his bike*
> *from the flaming tail*
> *of a comet."*

(Just one question obsesses the points along the route of the bicycle . ? . It goes back and forth between the Constellations, Signs, The cabalistic range of the infernal Zodiac. Bumps into two astrologists who have brought their astounding tranquilities to collide. Gleams in the glow of Mars. And melts in crazed eyes.)

(The café owner is subject to the atmospheric pressure of Mars. Among the bottles a war like refrain drifts up, more moving than that of some military body. For the first time God is worried and fears being swallowed up by years of fog.)

(God is afraid of his own imbalance, and remains inconsolable, over the loss of his vehicle. Don Juan is doing somewhat better.)

The Owner hears music. Or, rather, a certain rhythm. That of bees shoving castanets into the spotlights of flowers and sucking pollen. (Succulent!) A sparkling dust scents the milky way, creates multicolored trails, as if, instead of the electric lamp resting on Harlequin's stomach, Bengal flames shone at the tips of meteors' antennae, burst forth on the heavens' flowerbed, like the fireworks of dreamy celebrants.)

(A silence pressing down. Insular. Royal. Insolent. The exasperated and sublime mirror of this ascension! Don Juan.)

(Dionysian heights of worlds) (The galaxies stir themselves) (and call forth) The insatiable dance, Universe!) (Acte II) (The owner lights another cigar) (It is the hour of invading monologue)

The invading monologue.

(The café owner : (Am I questioning myself?) What does that mean to say? Am I lost? dethroned? envied? I hear it! Yes! I'm listening! I'm getting it! Am I betrayed? stunned? bowled over? scrambled? stung? gotten to? Am I speaking? Yes. I'm talking. I'm so screwed. My despair. These words that invade me. Yes. From an angle. Yes which invade me this way from all sides. Yes. And so I am. From all sides of my starry domain. God. Me. For the first time so very close to myself. I exist. I speak of my death. Of my death arrived here in this world in this century. Having every right to do so. Through speech. Through the multiple kinds of speech that gave birth to the world. I speak and revolve upon myself. Am I questioning myself? I question myself instead of just talking. Just talking, like that. About men's hope. Am I interpreting? Yes. I'm interpreting this speech that drifts from the café owner. Speech I'm beginning to believe. Yes. Me. The Great mute. I'm beginning to believe in other people's speech. As much as in that first speech I spelled out so long before this day. And in order to understand my plain speech. The whole of my speech: interpreters. Many of them were needed. From every horizon. From diverse possessions. Diverse passions. Diverse commandments. *"I'm the one who is" "Guessing?"* Yes. Like an impossibility (serious) of going beyond. Of understanding whatever it might be. Yes. *"I was the one who was"* Today, I should add: *"I am no longer. I'm beginning to live. Yes. Beyond the difficulty where that first pronouncement[18] had cornered me. Yes. In front of mankind. The credulity of mankind. Finally. I'm beginning to live. Yes. To live. Through the will of a café owner. I live.* Should I say. *I die. I see. I rave. I* say *I. Instead of just talking. I'm no longer alone. Another is coming* (other) (Other) *is*

---

18   It's a question of a "phrase." (The Café Owner.) [Farès's note]

burrowing into me. By means of a simple café guy. What prowess! My miracles? Through them I was raised to mankind's most sublime projects! My voice no longer carries. No. I should have a loudspeaker. Yes. What destiny? Hm!.. Hm!.. Destiny?..... (The café guy is (secretly) very happy with this word, and seems to sample with rapture the smoke that envelopes him. He is about to disappear. Alone (or appearing as) a beard floats in space, long, like a highway.) And that's when the sidereal encounter took place and, *in that vast ether, the former seat of (who?) (who's asking?) (who?),"* there happened the famous and historic recognition between Don Juan and Harlequin, new princes of the Earth.)

The historic recognition

"…Curious type of pleasure. Oh yes. Curious pleasure. Here I see Don Juan appearing, and with him an invading monologue. And all this I owe to a café guy's cigar. Still, curious. Me, that everyone thought was shut up in the wings of some theater where I only played secondary roles. Now I'm in charge of the whole works. You just have to look at this lamp lighting up the vast world. Truly, I could easily take myself for the moon. The awesome moon. The cold moon. The death-moon." "…….. It's true that I'm pale. Terribly pale. And that. Eating cotton candy has done me no good. But, today, it seems as if something is evolving in my favor. Something to do with the whole world. That I will have to do. I admit it. Yes. For the first time in this world I am going to h-a-p-p-e-n- Yes. On the moon. yes. On the terrible moon." …….. "I owe everything. Yes everything. To a curious café guy's cigar." ….. "However I'm only at ease in passing. Very much only in passing. Because of the narrowness of this stepladder I've managed to climb. Lady-Mine Moon has just as completely invaded my stomach. And I think, at this moment, there is only one being who can understand what it is 'to have the whole moon in your stomach' : the café owner : for certain, yes." ………. "I am going to happen independently of the roles they've seen fit to give me up to now. Lady-Mine Moon strikes me as attentive Yes too attentive to what is about to happen. Lady-Mine Moon awaits my death. Which absolutely can not happen since I am going to happen as I should happen in blazing clarity."

……. "Lady-Mine Moon is too close to my stomach. I'd better warn the café guy. Yes, the café owner."

(Harlequin hooks one leg on one of the steps of the ladder. Stares strangely at the earth. At a luminous point on the earth. Makes a loudspeaker with his hands and yells: "Hey! De la Vigne. Hey! You, *Casimir de La Vigne*." Finally he sees. He sees ten jittery candle flames that dance on ten fingers. "*I'm on fire*" Harlequin hears. "*My ten fingers are on fire*." Then. Space. The universe. The earth. Silence. Harlequin swings there, ten fingers above the earth.)

(At this moment (the whole time accompanied by a gypsy romance) Don Juan appears, dressed in a black cape, red velvet lining. Blood-red.)

(The café owner is once again set up behind his beer tap. He takes two sips of Ricard. His ten fingers still brightly blazing.) (He hasn't seen Harlequin yet. And, we imagine, will never see him.) (He just thinks how he would really like to see Harlequin. How he'd really like to have a drink with Harlequin.) (Don Juan? The café guy is somewhat indifferent, because Don Juan got what he wanted.) (Whereas Harlequin. As for him. Never. Never has gotten what he wanted. Never ever.) (The café guy drinks a third sip of Ricard.) (The glass is empty.) Atrociously empty. *"Que viva el boracho El boracho de mis palabras. De mis noches. De mis revoluciones.* (The café guy works the beer tap." *Ricard, Old Tap ! Some Ricard! That's what I want!*) The beer tap has a reaction to the Ricard. Violent. It says: "Who is this café owner who's put Ricard in my pump? My beer tap. I resent this. I resent it. I'm no longer a beer tap." And the tap lets a treasure of Ricard trickle into the owner's glass. *"No puedo vivir sin beber. Porque la vida es un sueño. Un sueño de un sueño, Arlequin. Espero tanto de ti, mi pobre Arlequin, que no puedo vivir despuès de tu muerte. Si, espero mirarte en pie."*[19] Then Harlequin spun around the moon, and sat, high up, at the top of the stepladder. (Harlequin now speaks directly to the moon)…. Lady-Mine Moon, I'm now sitting on your stomach and I

---

19 "I can't live without drink. Because life is a dream. A dream of a dream, Harlequin. I expect so much from you, my poor Harlequin, that I couldn't live after your death. Yes, I want to see you on your feet." (Farès translating into French; other Spanish passages are untranslated.) The passage suggests Calderón, in whose work there are several Don Juans along with the play "Life is a Dream." Later, as will be seen, the Don Juan is that of Tirso de Molina.

see the earth upside down in my stomach.. What a sensation! I don't think there's anyone more expressive than I, right now… I who hold the earth in my stomach! What a taste! A raw mixture. Sloshings of sperm and vaginal bounty, and also… Yes, these little sounds that enunciate their meaning, in my stomach? These tiny particles of some matter that resides in my stomach and wiggles. Wiggles. My ravings. Harlequin. yes. (Lady-Mine Moon) Harlequin. For the first time. So close to (Lady-Mine Moon). I play my role. I am my role, for the first time. What a delight. I am able. To caress the Oceans that heave in my stomach. The Oceans that I've always dreamed of caressing in my stomach. These Oceans that make (and have always made) the world sing. The formation of the world. Which the enchanters of the world have traversed. So long ago. The Oceans that swell with so many words. Yes. In the long wait for a shore. These Oceans that hurtle toward a shore. The shore where the man (the woman) dwells. Where the gesture of an unseen Commander comes to die. A Commander without statue. Weeping. At the bottom of Oceans. Of these Oceans that roll now in my stomach. Yes. Towards that place where…..

..... Land! ... How long this waiting was (my waiting)!

..... I was imagining (covered with rust.) (With that rust where you sometimes see) (Yes) (the hedgehog of the seas.) that I could (in this way) (like the Urchin) (deep in the rock) see (with a single eye) (open) the formation of the Oceans…

..... I was imagining (also) the rustling the hedgehog of the seas would make / Acidic palpitation (violent) of my lips (Open) (like the Oceans) (Toward the shores where there evolve) (and Sing) (and Live) (The most enduring wishes of man)

I was imagining (With that terrible imagination open to the Oceans' wind) the desire of the Sand / of the Sand become World /the Sand naming the World / the Sand inscribing the World /

I was imagining the desire of that desire naming the Sand / Where there appears (or advances) (or persists) / There where / in this clay of nomenclature a footstep is imprinted / the march of the Sand toward the World / Yes. / I was imagining. / I made this progression real / this advance of the Sand toward the World /

*My site of figuration in the world
in the march of the world where
the song of the Oceans endures.*

...there lives death.

(In this corner of the sky where Harlequin sits Don Juan comes along. Don Juan with the black cape and blood-red lining.) (The café owner is still behind his beer tap, working it every twelve minutes, ever since it started pouring Ricard.) (Don Juan has stopped now. He's looking at Harlequin. Harlequin who gleams in the night like an Indian cigar. Then, with a flash of his cape, Don Juan is seated on the rings of Saturn, the master of Time.)

"Oof! I mean, really, oof! I've just gotten free from the Commander. From the statue of the Commander."

(Don Juan wipes his brow with his cape. He shakes out his (long) hair, from which, like rubies falling to earth, come tiny incandescent flames.)

(Don Juan has black eyes. Black like olive pits. His lips are violet. As if, independently of Don Juan's Hell, they had stayed (Don Juan's lips) in the fridge. In the freezer.)

(... *Fuego! Fuego! Es el fuego que me quema Tisbea.*[20] *Alli.*[21] *En todas partes de este cielo. Es el fuego ! Tisbea. El fuego de ti. Tú, de quantas el mar pies de jazmin, y rosa, en sus riberas besa...*)

(Don Juan has black eyes. Black as olive pits. His lips, now, are red. Red, as if, out beyond Hell, they had stayed red with Thisbe's fire.)

Fuego! Marinos! Fuego! Nubes...Mi Amor en este cielo. Me ahogo en este mar.)

Sitting on Saturn's rings, Don Juan begins to be overwhelmed by phrases, all of which originate in a clearly determined period, a historical moment.)

However, among all these phrases, only those coming from Thisbe still interest him.)

(Don Juan even believes that he is going to see Thisbe again, because he can hear, or seems to hear, that warm voice of hers that cradled him on the beach at Tarragona—all the way from the rings of Saturn.............. *Fuego! Fuego! Marinos y Nubes....*

Mi amor en este cielo. Me ahogo en este mar,
Fuego !.........

    "Mi cabana se abrasa, repicad a fuego, amigos,
que ya dan mis ojos agua.
Yo
Quién
A ti se allana
Y de ti viva
luego que sin ti estoy
estoy agena de mi.
Pero !
En este cielo
No te veo.
Nunca !
*Por qu*é ! Por qué no te has

---

20   Without any doubt the café owner refers here to the *Burlador de Sevilla.* But. Really! Through so many Ricards and subversive intentions that the *original* text is, often, quite changed. In effect, simply put, *influenced.* (Café Owner's footnote)

21   (*allí.*) Farès, as will be seen, did not always write standard Spanish.

quedado, en la playa conmigo !"[22]
Tuya estoy !
Yo vivo
de ti !"
…… ……… …..)

(Don Juan is very moved; he thinks, immediately, of that time in history he lived through :

"No es
mia la culpa
Tisbea!
Yo
contigo
hubiera querido quedarme
Pero
en este tiempo
del tiempo
donde viviamos
No podia vivir
con mariscos
y la menuda arena
Alli donde el sol pisa
sonolientas las ondas
alegrando zafiros
las que espantava sombras.")

(Don Juan is now stretched out on Saturn's rings. The lining of his cape smears red on the star of time .[23])

(Without Don Juan noticing (his eyes turned toward that infinity where) (the stars), Thisbe has sat down on the last rung of the moon's stepladder where Harlequin is still perched.)

(Thisbe is dressed only in a scarf over her breasts, and blue jeans. Her nails have been done. Her eyes Moon-Blue. Purple lips. A bit like the

---

22   Also without any doubt Don Juan is one of those beings who prefer to conquer the sky without bothering about the sand. (Café Owner's 2nd note)

23   We must recognize that Don Juan understands his political place in literature. At least, he might have some regrets… (3rd note by the Café Owner)

inside of Don Juan's cape. Her right arm is raised toward the moon and her right hand rests on Harlequin's shoe.) (song for Harlequin).

(Harlequin has heard (listened to) (summoned) (made possible) the speech of Thisbe and Don Juan.)

(But, beyond these words, he thinks of the café owner who remains (yes, still) behind his beer tap. Asleep. Yes. Asleep and dreaming. Dreaming what he, Café Owner, *Café Owner*, in Tirso's[24] position, would have done with Don Juan..... Yes, what I would have done with Don Juan.[25]

> ... *"It's being a hidalgo*
> *Thisbe!*
> *It's being a hidalgo*
> *that has*
> *been my ruin!*
> *And*
> *the king!*
> *But now is the time*
> *Thisbe!*
> *The time*
> *of my eternity*
> *and*
> *of your*
> *own season."*)

....Yes: what I would have done with (besides Don Juan) Thisbe and Harlequin.

(thus : sad

the epilogue

of Harlequin).

(yes :)

(Harlequin's)

---

24 Yet another Spanish dramatist (c.1579-1648). There are also hints of Valle-Inclan and Lope de Vega in these passages.

25 This reference is exact (last note by the Café Owner)

(Epilogue)

(Moon)
    (death)
        (: I cross)
            (I cross over)
                (death) (and I say)
    (this)

Song for Harlequin :

    "Lady-Mine Moon!
    Why from
    Earth to the Heavens
    why am I
    now
    so changed
    since
    Thisbe
    (Yes. Thisbe)
    is at my feet
    (my foot)
    at my shoe's foot."

    "Lady-Mine Moon!
    Why do I have
    Thisbe
    (Yes. Thisbe)
    upon my shoe."

"Lady-Mine Moon!
Why?
?
Am I
  (so!
                 (far)
    (from)
                   (my)
  (shoe)."

(The café guy takes a piece of (deceased of (death of ! his dream of Harlequin's shoe.)
(Day breaks over the mountains of trashcans and all the world's milkmen in every country of the globe raising their glasses of milk to the health of every country in the world)

(Don Juan weeps for his eternity (the vastness of it) as a swindled hidalgo)

(while) (Harlequin and Thisbe) (Leave the moon (Lady-Mine Moon) for the rising (fluid) (ephemeral) (of) (a) sun (as) stuffed (with stars) as a (Guajiro) cigar

(is with fire) incandescent (it) (is)

the ! (end) yes
        (the strange) (subversive)
  dream (today) of (yes)
        a café owner (thus) and of
(no)
  (Little Cricket Flame) / Me
        (yes)
  Ogress (who)....
        (Fifthly.).

V

The Ogress

V...... Yes. I'm traveling. Doing quite well. This morning. Towards Barcelona. I who. Ever since this prodigious surging of the world on either side of my words. Is causing something I would never have dared to do myself except in a somewhat incomprehensible manner. A penetration, strictly material, into this world. Through all the material fabrications of this world. I have to add, even, (the confidences of an ogress are worth no more nor less than the confidences of an ogress: ellipse and explain'tion all at the same time) that Brandy Fax's railroad knowledge dazzles me. Without him (Brandy Fax) I would prolong (there's no doubt of it) my eons-long sleep in some Ikharshushen[26] cave. In this country where the true history rubs elbows with the most absurd human ambitions. And so it is with that ambition having to do with origins. Yes. In this country where I was one of the first beings to come into the light (and I say light, or glow, because of that linguistic disguising where I've always shoved my existence) of the world, the ambition of holding onto (of having) an origin has necessitated the creation of a sort of university of origins-instruction. The news left me stunned. As stated by (so long ago) the first Mediterranean litterateurs that I used to devour. Yes. An origin-teaching. A sort of cult of devouring. All told. And, while I was stupefied (Me, the Ogress of fable, "the dark-blooded ogress, as yet another poet says" (a more modern one, one who was full of taste and talent for me), and my (cult) I was also thoroughly happy.) But. Unfortunately. I had to. In some way. Become disillusioned. Because. Fooled by the recent arrival (I say recent from my point of view. For these horsemen who showed up towards the 7th. Then towards the 9th. Then (finally) towards the 11th century. Can't possibly be of an origin that predates mine) of a few horsemen come from whatever dunes in a desert country of some kind where there is

---

26   A lost village above Akbou. (Note by Farès.) Akbou is the home village of Ali-Saïd, a key figure in Farès's fiction (translator's note).

found a black stone[27] of some kind, the professors of this original teaching (about my origins) have halted their investigation several millennia from the true origin of the world and of myself. Is it? Cleverness on their part? Hypocrisy? Fear of seeing (along with their origin-teaching) the studious youth disappearing into the PRODIGIOUS-VAST abyss of my kingdom? Or else? Pure aggression on their part: desire to forget? Anxiety over an all-consuming urge whose warning signs they knew after having thrown themselves at that book (a book) published by Desert Editions, after a forty days' fast/forty nights without women? Me. The native ogress. Who was waiting for the advent of that man. And who was fooled by the scriptural virtue of that man. Who. Yes. Never stopped. Before me. Beneath me. Writing. And who. In this way. Tricked me. Tricked the native ogress (naïve ogress) that I was. For. I was amazed. Yes. Literally amazed to see. Before me. Beneath me. Spring forth several signs with strange serifs. Never before seen in this alignment before me. Beneath me. And which. Dazzled me!...... And so it was that (in my amazement) I was had. By this man come from a town. In a fast of forty days/forty nights of writing out of which came this book that repressed my origin all the way back into the childhood of the world and of men. While. I. A young ogress. Ready to devour and to make felt the sweet devouring of my lips to this man. I had to run. To descend into the greatest depths of the earth and of the day. To grow old. Yes. Grow old. Me. The young ogress. In my verbal and flesh-eating indigenousness. I had to grow old. Lose my teeth and my purple voice. Yes. In order that. Men might grow in the independence of a certain book. A book which. At that time. Astounded many. But. Today. And because books too grow old. I rediscover a kind of vital joy. On this journey where my old cave friend leads me. My friend from Ikharshushen. The one who. All through those years when I had to grow old and get to know the bowels of the earth. Was constantly concerned about me. And connived with me. With his thousand ruses. While. Grown old. Blind. Yes. Become blind. Blinded by that fifteen-century descent beneath the day and the book. I lived. Without looking. The earth surrounding my eyes. Demeaned. Driven mad by that man and his forty days and forty nights.

---

27 The Black Stone in the Ka'aba, Mecca. Comments on the Koran are restated in the third volume of the trilogy. This is an assertion of the precedence of Berber culture over Arabism and Islam.

Come from that town to write a book. This book that destroyed my naïve ogress's beautiful kingdom. And which. In vain. My friend of cave times attempted to rediscover. This writer, last among an offspring of seven sons. Whom everyone loved for his malice. Except me. The ogress. The now blind ogress. And who. Through these long years of sere earth. Had to accept the burnings. The drownings. Terrible home invasions. Of this child that I loved nonetheless. For. Just as in the days of my first sight. In spite of that cursed place I had fallen to. That child brought me life. Made me believe in another possible life. Darker than the first one. Harder. But. A possible life............ And that's how, in those inhabited areas where I was the PRODIGIOUS-VAST origin of the world, all those kinds of books (stories) were born, stories told though people do not really know where they come from. Clearly. From me. If I may say so. Yes. In all humility. Or vanity. What does it matter. Since all words attract me as much as blood that blood I drink (used to drink) in my day.......... This kind of book which circulates (circulated) in spite of and (roughly speaking) under the cover of that other book. The book of that man who came from a town and legislated several of the world's societies. His world's. And against mine. My world of devouring, so PRODIGIOUSLY-VAST.......... Yes. That's how those books (narratives) got circulated which recounted that *"there was a time when the ogress possessed a power."* Devouring power and power over life since I was (at the same time) the power of Day and of Light and since. During a night of tripled love. (Yes. Day and Light together with me out beyond the world and all of time and all the eras of the world.) I gave birth to the world and the universe. It was like two moments in the same shock which yielded the world. And then. With every precaution. The rest. All the rest of this first love that lasts even now. Despite the presence of the thing I most feared. The search for an origin more recent than mine. Starting with that which I have always detested: writing. Yes. That search for origins, focused on something that came more recently than I. More belatedly than this country (or place) I came forth from. Because. Contrarily to the man who was the origin (pseudo-origin) of the book (of that book written by someone arrived from a merchant town). I was birthed. ? . Is that really the word. I couldn't say. Because if I could answer the question of my birth. Then I could answer the question of what is the very life of my life: this flood of words through which men, women, children, the games of men, women and children gave birth to the world. The universe of the world and the earth. And where. Forever. I have roamed. In this way. Accomplice and origin of the words by which the sexual orality of life protects man, in spite of himself, from his own death. From that death that was written for him (revealed) well after the infinite birthing at the world's origin. From that infinity of words. And of languages. Where all books come to die. Despite their scriptural staying power. That has come (this staying power), as a formal matter, from a law. The same law that grew the Minarets of the holy land. Tied. In this way. To an alphabet's wound. I. Young ogress. In the virginal goodness of my Beyond-Death. Tied. I'm saying. To the exclusive talisman of words. Words which. For a faith. For a definitive faith escaped me.

I could have laughed. About all this. Tied to the writings of that garrulous man. Lost man. In my own desert.

I could have laughed. If I hadn't been dazzled by letters.

The hand kept working. Also like me. Bound. In a delirium of movement. Delirium and movement I hadn't known. Had never seen before. For. Delirium and movement were being born. As it were. On the spot. Right in front of me. Yes. I was staring. And I was amazed. Amazed by this miraculous swarming. *Miraculous?* Is that what I said? Miraculous. Which took off in front of me. Got beyond me. In the *miraculous* comings and goings of his hand.

He was writing, I guess you could say! He was writing. While I. Young ogress. I was staring.

I was staring and I didn't notice that I was being drawn in. To each one of his words. Terrible words. That he traced. He. In his way. Lost in his fasting. His forty days' fasting. Forty nights. And what this produced was absolutely prodigious. Extraordinary. Or. If you're afraid of prodigy. Bordering on prodigious.

The Koran

V'...... Yes. And so it was. Seated near me. I couldn't say that he saw me. Myself. More and more caught in this seduction. I couldn't see him.

What is certain. At the same time. Is that I did see him. As in those earlier times when. I could see.

He reached out. I remained dazzled.

Why? A gift like that, in this man...? I think I know why: his birth was attended by several sacrifices. Was he the object? the subject? of several sacrifices.

But if he was, in this way, the? subject or the? object. He was not. Himself. In his soul and body. The *Sacrificed.*

Very much the opposite. He was the *One Revealed.* If I may say so. The *One Revealed.* Because. In this far-off land. In these faraway places where. One day. He came to be born. There existed. In a coveted and thousand-year-old precedence. A matrix of several cults and adorations. The cult where the Feathered Bird and the Shattered Cloud mingled. That cloud that draws the other clouds into its plumage. The Gods of Sleep, in a way. Or. More violently sprung forth from Stone and Water. The wandering Beings of the other world. Those we called: the Desires. Come to pillage the hearts of men. And all the while the penury of those places brought forth other cults. That is how. This man was the *One Revealed*, in one of those cults. A cult of desert penury. Where were metamorphosed: the pirates of idolatry and a koranic destiny.

Yet the initial adoration was obvious. Even though. In his pride as the chosen one of the desert. Guardian of waters and of mystery. He was his own worst enemy. And had to feign ignorance.

A real complication because. As soon as he really grasped his own ignorance. He then ceaselessly. Throughout his imperious and prophetic life. Downgraded his ignorance into the simple assertiveness of pronouns. "*I am the one who is.*" He used to say. And he took up a presence in letters. In that far-off time. When. Though letters existed. Their use was only analogous to the vigor of street hawkers. Or to the arrogance of the warrior class.

For in every era and existence. There were. In the region where I was so terribly drawn in. Lyricists of the zeitgeist. A kind of being elected by my own law. By the prideful law of an Ogress wasting away.

Thus he came: according to tradition: "*among those ten thousand noses that drink before the lips do.*" Thus he came. But. According to the entropy of traditions. These "*ten thousand noses that drink before the lips*" were changed into ten.

A Prophecy and Transformation also challenging for our man.

Think about it. For a second. One brief moment. These *ten thousand noses* bent over the bowl or the trough. The trough now become the abyss of a *Tamenast.*[28] The sort of receptacle you use to gather the tribe's milk. For the tribe. In the far desert where liquid is so rare.

I could perfectly well have. In my status as buried Ogress. In hiding. Appeared at the bottom of the abyss. Or of the *Tamenast.* In the glinting of the milk. Beneath the eyes and faces obscured by so many noses.

I could perfectly well have devoured all those noses.

But I didn't. For the simple reason that. The noses didn't interest me. No. They interested me not. I preferred to see them grow.

It was then that the prophecy happened. When. In more modern terms. Terms more fitting for the speech of strange lyricists. It was then that the historic installation of our man took place. There. Right in the middle of those ten noses.

Make no mistake about these ten noses. The matter appears. Historically. In the *Genesis* of our…. transcriber.

Maybe. For a reader who is uninformed (however little) about the impact, symbolic figure or prestige of the noses. I should relate. Yes. From the very place where I live and do not see. From this place of prolific and daily wanderings. That. This figure of the noses is really impressive. Since. Fully turned toward the hole. The well. Toward the water. Or. In effect. Toward the water's coming. It whispered. (I'm telling you.) Yes. The prediction. This Pre-diction which. For me. Was the beginning of my

---

28   A kind of bowl (sometimes a drinking bowl slung over a camel).

seduction. *A voice perceived between Earth and Water was the beginning of that seduction.*

I could have. One should say. I could have. At that moment of power where I found myself. When I could reshape anything. Brutally intervened with that person who entitled himself to wish that seduction.

But. From that place where I dwelt. I watched over. During that period. The fashioning of every human being. Or. Male or female. Over their imperfection.

I could devour. In my domain. Whomever I wanted. Happily.

But what I didn't get. At that instant. At the moment I witnessed the man transliterating the world. Was that other way of constructing the world. Of controlling the world. Of improving the world. Independently of words and languages.

Yes. His prediction. The prediction of this man. Installed the terrible reign of the merchants. Yes. Merchants. That this prediction made use of.

The humble appearances our preacher later wrapped himself in were those of an imposter. For. In his era. In my era. And in that of this land that saw his birth. His lineage. The lineage of this man. Were given high and impressive positions. Bordering on chieftains. His status as chief. Chief of the tribe. And. Another excess. The ebullience and rivalries of the caravans that crossed the Peninsula and other lands where. As time went by. His "*Kingdom*" was spread.

I said imposter. Because. The prophetic fakery changed into mercantile chicanery. Then. Later on. Into cultural chicanery. A cultural chicanery so vast. That it was forever able to win over the inhabitants of the Peninsula and those of neighboring countries. All told. A prodigious dizziness. A prodigious going beyond.

It was in this way that he interested me. And also that. Strangely intrigued by his program of disorientation. I allowed the approach, toward me. As much as toward him. Of that prediction.

So much the worse for me. Because. Against my worship. Against the adorations people offered me at fixed hours. He deployed all his force and all his lack of breeding. What those close to him called. And those in many other parts of the earth and the world. Of this world. *El Nur.*[29] The spirit.

---

29   Strictly translated, "The Light."

His spirit. Against my own. The Koran. My love of languages, my love of the primordial beauties. Newly. Virginally. Consumable.

Nothing was left of me. But these caves. These caves where a few bitter poems huddled with my blindness. This is how. Dear Mqides. Or Brandy Fax. Bound by the truths of that moment. I had to leave the earth's surface behind. To inhabit only those regions men call cursed. Far from the starry shores of night. Removed from the clouds and drizzle of life. From where. Because of the courtesies and kind regards. That you have had for my ruin. I hope you can live. I hope you can find a way to keep on living.

PART TWO

The thrushes we call diurnal

VI

The Thrushes[30]

VI...... They could just have well been born in some other country. Elsewhere, not in this place. On the far prairies of the North. On the spot where. That murderous hill rises. Stripped bare. Deforested by the ancestral custom of fire. The fire you stoke deep inside you. At your edges. Like a torch that might flare with rejoicing.

Yes. They could just as easily have been born somewhere else. Far from the harshness of stones. In one of those places of omnipresence, of the abundance of the world and of beings. Those places where dwells the poetic belief in the atom, in the air. In human fullness, in dreams. The dream of a better way. Contrary to this world. They could easily have been born somewhere besides this world of murders.

Yes. May several histories be pardoned. All of them born from a serried migration out of war. The human war. The very war we profess. Whenever we speak of the world. Our world.

They came guided by their truth. At the instant of the most terrible. (Prideful.) Density of the earth. Our earth. The one we work for springtime bounty. Yes. The one that guided their migration out beyond sand and sea. Or. More southerly. Into the elements of sand and sea.

They evolved above Europe. Above the two Europes. Well above national and linguistic conflicts. In the springtime erection of a City. On the world's mother-of-pearl horizon.

The movement was traceable. Their movement. The one that carried an invitation from the other world out beyond war. A fluorescence above water and language. The allure of the ocean. And their departure. Free. Marvelously free. On the surface. On surfaces. On all surfaces, of all waters.

---

30   Thrushes are common in Berber (and many other) folk tales and sayings and appear in several of Farès works, including *Le Chant d'Akli*, 1971.

Then. There was a trek. The crossing. That crossing. Hard. Tense. Beyond that death.

Yes. Their life's reverse. You could have. At that time described their movement. Yes. Or. Appointed death. Their death. Beyond movement. Worked toward the negative. Against the negative.

> *"space*
> *yes,*
> *is sometimes lacking*
> *in movement.*
> *A space*
> *with hunched back,*
> *the space*
> *of The Thrushes*
> *in movement,*
> *The Thrushes*
> *without*
> *movement."*

This is how it was designated. Some time ago now. The space of man without life. Without movement. The space of man killed while in life. Gotten to, there where he had a certain expectation of his life. Of life.

These are the several stories or thoughts that, in this way, activate man's belief, or beliefs.

Men used to say. In the shelter of their beliefs. In the war-like tremors of their origins.

> *"Movement*
> *comes*
> *at*
> *the moment*
> *of a murderous*
> *autumn.*
> > *The open*
> > *thrush.*

The air
hard
as
a
rock.
*   And*
my being takes off
*   (outspread)*
*   in the sharp*
movement
of a war."

"I
see
The Other.
The one
from
my belly.
The One
from
my shock
from
my exile
from
my hate.
I kill off
the belly.
The One of
my happiness
and of
my breath
I envy
The Day
and
autumn

The world
open
like a
Thrush
Bones
thin
The olive tree
barren
or
burnt
The
body
puny
and
run through
The down
warm
and
the red
shadow
like
a
flight (the state of the world in the Valleys)
of
immolated
Thrushes."

"Here is my blood," said the Young man. "Thrushes from the South. The North. Or from the East. I call mine that region of the earth where man's conflagration grows. I make this autumn mine. This place. This year. This double movement of nineteen fifty-four.[31] This law of life or of death. Your movement. The activities of your war. My weapons. And my eyesight. I will reach. Some day. Your springtime."

---

31   The year the Algerian War (of Independence) began.

Men continued to live in the shelter of their beliefs. The Thrushes sparkled with power. Named in the unfolding of all the lands burned over. In their effervescence they dove over all the plains and valleys.

"Thrushes of the South. Or the North. Or the East," said the young man. The same man who announced his being. His soul. Or his murder. To the young messengers among the olive trees. Close relatives of fleet greyhounds. Diligent consumers of order and of the murderous powers.

"Thrushes of the South. The North. Or the East. Behold my blood.[32] Born of clay and wind. Inured to the pleasures of others. Of language. And dream. I dream of being among those who constitute the world. The other world. The one whose doors are kept sealed away from your magnificence. I offer my blood and my life at the entrance to your glittering. This rain of ruins that covers my time and my body. The time of shadow or of movement. Look. Shadow rushes up by regions. Over regions. Onto regions. Rain. The world. Thrushes. Young Thrushes."

Shadows ran over the whole extent of the earth. Like a flight numbed by the slickness of the air. Detours. And the flight. Resembling each other.

There were also. Several beings among the grasses. That grass that favored movement. A gentle movement. A violent burst above the ground. Not far from the rain. More dazzling than any storm. Or mood of the sky. Several beings were there, among the grasses.

One of them had a sad look. In the midpath of his belief. In the narrowness of his body. Thinning. Legs and knees frozen. Mud and water freezing his body.

A crying out. Further ahead. East of his body. He recognized the voices. "Thrushes. Young Thrushes. I offer my eyesight and my blood."

Toward the hills. The ground underwent a glowing. Parcels of land lifted up. Voices. Fleeting shadows. Toward the grass. Toward those spaces where the desire to live confuses being and day. Where man stalks each instant. The instant of his movement. Toward the other. He who was running the war. Up above the villages. And the nights.

The other. Planted before me. In front of my enduring. In front of its day. In front of our life. The other. Who exercised his power above

---

32 The original edition has "*rang*"—"rank," probably a typo—instead of "*sang*" (blood), which is more likely.

the grasses. There. In that place. That space. Where he braved the world. The world somehow other. The one we would have to leave. To become Oneself. And at the same time. To become all others. All these others who kept up the war. Everywhere. In all the forests of the world.

The young man said: "Thrushes. Young Thrushes. My power. The power that fulfills itself in me. By day. Among the day's beings. Far from my shock. My liveliness. My past. My exile. And my law." "Thrushes. Young Thrushes." "The cold grows. In me. The space for life. And death. Death, active among the grasses. And in the hill. And in the nights." "They're shooting. Yes. They're shooting. Over there. Just above me. On the other side of this wall. Just a few yards from my body." "Thrushes. Young Thrushes. I can't move my body. The other has touched my legs. Twice. Two burns. In the life of my body. The other. The incendiary. The one who blows up the world. The hill. The one who inspires war. The other. My being. My sight." "I can't tell you everything. Thrushes. Young Thrushes. There isn't space enough. My words. My legs." "They're shooting. Over there. Near me. On the other side of this wall. As if they're trying to dissimulate my death. There. A few yards away. From my blood. My eyesight. They're trying to hide my death."

There were several bodies. Barely hidden by the grass. In the grass. Several bodies stretched out. Chilled. Splattered with mud and reddish dirt. On the radio they were saying that the exile was coming to an end. That they'd be giving the land back to those who had so ardently longed for it, land conquered by the enduring of their bodies. The radio said spring was finally coming.

There were several bodies about. The radio announced that several frontiers had been broken down. But that there was no news of those who had passed beyond the frontiers. We reserved the right (the duty) to go to meet them. Or. To go past them. Or. More simply put. To walk behind them. You could take a weapon with you. It was open season. We were advised not to scatter our fire. The Thrushes were abundant. You just needed to bring down a few. Certain. One(s). Without wasting a shot. Yes. You only had to get one. Only. "Thrushes. Young Thrushes. My strength and my blood. There. Up above the world. In the instant of the world. That instant when my blood finally comes home. I'm cold. As a blade. Here.

Everywhere. Like a caress. Inevitable. Over my body. Thrushes. Young Thrushes. I despise death. My death. Death of all other deaths. Several. Bodies. In the wet grass. And this mud… This mud… on me… in me… Like my blood… (cold)… moving…over the ground… mixed into the ground… (Thrushes) (Young Thrushes) *My heart blushes to feel itself so scattered A shame As well Shame Among the grasses and my hands Or Your back (Thrushes) (Young Thrushes) Similar to your back Shame Spread Liberty Or Being: To Live Living One World's Faith This moment when my blood flees The Dream where the Other comes to drink He who held to genuflection Where War…* I see *(Thrushes) (Young Thrushes)* Over there I see On the main screen Before me Around me Yes (this being) yes First life that ran to meet the world A watch strapped to the left wrist and two wounds in the legs There gently

on the grass…

We need to be able to get out of the mud. Go deep, through the mud. No longer stare fixedly at the silvery movement The lighthouse beam

We should be able

They should have left already. Left the road. And returned to the village. To the tents. Or the huts. By that path. That one path. The one that follows. Very closely. The utility poles. The road. Very close to The Other. Yes. In his territory. There where he can't get at me. Without getting at his own heart. His life. My deliverance. There where he couldn't survive my murder. They should have followed beside the road.

The lighthouse beam Silvery On the hills. It lighted the land with Sinister light Men here and there A few shadows could be seen racing away Yes towards the thalwegs Down from the crests The line of the crests In the lighthouse's motion Silvery East of my body Yes

Have you Already? Heard the sound of the moon in the grass? The moon's advance? Did you know it's the opposite? Yes. Opposite! To the day's more definite movement. Did you know that the moon marches over the earth with astounding murderous legs? That's what I've heard

The guide now pressed the pace. Beside the road. We had to take a detour, three hours' march. Amid the earth's explosions. Amid what the 155s[33] sent and the fields of brambles To get back to the camp of The Other

---

33 Howitzers

At the far edge of his invasion Like a reassuring presence There On our right Our West Just as we were crossing the Eastern frontier The frontier that had Early On welcomed our movement The East frontier The One of our very enchantment *Yes I've heard it said That to live well inside oneself You have to go through the outside the Whole exterior of yourself Know the whole and the limits And see how to Live Beyond yourself* Like a gunshot Or a strange hypodermic (I'm cold) (I'm cold) Thrushes. Young Thrushes. Forgive me. I'm suffering. I'm really suffering. This very moment. By your side. Well beneath You. Thrushes. Young Thrushes. I'm throwing up. And my life. And my blood. The Other is no more *healed* today than yesterday. The Other is always among the grasses among hands among bodies. The Other has become more and more *crazy* Yes *crazy*. I want to live Thrushes. Young Thrushes. To live. Without murder or violence always staring at me. In my legs and shoulders. *Seeing. Thrushes. Young Thrushes.* Living. And seeing. That splendor that awaits the world. That I've been told about. More than once. Back when I was questioning the world. A certain capacity of the world. "One's being is not handed forth in mid-journey." That's how The World spoke or The Guardian of the world. He who was named the *Amin* Or the most certain being Toward whom march the men and women of the village Or toward the truth of the earth.

The *Amin*: "One's being is not handed forth in mid-journey. Exile is not anywhere. The portion of truth each man each being has within him or her is a disposition. An ephemeral disposition. Being is not given in midstream. Man is a migration."

The Amin:

"the inscribing throughout the world
the grass, a death
further on, the writing of the very being of a being
here lies Meaning."

VII

The Olive Trees

VII. It was hot up on the hill. In the bushes[34] that peopled the hill. Still hot. Shadow still hid. Down below. In the ravines. The olive trees. Under olive trees. Among the orchards. And fig trees. And other trees Here and there. At the foot of the hill.

All around. At regular intervals. Furious assaults launched from the ground. As smoke. As smoky tufts. You could see them bursting from the ground. Then escaping through the air above the trees. Not far from us. Bursts of smoke that came from the ground.

The guide had decided on a rest stop. There. Half-way along. On that hill. "We still have an hour before the shots start coming. Toward us. Toward this spot. One hour. We have to eat, drink. Then take off. On the other side of the firing. Across the fields. There. Down towards the bottom. Very close to their position. A stone's throw. After that we'll reach the upper village and the mountain. By then it will be night. Our night. It will go better then. We have to pass through the shooting."

The stone's exile. In this world. Where man kills. By blowing up the stone. Or the clay. There. Right above us In order to say: *"No place in this world.... No place... But this explosion of your land... Young men who will have... From now on... Only a struggle to live... A madness to circumscribe... A death to realize... No place in this world... Your footstep and Your Desire uncoupled... Our reign among the stones. The grass. And your fields... No place. There exists no place in this world."* The earth rose like smoke among the stones the thickets of the other ground of the other village of the other hill Which we saw Burning Beyond our position Facing us *"I'm ashamed... Man's rage as he burns his brothers alive Killing the world This appointment Or this time I'm searching for*

---

34 *"Les maquis."* The singular, "brush" or "thicket," signals to any French reader "underground resistance." "Le maquis," and related Romance language words in other countries, was one word for resisters against the Nazis.

There in the Inscription of the true Its faith or Hope Our century That of the Former World Finally present amidst the world Yes This faith in a new world There with Equity Equally life Equally land or game, love and illusion Ourselves Inventors of the word and its sound In the urgency of this world All that I would have made out of language if you hadn't killed my brother A pure elocution of life Of the glory of our glory Men living this world I would have put down my weapon As if caressing the world Our love My joy Your lips and my Present.... I'm ashamed This rage of man, who burns the world." The shots had now stopped on the other side of the hill from our position. We had to leave our spot and head down into the shadows. Down below. Under the olive trees. Near the military camp. In the orchards of the Upper Village. "There's nothing to be afraid of," the guide said, "they've been gone since morning. They won't come back here until they've scoured the hill we were just on. We have nothing to fear. Here. In the olive trees." The firing had stopped on the other side of the hill. The sound of trucks carrying the troops the war further into this lasting The Moment of The Thrushes among the olive trees There harking to the little noises of the leaves Stalking the river further off In the shadow of this hill giving Akbou its Name I see The Other spreading the panic of death amid the grass Mine That of others Similar to my own Thus amid the grass the Olive Trees Your olive trees *Thrushes. Young Thrushes. That time we were under the olive trees.*

Men were bringing the body. Wounded in the forehead. Touched, in the forehead. In that pain space, life of the forehead. A faint trajectory of tiny metal, a weapon escaped from the earth amid clay, waves of shadow and falling of a stone burst above the world in olive tree song *"Thrushes. Thrushes. This wound that bears my name. Mine. Name of all the others. Bearing my name. Up above the olive trees."*.........The Olive Trees That stone burst above the world The space of the murdering of physical enjoyment Enjoyment Ripped Away (ravished) That trajectory beneath the world Our world The one belonging to everybody In nature and also Presence This presence where we make the world happen *Thrushes. Young Thrushes. If I'd had the chance to remake the world. I will begin by naming the fevers vibrations human migrations So that nobody may be mistaken about the meanings of others So that nobody twists the meaning or the body the life of others So that nobody believes only in the word of one person But of many Many throughout the world* Two men were carrying the body in a group similarly dressed; in the shade, among the olive trees. *Thrushes. Young Thrushes. My blood where lives the world.* In green uniforms among the olive trees. Like a rustling in the olive trees. "Si Mokhtar's house" said the guide. Let's head for Si Mokhtar's house. "There, halfway along under the olive trees. Si Mokhtar's house."

Like an explosion among Olive Trees. Men shaped the rock This rock that they wanted both to contemplate and to subject to the movements of their desires Slightly bent over It Their lips among the stones Planted on them *"Being is not handed over in mid-journey"* the Amin said *"You must reach this world beyond the world."* The men now entered the courtyard. The courtyard of being (these men) where the world lives.

"Yes… A simple language game If you hadn't killed my brother… There in the grass… While we waited for our reign. Yes… Like a free creation of man out of matter. Matter that refuses and then forms… Yes. In this simple language game the world is born from… YES. The chosen one of Si Mokhtar." *"Yes. A simple language game the world was perhaps born from. Like a first word issued from the depths of the world passing through all the languages of this world."*

But it was necessary to rush the men (all the men who'd always been there; and young ones; young men; those who couldn't (yet) know the world, towards the work of war, in this quarrel of being and becoming, among the olive trees, the farm work, the tracking of resources, the robbing of time, the occasional illness, and

Yes. They had to construct the day: a new day; construct night; keep death within its own space; construct day, hope, in this ancient quarrel of man and the day, of a being and his becoming, this old quarrel of being and becoming, here, in this world, in this world where there must, ineluctably, appear once and for all, a new day, today. *"Man is obsessed by many stones… just as he was obsessed by many trees… And now the sign… stuck to him… in him… like a medal from other wars… What a mockery"* said the Amin *"There is no victory in this world… But a temporal decision stretched over the vast world…"*

The Amin had taken refuge at the bottom of this world. In the valley of the olive trees. A few miles from his village. This village he could see burning beyond the first row of hills. Above Akbou. A mile or so above Akbou.

He had left the village. And had come to seek refuge with Si Mokhtar. *The Chosen One. Si Mokhtar.* The one who was leading the war. He who was making a place for this war. Ever since the world (this world) the lives of this world had opened in his hand like a grenade. *"...Si Mokhtar"* said the Amin. *"...I don't envy your future, your becoming... Nor your being... Both sprung from this war... I still see, still see, many troubles coming from this war... Many troubles that will assassinate the lives that make up this war... Si Mokhtar."* And Si Mokhtar answered those (these men) who showed up in the courtyard: "Put the bodies down, over there, under the olive trees... They'll have to set fire to the whole area to get here..." said Si Mokhtar.

"They'd been surrounding us already for five years" Rouïchède said. *"Five years. And that was in nineteen sixty. Summer. I don't know how I've been able to get through this war... Get over this hill... : through all those years. With so much fire around me. So many fires."*

And Si Mokhtar told the men who had come into the courtyard: "After you set those bodies down... Station yourselves at different high points in the field... Yes... More towards the trees... And over near the road... I think They know you came down this way..."

The men ran to the various ridges. The olive trees. Twisted trunks Enduring in the World's fire. I saw your pain at the time The Day like an Old messenger in the world's active surging and your nerves must have been wrung once again that Day like a bursting forth of flint amid all the cubits of the world Each sparking The Day At That Time When The Day brought out the fire in every cubit of our world. Si Mokhtar's house. The chosen one of the war. Si Mokhtar. I saw burning (there, before me, before my face, my blood) every distance (cubit) we might want to cross in this world (each distance) attached to each body in the world skin burnt with each distance Man threw down fire above the hills "Napalm" *said Layachi* "It won't be long before we see refugees."

"You must die on the spot" said Si Mokhtar "We have nothing left... They've surrounded us now, the whole hill... It's better to die than be burned alive. Because They're going to use fire. Yes. Like in the old days.[35] They're going to use fire... You'd better die before the fire comes... Every man save one bullet for the end..."

The men had reached the ridges. At the edge of the road and field. Up at those sites or points where the other appears more clearly in the uniform of his times The Other He who obliges the war and requires war for a man to be born simply in his own place For a man and (his group) to be able to say to each other: "This is my land. It belongs as much to you as to me. Even so, I've always been its first and best inhabitant. But, you are teaching some other ideas. Other things I want to grow up with, I just want to grow up day after day without being humiliated without my life being gradual death By Degrees each day. Yes. I'd like that to be possible. That you might be able to say: the things I will teach you are of lower price than your own land than the Gift of your own land But they will be precious to you very precious outlasting these times For they will teach you a kind of patience The patience of your own birthing Yes They will teach you your own birth." Man had had to resign himself to the gift of the land But birth This birthing the other man spoke of he owed it only to his hatred Yes his hatred and something mixed in with hatred inseparable from hatred *Love* Yes *Love* so intimately blended with hatred: *"sometimes space was lacking, for movement; the space of Thrushes who couldn't move. ... Like a powder keg suspended above the world.*

> *This hatred for the world*
> *that I have in me   (hard and fast)*
> *like a*
> > *blade   that I*
> > > *aim*
> > *at you. Yes.*

I would have liked to be, the murderer of this world The One who lived above the world and held all the acidity of this world, there,

> *I would have liked to be a hate*
> *in this world. Distanced from lan*
> *guage and books. Closer to ac*

---

35   He is invoking a French practice from their 19th-century war of conquest. The French military suffocated Algerian villagers and insurgents by setting fires in the mouths of the caves where they had hidden.

tion. To the murderer in this wor
ld.
I have stayed too in love
with my field. The Olive Grove.
My song of youth
   hurried
   interrupted
in the brevity of this
   world.
   I would have
   liked
   to be
   (in this way)
   the
   murderer,
   of this
   world."

"the olive grove; in this shelter where I find my true place; the seat of my indifference; between love and hate; equal distances from the river; in the alluvial plain of my being and time; the rich plains of this exile above the trees; Thrushes. Young Thrushes. Like a young thrush above the trees, above the fields. Thrushes. Young Thrushes. A justice above and below the world. One justice. Thrushes. Young Thrushes. In the wheeling of the world. This being that has of a voice. Thrushes. This being who spoke of an apparition out beyond this world. A sharp being. Like a blade in the whistling of the world. Yes. Murder. Like a ram throat slit in its fleece. The world. The head cut open. Eyes red. Red. Circled with gold. This wool that cradled the body… Thrushes. Young Thrushes. I want a burying place for this body… His body. The man who first taught me to hunt among the olive trees. Under the hard leaves of the olive trees. To flap in the wind escaping his view. Yes. Thrushes Young Thrushes That murdering view. There. Way above the world."

The soldiers

VII'.

"I can say *at least starting right now* that she couldn't fight the coming
of that day.
Not my mother.
My mother who had come to live. With us
at Akbou. Because.
About my Uncle. No one ever had
any more news. No one
But me. Who tried.
From then on. To make his story known
No one."

VIII

Algiers

VIII. It was ten-thirty at night when they knocked on the door. They had jumped the wall. Climbed over the wood fence. The dog was dead. Struck down. A rifle butt across the neck. At the foot of the stairs. The five steps. Below the front door.

It was true he could have fled. The night before. Right when two men from the town told him that Si Taleb and Nourredine had been arrested. He had at the most one night. A single night to get out of there. He had to leave town.

That's when he explained, related, what he was going to do that night while Nourredine and Si Taleb were being tortured in Haut-Alger. That's when he took the trouble to invite the two men to have a drink with him in that room that room he had spent twenty years making as solitary and studious as he was at the bottom of that house a comfortable house whose every wall had been built upon his labors his jobs: day laborer teacher speaker lecturer: His work. Which he had lived for until that day in spite of various historic falsifications. Which he would fight for Yes As one fights for his fields his harvest His history For which he would fight any battle From the union battles to the summations for the defense and the political declarations Ever since those days when, as a School Teacher from the Rural Areas which he reached on a dirt path circling the hills, He had felt his hands and his eyes the eyes shone at the very pronunciation of certain words his hands reached forth like rope knots out above the olive trees Yes Toward those places where there flocked waiting for the new crop of olives The Thrushes The very ones who in the terrible fall of Nineteen Fifty-Four prepared for flight without stopping never stopped demanding a consecration of their flight There Above valleys With the power of olive trees The land never again neutral Blood Red Out to infinity Our flight The earth where everyone disports themselves Our flight like jewelry on the murderous impact of the world the young being A Migrant from his own lands Pinned to his labors with no recourse Who leaves the land And has always done so Toward the other lands other lands Europe Orient or Occident There the same annual migration from the other side of his world in opposition and in the disappearance of his world Young beings fleeing their world The asphyxiation of their world Inexorably seized Like a geological wound

like a wound close from now on and within and parent of an illusion of existence The Earth open like a leak

and the next steps and the body accentuated in the visible migration from their world (*Thrushes. Young Thrushes*). Everywhere. On the boulevards. The avenues. The train stations. The construction sites of the world. Paris–Hamburg.

Algiers–Miracle. Paris–Renault.

Paris–Madrid. Paris–Clermont. Paris–The world. ( ) ( )

Unnamed and Visible

Like a geo-graphic wound So mingled with my body and my steps Toward the territories That the door I push opening there before me so near me in my face on my face on all the faces of my bodies of our bodies of your body of my body the door? As I was saying turns there before me offering wind the wound of the wind the *cold* of the wind My being My life My Love

Unnamed and Visible

Like a geo-*metric* wound So splayed out before me and around me

That I see my loved ones My Familiars Paralyzed Like Thrushes Above the Territories of this world. (*Thrushes. Young Thrushes*).

like a geologic wound Active in language The earth's foam and Belly of the world There where the speech is delivered the address the man the other man the one like me and the woman each one to the other And

thrushes. Young Thrushes.

I am responsible. yes. responsible for the migrations in this world. for the unnamed of this migration. like a wound opened in the farthest part of me. that revels in me. that collides in me. that speaks in me. I'm responsible. Thrushes! Young Thrushes. And I don't know why? Thrushes? Young Thrushes. I don't know why?

The man had offered them tea with mint before telling them why he wasn't going to leave the town or the hill or the house he lived in He preferred to be at home when they came for him. Why should he leave? He would burn everything. Give them everything. That very night. And he would wait. At home. For them to take him away. He would wait.

His mother was wailing now behind him Very loud Her hand frozen onto The Other's clothes The one who was leading this war the frightful war of lives of nerves of fire set under the world She wailed in a voice he had never known a voice until now unknown in the ancient folds of vowels and murders There behind him A voice Completely plastered with age-old pain and fears with all the ancient fears that had dwelled in her despite the upheavals the places she had had to cross with him because of him from the interior of the country toward the sea from the valley to this little hill that resides There above Algiers pending its becoming like a witness to wandering existence among the shanty towns That house he had had built its island defeated by the day Where she now cried out with her hand frozen onto the clothes of The Other: "Tell me? Tell me where you're taking him? I want to know. I have a right to know. Where are you taking my man?" The man just tried to keep her from crying out: "All we know is we have our orders. Just our orders, right? I can't tell you anything. Your husband is smart. He'll do the right thing. Yes. He'll make out alright." *A smart man? My husband? Ever since the day they started the war! What does that kind of wisdom mean? That smartness. My God. My God. Since the day they started waging war. This way. Street by street. Road after road. Him. Already aged. Because of all those lives. All the lives that he had to lead in order to defend the valley this hill my blood Him The Man This man with whom I have shared I have lived through the world's terrible dividing up My children and my days Him A wise man?* "I just want to know where you're taking him."

They were everywhere. On the roof. In the courtyard. On the two balconies that overlooked the night sea October twenty-three '57 in the Clos Salembier that part of the City cut off from the rest of the town Now neighboring the new world Belonging to The Other and

Three of them were rifling through the room Abdenouar's room the fourteen-year-old son's the one who would remain who would become the oldest since Hmidouche had left and the father was going to leave and all the same you had to have an oldest son.

"No. I'm not leaving" said the father to the two men. "I'm not going anywhere. Because if I did they'd take the little one to make me come back. No. I'm not leaving. Besides. Neither Nourredine nor Taleb will talk that much. They might give a few names. Mine. Lots of others… You have to. Provided they find nothing here at my house. That's all… My name… What does my name matter… Lots of others will name me, too…" He added. Grudgingly. While taking a sip of tea… "Besides… If in a few days… You don't have any news of me… Tell the others… Those who get caught after me… To say my name… Yes… Say my name…Neither I… Nor my children will run any risk… no more risk… You can say my name without worrying about anything…" And he had risen approached the place where his written archives were kept his tracts his books and had slid open a wood board and removed some files from a space constructed between the uprights of the bookshelves and the wall files which he brought near the two men at the table there before them and they stared as if seeing this man for the last time Him the old man the unionist the one they would hear nothing about until the end until after three long months spent in the prisons the villas of Haut-Alger. Yes Three long months of intense interrogations both arms Yes broken Elbows gashed open Before this strange soldier an "Officer" as he said "I'm an officer. You have nothing to fear here. I don't like their methods. Oh I could take off. But what good would leaving do? For my honor My honor? My honor as a soldier? There's never been any honor in being a soldier. There is only duty. And I'd like to limit the damages. Yes. Limit the losses… While doing my duty… No more than my duty… And not my honor…" "You understand?"

They had put him in a cell. Alone. And the soldier. The officer who had no honor. The strange soldier. He was the one who brought water. And soup. He was the one who applied bandages and splints to lessen the pain of the wounds.

"Don't be afraid. Them, they take care of the interrogating. Me. I take care of the prisoners. And you, I've known you for a long time. Because here. I have. They. They too they have. Heard of you. Yes Many of your… "brothers" have mentioned you… But don't worry… They have nothing on you... Only your name... that can't be enough... that can't be enough... They'll keep you. And I'll keep you... me too... for three... yes... three months. Here. In this villa. Afterwards... You will be... like the rest Those who manage to bear the cost of their interrogations... sent to a camp... yes... to a camp in the South or West... deep in the country... or Elsewhere... Out of the country... On the north border of where you've been fighting... Yes... But don't be afraid... You can count on me... from now on... I'm not involved like them in torture... No... All I ask is that you say nothing... keep on saying nothing... and bear up under it... bear the cost of your struggle... As for me. I'll look after your wounds..."

The officer must have been about forty.

And he The father fifty-seven yes fifty-seven like the year itself like the day *Thrushes. Young Thrushes. Why did Hmidouche leave? Already? Or. Just now. Far from us. After three months of fighting. Three months. Almost like the father. Tell me? Thrushes. Young Thrushes.* Fifty-seven years like the night the day the forest.

Fifty-seven years like the night they came to take him There In his house At home like that Up on the heights that you see Algiers from Its luminous harbor Warm shadows In the distance a few movements and lights that show that other world The One my people our people leave for Those who flee war or misery Those who can still flee war and misery Land Land Splendor of my eyes *I shred the sea like a sheet hung above your abyss. I tear the water's salty laughter like springwater My throat and My sight. Land Splendor hanging at my very gaze. The guardian of the world. Of this world he has gone crazy. He sends us out in the world. He leads us to believe there exists somewhere in the world some place a site where the olive trees sing. Land O Land Powdery and Virginal Still Virgin to my accent Land O Land How can the migration be stopped Our migration throughout the world The guardian of the world Of this world Has gone crazy Land O Land* Those who run away through the world who flee the indigence of their world Lights moving beneath the sky *I see several letters setting fire to the sea There In the silence of the seaweed Several letters that speak of this world where I cannot live This world? World of all beings. This world? YES. Several letters setting fire to this world. The sand The stratum Myself My body in the flames of the world. I know more than four thousand beings exiled all over the world. Exiled in their routines. Their laughs. Their joys. Their tears. Their hopes. I know more than four thousand beings exiled in their work. Their loves. Their magnificence. And I know several Thrushes. Young Thrushes. Exiled in their pleasures.* YES. Powdery *Land Virgin Still Virgin to our pleasure.* Land Splendor to my eyes That night of the world That night When the men penetrated *Several of Them* that villa

The dog had been killed outright. A rifle butt across the neck. No yelp or barking. His tongue still caught in the trap of his jaws. Paws folded under his stomach as if running an interrupted running a race and the blow the hand the neck the hand that dealt the blow. "They killed the dog the dog" said Abdenouar. "They've killed the dog." The mother now held the son's face his cheeks against her breast. She was pressing her son's cheeks there Still In the doorway at the foot of the five steps where the dog lay. "They killed our dog" said Abdenouar. The mother pressed her son's cheeks "Don't cry. They took your father away. Stop crying. You mustn't cry in the glow of your father." They had blocked off the neighborhood. The street. A few silhouettes. A few cars. Civilian. And. Military. Several cars starting up. There. In the various streets of the Clos Salembier. *"Your husband is smart…"* the officer had said *"…he'll get out of this alright…" "…he'll be alright."* As if anything could be possible. Impossible. *"He'll be alright…"* More and more impossible.

The mother held her son. The old woman was there too. The oldest one. She who held on Now Almost blind At the edge of the steps *O Land Land* My vision and All these cries scattering in my veils My vision and My Blood From now on reunited in the dividing of this world I could have said Just as they were readying their weapons That my vision My life Would cost them greatly in human presence But

Yes But In that moment In the thrashing of the men's abduction The man's heart and his name gaping open I begin to fear Me An old woman at the edge of a vision

They called her *Jidda* Yes. Just *Jidda* The old woman That's all Who wore several veils various cloths blue and white dresses And Shrouding her face a very cool weave piled on her head like a turban *Jidda* Who for several years had done nothing but draw Alone In the room the father had set up for her Not far from the front door Several colored drawings Like wandering beings. which she multiplied during the days the nights over the walls Which she hung all around her like the only possible confidants of an old delirium conceived in the distress Yes of a single bit of human luck Her son The Husband dead long before the country had seen this war The war that would have pulled him from the depths of his village to hurl him into the middle of the street or toward the camps[36] In the officialdom of the camps created that way In the very land the sky the very day belonging to those who Were already living a kind of resettlement In a seasonal formation of regroupings around the olive groves or the fig gatherings or the ploughings or the springs in that opening moment of the prairies the pastures decided on

She kept living there for several years with only her day-to-day worries Those drawings that decorated the walls of her room her bed her brain In her brain they also decorated In a thought that was sharpened by madness The many desires of those whose birth she had witnessed Whose flight she had witnessed Far from her And whose coming home in the shape of colored silhouettes But Islam We've been told Islam Thus she had transgressed By herself From this room where he had lodged her The Holy scripture Which nonetheless she worshipped Since she believed that these drawings her own drawings came directly from that book run through with threads of gold Which she never failed never failed to bow to several times a day While all around her On the walls On all the walls of that room the colored silhouettes of human beings danced "Mother. Jidda is outside. There. At the top of the stairs.

---

36 The French broke up villages, to both punish and prevent insurgencies, and created resettlement camps.

"I hate this war."

Mother
Jidda has fallen
over here

Mother. Jidda went outside. She's over there, Near the stairs."

I hate this war. All my streakings through the night the nights My first works Those I distributed everywhere in the world So that some gratitude might arise from it I hate this war The mother now stumbled over the Dead dog Before drawing near to the old woman *Jidda* She whom they'd named that way as if they had found her already before them already in front of them that way covered with blue and white veils *Jidda* She whose eyes no longer recognized anything more than silhouettes traced by her hand that her brain or memory or nerve fibers presented to her not in images or thoughts but in a sort of instinct already inured to the reign of dark beings in the world this side of the world in this shadow where the world constitutes itself Beings of nightmare and dream living at the edge of the world Awaiting a gaze a first glance this first glance that might thus hold them above the shadow.

Sometimes she said: "The world is narrower than my head. Much narrower. Look. I can penetrate. Whenever I want. Depending on the distances I want to cover with my head. In the other world. Much more vast. Than this world."

She added. As a sort of confirmation that she felt was superfluous since what she thought and said appeared of such paramount truth to her of a truth that could never at any moment of this world or of the other recognize its inverse or hide another truth or a more global entire truth more able to account for what she was thinking Her truth as if a paramount truth of this world and the other a truth than which none could be more general considering that this one this truth that she took as her own could only be found in this solitude borne along in solitude meditated in solitude and that it could not serve for any other demonstration or proof than the one *Jidda* herself desired: this truth; her truth; her beings: "Look" she said. She added: "These beings that used to be of this world are no longer in this world. And yet they are still part of this world. Therefore they exist above and beyond this world. Out beyond this world. Right?" Abdenouar laughed and said standing close: "There is only one world. This one where we are. That other world. It's That of the others. It's not ours. There's only one world in this world." "The world of the others" said old *Jidda* Since Abdenouar had called it that "Yes. That of the others." "No. *Jidda.*" Said Abdenouar "No. Mine. The one where I exist. The one where we exist. How can you talk about another world? Shadows. Shadows of shadows that you pin up on your walls."

The mother had hurled herself toward the old woman dressed in blue and white veils as if (*Jidda*) had gotten up to take a few steps at night like a sleepwalker in her unbalanced peril that no one should try to wake her from So close to her madness to a madness everyone will inevitably tumble into really tumble once in life Death This madness of our world Death-Madness she had already signaled She The Old Woman at the edge of the stairs *Jidda* Madness she had already signaled in the drawings pinned on the walls and a madness about which nobody had been able to think couldn't think that she Already knew a few things. Yes. That she Already knew a few things.

"I hate this war" Abdenouar thought "just like that woman, before the stairs. Yes. She's crazy. Just like that woman. At the edge of the stairs."

"I hate this war."

The men had reached the crest of the field At the end of the road and field. And those spots or points where the other appears more clearly in the uniform of the day The Other He who required this war so that a man might be born at home just simply at home and be able to say:

here is my land; it belongs to you and, although I say it myself, I've always been the best and first inhabitant; but, here you are teaching other things; other things with which, among which, I want to grow up (I'm going to grow up), simple as that. Day after day. Without being humiliated by that or feeling a gradual death a death *by degrees* every day; yes; I would like that to be possible; that you might be able to say: those things I'm going to teach you will be less costly than the price of your own land than the *gift* of your own land; but they will be very precious to you, beyond these days; beyond the nowness of these days, because they will teach you a patience a rigor a faith yes a faith, that of your own birthing.

but he had owed only to his hate Yes his hate and to something inseparable from hate *love* Yes *love* the story of his birthing

being is not given to you in mid-journey
said the Amin
the Aged Teacher
you have to go well beyond this world
to reach that other world
that of being,
mankind's place.

we used to know the legend that
gave birth to The Day from several
drops of Dawn
but the Aged Teacher would say
man is a migration
a migration in this world
and we listened
to the world
the migration
of our world

IX

Paris

IX...... They saw the father again in the year 1959 in Paris. The family had left Algiers because. After the Paul Cazelles camp where he had remained since the end of his interrogation. The territory was off limits to him. And. Since in those days, and as in every other time, irony had settled over the human tragedy. They had liberated him to France. Paris. Where his family had had to find him. Or. Rather. Arrive before him. Almost at the same time that he did…

Of course there was no more old Jidda. And young Abdenouar had a strong feeling that. From now on. He would me missing what he had thought a necessity of life. Those drawings she sketched and pinned onto all the walls of her room. That he had loved to look at. Because of all the distortions that made up the people and landscapes who, captured in bold colors, seemed to have broomsticks instead of legs and entire brooms instead of arms. Different kinds of beings situated that way in the madness of her world like scarecrows in a field where fugitive human beings were transformed into sparrows or titmice who wheeled, eternally, around them in the air.

All it took for Abdenouar to feel alone was the disappearance of these pinned-up drawings; and, at the point of leaving the town, without even being completely sure that his father was waiting for them, further on, on the other side of this sea that he'd always had before him Always there rising like a wall, from his balcony, solitude, his solitude had climaxed; as if the world had become, suddenly, murky murky so murky that you could no longer guess or perceive him or her who was holding it up had held it up from then on above the shadow, near that fleeting luminosity which *Jidda* The Old One had known since the first moments of her craziness, and whose secrets she had woven, day after day, in her room, all around her, on the walls.

A berth had been reserved for them, at Algiers, and a train compartment for Paris. They left the country and the city in mid-November and the whole world looked to them like a rain-soaked ball full of drizzle and fog sewn together with needles, poisonous and invisible pins, fallen all around their eyes.

By chance, the villa Yes That villa perched by the shantytowns, had not been requisitioned and they had been able to leave within its walls the things that didn't even belong to them anymore (they were leaving the country without knowing at what date what moment what place of what day or what night or what season or what life they would be able to return) *I had thought; you had me believe in a sort of game in this world; a game wherein I might grow up. My head is still ringing with your games; you had a frightening way of showing your drawings; a completely furious manner; as if your drawings were made of pine needles; those needles I brought back to you after high school; and your eyes; yes. Your eyes. With their* animal *blue. With their gaze, they burned those pine needles; those drawings that made the room revolve just like my head around its own walls. (I should add there, in that evasion, in the destruction of your walls, the multiple joys or enchantments that came with your footsteps, in that room, or mine, my room you came to worried about the teachings you saw reflected on my eyes and my lips, yes; I sensed your worry, but also a diabolical agility; yes,* diabolical; and your agility was that (I can say this) even though that word, or affectation, with respect to you, is fairly meaningless; *diabolical*—if only this word could mean the *ease; yes, the ease;* of that truth—*your truth*—where, in one gesture, you moved your arms your body, your drawings heavy with flames and intelligence, your eyes, there, turned toward me, *blue, miraculously blue; and that ease, that agility that I felt to be troubled because she was discovering the cracks, the injustices, and the disasters: those wise apprentices now turned away from my body, my blood, my sight, from my character, or my being; young; still Young and already False; False; Beyond what is allowed; in work and adolescence's disguise; that work that was supposed to*—this is how they made me believe in the world, this world so different from the world where—*in this room*—you were evolving—*alone and human, human... make me grow up in this world; while. Now.* On the day of exile of departure and migration. *I remain so deprived by your absence that I emit no word thought or feeling desire for return or for progress forward, here, in this world where, in spite of yourself, in spite of me, you left me waiting for something that—and, naturally, I can know this—will never arrive).*

You shouldn't have, given the casual air of this world—your world—left me, this way, alone in the world; despite the possible appearance of that being whom I love and hate for not having been able to send me back—*or send me*—toward *your world:* him, *the father,* summoned *by me,* in the long nights—*all my nights of patient vegetal reconstruction; a difficult reconstruction because, with my mother there, I could only think of You, my two beings of the world who guided*—visually—the opposition or distinction between the two worlds; *You, the two beings ripped from my world, and because, over long nights*—all those nights when I struggled to reconstruct a person: *myself—I had to call, beyond any anguish of mine, beyond many anguishes, on a certainty of existence situated beyond any* real *existence,* any palpable existence; *yes, wounded in my truest center, at that site, a locus, of personal distortion:* I begged, *over long nights*—all those nights when I had to, without considering the weakness that, on the day of your death (Your Death) will seem even more acute and irreparable, I had to (yes) all alone, as alone as squirrel or hedgehog, rebuild my personhood—*I begged for a possible renewal of my life, and the lives of others, of all those others I felt dying in me, dying dying, as if they were dying in me. Yes; I had to bring back each needle of that rain that flashes through the ship, the world, the bridge and the language where I now exist, where all the others are found, impatient for the day, for murder, for luck, for lies.*

Still, you should have told me warned me told me… something about
yes; something very close to this flight or state of loss where I find myself; you should have told me that

They were expected at Gare de Lyon train station, in Paris, and, after that, they would go to Levallois[37], in the inner suburbs, to live in Levallois, waiting for the father who, after leaving Paul Cazelles camp (November

---

37 Farès clearly knew something about this Paris neighborhood as a thirty-one year old—and he moved there with his new wife in the very last years of his life.

12, 1959), was supposed to be liberated in Paris, assigned, sort of, to a residence in Paris, where they'd already found work for him.

The father, the old unionist, who'd been told, on his transfer from the Paul Cazelles camp to the prison at Fresnes: *"Of course it's alright if you're a unionist again. But: always respecting the law. Yes. On this one condition. You have to stay in Paris. Your wife and son will stay, like you, in Paris. Stay away from politics, the FLN,[38] subversive activities. One day, for sure, you'll have your Independence. So... We got you a teaching job... You can continue your research here, peacefully... What do you say?..."* And the father had said nothing; except: *"I have a little trouble believing that I'm free; yes, free; after being in Villa Susini Only a few hundred yards from my own house; that I've been interrogated, tortured, sent to Paul Cazelles; that now I'm being sent to Paris, off to Paris, where (already) my wife and son are waiting; that I'll be working again; I have trouble (some trouble) believing I'm free; yes; free; I'm going to be free... I'm having some trouble..."*

They had to turn the villa their villa over to some friend or neighbor so they could leave for France. They had to leave right away because they didn't know (at least that's what fear did to you; yes, fear; you could suddenly, just like that, not know anything anymore...) if the release order *(that's what they called expulsion and assigned residence in a certain town, beyond the Mediterranean)* would be valid much longer; or if some over zealous soldier would interfere with civil decisions and military prerogatives. There, during this brief moment of hope, a moment that appeared, and was nourished, hovering above murders. They left three days after the *release* of the father. Three days. Yes. In the middle of the war.

---

38 The militant group fighting for Algeria's independence, and, later, the ruling party in the country.

Yes. Being is not given to you in mid-journey said the Amin, The Old Teacher. You have to have gone the whole way and the distance whatever distance separates and you have to understand space beyond separation understand the space where the other life could have been built the other life the one you desire the one we all want to achieve some day: all in one day. Being is utterly an other place outside of oneself and with a duration equal to the birthing of another world: there, that is why I linger or delay my going out into the world in the long age of this world.

X

Abdenouar

X...... At least that is the way fear worked; fear of yourself; yes; like an obsession deep inside your being; an active, present, obsession, as if you were able to see the fragile limit of your life, here, passing through your body; as if your body were "*limit*" a limit of resistance and lasting; as if you had to learn to hide your body, the way you learn, just as surely, to hide your heart. At least that's how the city appeared, powerful rivalries of people and places where time seemed to take hold of each being and transform the person's legs into the hands of a clock; you had to find a way to come into contact with this place: to disguise your foreignness: avoid gossip: and quickly comprehend, in order to sidestep the massacre, and reach some clear horizon. This apprenticeship lasted two years; Abdenouar learned quickly, very quickly. *"This world; yes! This world. Nothing but this world we're living in. You could have*

> *told*
> *me*
> *all the same*
> *that this world would end up*
and inevitably
> *seeming more empty to me than the colored spaces of your games*
or drawings;
> *and that I would no longer be able*
despite the whirling solitude in which I see the days dance their shadows (the shadows of your days; yes. Those in which you held forth in the world) that I would no longer be able beyond you Jidda *to uncover some refuge in this world; no What closeness or what opening was I supposed to live in? Today and all these other days when they come tell me about so many disappearances and abductions? No; all I can do is focus on each person's lot, on the individuality of death or of the day; walk, understand, and avoid that other wounding by the world, the one you never recover from: despair,*

or being's flight from this world; here, in these streets I roam; the tasks I perform; the war I wage; and your face your face Jidda; *these blue white veils that stirred the mind the fragility of the mind and the insufferable presence of death or madness[39] that shaped your drawings";* Yes. Like an obsession deep inside. Their arrival would have been more brutal if the father had not, in fact, come to find them at Levallois two days later. An attenuated joy. Suspended in murder. The murder

of man,

my fellow.

---

39 The theme of old women driven mad by the war persists in Farès (see "the Aunt" in *Exile and Helplessness* [*L'Exil et le désarroi*, 1976, volume 3 of the trilogy]), and it is important to remember that, as a psychoanalyst, he treated survivors of the war and its aftermath.

*the Old Teacher
off in some
part
of this world.*

The Old Teacher was talking about a
distance equal to that of two worlds
where neither one was the far end,
rather, an exactness, or, adjustment
*"you'd have to be able to perform
this gesture of the earth; or, its
movement towards"*
*"the earth (this earth) will take its
place on a site; in the fullness of man and*

*his desire; as in that Saharan legend of
the two stars who shared the same goal:
to capture the gaze of the shadow fallen
over the other side of the world."*
You couldn't avoid the Old Teacher's sayings
because, coming at you, or, into you, they
opened up the cracks of your being, yes, they
opened you up and, despite that pain you felt
entering you, you became part of a happiness,
realized in this world.
The Old Teacher also said:
*"You'll never go the distance, alone: you will
have to be several, and given to the world, all
at the same time."*
, he was speaking of that distance out beyond
this world, included in the two worlds,
without end point or beginning, included in
the two worlds, at an equal distance from the
two: he said:
*"no one will be able to reach that place,
alone."*

One day *hope* came to this world; and said

"No being in this world has as much spirituality as I; no being and no non-being, as philosophers would say; no non-being; because I am at the same distance from being and non-being; Me, from any hope in this world."

1962

Hope had in this way hurled enigma into the world, and the world or the inhabitants of the world (this world) didn't have time or the chance to beware. Therefore *hope* stayed forever clamped onto human speech

"Being is not given to you in mid-journey" said the Amin
The Old Teacher.

"... one of the essential conditions of my
soaring rests in the vastness-vanity of the
rich man; or, in the coarseness of the poor.
Man will never conquer hope *since I can't—*
no matter how you phrase it—die,
"both being and being not": I am too similar
to man *for him to vanquish me*
  one day. *"*
Thus did Hope think.

1954.

Hope came into this world, amid
the scattering of the word and of men.
There is no doubt that Hope was fully
able to comprehend the places and the
acquittals of this world. It soon had to
share the tastes and the words of these
men who, just like it (hope), were on a
quest for being. It had to become man,
to arrive at some form of being, in this
world. Hope.
No doubt at all. In this world.

Acting with the certainty of the event
of the advent that's the spot I occupy in
this world; that is why they call me
hope in this language that occupies
mankind

1954.

... Agile old man; old one of language and agile rages; we learned of your birth back in the other century, back when people landed more consistently in our territory; yes. We used to like to believe the old man existed; an old man whose power resided in words of wisdom given to the youth of the village so they might learn to distinguish that distance that equalizes; yes, that makes any trajectory equal. He didn't like things that wasted time.

1852.

1862.[40]

"Ten years the Old Man; ten years, in the last century; ten years, an Old Man of language and agile words."

His birth had corresponded with the country's first losses. He had been born on the west side of the valley, above the upper village, not far from the world's consciousness of religion, on the spot where the memory of the world's first thought still echoes, the thought that worked its way along the oceans, the moons, the stones, the one that coursed over ploughs, pastures, acres, that armed eyesight, smiles, nerves. He had been born into the world's conflict, this world's conflict, the conflict that attacked the old world, in this world still. So what should we do? Understand conflict in the present world.

---

40 Counting back, 1852 was an important date in the reassertion of French military control in Algeria.

1872.

"Twenty years the Old Man; twenty years in the other century; twenty years, Old Man of language and agile words."

The war had made quick work of stripping the old world of hope. Old World was bound to die because Old World had, in truth, lived too long, in this world. What should we do? Understand the new world in this world. Win the other world's war.

"being is not given to you in mid-journey", said the Amin, the Old Teacher.

"Win the war in this world?"

The news had terrified the old world, because, *"man is a migration, in this world."*

many men (too many men) were absent from this world. It would have been best to be able to round up some troops. But the territory had become *bald*; yes, *bald*; like the villages; over there, high in the mountain range: they had razed, torched, burned, exterminated, the villages; *there, high in the mountain range.* It would have been good to be able to raise a force.

1882

"Thirty years the Old Man; thirty years, in the other century; thirty years…"

Many men absent (dead) in this world. Old World will have to move on. It will have to understand the war: the New World. Old World has to understand the New World.   The news had terrified
Old World

"Old world; all I can do is focus on each person's lot; on the individuality of death or of the day; walk, understand, and avoid that other wounding by the world, the one you never recover from: despair or being's flight from this world; here, amid the streets I roam; the tasks I perform; the war I wage; and your face J…"

The news had terrified
The old world.

1957-1959.

"being is not given to you in mid-journey" said the *Amin*, the Old Teacher. *"Man is a readiness. A migration in this world."*

XI

The Old Teacher

XI...... "There are always people who will say. Who want to say to me. That they don't understand me. No. They don't understand my words or the form of my language. It's their strange way of eluding the *Old Teacher*... I would like to have (already) lived for several centuries in order to be absolutely sure of being at the zenith of my understanding (I'm talking about centuries to come) and thus to leave, in complete tranquility, this world—after having conversed, one last time, with the *Old Teacher*...... Abdenouar? Who can really tell me about this Abdenouar. This Abdenouar and his red hair. He disappeared in 1961. During the silent demonstration, in Paris.[41] A disappearance among disappearances. It seems my speech is incomprehensible. Yet the work I'm doing is simple enough: I'm giving a burial place yes *a burial place* to this migration, *in this world*."

---

41 What is sometimes called La Manifestation Silencieuse (with ironic comment on French official and media silence in the aftermath) took place on October 17, 1961. The most famous of the 1961 demonstrations, and, like most of them, organized by a branch of the FLN, it was ostensibly a protest against an arbitrary curfew. Two to three hundred were killed, many "disappeared," beaten to death by police and thrown in the Seine. Note: "I'm giving a burial place..."

The Thrushes

They could just as well have been born somewhere other than this country. Other than in this area. On the far hills of the North country. On the spot where

your face or footsteps there, in the half-light behind you; death, between my sweetest moments of daydream, present death, death wandering in the sand and the shifting of my hands; I fell from the corner of your mouth, in this mad silence where—as if you could create some happiness for me—I listen to the most whispered of your words, spoken in the complicity of our world, yours and mine, where I struggled to live by understanding your words"

" "

; as if that world you ceaselessly bore witness to existed; yes, existed; *that world? Not the stuff of memories; For who would tolerate memories like that? But this world of continuous life; or perpetual life; or:* irreplaceable *life (that word) (a monstrous word).... a word so discredited... and yet so valuable;* yes, this word *that speaks eternity yes* Eternity *or* Rapture: *this word* ... eternal *life;* this life

"being is..."

And to think that you had to disappear from our sight before I could understand something (not that much, to be sure) in your words;

The Old Teacher.

before I could point out a few dates or places that trace and scribe that terrible movement (slamming together) of Day and Shadow, both issuing from that migration of words and beings throughout the world; before I could go back to some prior state and say Here, this is the moment when

No

I marked its progression in the silence of those years when man relearned to live in a terrestrial hell; the silence that loomed over the two wars; its rise; the inevitability of the industrial rise: the war that gripped our land (Thrushes. Young Thrushes.) that landed (like a whiplash) on

*the Old Man (Old World); the Old Man of the last nineteen years: 1871[42];
Old World; they could just as well have been born in some other country.
Elsewhere than in this area. On the far hills of the North country.*

The Old Teacher had to give way under the shock. In the valleys,
plains, villages and the tormented foothills of the mountains they had
left lookout posts, mustering points and military intelligence. After the
war men were meant to live in peace, learn to read and write, listen to
speeches, and keep their heads and eyes down. Weapons vanished,
confiscated by administrators made suspicious by so much Yes, men
kept quiet or muttered only a few words, words empty of meaning but
full of life for them: they would say: "Yes, Administrator. Sir…" "very
good. Administrator, Sir." Or else "Yes. I'm working hard. I can do lots of
things; and, above all, I have a family to feed; I'm a man at peace." Then,
talk began about certain men who lived underground, their eyes buried in
rocks, heads covered in dirt, and the talk was in the third person plural, the
pronoun that surely suited them best. Their existence was in the vicinity.
Yes, the vicinity of other people. The ones who referred to themselves in
the singular. They said of those others *"They…"* while adding one or two
words these singular people did not actually believe, but the thing was
to show that *they* were set apart on the silent perimeter of being or of the
land, in those places where life barely brushes the belly-life of a man, a
man who, from one such brush-by to another, is able to nourish a new will
power for mankind. The women knew movement, the Shadow's chorus.
They had suffered much loss of life in the other war. The 1871 war. And
they couldn't come to grips with these times these times that so insidiously
tallied the skin the nerves the bodies of all the men. They tried to reflect on
it. They tried to forge new words or new ways of broaching or breaking up
this new world. The enemy was hopelessly over-armed. The women sang
Yes they sang day and night they sang the son beyond the sea or the other
one fled from the coast to the South, hidden in the desert's warm zones
They sang and their bodies twisted like vine shoots in a brush fire. The
Old Teacher lived several miles above the Upper Village. Young people
came a few times to pray with him. The adults came only once a week, to

---

42 Again we count back to 1852. 1871 is, itself, significant as the year of the Mokrani
Revolt (against the French). One of the more important armed revolts, it started in Farès's
region, Kabylia.

talk about land in that village or the other. They had to figure out a way to keep on

living. Men accepted the administration, identity papers, the census, school, but on no condition would *they* accept serfdom. "*They* still think they're free" said the Other. "We'll tell them that *they'll* never (you will be) be slaves, but *workers. Yes*. That's what we'll tell them: *You will be workers.*" And that worked because what workers respect the most is work, theirs, or other people's, respect for the world and the land, the man who furrows the land. It worked like a charm. Men had accepted this bit; only the Old Teacher became thoughtful, as one who had heard everything before. Here is what he said: *"We're going to live according to their world; since there's nothing we can do but live in their world; but we are going to be healed; yes; healed; we have to learn how to get well; because our world is too old; within our being; yes; within our being; we will put time to use; time; now the only ally we'll ever have in this world."* What followed was the Old Teacher's parable; a kind of linguistic construction, winged, beyond this world and its time. The men listened because the Old Teacher used the ancient language, the one that changed every being into a hope charged with life, like shells full of birdshot. The men listened because the Old Teacher was telling them of their being Yes of their being the being so wounded during the course of the last war, the one of 1871. The men listened. That night they'd decided to exclude the representative of the administration, down there, at the gate of the Upper Village. The Old Teacher said *"We're going to invent the Thrushes yes The Thrushes, at the threshold of this world; the world we want to conquer, because, there is no other solution for us, but to conquer this new world."* And the men understood because *Thrushes* was the other name of that young man, the one who, in his fragility, makes the narrow-minded world move. The Old Teacher said *"We can't escape our beliefs, men of the low country; because we've got to comprehend the farthest and sharpest meaning of those beliefs; no belief is, in this world, negligible, the Thrushes are one of the beliefs of this world, in this world; isn't that so, men of the low country."* The Old Teacher[43] knew every language; but what he didn't

---

43 The translation has consistently been "teacher" (*maître* can mean "teacher") because, despite this brief Islamic reference, this figure is unlikely to be a *fqih, imam, marabout* or other Islamic spiritual master. The more secular translation is consistent with everything

realize (because of his Koranic overtones in this his thirtieth year) was the power of such speech; he only meant to interest men in the hope of a new world; yes, interest them simply, in the hope of a new world; he was to learn something, later, in this world (as he started to age and lose his sight) *"Men ran to the different crests of the field. The Olive Trees. Twisting trees Enduring in the world's fire." "I hate this war,"* thought Abdenouar. *"Jidda... The Olive Trees... This rock burst above the world..."*

Farès writes about Islam, the Koran (see "The Book" in *Exile and Helplessness*) and Arabism.

"being is not given in mid-journey" said the Amin, the Old Teacher *"Man is a readiness; a migration in this world."*

The Old Teacher

The Olive Trees

Men went on living in the shelter of their beliefs; the olive grove, the trees, struggled on in the world's fire; men chased after their being, soul, day or murder, in the conflagration of the world.

The young man said *"Thrushes. Young Thrushes. From the South, the North, or the East, I offer my blood and my sight* The very man who designated life, or death, for the young messengers of the olive trees. Close relatives of swift greyhounds. Diligent consumers of murderous powers and of order.

The searchlight swept the hill and the military scouting posts; the land climbed, not far from their position, humped up, while they hunkered now in the grass, sixty yards from the searchlight, just before the first strands of barbed wire, a couple of feet from the minefield before the road, yes, the one that ran along the Eastern frontier.[44] from sea to desert, the tar road, long, sown with traps, mines, signals, men stalking other men caught up in the same death; yes, the death that caught the young man, running along, just as the road seemed deserted or conquered *reconquered,* just as the young man wanted to dance to the reconquering: Lounès yelled out hide yeah they're firing right in front of you; get down; the young man couldn't hear any more: *the tar road; I'm dancing on the tar road; imagine a thrush who found a whole pavement of olive trees; yes, olive trees; for him alone; what would the thrush do?* The young man was dancing at the edge of the road through the olive trees after crossing the first block, the first electrified fence; he was dancing, machinegun in his right hand watch on his left wrist; he was dancing; *Thrushes. Young Thrushes. I'm on the other's territory; the land the other administers, while we're creating the world. Thrushes. Young Thrushes. I'll surely die in this world. But Thrushes. Young Thrushes.* The young man kept on dancing on the tar road. *I'm drunk Drunk DRUNK on this world."* You could see the rounds' trajectories. Yes. Glowing. From the door of the blockhaus.

---

44 Logically, the frontier with Tunisia. On the Tunisian side were camps, military and otherwise, set up to support the war of independence. Farès temporarily gave up his student life in Paris and went to the Tunisian camps near the end of the war.

Men were chasing after their independence, on the very edge of the accords; over those three days when the accords[45] were to be signed

night of the 16th and 17th

to the 19th of March

62

---

45 The Evian Accords, ending the war.

"Independence! Like a blade against my neck; the wind that speaks to us whirls up in clouds*; I see your hand your shoulder your laugh my lips your eyes; the day flows, here, sweetly, from my loins; I see your sex your speech your legs the years yes the long beautiful years opened to my work my abundance my days; I see: I needed only one day to know love; and, today, I hurt; terrible pain: I see: Independence: I am Independence: I say: come closer Independence: and I bite my cheek; yes: independence Our Independence in one day!"*

Never was war more deadly than in the few days just before Independence.

Those three days when from East to West North to South the frontiers were *torched.* What would the Old Teacher be saying, in whatever part of the world? Yes, what could the Old Teacher be doing, in whatever part of this world? You could say: that we've deserved our world Yes in whatever part of this world: you could say: we deserve our world.

The Old Teacher, in whatever part of this world.

"Our experiences of life come about in the shape of catastrophes. We must deduce, from catastrophes, the way our social system functions. It is when crises happen, economic depressions, revolutions, wars, that we must, on reflection, discern "the inside story." Already, then, reading the newspaper (but also the bills due, the pink slips, the legal appeals beneath the flags etc.) we sense that someone must have done something for this visible crisis to arise. So who did what? Behind those events that are announced to us we presume others which are hidden. Those are the *real* events. Only if we knew them could we understand.

It is only history that can teach us about these real events—to the extent that the main actors haven't succeeded in keeping them secret. History gets written *after* the catastrophes."

Bertolt Brecht
"Les Arts et la Révolution"
—article in *L'Arche*
(Travaux 9)

XII

Barcelona

XII. The approach to Barcelona was gray, endless vacant lots, warehouses, major roads and children throwing stones at the train's windows. A lowering sky. You could almost touch it. And then I remembered. That an esthetics professor had said That what constitutes the beautiful. Is the possibility of its existence. Which is to say. Its present inexistence. Such was the beauty of the bas-relief the young man from Gradiva had fallen for. The love quest was rooted in the statue's imaginative duel. The imaginative duel of its foot. And in the desire—not recognized as such—to make love to his neighbor in the next apartment.

Therefore. I can say. Persuaded as I am that inexistence is the precondition of beauty. That I had. In some way taken a vow of beauty. Since. I had said to myself. Through some unknown power or desire: I had told myself. That I would only reach a state of existence if I succeeded in making this more evident: At the spot in the world I then occupied. Whatever made me "live" or (though there is still no such word) "unlive" or, simply, "write."

The problem was formidable. Because. At the same time. I understood and asserted the derision that held me in the world, a derision which came from a *historical* incapacity to exist in the pre-existing forms of social and political life. And. In addition. I affirmed history's value, the value that every country, in its own time and place, must some day achieve.

Thus I arrived at the following. That, instead of upholding a historical and psychological form of *Myself.* I had to activate the lateral form of a self which, in this way, was no longer the origin of anything, rather the moment of passing through an ensemble much vaster than the self.

That's how I began to write.

What remained was the ENORMOUS difficulty of nourishing this me. For. Ever since the last time I'd seen Conchita,[46] in Paris. And. Later. That Ogress in-dwelling. So to speak. Beneath the world. And above the world. It had quickly become apparent that I had to nourish myself in a more lively and *worthy* way than the means which had. Up till then. Kept me alive. Because. Meanwhile. I had ended up brushing against the most intense craziness. The madness of a monumental articulation of quotidianness. Yes. To better explain. I had become: *a sociologist*.

Others. Would have rejoiced in such a hard-working consecration. But. Given the slight worth that contemporary sociology had accorded that perilous part of the world I am from. And that sociology was content with a world made of socialized categories and hierarchy. I really had to discover a social locus from which my elocution and my work were still feasible. That is how I chose that trip. That voyage equidistant from Conchita and the sea.

Yes. I went and found Conchita again. Around five o'clock. Of an afternoon on fire. At the bar of the hotel where she was working. With a switchboard operator's cap on her head. "This is all you could get, for work?" "Yes," Conchita had said, "that's about it. And giving a few French lessons at sixty pesetas an hour."

She had changed, slightly. Her hair was redder now. And longer. Her hair was wavy now, quite different from what I'd known three months before.

"It's the phones that make your hair curl like that?"

It seemed I was entitled to a *bien largo* coffee and two soft kisses from Conchita.

The Hotel Barcelona was a four-star place. Where rooms cost 700 to 900 pesetas. The equivalent of 80 francs. I waited for Conchita for ten minutes (she was changing) and, like two flush travelers come for a Barcelona afternoon, we strolled (Conchita and I, and I and me) through the hotel lobby.

Oof. We were out in the street. A gorgeous day. We went up the street. Toward the apartment where. Conchita. lived.

---

46 The first encounter occupies about a third of *A Passenger from the West* (*Un Passager de L'Occident*).

XIII

Barcelona

XIII. At ten-thirty at night, we were on the Ramblas, near the Tapas Canaletas Café. Ever since I've been in Barcelona Conchita has feared one thing (the Ogress): getting fat. *She thinks. Yes. She thinks. That the afternoons, the nights, the days of love making, have made her hips spread. But, the way the tapas are presented on the Canaletas bar, Conchita loses her decisiveness. "One draft, or two?..." "Two drafts and an order of mussels..." Conchita laughs, while some "culture of up-to-dateness" has plugged in an implausible TV, at the end of the bar. Conchita's eyes have changed since the afternoon. Now they are circled in black. Wildly green. Green and yellow. Limpid and loving. You're shaking. Old Brandy. You're shaking like a thrush about to be seized. Like a thrush they're hunting. Like a thrush they're going to panic. You're trembling; and yet, you love-revere the flight of thrushes and olive groves. You love-revere the crazy weightlessness of their love. Who? Barely tangible. Who can imagine what goes on between a thrush and an olive grove. Who could believe there's a connivance there. Their connivance of fluid happiness. Only slightly earthbound. Slightly frivolous. Slightly dangerous since a thrush. Yes. A thrush. Only rarely makes it to the other spring season. The other spring. So you imagine a long string of thrushes playing in the wind. Rolling the wind. At the same time you imagine, in the mad flight of thrushes, a young partridge. Yes. A young partridge. A partridge that steps and searches the wind. The grass. Right beneath the olive trees. Or perhaps. A being without fur. Being with no ears. Climbing through the different forests of the world. You make out the plaintive being in its carapace of quills. A being of the blood river, of the plains' red glow just as, at the moment of coming to life, it had to grow up in a clearing, at the crossroads of men's varied ventures. A being the serpent will scare. (Yes.) That sulks within itself (thus). That sulks about itself. The hedgehog. Three beings. (The hedgehog.) (The Thrush.) (The young partridge.) Whose existence not a single one of the people you watch eating/drinking at Canaletas is aware of. Nor suspects its existence*

  However

Yes. Three beings of language and of blood. Have you grasped these manners? These ways people have of strolling the Ramblas or the quais near Châtelet, when you're in Paris, before the bird cages, the parakeets, the titmice, the long-eared animals, the partridges: you despair of living a new life; while at the same time, you might drive an eighteen-wheeler from Yugoslavia to the China Sea, you (yes, in this way) you (yes) might wrangle a twelve-seven (12/7) with the skill (yes) of a typist, you might stride with a Mauser in your hand, two cartridge cases on your hip with the same precipitation as a wadi in spring spate. Yes. The Ogress exists. Because you can sense her pounding the pavements of the cities and the desires of their people. Because you can see her devouring the windows of the café-bars. Of the sandwich cafés. The beer cafés. The bar-cafés. Yes. Because you see her opening mouths. Because you see her devouring from one mouth to another, biting down on the nourishments of anguish and of nothingness. And you hear her speaking horribly (horribly) in a TV set. In the clank of an espresso machine. In the gulping of a Metro entrance. In the bus stations. You'd prefer to know something different. Something other than a momentary dazzling exaltation. You'd like to chase after delirium. Go right to the end. (All the way to the end.) But you're afraid. You're afraid to be, at the same time, here, with

  and absent from
  Paris
  Algiers
  Akbou
  Collo[47]
  Port-Saïd Square
  your street.
  You're afraid
  to be stunned
  by
  what

---

47 Birthplace of Farès.

devours you
and grinds you up
You're afraid
to live through
a devouring
of the life
that
lives you
and
deploys you.

You're afraid
of being
and
not
being.

Of being
simply
here
Or
being
the way you are.

With no
sense of belonging
in your control
or…
Yes.
You're afraid
and,
at the same time
you can see
to the other side
of this delirium

you behold.
That you'd like
to hold on to,
there,
at the end
of your reach, your lips, laughs, steps, (for you step always) your
running (for you burn through your time) words (for you talk all the time)
blunders (for you're fearful all the time) charms (for you dazzle the whole
day) wants (for you desire the day long)
You would have liked to live,
even before coming into the world.
You'd have liked to be author
of your birth. Yes. And that way
you wouldn't have had
to assess the many steps
you'd take in this
fear (yes. Because of your youth. A youth
that doesn't want to die without a chance to be youth.)
of seeing the world
(yes, the world. The one you know)
despise you. And you're dying.
You're dying from a love too
great. Too greedy. And immediate.
So you're afraid. You're
afraid of not doing
enough. Or too much. Too little.
Or poorly. Or falsely.
You're afraid of being
nothing more than
the revelation
of what
doesn't belong to you
what
belongs not at all
in no way

to you… Tireless worker in the other language[48] *Which you respect in its slightest folds, strengths, disputes, revolts, absurdities, rigor, joy, delight or vanity.*

> *You're afraid.*
> *Yes.*
> *Afraid that you*
> *won't be pardoned*
> *this subversion*
> *or*
> *this*
> *taking over*
> *or*
> *this*
> *appropriation*
> *through*
> *the fact*
> *that*
> *you*
> *are*
> *a poet. Yes.*

Poet of the wreck, the sharp word, the anecdote, the myth, the street, the war, the train, the stupidity, the plain, death, games, paucity, shadow, exile, earth, and nothingness. Yes. Because you imagine that Harlequin's suit is cut from the suit of words and not from the parted-out cloth you see in books, in cinemas, their screens open for the show of those in love with war.

> *Yes. Because*
> *you persist.*
> *Because*
> *in your emptiest*
> *flattest*
> *place*
> *you use*

---

48 Through all Farès's oeuvre, interviews, opinion pieces it becomes clear that he has no neatly packaged anti-colonial view of the French language.

the word that suggests
deception.
The name.
This name
you grant
to a future
you
are not.
You who
point out
to the Foretastes
of the world
that which
you can't
(haven't been able to)
attain
all at once

happiness, lucidity, dread. Yes. In the murmuring or ... In the
murmuring of that maxim wherein man .....

... ...

Ecstasy of self!
and of the blood (quick) that blackens your fingers face loins eyes
while
here,
in the foretaste
of the world
resides
not man
but
the child.
Not
words
but
form.
Not

meaning
but
childhood.

. To believe.
Yes. Believe.
That your mouth
is the narrative,
(the telling) of an energy filling that place where you were born.
      . To believe.
Yes. Believe.
That you do not
breath only to
attain
not
      the question or answer of a being who dwells
in the
Foretaste
of the world
In the very
space
of that taste
 you chase after.
The space
before space.
In this Fore
      (Taste)
of the world. Yes.
Poet of an
anterior
naming. But
one torn off. A throw-away
name that
you give
to define

that which

(in you)

Doesn't ………… you. That which remains incomprehensible in you. Not to others. But to you. So you force yourself to denounce the wound so that the word becomes plural and equal to that Foretaste (of world)

    you're looking for

    and apprehend.

    A being

    whose

    sole

    enigma

    is to be

    a

    profusion of

    existence. A profusion of which you like to grasp, not the guarantee, but the horizontality,

    or[49]

    better (there,

        where,

            precisely,

        an excess pulls away)

            the permission

Yes (tied in this way

    to what is permitted,

        to the act of a permission

            whose movement you would contemplate)

Thus,

    (avid and close)

    you would speak

    (in the natural ease of offering-words)

    this happiness

    (which you were) in being (together)

        to (in)

---

49 The original has "*où*" ("where"), but it is very difficult to make sense of this. The translation assumes the homophone "*ou*" (or). There is only one other homophonic typo in the novel, and the justification for its translation (its correction) is too tedious to footnote.

this (Fore-) (Taste)
 of the world
   There
   where
   with the str-
 ange pleasure
  of the hedgehog
   or
  the thrush
   You
   imagine the bar of a café on the Ramblas as imaginative
as an olive grove where you might imagine that other life you could have
had
   if
 Yes. The war. That uncovers life.
As incomprehensible as that moment which
  Yes.
  Sly poetics of fraud.
and so you dwell like this
  at the bar
 of a Tapas Café on the Ramblas
  within the love
of one life you're living.

.......Conchita

149

...... Conchita left the hotel at three: "I'm hungry. I'm starving." "I was thinking," I said (we had to go down the Ramblas, dodging cars) we could have lunch near the port. It's such a nice day."

"I'm taking off my hat," Conchita said, "it's going to fall off." She was wearing a beige hat with a mauve brim. "It was so hot in the hotel." She shook out her hair. "I'm so sick of sitting all morning in front of that switchboard!"

We crossed the Plaza Cataluña with its swirls of pigeons. We stopped in front of one of the Ramblas kiosks where the display included, along with detective stories and pornographic novels, a few volumes of Althusser, Michel Foucault, Freud, in paperback editions that were quite pretty and not expensive. And we continued on down the Ramblas toward the port.

"You have a good morning?" Conchita asked me.

"Yes."

"Near the port. We'll take a boat to get across the harbor."

Unfortunately, there was no boat, and we had to take a bus over to the Barceloneta. "I'm dying of hunger," Conchita said, while pointing out the little port streets through the bus window. "We'll have lunch near the beach."

We went by several shellfish restaurants before heading in back of all the kitchens and finding a big room with doors open to the sea, facing the sandy rolling waves that spent their force fifty yards from our table.

Conchita ordered one and a half paellas and a bottle of red wine.

"Can I have lunch with my hat on?"

The question was only one more coquetry, added to the paella, since Conchita immediately took her hat off, and let her hair down. "I'm hungry."

The paella was very good, full of shrimp and, already, on top of the joy of looking at the sand, the sea, the sky stirring with clouds, all kinds of words started to flow toward the future, accompanied, drowned, melted by the red wine—slight spaces where plans for the future try to blossom, while in the distance, buried in a memory that is always there, battered by marvels, there trembled that electric lamp resting on Harlequin's stomach.

Facing the beach, against the unquenchable blue of the ocean, we could see, on the lookout for any anti-imperialist move, an American boat (aircraft carrier or cruiser). Disaster. Conchita said: "I'm going to quit my job at the end of the month. You have to stay in Barcelona. Sort yourself out. We'll take a trip to Valencia."

Before me I saw Future. And I saw nothing there. Nothing that could keep me from staying in Barcelona. Going to Valencia. Unless it was the lack of Yes, Cash.

"How would we go? To Valencia?"

"By train," Conchita said. "Easy, on a train. Last year, in March, I was in Valencia, at my aunt's, and I took the milk train. Not expensive. It stops everywhere. And it's got second and third class. So that's how. We'd go by train."

I was looking out to sea: no train there. Waves. Waves. And that aircraft carrier or cruiser shifting in the distance, before us. I asked: "So what is Valencia, in the month of March?"

"It's great. I'll show you. You'll see. There's a huge festival. They burn everything up."

I looked at the sea and the American aircraft carrier. All I could think of was that war going on, today, everywhere, in every country in the world.

"My love, you have to come," Conchita kept on. "It's really beautiful, the *falla* in Valencia. The people, the Valencians, make huge mannequins and representations of real life. It all smells like gunpowder. Like cannon blasts. And they blow everything up all night long." I began to be intrigued: representations of life, that you burn. Mannequins. Gunpowder. Many years since I'd seen something like that Me Brandy Fax, 5. ( ) ( ). Especially because…Yes/in my old Kabylia where I once lived/my first years after coming into this world/there existed/yes/for a long time already/festivals like this/celebrations where all the villagers acted out "representations of life"/festivals where/suddenly the social order was in play/played out as farce/in the very streets of the villages/yes/festivals that today's country no longer wants/nor is able to put on/festivals of childbirth and social delirium/

festivals that could be the festivals of a country gone mad/carnivals of a crazed country/yes/well before Christianity/well before Islam/well before all colonizings/independences/this carnival doesn't exist anymore: and yet/"Yes, my love. I will come in March. To the carnival of mad countries. At the sea's edge. In the murderous flames of the mannequins being burned. In this new country where I am now, and to which I belong, just as much." "Fabulous," Conchita said. "We'll stay with my parents." "But— there's still the question of money." And I imagined (however little) (Me, Brandy Fax) waves rolling hundred-weights of pesetas toward us, and upon which rested, unsinkable, a huge sign, artistic propaganda: "A trip to a *falla* is a voyage to Valencia." "I'm going to write," I began, with a miraculous shrimp on the tips of my fingers instead of the monstrous pen that ceaselessly sears my temples. "I'll write to some friends," I went on. Thinking I was owed for some articles and stories. Which amounted to very little. Otherwise, I'd have to borrow on a grand scale. Mobilize a serious bite. Like the kind of cadging I imagined from the voyages and writing of Blaise Cendrars. (*…language is born from life, and life, after creating it, nourishes it. The ancient idea of a language miraculously bestowed on man or artificially organized by mankind has left its trace in a certain brand of linguistics that treats language like something independent and transcendent, and lends an internal necessity to its laws, not just its phonetic laws or pronunciation as this is linked to speech organs, but to its morphological or grammatical laws, its vocabulary and semantic laws. Now, it is wrong to think of language as some ideal entity that evolves independently of men and follows only its own ends.) (Living off language. Sustained by the life of words. A lesson I remind myself of. And which (me, Brandy Fax ( ) ( )) drives me on.)* "I'll write some letters," I say to Conchita, "precious-stone letters. Maybe that way I'll get thousands of letters from every friend in the world." "I'd really like you to see the countryside around Valencia," Conchita said. I lit a cigarette. Conchita said: "Don't worry. I just want you to be so happy!" Conchita took my hand and her eyes swept over the sea, the waves, the clouds staggering high and white, the paling sun, the afternoon fleeing toward dusk. "Let's walk along the sea and on the shore promenade. Before heading back and writing your letters." Already Conchita was on her feet.

The paella cost 130 pesetas. We crossed through the main room of the restaurant, then out to the beach.

"I'd like it so much if you could live with me in Spain. You have to stay."

"But what would I do? In Paris I can always figure out how to live. I know people. I have my Algerian residency card in Paris. …I'm not a known writer; I have some tough years ahead of me. Really tough. In fact I think the tough part, for me, really starts now… Before, there was the war. Independence. All that, that was rough. But it was sustained by meaning. Today, it's different. I see my work and my life as the creation of a meaning. Do you understand? A daily creation." "Yes," Conchita said. (She had taken my arm, and our ambling was glued to the sand, to the flaming movement of the sky, in the day's ending.) "How is it you're not dead already?" Conchita asked me. "I don't understand how you can still be alive. Your beliefs are in such opposite things. You believe in love, and you believe in violence (Conchita was looking off to the farthest touching of earth and sky. The most intimate. The most mysterious: that horizontal meeting of water and sun, sea, and dusky day). You also believe in a great deal of tenderness and, at the same time, you dream of more. When someone looks at you (this is how I saw you) they have the feeling you allow every kind of dream. But. Quickly. They notice that you only allow yourself the dreams of others, and you don't allow yourself your own. As if you didn't want to speak them. As if you wanted to hide them. It hurts me to think you're afraid to speak your own dreams."

Then we were leaving the sand to get back on the promenade. Conchita's words gave me back a moment of savage truth, a truth wherein dream cannot speak its dream, but where dream tells how hard it is to be dream. For dream to be dream, this belongs to a reality whose illusionary facility is too bastard to be aspired to. But this difficulty the dream has, to be dream! Conchita had hit it on the head. On that spot, the intimate spot where you try to stay alive: between the reality of a dream, and the dream of a reality. In other words: crapping out.

I replied.

"No. Conchita. I have no dream to tell. Maybe nothing at all to tell; and that's why I'm so afraid either to dream, or to speak. To discover this nothing. Accept this nothing. For me this would be: dying. But, my death, it's something I want. Through others. Because, it's the only thing they're capable of giving you (of giving) for free. The only thing you have a right to for free. Nothing to pay. The rest, you have to pay. And dearly, to have it. To live. To create. I'm giving that a try. That's all. Yes. I'm capable of paying dearly for a creativity whose fragility I fear, the fragility it condemns me to. The most daunting thing is that some people think it's easy for me to make words obey. What's easy for me is to endure the thing I align words for. That's all. Because I really see nothing else that can keep me alive."

We were on the other side of the shore promenade. There was a café. I asked Conchita if she wanted something to drink. "An orange juice," she said. It was an old café where they drank small glasses of wine with one hand and rolled dice with the other. We stayed only long enough to drink an orange juice and a cognac-and-coffee. We continued our walk, along the promenade, above the rocks.

"It's unbelievable, Conchita, that you can be persuaded, at the same time, of an incredible vanity about yourself, your desires (I mean vanity in the sense of a pure loss of self and one's desires) and also hope that something is born from you and from those same desires."

"There's always work," Conchita said.

"Right. Yes. And that's what I do. That's exactly what's left. I work. But, try to imagine that I've known, very early on, beyond work, something else, something like a force. Like the force of the sea, for a fish. You couldn't say the sea holds back the fish's progress. But you also can't say the fish trifles with the water, that it costs him no effort to live in the water. Well, that's what I have known. Something that surrounds work the way the sea surrounds the fish; something that kept me warm; and I never even asked if you had to believe or not believe. I lived in that warmth. That's all."

"But, my love. It's really because you loved. You were simply in love with what you were doing. Today, you've *fallen* (not just with me) in love with the letters you trace. And, at the same time, you're a *fish.*" Conchita laughed like the waves splaying themselves on the rocks. She said: "Come on. Let's sit here and watch all the red of the sun." Conchita could really hit home when she wanted. She went on: "You should realize that you're in love with the way you envision life. When you recognize that, you'll be able to live in peace." "Impossible," I said, "love exists. But, it's too enormous for me, today. I need things that are precise, clear, intolerable. I used to be someone who believed in a lot of things. Did you know, for example, that I taught peasants to read and write, who had worked so long with picks and shovels and ploughs that their fingers were so big, so swollen, they couldn't hold a pen? The only diploma those peasants had was the *tractor-diploma*, they used to say. A degree in tractor driving. And I was giving them lessons, along with a few friends, while it rained bombs all around us. You see, Conchita, there are choices that got made in me. They've grown. And they're killing me. For sure, a falla celebration, you can always go see one. And I'd like to, in a different time. I'm nothing. I have nothing. I'm finding it hard to get any work now. But I insist on certain things. Or certain things cling to me. It might even be that I love you because you make me run from whatever is holding on to me." Conchita's body stiffened. She said: "You're wrong. I would follow you anywhere." There, shyly, I fell silent. Conchita kissed me. She said: "Now we can go back. You're the most honest liar I know. Let's go."

We left the sea's edge and, after following along the walls of the port warehouses, we headed toward the bus stops, taxi stands, the lighted signs, restaurants, alleys off the Ramblas. We remembered our desire to take off for Algeria. Conchita said, "I'd really like to know Algeria." "You'll have to wait a good twenty years." "Why?" "Because the Algerian government types and nationalists have no sense of humor. Because their desire is a uniform population. And because this type of politics tends to last twenty years, minimum. Ten times that, perhaps, yes?" Conchita understood the allusion, but what interested her was not knowing what the Algerian government was like, rather what a country of Algerians was like. "Algeria is a country born of several wanderings and rapes from which there eventually grew not humans, but human dreams. Thus for twenty centuries or fourteen centuries,[50] according to what is believed, Algeria has been searching for the man or the woman who might recognize her as having sprung from herself, not from some Islamic, Arab country or other. Algeria

---

50   Since Roman and Phoenician times, and the Arab invasions, respectively.

is so constituted that she has not attained full satisfaction from those who currently call themselves her masters. And this doesn't derive from these lords. But from the delirium Algeria was born in. Very few people can recognize their true ancestry. That is the question in today's Algeria."

"I would really like to know what the Berbers are," Conchita asked. "Los Bereberos!" she added. A smile on her lips. "Los Bárbaros," I responded, "Los Bárbaros or Los Bereberos son mis ascendientes... ; hombres sin cultura y sin existencia... " "Pobrecito," Conchita said. I rambled on,"The kingdoms of Espagne were Berber kingdoms because it was Arabized Berbers who crossed the straits of Gibraltar. The Berbers who set off for Spain couldn't resist the beauty of Spanish girls, nor Islamic ornament. There is even a very well-known Algerian writer who cites Andalusia as the real ancestor of Algeria. The Berbers became kings and ruled over the countries to the South. Do you know the Arab poetry of Granada?"

"No."

"They are poems about leaving Spain. The ones who left Spain had the feeling, forever, of exile. The country they were leaving had been their country. Maybe that's what makes me feel so good when I'm in Spain. Today..... Los Bereberos... Los Bárbaros...; the latter means 'those whose language you can't understand.'" Those whose culture you don't know. You are always the B(e) (a)rb(e) (a)rian of someone. Nowadays, with the kingdoms no longer there, every Berber tries to figure it out by himself since, collectively, he has been too affected to become what he has never been: a single people. Or he works in a café. Or he gets Arabized."

Conchita laughed, wondering what there could be in common between the survivors of a people who never existed as a people and the buses, cars, red lights, tapas, quick kisses, Barcelona, the rest of Spain. I said: "It remains for each survivor to believe in an illusion, to make himself believe in the illusion of a dream that nobody, governmentally speaking, can put up with. To give birth to a nation that has never existed."

Conchita: "Israel."

"Yes," I replied, "minus international Zionism (a catastrophe)." Conchita said: "I'd love to have a cacaolac (hot chocolate)."

"We went into a tavern with hams hanging from the ceiling and two grey pig's heads. I asked for a glass of *tinto.* "I can't even bear to look at a map anymore, the dispersal of a very ancient existence being so obvious. 3 oceans; a frontier of sand, the reaches of a dispersal that the centuries, by turn, have all aggravated."

I started to draw a map on the paper tablecloth. "To start, the first shore, the one open to the Mediterranean, a place of turnings and appeals from the cool wind. From West to East. From the most present to the most absent. From the Atlantic to the Red Sea...

The movement of resurrection needing to be the reverse of the movement of destruction. A strategy will have to come into being: the power of the dead. An old problem in North Africa. One which, with each social, historical or linguistic mutation, continues no less present. They call them. The Sioux. Clothed in absence and prestige: the ancestors. They are granted only enigmatic rights. And for good reason. Speaking, after their death. Before. Without any doubt. Complete silence. What reigned was absence and patriarchal thinking..."

Conchita was beginning to wonder what was going on with me.

"...Yes. I'm the guardian (old dreamer) of a madness whose full scope I deploy but whose causes I do not espouse. Being too winded for that. And because I'm immoral. But...... I'm still sensitive to.... The Landscape."

Silence from Conchita.

" ... However I have no pretension of hegemony. Unless you're talking about the right to bring back that moment when (XXth century) disappearance is finally complete. I'm not making up a history. I'm citing places that are findable geographically and socially. But what country will accept this?.... In several countries I could name there exist kernels of that vast, outdated collective. The histories of the ... that have been written up till now are false histories. They have been written only by people who weren't ... and whose most awful (fond) desire was to see them disappear completely. This history was never written by the ... for the simple reason that they have never thought of writing it/never thought that a writing could protect them from their disappearance. Even today, many can read, but only in the stars, the footsteps of the wind in the sand. One of them did try to write and this was not a writing... but something Islamic. He wrote the Koran in Berber... (...) using an Arabic system of transliteration. (XIIth.) ...Since then, a few squibs, a few turns taken, almost nothing more, in the direction of affirming something other than being completely swallowed up. They had to go looking among others, for what seemed to belong to themselves. We have always been "dazzled" by the presence/life/customs of others. This is how we've been able to "tolerate" with lots of irony— linguistic but not only that—the various tribes that disembarked on our lands, and this up until quite recently..." (I was looking at the map of that unfinished country.... And: ...As hard as it is to realize you're from a country without the official outlines of a state... It is just as comforting to think that, in this way, through this manifest exclusion from the territories of the established order... It is possible for us to think (us, the cultureless and exiled) that we belong to all the cultures of the world... That there isn't a single one of the world's cultures that is fundamentally foreign to us... That we are (have been) situated, for a very long time now, at the meeting places of all cartographic currents ... That we can succeed in many literatures and languages... Without any part of us being eclipsed diminished humiliated or aggrandized... We have always been this way... Borne along on different human hopes... And this... In spite of the fact that... Today... We are so *irrevocably affected*... Struck in the site of our existence and language... For... Even if... With a bit of luck... We could make out or retrieve some trace of that Former World we came from... The wound would only be that much more noticeable... More devastating... Sharper... Like that which... He... Brandy Fax... Well knows... When he touches (perceives) (discovers) certain origins...)

"You shouldn't drink any more," Conchita said. "It's not good for Berber morale."

"Oh I know! But the Berbers have always been steeped in the wines of Spain, like the kinglets in Shakespeare, little kings of tragic and murderous countries. Kinglets of a madness where incest wears political finery. Poetic finery."

"You're drunk."

"No. I haven't finished my map. My real madness." I was drawing the southern border of that inexistent country:

"What's terrible is that the madness rushing through me has its reality. Palpable. GEOGRAPHIC. I'm no ordinary madman. I'm a map-making loony. And I drink to this new cartography…… And now we'll dine, my love, and we'll drink a young wine, one you'll love as if we were the last heirs of the decomposing of North Africa's and Spain's histories… I'm very… I'm very much in love with you…" and I bit my tongue until my throat swelled.

"You're not taking your map along."

"No. My love. I'll start it over again every day. If only for you. If only for me. For those who don't want to believe in it. Because the teaching of cartographers and madmen has been ignored. If only for those who force open the hidebound laziness of sundry politics. Dreams. Ignorant sciences…. For those who dream. Yes. Dream. Of belonging to a real status. Not the status of political exiles. Dangerous political exiles… But. YES… For those who believe. Still believe today. In the freedom of intelligence and culture. Even if the reality this freedom delivers is owned by the dizzying demands of life… What country will discover. Beyond the political exiles (No more than a contemporary limitation) the cultural exile. The impossibility of belonging to the confines of a nationalist perimeter. Who will recognize *that* status beyond the status of the stateless."

…He was striding toward that recognition. In that city where his lover lived. A city of varied routes. Different countries. Different continents… The status of cultural exile should look like the status of a port, of long and medium distance haulers….. Barcelona?... Yes… Perhaps… In another time.

XIV

The Inscription

XIV. A pilot revved the motor of a launch full of harbor trippers, come across from the beach and the Barceloneta district.

Above him a discussion rang out, a discussion that lifted him on a wave of vertigo to the port of Algiers. There were, on the boat landing, some pay-telescopes. Algiers seemed close; he would have bet, with someone else, seated, like him, at his side, that, with his eyes glued to the lenses of the two telescopes, he could have made out the entire Port-Saïd Square, of a June morning.

The departure (the sound of the motor) of the launch made the gulls wheel above the sheets of diesel on the water, he groped for words... a few words... stammered... his head bothered by the slightness of the winter sun... a shock... within him... lasting... several leaflets floated in the Barcelona sea... and, further off, to his left, at the dock, a warship, machine guns tipped up to the sky... this shock... this reality taking place inside of a reality... becoming... slowly... more real than that reality... borne of Matter and in a form... in an active form of war... like a spinning... a moment of labor, or dizziness... the water penetrating your limbs with every vibration in the air... in this reality that imposes its moment...; how (yes) how? To talk about that being who... there... more distant than I am... more me than me... in the very absence where he tells me his history... his fever... fever to one day be more real than I am... while I envy his (absence): ...while I know he's speaking to me... *constantly...* Yes... Coming toward him the way one comes into the world... and leaving nothing out from the impossible diction of a being who... was... is... in the process of reaching his lookout post... through language... all languages... Attaining that word which speaks... That...... kills. Yes. Telling. Despite the dizziness. This reality of a tombstone existing nowhere *nowhere...* since... A reality of two worlds. Of two worlds... Of the one deepest buried which... through its absences expresses the anteriority (outcast) of a life… Yes. The Anteriority… And. The Other… Anteriority of the revival of the deeply buried… (of that which is truer than you)… in this practical work of war.

No other determination but that (those) of a confrontation (open)
between this reality of a vertigo and that (in myself)
     which
            loses
its grip
        in
           one
              day.

"I can now say that the grass is growing there, after the snow melts; that, at the very moment of independence, in the beginning of spring, 1962, the napalm treetops met a new spring, one not deafened by army trucks; that the roadsides from Maillot to Akbou (and many others) were starting to see the resettlement camps open their hedges of barbed wire, the damaged inhabitants getting back to their mountain villages."

"They took with them roof tiles, door jambs, window frames; some carried wicker baskets where, instead of a harvest of olives or figs, they had stacked bricks."

"Yes. Who could have foreseen the alacrity of that day."

"It had taken so many murders. Still. The alacrity of that day."

"That is why grass is growing on the rock."

"It grows there in a state… that's not… wild… nor domesticated… It grows there in a nascent state… Yes. How should we say this?… And the sap that runs up the grass goes on spreading the birth of other births around it…"

"You can see… (if the reality of a gravestone strikes fear into no part of you)… right next to the grass, the shadow thrown by Si Mokhtar."

"You can also see (again, only if you can arrive at the reality of the tombstone without fear)…

But, more important, we must demand that is demand an explanation of it all from the young man dwelling at the back of the cemetery (a young man because) (yes) (just like the one who named me one day with this first name designating life, this name of my own life) the tombstone—not Uncle Saddek's—Because no news of Uncle Saddek has ever reached us—but

That Woman's (Yes. The very one who died a short time after March 19, after a crowd vengeance was sparked in the Akbou marketplace That day when a few men were stoned, just as in the worst times in the reality of those days.)"

"I can say that Rouïchède has become the guardian of the hill. And that he dwells at the back of the cemetery and sometimes tells the tales of various lives, various graves."

"And I've also seen Mokrane again.[51] The very Mokrane who. As proud a student as he was then. Has become timid. Yes. Timid about his life and that of others. Mokrane whose pride I never once envied. Nor. His education."

"Coming back to Akbou was so hard... so hard..."

"There were so many murders... In the village... And by that hill at the edge of Akbou."

"And the end... So... brutal..."

"One day... After so many years."

"Eight years... and those others years... that we knew, too, in the war and in that murder of ourselves... Yes. Of ourselves."

"All those other years when we had to search... Oh how much we had to look... For the shape of an enduring... To learn to bend our language... The language of our languages... Learn to dissimulate our vowels... our syllables... to make them imperceptible... hardly identifiable... to whisper them... to hiss them."

"That's how on that spot, on the very site of our dissimulations, this hissing-poem was born... Poem about the vowel that dissimulates our tongue... The vowel that helps our language endure."

"This poem continues as the ventilation of our language. For many were astounded. Astounded by this hissing... Some... among the most ignorant... went so far as to write that our language was a kind of mishmash... Incomprehensible, our language...What they didn't know was that we had only continued to speak in our tight corner. Yes. Wedged in our

51 Mokrane and Rouïchède appear later in the trilogy. They are among the figures who, as Farès says (interview with Peter Beatson, in *Fountains*, no. 3, 1979), "pass through" (*traversent*) his work.

mountains; wedged in our villages; wedged in our waterways; wedged in those efforts of ours; wedged in our fields… Our only claim was to be able to speak among ourselves right in the middle of all that surveillance."

"And we weren't trying to free ourselves from all kinds of surveillance."

"But we desired merely to live among all that surveillance: so many veerings of history had we known."

"In fact. A very minor thing. It's a question of very little."

"A slight furrowing of the lips. Like a lactation. A seeking out of movement…there… within you And this š … Such is its designation. This hiss… that unfurrows our tongue."

"Therefore   *in*
I   *that place*
wrote   *accessible*
on the stone   *to the unfurrowing*

                          of our
                          world
                          between
                          the paths
                          among
                          tombstones
                          and
                          the groves
                          of
                          olives

the inscription
        of
    the name
        ta-   *1938*   *in the swirl*   *larks*   *of the rapid*   *1962*   *Yahia Ou*[52]......

                                    of spring

---

52   *"Ou"* means, in Berber: belonging. (Note by Farès.) The above pattern resembles several Berber symbols, including those for various trees—among them the olive tree. Berber *"ta-"* is a marker for feminine nouns.

"The stone's exile in this world. Where man does his killing. Making the stone explode, or the clay, there, above us, in order to say: 'No place in this world... No place... But this murderous conflagration of your land. Yes... A hardship to live through Nothing but a madness to circumscribe... But a death to achieve... No place in this world... Your footstep and your desire

uncoupled... Our reign among the stones, the grasses, and your fields. No place. There exists not one place in this world.'"

The land rose through smoke amid stones and the brush on the other side land or villages from now on set ablaze I'm ashamed:

"This rage, man burning his brothers Killing the world This designation Or that era he seeks there in the inscription of an Other World His faith Or Hope Our century The one of a New World Finally Yes Finally Present in the world Yes This faith in a New World Equally there Equally Life Equally Day Love Play And Illusion Yes The World Finally The Century of a New World"

The land rose through smoke amid stones and the brush on the other side Land or Villages from now on set ablaze by the thrust of the New World.

MEMORY AND THE MISSING

VOLUME II OF THE TRILOGY: DISCOVERY OF THE
NEW WORLD

TRANSLATION OF *MÉMOIRE DE L'ABSENT*:

VOL. II, *LA DÉCOUVERTE DU NOUVEAU MONDE*

BY NABILE FARÈS, SEUIL, 1974

TRANSLATED AND ANNOTATED BY
PETER THOMPSON

PART ONE

Dahmane

I

As I left the station, amid the lights and streets that made up my first glimpse of that city, and of that country I'd been sent to in the hopes of soon seeing my father arrive from Camp Paul Cazelles, a vague thought burdened me, like a warning, or like a pit suddenly gaping before me, a thought that filled the night and that place where I'd just arrived, with my mother, from Algiers.[53]

My eyes seemed to whirl in their sockets like squirrels caught in a cage, whose paws play out an unenviable sham of freedom, spinning away before you, at full speed.

But what I had feared was something else, because the departure from Algiers had not been all that "simple": a car had come from the radio station to take us directly to the port, and, as this car had been followed by another car full of police and soldiers, it was natural that we (my mother and I) thought things were not all they seemed and that, instead of taking us directly to the port—they were taking us *Where?*

I'd rather not remember where *they might have (could have) taken us.*

More important to be able to reconstitute—starting now—the history of this skin.

This old skin that cracks in you like earth like grass or like
This old skin.

(my being is now ever open—suddenly, just like that, like cracked wood—and I envy those people who don't believe in the *reality* of this skin, in its temporal insinuation here, as if, once arrived from the other side of the river or the cold waters, you ran into your own skin, your face, gestures, territories; as if this skin spoke in you, and spoke you)

---

53 This continues an episode in Abdenouar's life, directly from Volume I. It is also much like the story of the boy Yahia (Farès's first novel), who comes from the village of Akbou to Paris. Among those beginning to pay attention to *Yahia, pas de chance* is Nassima Metahri, "Complaintes des hors soi," in *Nabile Farès—Un Passager entre la lettre et la parole* (2019). Needless to say, there are elements in this scene that reflect Farès's arrival in Paris, as a student, during the Algerian War.

And then, too, there was that house we were leaving; that house where I'd been raised by you yes you as well as by my mother and father, and my brother whom I never saw again after he left in August, 1956.

That's the way it is. People live and at a certain moment, when the country begins to have problems in the fields mountains rivers roads days nights trees and desires, they screw off, go off in all directions.

It's hard knowing that; but, nothing you can do:

that's the way it is. Men leave in every direction.

Right here.

Near me.

I am on the point of believing I'll live my life, at present, in fore-shorten-ing

Yes, in a contraction of time and hope, and that, having tasted and understood or killed off certain things, I will disappear from this world, thus (*I think they'll never hear any more about H'Midouche; that I'll stop living in Clos-Salembier; that I couldn't take that any more*) thus, to my great despair because who—after me—will think to talk about *you* to bespeak the joy of this very *you* yes *you* You who, in all the years you were among us never stopped pushing me forward in this—

yes I came up with "pushing"; but I should have used or discovered some other word—a completely different word—a word that would be the opposite—and I should have written with no regard for myself and what might happen to me later: *Conquering.*

yes, this word,

You, *who never ceased conquering me in this world.*

we might as well say death, or, more present than death, this kind of active disappearing that is all around me.

There exist very few beings with whom you can speak in complete quietude; or rather, with whom I could speak, after that—or even *way before that*—in complete quietude: And this is *your* fault

you always led me to believe yes *that one could speak*

maybe that's what suddenly opened that space around me, when

speaking, simply speaking: reaching the other person through language, through his own language, so that it deconstructs: the confectioners of histories

I came here, through hearsay, in the end because I only knew the country this country through books or the speech of the people who came home every summer

Yes: *you should have told me one or two things (quite a few things) instead of leaving me this way, my head rustling with words so* portentously *uttered* back in those days when you gave name to the goatskin[54]:

The *goatskin?*

That's what you called the danger that was trying to drag us toward drowning because, as inhabitants of the hill that terrible hill above Algiers the bay of Algiers, we had to hold the line against the occupier[55] and because, constantly involved in the outbreaks of death's little game, we had to disappear, in little groups, into the occupier's midst. That's the name you gave to the risks of a land being born because it amused you to spell out the origins of all births and because, not wanting to say any more than those words you so *portentously* uttered, so *intensely* present for you, you anticipated night death disappearance: goat-skin?

You gave name to our exiles or migrations all the while knowing, having just broached that primal language of the other world, that our time among the living would be dear,[56]

that,

yes. The goat-skin?

The man yes that man—close to me—yes, that man I'd gotten used to speaking with—every day, within our limits or respective territories. I

---

54 This Berber image was first inserted in Volume I, *The Olive Grove*. In the present volume, as in all three, elements of Berber folklore will appear, sometimes as simple emblems or archetypes rather than as fully developed myths. "L'outre" will be partially explained by the character Jidda; see also Farida Aït Ferroukh, "La Langue mère dans l'oeuvre de Nabile Farès," *Expressions Maghrébines*, vol. 17, no. 2. The central image is that of an inflated skin, like a wineskin.

55 The French

56 The entire volume, indeed the trilogy, gives free play to our imagination about "absence." There is much for scholarship to say here, and Farès's friend Flavia Buzzetta makes progress: "Des Mots et d''heureusité'—Dialogue avec Nabile Farès," in *Nabile Farès—Un Passager entre la lettre et la parole* (2019). Farès discusses what he sometimes calls the "ab-sens" ("without meaning") in a lecture, "Du Sublime et de l'ab-sens," *La Psicanalisi e l'arte* conference, Rome, 2015.

couldn't break the law, join directly in that movement of his, that is *abreast* of it—yes, that man I was used to talking to was no longer there,

gone

and I,

meanwhile

throughout those two years

when each evening I had felt his heart beating

here, in me

beating

softly; as if I could touch his heart though he had been hurled far from us, so far that—

It is Dahmane

And so: *it is Dahmane*. These words have a manifest power of disintegration. The words, or their reality as words. Their reality as words. The reality that lodges them somewhere, within you or outside, and sends them at you in little blows, like bullets. *The reality of words?*

What does it matter? Because it's in this way that:

You have to cross over the river and, she added, *the worst is that you'll always learn soon enough what the river is:* It was Dahmane who first came to let us know, yes; *Dahmane* whom they'd arrested along with him and then let go a few days later.

Dahmane who came and told us my father was still alive: that he'd seen him with some other men in the courtyard of the *Villa Susini* Father had signaled to him with his eyes... *Just something so I'd come back and let you know. ...They were leading me toward the villa's exit: I was able to go through the gate and find myself on the road, above the new town, and take off toward you... Yes... To tell you your father was still alive... alive... in spite of everything... alive...* Dahmane's eyes were wild, almost red, red, reddened. They had beaten him for two days. Then, when they found out he knew an officer in The Redoubt[57] they let him go, telling him to come back, back there above the bay and the city to Algiers, every ten days. Yes

Dahman didn't know what to do

or rather:

---

57 A thickly settled area near Algiers

Knew the one thing to do Yes leave Leave

But those crazy eyes of his crazy

"Leaving the Old Woman; leaving the Old Woman... and my sister... How can I leave the Old Woman and my sister? How?... and his wild gaze trailed on my mother She who's seated in the taxi, right there, near me, and whose tearful breathing I can feel. Hamid puts the suitcases in the taxi's trunk Cold runs or is it fear runs along my skin like a light sweat while Hamid closes the rear door of the taxi next to my mother Hamid has a kind of smile for us when he climbs in we have to play it cute with life make believe you're being born in the midst of it without a gram of terrorism and advance in the sun as if we are the sun Yes us, and burning everything right up to the eyeballs the whites become red *Red* Mother seated looking at him and his words his words speaking to her of that other man that man they had come to take from us, at her house, in front of her, in the middle of the night... *they can't stay, stay, on alone at The Redoubt... especially if I leave, and I have to leave, right away... they could, they could grab me again tomorrow and no one will ever hear of me again* I KNOW WHAT THEY DO TO MEN IN THAT VILLA I KNOW[58]... *and he looked at my mother* to let her know that it was luck a real piece of luck that he'd been able to see my father Alive *there in the courtyard* among the bodies stretched out or standing along the walls of the yard beneath the three machine guns of the gate, guarded, herded among the searing cries that rip the chests of the men penned in the walls of that yard *"They won't be alone,"* my mother had said, *"they won't be alone. The women will come here, to Clos-Salembier, and stay with us until until"* and words had failed her because Yes Terrible Morning when madness drained the words of Dahmane and this strength of my mother's I now saw understood perceived Yes for the first time "he's alive... he's alive, but how? How can he be alive? A few hundred yards from home, from me who can't do anything now, like every day, before, not able to do anything Who would you see? Yes *Who is there to see?* In this town where no one can do

---

58 To clarify this and what Dahmane says later, this is torture by various arms of the French military—a torture regime to which, after some decades, many of its actors have confessed. Relevant to the effects on Dahmane and the "experience of depersonalization following torture" is Maya Boutaghou, "Peau noire, langue blanche: Nabile Farès, Frantz Fanon et la réalité des mots," *Expressions maghrébines*, vol. 17 no.2.

anything any more except let you in share your helplessness promise a few phone calls and a watchfulness extended over the city and also lost there *Me* in the hell of this land this town where they've seized…"

"Dahmane? Dahmane? How was he? They didn't let him take anything with him and they threw Yes Two of them threw cartridges in the hallway Yes spent shell casings to show that here there was some sign that the things of this land still moved like clockwork."

"Yes, Dahmane? Dahmane? How was he?"

Dahmane's voice was red.Ow was he? hhhhh

Like his eyes and his weeping, above the town; in the red morning of the city; where the sky the Blue Sky of Algiers was terribly red, acid on my eyes and his eyes and my hands my eyes my red hands above the city

Dahmane?

Before nineteen fifty-four and during the three years following nineteen fifty-four Dahmane? Until that day they took Dahmane the city THE WHOLE CITY had belonged to me Yes B-E-L-O-N-G-E-D—despite Yes despite that other side of the city the part we weren't allowed to enter because of our look our legs our eyes our voices our hands because? Because of I don't know what deformed or unformed or Yes excessive element in us Yes because of a whole lot of things that, still, weren't staring me in the face the way they do now, looking always in me, as they do now, for some Difference, it seems, Something different that didn't belong to that other side of town to their humanity in short, Below us below the shantytowns of Clos-Salembier a horrible neighborhood with shantytowns spilling down the hill toward the city from every side an underserved wild place city of a murderous liberty Clos-Salembier Nadhor City as the poet said City whose every square yard harbors six pairs of legs along with furious impulses to splatter life beyond the alleys and gutters full of bodily disease and then further out and all around

In a sense, our part of town, *there*, avid of its asphalt, its sand, the breath of its laugh and its breeze, with us still dispossessed of our names *One day you'll have your freedom or your Independence and You'll be on top of things while I, buried under some garbage dump or dissolved in quick lime in the basement or crawl space of some police station, I'll bang (Yes, I'll bang) my parts together, take off in search of my limbs scattered over city and sea, each star, each shift of the ocean, each dust mote stinging your eyes your eyelids setting fire to the wind; each word that—Yes, my nerves swelling the sky like branches—each word I try to utter in this frenetic search for myself for a self completely blown apart in the conflagration of this world* Yes in a sense the city belonged to us, I would say *or rather* in a certain way: the city belonged *furiously* to us like Dahmane Dahmane who spoke then with those red eyes I'd never seen before: *furiously red* and his face torn right off yes as if they'd ripped the whole face off at once, with one blow of a—

Dahmane said: *There was nothing I could tell him; in fact I was amazed to see him since they hadn't asked me anything about him, no, nothing, even though they knew perfectly well that I worked with him… for him… and then the broadcasts on Clos-Salembier and The Redoubt and on all the camps full of our young that he'd set up even in spots yes spots where few of us dared venture; no… they didn't ask anything about him… they did interrogate me about a man they knew only by the name Si Mahfoudh or something like that Yes, that's it, Si Mahfoudh they kept saying Yes;* "Si Mahfoudh, it's clear you've heard of him" *and then they'd hit me on the top of the head right there* (and Dahmane, with his right hand very very gingerly touching the top of his head where they'd been hitting it) *with a lump of rubber studded with nails yes covered with nails they'd driven in big nails and the heads of the nails hit you every which way on the top of your head because they didn't hit you with a sharp whack but with careful little blows just so, on the top of your head, and then they'd shove your head in a pail of water there in front of me at the end of the bed where my head was hanging off, above the water, while they hit me and I heard a dancing each syllable entering in a dance into my head or each nail like a shot with a needle all the nails on my skull like shots* "Si Mahfoudh, you have definitely heard of Si Mahfoudh" I HAVE NEVER HEARD OF SI MAHFOUDH *and I drank the water of my words of their bullshit* I WAS NAKED *naked* NAKED THE HORROR *naked* ALL THEIR SHIT *on my* NAKED *body* Dahmane was trembling. His legs. I saw his legs before me, moving; his hands wringing before us like his reddening eyes his eyes furiously red as if they'd held the embers yes THE EMBERS of his shame his hate *the embers* he was scattering there before us While my mother

175

took Dahmane's hands: "*Don't be afraid of anything...they won't be left alone... you can tell them, now, to come here to Clos-Salembier*": Every day I will kill off some part of the happiness in me or in you so that no one can ever use this word again; yes; so no one can use this word "*I can't stay here*," Dahmane said. "*I have to leave I have to kill someone I have to learn to kill: they killed my soul: they killed my body What will I do without my body? They've killed my body I'll have to learn how to kill out there; I'm going to be a killer out there I'm going to kill out in the city: in the streets: all the streets of this city; I'm going to be a killer*

Mother why weep being far now from the city while the taxi takes off and Hamid... You were trying to calm Dahmane You grabbed his hands, his head, leaning against these words: I'm going to kill.

You said: "*You should leave. You can't stay in town. Don't be afraid for them. They'll be taken care of.*"

Damane said: "*I don't know anything, myself, about Si Mahfoudh. Absolutely nothing... You can check... there's no one that works with me by that name... no one... You can check... Twelve hours a day... That's a lot, twelve hours a day... A lot, right? I work twelve hours a day... and my mother is old... in The Redoubt... I have no time, you understand?*

Yes.

No time for any Si Mahfoudh."

And yet. I well knew

Two days before that night they took my father away that night when father had opened the mailbox, there, in front of me

Earlier—an hour earlier, at the most—a man had thrown an envelope into the box

I had run from the foothills of Nadhor City when I saw that man throw something into the box. I'd run, and I'd seen an envelope.

My father had come at the usual time, after that, and opened the box.

I was next to him: I could see the envelope The man could have stayed or knocked at the house or rung the bell but he had taken right off and I'd seen how he moved

On the envelope: the name *Si Mahfoudh*

I could read the name Si Mahfoudh on the envelope and then watch my father open the envelope as if it were meant for him but I know his name is Si Taleb not Si Mahfoudh Yes him Si Taleb who didn't like these words said too loud after a certain hour in the evening; who organized pedagogical workshops for the new teachers in the Clos-Salembier school, the school where the kids washed up in waves of sixty or eighty in shifts, part-time, because of that galloping overpopulation of children in the least well-fed parts of the world Clos-Salembier the Reef of the world a New Zone Island and Hill where all the throw-aways of modern life washed up life and under-life: Four times a day, at 10:30 and half past noon, and later, at 3:30 and 5:00, we heard the shouts and cavalcades of children freed from the schoolyards flying through Clos-Salembier like migrations of birds through the vines: book bags turnstiling before them as if, in that moment, they were learning to live again or to defend their bodies: Clos-Salembier, the place where silence and anger wandered aimlessly before crossing that strict colonial line and tumbling down to the city there below the hill among the abductions and bombings and explosives thrown into coffee shops Clos-Salembier The envelope held a letter my father opened in front of me. *Then I had a name; my name; yours; the one written on the envelope on the town; Si Mahfoudh As if this name had been written on every sidewalk of the city, this city, Algiers, where, for the first time, I sensed my name welling up, like a caress of wind or heat, there, deep in my voice, my mouth, my throat. My name mixed in with all the city's streets store windows intersections bars cinemas houses, apartment blocks. This city whose vibration I felt a whole new way now that I knew, yes, I knew: I belonged to that city's shadow. My name, mingling with the evening with the night sliding over and through the city The city indefinitely Loving but also Crazy.* Thousands of stars over the city. Far off, the dim immensity that I know and feel to be forever luminous, over-spilling the night, the darkness, my gaze: I've always been able to imagine what kind of life can *stir* can exist under the sea especially from that bedroom I had in that house in Clos-Salembier my window open to the sea's wall with my ever mounting drunkenness and yes—

I knew Very Early how to navigate through the city with Dahmane, even though the city—in effect—didn't belong to us Did not BELONG to us.

The wind's gentle gaze. The stars roamed before my eyes like stones far above my body my eyes the city Seeming to stay hung there like thousands of eyes above the night deep in the night This night when I take off I take flight I take my territories my words my speech or my terrors That night: I laughed Yes laughed because as I closed these city eyes one by one, blinking rapidly and crazily c-i-n-e-m-a-t-o-g-r-a-p-h-i-c-a-l-l-y Yes like those old movies we'd go see with Dahmane Scenes where the bad guys (the theater was the back of a garage where they projected the cavalcades of the bad guys with disastrous speed but with no sound) cinematographically, images upon images on the pocked screen of the garage: In this way I could multiply the life or the sight of the stars (the sparkles above my eyes) by multiplying the speed of my blinking over the screen of the bluish depths of the night

Sometimes I killed several with one blow (one eye-blink) and then, further off, in that fixed but moving and fluid panorama, other stars appeared, more feebly aglow or almost dead according to the state of my eyes and laughter, in that race where I felt a luminosity bounding over the city's every shadow, the sea's luminosity out there, before, below and above me just as

Mother weeps next to me, right now, caught in this spot, and on the other hand:

she should never have left our city despite the hell of it and the bite it took daily

I can well sense that's what she's thinking she's thinking she should never have left our city and that my father, one day or another, was going to come back: yes.

And I know that is our curse.

Not to leave our city, like an order among those given in the form of hand-outs: the FLN should have written: IT IS FORBIDDEN TO LEAVE YOUR CITY.

But how to make such an order work:

Clos-Salembier, and all those soldiers who come back to your neighborhood *Ineluctably* since while part of the city belongs to them the other part, the cellars, slums, Moorish baths, colonnades, terraces, doesn't belong to them   It is forbidden to leave your city.

That's what is making Mother cry. Because not a word comes to her. She can't even, any longer, desire, see, love, understand things *Unconsciously*.

Yes, because nothing is familiar anymore, and, among all the things, yes, among the streets of our taxi ride, the store windows that shake on the right under the yellow lights, the people walking under the colonnades, grander, richer colonnades than those of Bab Azoun Street, She no longer sees anything but her distance from each thing, a distance that each word and sigh measures and each shadow or patch of light lays out before us this way, like a skin, like the goatskin, in some ways.

The goatskin?

Mother weeps in this country we come to in this strange way, by breaking and entering.

It's scary to see her crying because you sense you realize that what is making her cry is something terrible in the world: love; yes, I see that, in her tears, precisely because I feel a desertion within me. Yes, a desertion by love, as if this movement through the city, this other movement away from the city, from our city, was hollowing in me, or in us, a kind of desert aridity, a kind of pit of thirst, or of desire that lacks any matter.

Yes. My mother is crying, there, next to me, in the night in the back of the taxi, while the city stirs among its streets, unrecognizable, the windows, the sidewalks, and that terrible smile Hamid was wearing, up front, in the drive through this city.

Breaking and entering? We enter this city like burglars, in the same way that, for some time already, we'd had to live like burglars in our first town.

We couldn't *immediately* find a place in that city. We had to live on the outskirts in order to really live in it, beyond the expulsions and slums.

I now know that is our curse, above and beyond loss and delirium: to have lived as if breaking and entering.

That is how we were given a world, an entourage of mésalliance.

Each being lives according to the law of many others, meanwhile you, because of the very impossibility of your dialogue, had already left this endless world.

I might say

Here is why: we weren't made for this world, for its horror or bias, because all we can do is live on the outskirts, on the hills or slopes, between the springs and falls, and shivering in winter, clinging to our bewildering hopes, like those of his eyes, Dahmane's eyes, red, red, and with me not knowing, I who had to wait until the wound or bite became intolerable for...

Mother to tell me: "You must not weep, this side of your father" and that they'd seized him "the *pathetic jerks.*"

They had seized my father, the very one to arrest in order that, sooner or later, this country would have no hope but that of the terrorists.

The terrorists? Everybody will become one someday because that's the way it is, war goes on forever, caught within the new Order.

The new Order?

Yes, the new Order: distributed among all the religious, language and national rivalries.

Yes, scattered out there that way, in the world, a thousand murders thrown out into the world, to wash clean the new Order.

"*You mustn't weep, this side of your father,*" Mother had said.

I learned not to cry in public. Only intimately, in the roots of the day and of powerlessness: as if breaking and entering.

Yes, in that burglarizing where my being was all bound up, in that desperate searching for the day of death and my anger my life; yes, that burglarizing I still dwell in, in the fracturing of the world, its violence bound to my body or my habits: other selves, since that's the way I had to live, in the découpage of the place, within the alien nature of the city or the voyage, in several degrees and removes from that approach or truth which *you Jidda: inculcated in the young man or, as you said, he who must never die because you said you knew, quite precisely, the quantity of words you'd have to bring together to keep the young man from dying;* pure tenderness for me, you were counting on your own words; *Words you knew so well how to insinuate in me, like a skin well supplied with flesh, a vibrant hope that runs through my nerves, my body, my deliverance— yes;* All the same I learned something else, something else that made me understand (still helps me understand) the other realm of this world where you live (*wander, haunt the world*) all alone; yes, alone, because in spite of this belief you've succeeded in furthering in me, beyond other types of readings, teachings, manners, I could never rejoin you; *yes, rejoin you there because: should I be clear, now, about the impossibility of reaching you; my desire to, walled off there, in the world, daily, do I have to, Really?* I could never find you again there, despite that second (or because of it) (its duration) that resides in us, stirring, that prospect where desire and murder both unfold, the shimmering of my presence, or this memory of you:

my father comes in and says:
you have to help me straighten up the room downstairs
my father is tall.
Blue eyes stare at me; yes, his blue eyes: like yours
Blue.

you have to help me straighten up that room, and he steps toward me, toward himself, toward me, slowly

my father is near, now, closer to me than I am myself, or, more exactly, within me, advancing, like another myself, about to spring forth or about to speak, talk to me, me who

what need pushes me to disclose these things; I could just as well have carried them off with
me in the secret of that disappearance where the murderers of the day and of the world have
the right to kill in complete peace
ah, if I had been something else
no matter what else
tree or plant
no matter what else
rather than
yes;   rather than
what?
and if, from time to time, I think about being something other than what I "really" am
it's by breaking and entering that I think about it
yes, by burglarizing

really: father always talks about straightening up the *room down below* "I have to show you a few things. Letters and papers that a man: Si Mahfoudh *Father said Si Mahfoudh?* Will come looking for: if they come to take me."

Si Mahfoudh?

The taxi wheels around the square, the wide avenue before it, at the end of which an arch, grand, lighted up, and Hamid there, still turned back toward us, speaking, yes, speaking;

his lips are moving

yes, moving:

they must be saying something about the avenue and the arch, down there, all lighted up because of a holiday; yes,

that's what it is: a holiday

in flashes, I understand the lips' movement

I understand, but?

Hamid, turned to face us: the war?

What war?

So where is my father? Where,

in all the world,

this world that's making war on a part of us yes; *Can you guess?*

Hamid speaks again

But how can we understand Hamid's words

For how long now have you not been back to the country?

I know, it's a mute little dialogue

where the shadows of our obsessions speak within us, almost freely, while on the surface of our lives, our contradictory outer appearance, the murderous dissimulation of our exile trembles

Hamid, Hamid, I hate you; yes, I hate you, yes, despite your picking us up at this station, despite your attachment to my mother: I hate you because of what you know perfectly well and which, Hamid, *is killing us;*

"Two years," *Hamid says,* "two years since the day they wanted to arrest me. Tomorrow will be better, you'll see, it's different here, people actually want you to tell all, it's not like back home, right?

I can imagine, it's not like back home, they're not savages here, you look like decent people, and of course war, well, it's bad for everybody."

Hamid disappears behind mountains of phrases I could neither hear nor understand because

father (yes, my father) was there, deep in me, behind Hamid behind the taxi driver behind the arch, the avenue, the lights yes behind because they had promised us—I'm saying promised—my father's arrival within a few days?

This proximity where father (yes, my father) kept drawing near, and scaring me, yes, scaring, like that day he scared me, yes, that day, then, through Dahmane Dahmane Your reddened eyes over the town Your eyes

I never got over their seizing my father; no, never. Because I know what happened afterwards, in my head, in my movements, the very movements through which I inhabited the world, and my body

This body that followed me ever after, as a pale reflection of my helplessness, because that's when I started my long wandering in it, through all the days that followed my father's arrest.[59]

Yes, I know what went on inside me, in that place where father had left me, and where *you*, underestimating the immense pain ahead of me, *you Jidda, you also left me.*

I then had to rave yes *rave* before finally understanding the law *that law* of my *raving.*

I raved. The same every day, all those days, those days when life could no longer be the same, infinitely opening out, now only open to the temporal wound of my age, sixteen, and starting then the search (ongoing) for my own sanity seized, torn apart by those days when the hope of seeing my father again died hour by hour, and after his downfall the hope of seeing yes seeing *Jidda*, yes *Jidda*, who until that moment had breathed life into my life.

What to do with those days, yes, what to do with those days when, hour after hour, the fate of everyone I loved in this world was confirmed: their flight, far, very far   far

from my sight my reach my apprehensions or ravings they eventually led me to The Redoubt and Hamid's brother's place the one who had set up his office near the Gulf and insisted on giving me an injection, and

---

59 With some compression of time (since the arrest followed the war) this also reflects Farès's feelings when his father was imprisoned.

then more, over several days, because I was still delirious far far   far
New limits within which I had to learn to live again, in distress from that
cataclysmic disappearance of my being, as if each instant of time was
impossible, yes; impossible.[60]

I had to learn to live up above my raving. They could always call my
name, at school or elsewhere, but I became deaf, *dazed*, a thousand miles
from the place where my name originated, the high school was built on the
other slope of Algiers, near the El-Biar hill, and I would not recognize my
name, as if by abducting my father they had removed any possibility of
understanding my name, that's how the syllables, the sounds work and I
had to *live* up above my delirium, in this incomprehension of myself, years
and years in which I had to grow up and be.

---

60 This resonates with—though written before—Farès's work as a psychoanalyst. For
another medical analysis of trauma in Farès's writing (and these pages specifically) see
Karima Lazali, "Une Poétique du trauma," in *Nabile Farès—Un Passager entre la lettre et
la parole* (2019).

II

How to understand these mother's words?

I was sitting by the window in the kitchen, and I watched the two kittens, the ones just born three months before, before my father was arrested, and I watched them play on the stairs with a tuft of yellowed moss; once in a while they would scratch each other because their paws flew out at this tuft, one rolls or falls down two steps while the other is already at the bottom running after the moss; they can play like maniacs now that the dog isn't there; even the big cat sleeps near the dog's spot, on the rucksack that no one here has dared throw away: I've never left the...

Nor has Mother? I can perfectly well understand her words on the difficult plane of keeping myself alive, yes, because I think I will stay alive, I'll construct a road-block before your death, the death you left trailing behind you, me, inside me too, the streets, the death that rends the whole world just like the perimeter where you were wont to produce your movements.

Jidda? Look (yes, see) Hamid, there in front of me, *while the kittens run before Jidda,* "You'll get to know the city" *whether they go after the dress style or the veil* "You're going to live right near the center of Paris, where I work, near Saint-Lazare Station."

See, yes, see, there, right in front of me, Hamid, yes Hamid, who hides death in his smile. Hamid, yes, this other Hamid the one who left the town before *H'Midouche* while my mother weeps, still, leaning on my shoulder, still, the same, so sadly

While we're waiting to see my father again, that he might appear to us, that

Hamid.

Hamid, I hate you.

You understand. I hate you. Because you are passed beyond my age, this age where the main thing is to understand how to grow up. I'm cold. Dahmane, Where is Dahmane.

I'm cold. Water?

The river? And that wild dash through the streets of the other city?

I'm cold.

Suddenly cold; and this rain falling, as if it were falling on me, and freezing me, and this desire to shout that comes over me; that swells in me; that makes my legs shake; that rises; that opens the rear window of the taxi; that

You'll catch cold; and your mother

and what the hell does it matter if you're cold? What the hell can that matter, that you die of the cold, here, while I'm straining to cry out everywhere, here, from the bounds of this window, toward the other cars there, turning, like us, around this square,

Who me?

Me?

Since I have no place nor landmark in this city, this passage that's empty of our love, I know nothing, I see nothing, hear nothing, my mother didn't once leave the boat's cabin, no, for the whole trip, not a single time, and I stayed next to her because her body was burning with fever, as if she bore all the world's fever to press it onto everyone else.

I heard a few of her words even though I was struggling to keep my eyes open wide open upon our flight.

I heard a few of those words: "*la ilaha illa Allah wa Muhammed rasu Allah*" and I felt like tearing at God, to hear more of it, because, with the fever, she muttered between her words: "*la ilaha illa Allah wa Muhammed rasu Allah*"

She muttered between each of her words, and her body stirred: "*la ilaha illa Allah wa Muhammed rasu Allah*"

I heard the sound of waves and machines all through the cabin, but all my mother prayed over was: our flight, yes, this flight beyond resting beyond world beyond words beyond us.

Between her words, I heard the sound of her respiration, wild, old, yes, old and wild like that skin, the goatskin?

It's no good trying to flee somewhere, it's waiting for you. You can't get outside the goatskin.

Why pray?

Why mix something else with the goatskin?

Why say these words the skin cannot comprehend?

Mother, why pray? It does no good.

Because what's really magic is elsewhere, deep in you, like your heart, or upon you, like your skin.

You have to discover this skin, to climb out of it. The true skin.

My mother says: *"There is no God but God and..."*

But there is no other thing but the skin, the very skin that engulfs everything.

The skin?

As for me, it had been necessary first to understand others in order to understand me, for me to understand me through others because they said all kinds of things about me, no doubt because my skin wasn't like other people's, most other people, because of its whiteness, such whiteness, making it distinct from other skins.

It had been strictly necessary that I understand certain things because, among many items, I was the only one in that skin, the only one, not H'Midouche, and my red hair, almost red, red, yes, like Dahmane's hands and eyes, over the city.

That's how it was. Mother's useless praying, because you don't just get out, the way you want, out the goatskin since, according to what people say and Jidda always reminds me, the skin existed way before, as if we, ourselves, only existed to stretch or explode the skin.

This is why I want to know, more than anything, something about this skin, because you can't be like me—and not question, all the way to the bottom, the lore of this skin. That is why I. Someone gave the order somewhere, up in heaven, or in hell, and the horror happened, with no *real* reason for it, or else, maybe, out there, like

the shadow of your face
in these streets,
and my skin, my footsteps,
my prayers,
pressing against
the skin.

This is how it is

    :

            it's no use running
                my legs
           are caught
               in the hide
           of the Goatskin.

That's how it is
:

I couldn't understand all my mother's words, and before, well before in that place, yours, those you constantly sank into me, beyond me, in that kind of *natural being* of myself, the one whose extent and even name I was unaware of, the name before myself

Emma? Nothing is anymore all the same

nothing

the world? The one that could slam against your coincidence in me

That could brutalize *your desires* or designs while I won't have reached my half-way point yet, in that painful distancing where

I've nonetheless learned not to open my heart *doubly,*

for there came that moment when I no longer knew who I was

one of those moments when the world (or the city) was shrinking (this city) (this Upper City)

so fast that I had to run

toward the port.

the port?

I forgot everything, and I crossed the city, my skin on fire, my heart gripped, head gripped and
    worn down by what *you* say: the goatskin.
      The hide of the goatskin?
        Who is saying *goatskin*?

      Me?

I forgot *everything*
/:

Me and the Goatskin?

the goatskin?

for, there came that moment when I no longer knew who I was, one of those moments when the world (or the city) (or my thoughts) (or my space) (this upper city) (Clos-Salembier) was shrinking so much that I had to run, run all the way down to the port

to buy some cigarettes

and drown my brief attempts at life in the view of the rocks, the harbor that protects the city

and me, *wiped out*

while I would have liked to mash

the city,

there,

with one fist

like an insect

a tiny one; while I would have liked to be *Master of the Place*, and act, ACT, without my being aware, against my pain or my kindness, make the city EXPLODE

from the inside

BRING DOWN THE HLL

and watch the days come to life

or your Clos-Salembier games

this laughter or wordplay where you caught up with my ignorance of *your* world; that one-*of yours*, Jidda, you who wanted to amuse me with the city, with no regard for its modernity, its turbulence

Walking once more with your impenetrable veil or your face up against the walls, like my shadow, the gigantic shadow of your face over the streets

And me, What, Me?

I have two legs, two arms, a head,

But I also have this color in my hair and my skin.

It isn't me What Me? that focuses on these colors, it's everybody else, Yes The Others Who have insisted on these colors

H'Midouche, too, was white, had white skin that is, and hair like most people here, brown.

But mine, Mine? It isn't me insisting on these colors, but in the end

: you don't extricate yourself any way you want from the goatskin.

Jidda is the one who says that because

"Where do you think we all come from?"

"From the mountain?"

"From the grass?"

"From the word?"

It's no use Jidda speaking into my ear

above all her words that thumped against my temples without allowing

me to discover anything at all

that might put me at rest distance me tranquilize me.

Absolutely.

Nothing.

Nothing explains Nothing.

Nothing.

Always words upon words and me *What... Me?*

What... Me?

nothing. All the same I do have other things in me or on me beside

these colors

well, for example, Malika

Malika doesn't have anything against my colors.

Just one thing:

When we go out in the street, leaving The Redoubt or Clos-Salembier

she only asks one thing,

or rather:

only does one thing

But Malika, people are going to stare at us.

What the hell do you care Malika says *what could that possibly matter*

to you: you, Red.

My eyes are burning.

What, you didn't know: that's what they call you:

Red.

You, they stare at you all the time.

It's tough, tough

what dwells deep in my head: like a non-understanding stone.

Go on in town

like me

and you'll understand.

You Will Understand: one of those moments when the rocks in the port resembled the sea's aborted dream, the many kneelings of man, hurled there, like a block of shadow on the waves, only a few yards from the rumble and other sound effects carried aloft by the city

So I couldn't
but consent to a return
toward you,
Another cramped quarter
of myself,
and hope
for that aptitude
wherein your voice
sustained my being.

I did return, barely heeding the city's hum, I ran, yes, through the event of your face on those streets, nourished by the shade that you edged with porticos along the boulevards that circumscribe the port. I ran, in the annihilation of my headlong desires, desires cast, like my eyes a moment before, down into the city, in a gesture of abasement or defiance, onto the rocks or the waves glowing there from my war, down in the brutal fault-line of this world, a world which, running against all our witness of this existence and its murders, refuses the advent and the sight of our bodies, our bodies among the porticos and the bounty of our streets, our bodies, and refuses you, stretched out over the city, refuses independence, or my colors, You toward whom, in spite of my flights and perjuries, I ran, like a tree seeking its foliage; I ran, toward the leaves where, through pathological tenacity, I was able to hook my arms, my hands, my words, my words? as if toward branches, branches covered with all these words.

III

Who else?

Yes, to whom else could I come running back, since, so much earlier in your language I was, so to speak, *already* discovered:

Malika asked questions, not in order to know, but to confront.

Malika? I'll tell the whole story.

Absolutely everything.

I have nothing more to lose since my limbs are already running with water, as if instead of veins and muscles, territories had sprung forth.

Maybe that's where it is

the Goatskin?

The territories or, the Goatskin?

My brain is already humid, like foam.

Someone is walking, here and there, someone walks, and perhaps it's you, hard and delicate,

in the Chetma night.

Shadow of the light spread over the earth, my limbs, and this mimicry of colors that, starting with the whitest, uncovers the deepest black.

Kahéna?

Veiled shadow of my raving.

Toward you that lover, or Jidda, pushed me, when, in the delinquencies of my body or mind, I refused, or lived the world's refusal, this world that had absolutely no use for me.

Starting that day I'd have liked to kill

but my mother forbade insurrection because

as she said

you, you ask only to live: yes: just that: to live

I could fully understand what my mother meant but

that's not enough either: living: just living or rather: understanding.

But understanding what:

Living?

Her body shakes, while the water continues to hasten our flight, everywhere, far from this cabin where mother patiently awaits the sunrise.

I'm still wearing Dahmane's coat, a cast-off given to me before he left, because *he* knew,

Dahmane

that we'd be leaving the town

take it, now

I'll be wearing something else; you'll need it more than I do: the town gets cold in November,

like the river.

I could always watch Dahmane leaving, like H'Midouche, and still believe that for one day

Malika owned me

Mother had had to shorten the sleeves and bottom, so that I didn't disappear in it, with nothing showing but my red, red hair.

Malika knew that coat, and she owned me, with her cigarette packs and her photo; I only have to look between the lines in her forehead and her smile to believe I'm once again sunk in the dunes.

This is how it is:

Dahmane is chasing after something we no longer have

even the sea

has been taken from us

because: we always have to burrow in the dunes.

How it is:

Someone yells, right there, close by, seated like me, beside me, yells with the desire to plunge a knife in my back, slash, right in my neck.

Try to understand, a world that wants no part of you:

try?

Someone yells: me?

Mother says I should sleep while Hamid, *Jidda,* is still turned back toward us, elbows on the seat back, and the taxi continues on through streetlights and traffic signals like a somber man through a rainbow.

"You'll be a goner if you listen to the old lady."

?

She was surely trying to say this: *?*

or: almost nothing

because: either she understood full well and could only approve of me, *or* she didn't understand and didn't want me to understand, and was, *neither more nor less:* jealous.

Right, Jidda spoke hardly at all, but *me?*

me? *I* couldn't get along without her: absolutely not.

The proof: the day they sent me off to high school, supposedly so I could learn better.

Nothing I could do; it was her—her they wanted to separate me from, from her,

Jidda: whom it takes a long time to understand and yet,

today

despite the water flooding my mouth and limbs I see everything,

yes: everything.

The high school? and beyond it a school and the cries I hear all around me, rising and clanging against the cabin

nothing, it's nothing

you must have had a nightmare

it's nothing; and I'm not red

son of someone red

whatever were you dipped in?

your mother must have slept with the devil or with the Djnouns:

come on, what the heck were you dipped in

son of something red?

oh it's nothing: my father's always been in the union but that doesn't make me *son of someone red?*

Where has your mother

been sleeping?

I'm afraid: I have red hair

As you know,

and white skin

white like a black child

You do know who the *red* child is, right?

Mother says I should sleep a bit

since tomorrow we have to arrive on time to meet Dahmane

at six

in the Redoubt.

Dahmane, who is due at six, to tell us how he's leaving.

Dahmane?

Yes. Dahmane, because Dahmane is taking off and I'm staying as if I have nothing else to do but stay in Clos-Salembier and wait for father's return.

"No, wait till your father gets back, because I don't want to—I can't—stay here alone, you understand?"

"Yes, Mother,

I've already enclosed my life in this waiting, innocently, or unaware, to the point that, whenever I think of you, I see only the waiting that could deliver me, or satisfy me.

That's the way it is,

I've played it all wrong; I should have left for the mountains, for those places where a man knows who the enemy is, has known for a long time, unlike here in the town—and died there.

But that's how it went, I preferred staying here, getting in your way, as in that dream where"

There's no doubt H'Midouche is dead because, in all this time, there would have been a sign of life

Yes, there aren't a whole lot of solutions to this, solutions, *I mean to say*, that are *entirely* satisfying.

Praying?

And why pray?

Praying does no good; mother is wrapped in four blankets (two of them mine, from my berth) which don't keep her warm but do keep her from falling.

Her body shakes and I can't find anything to say, even though my head is full—really full—of all kinds of people—yes—exactly—as if this cabin held the whole world.

I must have slept.

A few drops of sweat there, on my forehead and fingers which nonetheless feel cold, cold, like a chill all along my back, thighs, legs. I'd like to be able to feel Malika's skin, now, in this cabin where the pale rays shed by the night-light mixing their bluish tone with the white and green of the cabin situate me too close to my own death or my mother's to not feel like *killing*.

Mother cries out, but nobody can hear. There's no one that could intervene on this level or, rather, could *hear* on this level,

Unless

Him?

Yes: Him.

I don't need anything, no, nothing, except your veil to help stop Mom's (Emma's) trembling.

I don't need anything: except her very body, yes, hers, the one that so many times has made me prisoner. The one where I have been (set to it) against the whole world, and which turned me away toward the desires of others.

The one where the father is absent, because here I am not able to understand what father did.

Mom's skin is soft.

Her body seems to relax or find calm under the effect of your veil yet I don't see you I don't hear you I don't listen, all I am is your veil and I open Mom's life outwards, toward a beyond where I am not found, no—really—: I'm not there.

Someone knocks at the cabin door Someone who opens the cabin door though I didn't say anything and am bent over Mom's body Someone dressed in white like the cabin steward but who isn't the steward.

Someone set against me who is coming to see what I'm doing. Someone I don't or don't want to recognize who is opening the cabin door wider and wider.

This door that doesn't open onto the corridor or the deck but on the mother-sea the high sea flooding between the legs and

Mother cries out while a single word lodges in me like your veil bearing me up yes: Mom (Emma) I'm running to you, Mom (Emma) don't be afraid, I'll protect you from him,

Yes: him. The one who so suddenly opened that door onto the sea.

Mom don't be afraid of anything, I'll protect you from him: I'll go further than he did into the country, much further, and unlike him I won't get captured, and there'll be no need for me to come slyly back this way, and rip the door open on our flight.

Mom don't be afraid: I'll show you other things, sweeter, less painful than what he subjected you to there, in our old world, as if that world were to last always.

Don't be afraid of his returning, no, there's nothing to fear, because you've suffered just as much as he, and from him, as he could ever have suffered from you, or me.

Fear nothing: and don't pray before him or for him because really what do you know about him, what do you know about him.

Mom (Emma), I'm able to say these words again, here, as if secretly, yes, without his knowing or even you, because it's obvious, your body is trembling, and the walls of the cabin are still white and green and dimly lighted by the: so I press I press your veil here, on Mom's throat so she'll yell out again and again so she'll say no: I won't forbid you to be an insurgent: no, I forbid you nothing: you will stay in Algiers while I go look for your father in France: you'll wage this war because it is yours and you no longer know where you come from: so take up arms, Dahmane certainly did, and battle the whole world, your father, your brother, your country, your dream, everything: and leave me alone: that's what I wanted to hear my mother say: just that: that's all: that's everything.

My mother says: you won't leave with Dahmane, you'll stay with me, and you'll come look for your father with me.

Nothing more to say, Mother

Nothing but this: Mom who leads me away from father and toward the house of love.

What else?

H'Midouche tells me: you too, you'll have to take off because you love them too much: you can't stay on at the house with Jidda and the dog simply because you love them while outside the house they insult you and make fun of you.

Nothing to say?

Right, you have red hair, so what? You're not going to stay home just because of that?

Nothing to say?

Nothing. I have nothing to say except: I flopped my head into your chest with a violent blow where no word was possible only my anger the anger of living among you against you in that sad and despairing place: anger of your indifference. That is how I lived though I was sixteen, because, in history's odd venues, time takes fantastic shortcuts and throws it all at you at once, without blinking.

I didn't want to fight but I wanted to understand and that's why, Hamid, I hate you, because you're the other face of my age, the age when you learn to smile despite death, or indifference.

Do you really want to know?

Here, then: a few drops of sweat on my forehead, my fingers frozen, a chill in my back thighs legs while what I would like to feel is Malika's skin here in the taxi and to have my mouth full of sand as in those dunes and that Malika's warmth would come over me You think saying: I don't know anything about it, absolutely nothing But I have only one thing that counts, one thing to do that is to not sink into the pit to not drift down That is everything Malika, do you hear?

Him?

Look: everything is flying away, in every direction

But we will continue, yes: we will be, and They can commit whatever craziness in the dunes, and even there, in the Redoubt, or Clos-Salembier.

No more inward gazing but a look fastened outward toward the dunes the sand or the mouths

Malika?

Him: in any case I'll separate myself from him because I'm not alright with one thing: his silences and my confusions.

Do you know, Malika? You know he only spoke to me in moments, disastrous ones, when, inescapably, he *needed* me: you understand?

I've never admitted that, in this place where my love dwells or my desire to be yes with those I love or live with Never

Malika? Your water-splash laugh on that mouth and those lips passing over the soft paths of my grasses or hills your lips opening like a trickle of water under stones the depth of your lips that calm other that dwells in you and that I want to grab and breathe life into and steal like a thief who flees death in the hills.

If there had been no Dahmane? Here, among us, to lead us on? Were love and breath possible in the Chetma night?

The other man? The one who came from the other land, the one who marked our country the way you mark a being or a skin? The one who pulled at the territory and opened up the Goatskin?

Do you know?

Malika: who he is?

Who?

I want to know because his body trembles as if animated by absurd prayer.

Malika? I saw her yes I saw her before we left, at Clos-Salembier, take up the rosary, the one made of watermelon seeds even though watermelon seeds they are not?

Malika? Do you believe, really, in all those things: the seeds you let fall through your hands to go and stitch themselves again in the ground or in the sons of God?

You believe in that?

Malika lets her bare feet play in the sand, and her hands smooth her legs, brown like her lips. This is exactly how she is, while the dunes change their skin and turn black.

Dahmane yells far across the seaweed on the heap of seaweed that dominates the bay a large stretch of ocean far from houses lights cars Malika?

I saw her I saw her and I also saw that other man the one who waited for the country to wring itself there before you or us and smother us.

I would have slapped that smile off you if Mother's head weren't resting on my shoulder if I didn't have that cloud before my eyes or those veils drawing your face near and then far like a pit I didn't want to fall into where I don't want to fall...

IV

Mother said:

"Don't shut yourself in with her, in that room," the old woman, so inoffensive, and my mother jealous of her power

What did my mother mean?

Maybe this:

"you'll be lost to this world, if you listen to Jidda." Since clearly this is what she meant to say:

That there existed—*there had to exist, for me*—a radical loss in listening to Jidda. A loss of this world, the world of things and their proximity in language, a proximity that Jidda knew despite what people were wont to call: *her feeble spiritual health*. The loss of the meaning of things, of those multiple senses by which one could read or listen to the meanings of things. And, certainly, in the murders of the last three years, Jidda spoke little and her striped and multicolored silhouettes proliferated on the walls, the silhouettes of her world, her world of an ancient agility now lost in the bounding of this world, this one, that carried everything away with it, that had ravaged everything ever since its appearance in the interior of the country or the coasts or the towns, had opened the bellies of men and women, like goatskins.

Yes. Anyway that's how you heard about this bounding that had opened various bellies throughout the country, bellies known as Wilayas or Insurgents, the leaping that had surprised most of us even though we might have known that, one day or another, the Goatskin would regain its speech, the very Goatskin that would bring into the world the sons of the dead land.

A waiting, as well, but death.

For there was a death all through the city, Algiers, Wretched-Ville of so many people, those I climbed with, in a hurry to infringe on the law of life's stifling, and to find, glued to her childish attempts at drawing, Jidda, yes, she who restored my life with just a brush of her veil.

That's how I would surprise her, or rather: how she used to sweep me away, how she hurled afar the impossible colonial existence, enfolded me in her beliefs and the world she dominated, talked to me, initiated me into that other language, the one destined to overflow the Goatskin.

What could I understand of it?

I watched Jidda's pencil, and heard her voice and the hand that smoothed the design and the color.

The world would almost instantly spring open, really, and inside it the various seeds of life were germinating, the ones that cause the other seeds of life to grow.

She also initiated me into

The Cycle of The Gaze.

At least, what she called

The True Gaze. The one that, the opposite of ours or perhaps like ours, creates while it sees.

God? She thought not a whit of God, or a Cause. No.

It was much more simple than that, or more exact or profound than a simple or unique cause. For Jidda could not think in terms of a single or unique cause.

Because: one day: this.

"Every being is within," then, in all the innocence of her truth or her voice: *"The 'whys' seek the 'whys'? That's why they exist, the 'whys'? But—Us?"*

She traced the lines that would open the Goatskin, or the different bellies of the Goatskin.

I used to stare at the lines to understand: but, nothing.

I needed her voice.

That voice saving everything. Destroying everything. Destroying hate. Fear. Death. Obsession. Recklessness. The voice that unites. That puts the clothes on. And the make-up. And washes away.

"But Us?"

"Look: here is the surest path from one point to another: Night.

Yes. This line that binds the different parts of the Goatskin is the Night: The Origin of our world: Black Light."

"Take the white and the black," she said, "Or, your own skin. Already you can read, with no effort at all, the enigma of this world.

This is how it is. The enigma is within us. Upon us. Upon you. Like a skin. Your own skin."

Could I begin to understand? There on my skin, what the old woman was saying?

Of course! But was that the gambit, or the reality, of this world?

The Black child?

The one who lives, there, squatting beneath us, and coloring our skin?

The Black child?

A few words arrive from the Southern land.

From the borders of the Southern land.

"Sit down."

Jidda says.

Her veils. Her white veil. That thin veil over her mouth and lips, that comes to its end over her mouth as in the desert.

That wraps itself above her vast head of hair, over that straight hair few can see.

The Black country?

So near?

What do you do to approach the Black country?

In the school's playground, during a few of the games, as dust and sand was devouring our feet, I heard the yells that were part of the game

: The game of the Black child.

They threw some phrases my way, whose mixed messages I was supposed to untangle, like the slave caught between his Master's different wants.

I could! Next, sit down

near the Teacher.

"Look at these fists."

He held them before me, clenched, ready to box either temple.

"The slave is white:

He isn't Black."

"The slave is white:

He isn't Black."

I had to squeeze his two fists in my hands.

I had to repeat after him.

"The slave is white:

He isn't Black."

Such were the sentences whose heedlessness I was supposed to translate:

"Why is the slave white?

And not Black?"

And me?

To go against
Jidda.
Opening the place up
Because our world is not
Jidda's; She who spends
all her time drawing
:why is the slave
white?
Because he refuses
The Black child?
Could this be
the end
of the enigma?

In the school's playground, during a few games, while the dust ate our feet, I heard certain yells that were part of the game: the game of the black child. On the playground, they called me Kahlouche.

I lived in full sun, set against the wind from the South.

Kahlouche?

That signifies color. The black man, the one that occasionally appears in the hills or raw plains of the North Country.

The man who crosses the desert vastness and comes toward us to explain to us our heedlessness.

On the school playground: warm sun.

A wind that flaps our clothes and covers eyes and legs in dust.

A wind from the southern land.

On the other side of the playground is where the caravans pause, the ones that leave the last spots in the North Country to voyage across sand to the South.

In-Salah. And such is the route of the caravans of old, devourers of slaves.

I'm often asked. In a shockingly abrupt way, and I have to answer. In my own way. With stones or fists, depending on the age. My strength. Or my distances.

"You come from In-Salah?"

The road I'm on? The school I'm in? The village, the town I'm in?

What does the Northern village I'm in matter?

Or the frontier village I'm in?

I always respond with force. Since, *really*, I don't know where I come from.

I found myself to be alive, that's all, several times, and between times, between these moments of discovery, nothing—just a sort of monotony without illumination, despite a beating sun, a sort of toil of my being, or lack of being, while awaiting that other light, the one that will illuminate it all.

No use for Jidda to stare at me or tell me I won't escape the enigma: with all my strength I want to escape it But

Too late.

The enigma is inscribed within me. Ever since my divided birth. The division of my skin and face.

Ever since the divided country: that's the way it is

the goatskin is black in color.

black?

and me?

In the middle of the goatskin.

"the goatskin is black in color."

What to do?
The rumors keep coming, and the insults, the rivalries.
However:
"We are all a mixture.
Mixed in blood and skin."
According to what the Teacher says.
The slave?

But the children at school, those who belong to the well-dressed body, protected from the light. Or, from the raw, hard blaze of the sun. The school's children do not understand *mélange:* brown skin and fine features. Or white skin, the white that makes skin black, and red, red hair, like Dahmane's eyes.
Dahmane?
Wrong. Mélange exists.
They don't teach mélange at school.
No. They build right over it. In an imbecilic way, as if it were nothing. As if nothing existed. As if mélange had no importance.
Wrong. Mélange exists. And it works this world. Makes the world come alive. It, too, engenders the primal couple at their first contact with the Goatskin.
The Goatskin.
Jidda has just sketched a few new lines.
A sort of animal with no body, head and limbs cut off. An area where you guess at the burgeoning of a neck and some limbs.
Jidda hesitates

   :

  or *me?*
With her left hand she touches the veil on her face, near her mouth.

Then she looks over at me. Open my eyes.

Blue.

And speaks again.

In me.

Like speech

Issued from me.

That speaks and says:

"Look. The expanse, the scope, is all present. Yes. *Immediately.* And without the existence of any 'why.'

Look. Do you think you can live outside of this scope?"

I can't be next to Jidda except, automatically, in not participating in her world.

Besides, as she says herself: I am part of the expanse:

Thus:

I gaze.

"If one could understand the pages of the book that lies open in this expanse, that would be a good thing."

"The animal's skin : that is the meaning."

"Look."

"The book divides the world or this expanse into several sentences that run like rivers. I can carry you off on one of these lines. But be careful. There's no way out. No exit. Except the stream's flowing."

"Don't look for the way out. Instead, the other world. That's what you must look for. The one that makes this world live. And the animals, books, stones, men and everything else."

Jidda speaks:

"I didn't invent war, or this world, already ripped like skin. I invented none of it."

Jidda says:

"Here; there is war.
and the men who struggle in war."

"Here, there is the book
and the lines in this book that cross through war."
"Here, there is the river.
And, beneath the river
the two kingdoms.
The kingdom of the game
and of the Earth."

Jidda adds:

"We live above the river.
Without knowing what is below the waves.
Yet: in the simple, movement
of the water: we know,

yes, we know."

Jidda points her right index finger at the drawing:

"We know there is something below the waves. Some face, some land. Or field. Or word. Or world. Yes…"

She traces the last few lines. Beneath the faces in the wave. Those that observe. There's no doubt about this. Those we call: *the inhabitants of light.*

Jidda, I would just like to be able to cry out. Cry out unto hell. Open up the masks of other people or of Hamid, and stride forth straight, straight, to you, in the midst of the river.

I'd like to be able to read through fears and rages. Read without fatigue or anger, and be happy, and know the joy that uncovers and brings forth.

I would fasten my lips to your lips, and take on my life. My words to your words. My hands fastened to your hands. To lift the whole city and see, really see, beneath it, just as under the river, the traces of your presence or your voyage.

The water is cold, cold, beyond any bone, Jidda. Far beyond.

The river's water? Every being must cross over the river, but how? How is it done? Over across the river?

"The Goatskin is black in color."

PART TWO

The Enigma

V

I will start with the multiplicity of the two signs. Those two signs where your inscription told me of the enigma of my birth.

The simplest thing is to just cite the nearest moment of dissimulation, after the attempts at living transparently. Soon blocked, these attempts at transparent lives.

The territory was too brief, one or the other had to give up his place: that will have us wandering far very far in our childhood in this world.

The territory was too short, or the people too brief in their defense systems: it would have been necessary to invent—*reinvent*—the roots of the territory.

Wasted effort, men were listening to that other sound, the one coming not from the Goatskin but

What does it matter: men no longer heard the heart of the Goatskin.

Being clandestine?

Astounding, the rift between my father and me.

An astonishment mixed with fear, because, suddenly: his name must be hidden in order to follow in the footsteps of the Goatskin?

Nothing: later on I learned the word: being *clandestine.*

I understood H'Midouche's flight, or his strong will, after he left for the hills or the clay surrounding the towns like a sheet of velvet spread over the love of life.

Is there such a thing as cold velvet? *A cloth, or a warmth, more sizeable than the stomach?*

Yes, there, between the town's knees

like a scent in the clay.

Is there a word, a human word dipped in oil like a doughnut? A word held out to you like a doughnut?

Tell me. I've longed to know.

I understood a little better my father's concern; the false name that shuffles among other names like a letter in the post offices.[61]

---

61   This, like much of the trip to France in the foregoing, echoes Farès's journey, as a student, to escape the war. It is possible that at times he disguised his family name—that of his very prominent father—or was tempted to.

But: *man is an odd affliction for his own people… He dissimulates, and he wounds the other, there, right in his being, or heart, and then he forgets…*
    Just the right amount of secrecy, or
        let's say: innocence.
    a man amuses himself with words,
    and dies of them just like that, like a dog with a grenade
        for
    a man is an odd affliction for his people.
With a false name.

Thousands of stars over the city; in the distance the immense, somber blue that I know, and that I sense as luminous and overflowing the night the dark our gaze: "You've got to help me straighten up the room down below," my father says and his voice shocks my hands my eyes that voice never asking but requiring naming deciding. There you have it

I turned on the light. The dog was already in the room. Near the sofa. Up against the chair and the table. I opened the room up. There. Where all his books were. And that bed I loved to read in. While father was working. There. Almost right in front of me. For as long, almost, as the night.

The dog was already in the room. Near the sofa. Against the chair. And the table.

I left the door of the room open. Open to the yard. And the town.

His books. I saw only his books because: a few times, after reading, father would talk. Lying on his back. Yes. Without turning toward me. He spoke of certain genealogies. His hope was to put into books various branches of the leaf that he said was us. Or, our family.

I strained to understand what that was, a genealogy.

He said we had been there a long time, but that it was hard to trace the different directions, after eight or nine generations.

What did that mean: *eight or nine generations?*

Since we'd been here. In Clos-Salembier. There were no more for me. Of these generations.

What existed simply was. Clos-Salembier. The area of the town. Jidda. Emma. H'Midouche. Zineb. Dahmane. Smaïl. Yellow-Teeth. Malika. And a few others.

What did that mean: *eight or nine generations?*

These generations that filled out several leaves. That my father was gluing end to end. Respectfully. As if he were dealing with the very life of these generations.

I used to look at the shelves where the books were. My father read often. Besides the newspaper. *Republican Algiers*. Bought every day.

It was only later that I knew.

Later? To be precise, the time of the Great Strike. The one that was going to blow everything up. The high schools. Universities.[62]

Yes. It was only at that moment that I understood that. What father was looking for. Was a reason to live. Inside the territory. Probably that. A reason to live.

The one I seized when the Strike came. The one that sustained us. For several days. Above the whole town. Like gods.

Yes.

Like gods.

We thought we were opening the world's eyes. Just like that. All at once. Nothing to it. Simply by holding a Great Strike.

A real battle. Out in the open. And with open hearts.

That must be what that is: a genealogy?

A place to be, or believe. Maybe it was really something else. A kind of appeal to the future. Or the enigma of my own future.

What must Dahmane think.

Or *Jidda*.

That must exist in them *also*, like a sort of thought.

And in Smaïl?

Yes, did this kind of thought arise in Smaïl?

And Emma?

In Emma? I didn't ask her much, until after father's arrest.

How was I so unable to see, through all those thoughts inscribed there before me how could I not: a voice makes me jump I'm no longer in that room the table is as small as the dog and I think I'm starting to know fear, fear or a furious desire to live there. No doubt I will live again in other forms of being under other first names because that's the way it is

---

62 There were several strikes during the Algerian War (for Independence), but the Grande Grève of 1956, initiated by students, impacted Farès and is probably the one mentioned here.

with death that unifies and disperses life because that's the way it is with every belief or effusion and because in the first moment of understanding life there whirls death's enveloping childhood, like a circle (The Madness Game, or History, of a world) that inscribes the reasons—like an articulated swarming from every direction—to live or to hope while my voice rises in me while father is there while he is speaking out against my fear this fear I have of him while mother weeps while Hamid while in the distance father speaks while in spite of all these words I bring forth the terrible gulf of the light, me enslaved to yearning speech tied bound this way to the world's chorus, as madness approaches, naming the space, like an ancient ritual, old older than this new land that blows up the young limbs of the war around us Yes Come-See here, the pit of the writhing being because I have indicted man's most complete submissions in order to liberate his song of human lands Come-See or Hear for Word is Act now ripened more than Enigma-Terror :

> *water*
> *had flowed.*

> > Yes.
> > Water
> > Blood
> > Life.

> *water*
> *had*
> *flowed.*

> > Milk
> > had flowed
> > like water
> > from the leather
> > of the Goatskin.

> *Conversely.*

> ... ...

> > *Water had*
> > *flowed*
> > *like*
> > *milk*
> > *from the leather*

of the goatskin.

> Who can say
> what
> the goatskin is?

A stomach?

A woman?

A man?

A history?

A country?

Because it's not enough to know the word for a thing but all the names of all things.

What was it that Mother meant when, without trying to speak for Jidda, she kept on transmitting the language of her night, her day, her life, dispersing the words and the meaning in order that, removed from the language of my father, I might understand the first or even the antecedent meaning of things and beings, in order that, free from preaching or divine eagerness, I take into myself (I learn within myself) the desire and the death of living, before even starting to live.

It was in that way that I was *d-i-s-a-r-t-i-c-u-l-a-t-e-d* since I remained seated among them all, living an amputation whose secret my mother wanted to hold on to, while Jidda restored the veiled parts of my being to me, in her diluted and resplendent language, a fertile and free restoration whose laws I was then to know, in complete freedom to perceive the false verity of my birth (we are all "the other being" of someone) and to express Jidda's agitation as it guided my limbs my voice my lips over the dislocated territories of my adolescence or my history, the language of another language wherein the spilled goatskin signified the flowing beyond territory the other life or the life of a country in pre-birth, a language lacking clarity as it happened since it still muddled its bearings and surroundings as in that moment with Hamid when the disappearance of your face in that place my eyes watering up while I watch the lights and streets on both sides all stream away from the taxi windows Yes The first word does not exist only the word doubled, for you used to say that was your first name *"Abd Nouar"* For you were born under two signs, that of your enslavement and that of light Your name opened toward two

meanings that of genealogy or that of history[63] *"This world is not unitary.*
Single. Unique. Without divisions. That is false. The true world is several.
That's the way of the true world. The other one. That of your war. Is not
the real world. Harshly I laugh seeing you running off to your appointed
place. What do your Independences matter? Since you will reject what is
multiple. Yes. You bear the name of the former slaves. Others, too, have
this same color or name. But the country the country? For one day the
slave will be free. Yes Jidda the name of the slave will be free": I could
have thrown everything over. Tipped over the table. From the very first
moment. Down below. From the balcony rail right down to the ground. Yes
I should have thrown it all over. And the sky with it. No longer exist. Yes.
Not be there. And NOT KNOW ABOUT your spells or your domination.
Because. Soft traces of your world. Your lips' caresses imprinted the earth
like a book open to everyone. Yes. A more open book. More ancient than
that other one. The one you opened only in the morning. In the solitude
of your awakening. In the impossibility of your pages. That you flipped
through. And revered through simple inadequacy. That you liked to cover
with the world. In the clothing of your desires. That I would have liked
to burn to discover the other kingdom. That I'd have liked to burn. Burn.
Like this land. Or this town. That continued to shine. Yes, Facing us. Or
among us. On the other side of our wall or town, or legs. To take you
through the town and show you all those places you oh my madness now
spread over the town you are no longer and where I chase after you as after
my life taking your life for my life, while the sign flees ahead while the
word links to the name while the slave changes skins while the Goatskin
flees the world and the town opens in me and my hand takes up arms to
make the *world* happen Yes Jidda I was born under the sign far from the
sign under the sign like the site or the very emergence like the killer of
childhood the murderer of master and slave That is how, Jidda, I listen to
the progress of the Goatskin Those who are carrying my people toward
the infernos of this world Those who open my mouth my lips or my hell
Those who strike or give witness from the other side of this world Those

---

63 "The name" in the trilogy always addresses Farès's rejection of simplistic notions of
nationality, religion, language. In his view (conversation with this translator) the work of
Abdelkébir Khatibi most urgently in need of translation was *La Blessure du nom propre*
(The Wound of the Name, or The Wound of the Proper Noun).

who destroy the sanctuaries or the towns Those who cut the throats of sheep and their wool Those who burn the world or the land Those who Yes Jidda This is how I hold on to my place in the world Toward the site of murderous glare in the abysses of This is how my feet swell and how my voice As in the butchering of the beast when they blow under its skin or tear the skin away with their fists That's how the head is still in place despite the long thin gash That is how they divide up the limbs among the living gathered there and they hand forth that is how the Goatskin is born yes the Goatskin the Goatskin and me? Me? as I run, run to find Yes to find Dahmane... in the impossible place of his death Dahmane toward whom my legs still strain so he might run because what if there's a slender gap between life and death it's in that space that I want to find Dahmane in the last iota of human gratitude in that space where evasion is still possible A game of shadow or helplessness.[64] That's how I'd like to find Dahmane sitting on the bed in the room down below where I used to like to read have our glasses of tea and talk until the first lamb of day: Dahmane always says funny things when we're alone of course or with Malika or in town looking for some spot to spend two or three sweet hours Near the first Casbah streets near the square two cafés deep in a courtyard where the ankles of the night take up dance It's in that place or those places where the messengers from other worlds live those who nourish despair or *ennui* not with rounds of tea but with smoking and jokes: two zithers and a flute opening desires and souls toward the shadowy streets where rooms are yours for the tidy sum of five thousand francs: Dahmane and I We drink our tea in a corner of the room and watch the others the rich ones and the poor taking their pleasure for five thousand francs Now there's something ridiculous says Dahmane: pleasure for a thousand francs All you have to do is look behind you to know that the best pleasure is what you hold in your eye through love or because you're super at something or just plain liknable Look: Some day I'll introduce you to Malika You don't know her Malika who'll spoil you just to make you happy Yes Unbeliever there are people who think about the happiness or pleasure of others the

---

64 Though "désarroi" is translated elsewhere as "confusion," here "helplessness" is adopted, as it was—on Farès's suggestion—in the title of Volume III, *Exile and Helplessness* (*L'Exil et le désarroi*).

real happiness or the real pleasure of others I mean That's all there is to it
That's the way it is.

It kills me, this bit with Dahmane, because I just have to wait for him
to finish the story

Like that: for your own pleasure.

Hamid Dahmane she'll pull the Narrator's trick on you the one that
underlies your fever in the course of your wanderings the one that projects
your childhoods and establishes them, founds them, in the first spurts from
the goatskin or the stomach in her special places where she knows to lead
you despite your power like that day Malika She will splatter you with
history and presence with simple gestures of her body and her love.

I have some trouble moving because every motion takes me beyond
the river and because through effort or shyness I never quite reach those
scenes of spring-like creation while I, I am the one who Me who opens
my name up burns it or invents it anew One more time While I am in
fact included in this pursuit of man and of the other I can't quite reach
the slopes into the river While the water continues to flow over me in me
While my sight weakens weakens While I no longer see you Jidda No:
More than my picking up a weapon And shooting There Everywhere in
me At the town At Hamid At you Or Mother who is still crying At the
wheels and At the lightbulbs of the square where All around me are turning
The thousand riches of abandoned childhood... Or the town that explodes
around me like the thousand riches of abandoned childhood Yes: I should
have thrown it all over and strangled the cats at play in the courtyard
Suddenly Just as In the school's playground Also I should have Suddenly
strangled the Teacher's game The Man who called me Kahlouche While I
was busy inventing all sorts of other words I should not have let my father
come in and strangle my mother There in the cabin Before her weeping
in the town and I should have followed you Dahmane Dahmane Before
leaving in this town From this town In this town Before leaving in this
town.

VI

What is there to say?

Yes what is there, so that all might become clear again, with no part of my being wandering from me, playing by itself, set against me.

What is there to say? Yes: while flight has already taken place, and I can still hear her words as they reach me, without the slightest possibility of pulling myself back.

"Speech is the daughter of war, and against usurped meaning; and the day you understand her words, you'll have no desire but to flee, because you'll then need to understand why the country is a killer."

The country kills?

Dahmane is there, in that rivalry between my mother and the land! Dahmane: stretched out there, facing me, in my father's room, looking at the long lists of genealogy.

What is there to do now, yes, do with all these genealogies?

Yes: query their meaning and their names? Completely futile: one is a usurped meaning and, in this country, each time you trace a genealogy you tend more closely to god.

Yes: all genealogies trace back to the One

Therefore: they're *false.*

Take, for example, a few families that live right here, in Algiers, or a ways from Algiers, in the interior, in the mountains, and you'll be surprised, yes surprised, to see how many families jealously guard their genealogical folk, more jealously than they do living people, preferring the simple phantoms of those endowed with power and abilities supposedly greater than those of the natives of today.

Yes, you might well go from surprise to surprise and understand, suddenly, that this country's life has always been subterranean, hidden, clandestine, little known and, in sum, timid—only reaching the surface of the world here and there, and never, for all that, entirely asserting itself or definitively making a mark.

The lines of this country are terribly intertwined, and it's a disagreement or a great misunderstanding about our origins that persuades everyone in this country to seek his ancestors anywhere but in the place where he should always have felt their presence: in his brother, or in his neighbor.

Once—one afternoon, I mean—Hamid's brother showed me a genealogy, mine I mean, or rather—but all this is so foggy for me, even though every now and then I can retrieve the lucidity that voyages, departures or distance seem to churn up for me, mixing in so many things, memories, dreams, or pure inventions—rather I submitted to Hamid's brother a kind of genealogy, the one I was capable of perceiving or believing to be "real" in terms of my world and the one we're in since the war started because Mother—*yes, really her*—had someone call for Hamid's brother because of that sudden impulse I'd had to throw myself from the balcony and because—it's Mother who relates it to Hamid while I listen to the beating of my desire—I was yelling

> "I want to be in town
> in town,
> down there, way deep in the town
> with Dahmane."

and I knew who it was that was yelling, for ever since the night of October twenty-three, nineteen-fifty-seven, till December thirteen, nineteen-fifty-eight—from the moment the letters started arriving regularly from the Paul Cazelles camp and Hamid's brother—I knew there was someone in my head who was recording absolutely everything that might happen in me or around me: a great emptiness or relief in me whenever I return from Hamid's, or from his brother's, because at those moments I have the feeling I could reflect all over again—*that's what it is: r-e-f-l-e-c-t*—somewhat about myself, and also open my notebook, the one where I write thinking about *Her* or *Him*.

Hamid's brother drew near, there, in the bedroom, and I was able to say, or whoever it was in me that can speak because then I had the feeling of not being able to articulate one word or actual sentence: I DON'T WANT TO GO ON THIS WAY, BLOCKED; NO. I DON'T WANT TO STAY ON THE BOTTOM OF THE RIVER, UNABLE TO SEE ANYTHING AT THE BOTTOM OF THE RIVER; and Hamid's brother drew near and looked over my shoulder at what I was writing or drawing: I was happy—*at least I felt I was happy because the little man who lives inside me, I sensed him almost laughing, I felt it so strongly that myself: I had to laugh, yes, laugh, before Hamid's brother who*

—to see that Hamid's brother could read or understand what I was drawing: I was happy, and waited for him to say, too, that he was very happy to be able to read and understand its design.

Better expressed:

here

:

Even though it seems to me you can't understand at all, for other things would be necessary to make my language clear, like Jidda's or Dahmane's when he would talk about Kahéna[65]: But also, you have to treat my drawing gently because each line is alive, living,

living, so living and alive that I can make out certain cries or phrases, I can perceive a certain desire and know thus that I am not alone but part of a great number whose every gesture, wish and personality I must value at every turn, at each evocation or apparition.

Thus:

what Hamid's brother saw

on the notebook and
Also this

which completes the other.
Provided I can
inscribe other

---

65   The Berber warrior queen (7th century) who, importantly for Farès and Berber history, fought the Arab invaders from the East.

things which, no doubt,
belong to the drawing.

Here:

and: *"the slave is beyond the river."*

This saying around which or in which the whole world plays out, because I'm not inventing anything and merely affirm that: in that phrase are inscribed truth and enigma; in fact within it the world must open wide, and exist, so that the slave can be across the river, so that we might be able to speak beyond the river. Hamid took the notebook without really looking at me.

I wait because I CAN'T STAY BLOCKED THIS WAY BEFORE OR IN THE RIVER'S WAVES. I CAN'T STAY IN THE RIVER'S WATERS.

There's no half-way understanding.

: all, or nothing

as in love or war.

: there are no good half-way measures or intentions, since what counts is understanding that

: Country? : only half understood

so then : this, in all simplicity

: *the country kills*

Understanding why the country *kills*, while I know mainly its soft passage beneath the seaweed, the smell of salt on walks by the sea, the taste of the sky, and the winks answered in mirrors, there, spreading on the waves, in a multitude of shattered suns.

Understanding why the country *kills?*

the goatskin is black in color.

I would like to question Hamid's brother so he could help me understand what I'm doing all alone this way:

Me : before the river.

That's what I'd like to understand; and that impelled me to trace out other drawings to complete the first drawing—*yes, I don't say images, because the lines in the drawing are stronger than the passages within an image, and the drawing comes from me, whereas an image would come from somewhere else, as in a dream, yes: a kind of dream; here, it's not a dream; the complete opposite of a dream*—because I was unsatisfied—*I felt myself to be*—before the river, but the phrase says *beyond* and not: *before* or *at the edge.*

Hamid's brother sat in the armchair by the bed and took, from the left inside pocket of his jacket, a blue pad, small, the size of a wallet; next he took out a pen; then he came and sat on the bed, next to me, turning his back toward me, so that I could see what he was about to do.

I was content, and the little man inside my head was happy too, I could feel it in his way of moving in me and bursting out laughing, silently, but laughing, as if all he was invented for, this little man, was laughter; yes, just as if that's all he was for, laughter. And he, he started drawing and I felt something, in me, opening up, opening, in such a warm way in my insides—it had been a good *seven or eight months since I'd spoken with Jidda, and, unable to do anything else, I had remained rooted on myself, seated, completely unable to*—that I thought I was being changed at that very moment, according to the marks Hamid's brother made, all the vessels and veins nerves of my body too, and that I was being given another sense or feeling of my existence there on the hill, Clos-Salembier, and the attempts at transparent lives there; Yes, he too, as if by game or memory trick—*but memory of who and what*—held his pencil slightly tilted to the right and began to draw, before me, deep within me, in me, on me, yes, he too, began to draw, and I felt, as in that earlier *Jidda* time, that I could speak again someday, yes, that I could *re-new* speech, not just in the far reaches of me, but on the surface, reaching the surface, reaching others, other beings, those I'm literally cut off from, distanced ever since *you are no longer*, and whom I've tried in different ways to rejoin.

It's a fact: and very suddenly I saw what was going on, for, the more his hand sketched in front of me, and traced the movements of my body and those of other bodies of people close to me, immediately my eyes opened to something other than my own impossibilities: what I call: my impossibility.

There: all he did was write my name on the drawing, and I understood that

:

it was me; Me, who was supposed to cross the river.

and answer:

while he: a second time
simply
this
:

and me: that's when I knew

that it was the river, yes, *the River,* or *the enigma* that the little man in my head had confronted me with when he began to play all by himself, alone, independently of me, and I knew that by his frightening independence he had replaced my activity with a spectacle—painful, close, too close, and at times unbearable. That's when I understood *the river,* and *the beyond,* and the silence opened up in me, and this joy sprang from my fingers and, abruptly, I tore up the paper and its drawing of: Me-before-the-river.

Yes : my impossible : I tore up my impossible there, and Hamid's brother said: you can't: that's it: you can't: and I heard *deep down, here, deep, and even in front of me, here*, H'Midouche's voice saying: nothing could be easier than crossing the river: there's nothing to it; and I could almost read H'Midouche's words or voice: no, Abdenouar is not alone, beyond the river; many people are beyond the river now: many people.

Who?

Who: beyond the river?

That's when I understood that the drawing had begun a long time ago, before Jidda's arrest and death, and that—*it would take me so many lives to find the chronology of all this*—Dahmane had always known a lot about genealogies, and that, while my father was still with us in Clos-Salembier, he used to talk about this task, how it would end up being of little use despite the fact that he, my father, wasn't trying to establish common ancestries, but the routes and itineraries of migrations along which the tribes of the old country had dispersed, or the tribes that had come along later and mixed their names in with much more ancient names.

Yes: even before Hamid or his brother came along, or the little man in my head came along, I had known things and had some understanding of certain things taking place at the time.

But?

The common ancestry?

Here's the principle behind it: each branch has through common branching an astounding concentrate of Koranic founders.

Here's the cause: it's the *marabouts* who keep the written relations. There are real relationships, but how many of these compared to the hundreds or thousands of imaginary relationships.

I noticed one thing, *violently*: because

YOU ABSOLUTELY HAVE TO be from somewhere JUST WHEN you are expelled from yourself over all the territory

Yes: I noticed this, and maybe it's a cause or the effect of some cause since I clearly saw that, for someone like me, who has no relationship except just wherever I am, relation has been no help to me, while language, yes, *yours*, announced to me in scraps and fractions, *it*, this language, accomplished everything, even unto those moments when my sanity thinned out so badly that I felt myself getting smaller, *insignificant*, almost as small and thin as a nail, but in such an inward way that nobody—except maybe Hamid's brother—certainly the only person— knew anything about it—something or someone was holding forth inside me, and, to my intense satisfaction, was tearing down my isolation.

The goatskin is the bright land.

Yes: *It* accomplished all that, because, surrounding all the dislocations or losses, surrounding all the wanderings and migrations, there was this envelope, this first fact given by the goatskin, this first step, this envelope that reunited everyone.

Of course, there was expulsion, and in the aftermath it constructed the different towns, roads, points, fortifications, farms, and villages on the outside of the goatskin, but.

The full name, that's what I could *really* comprehend, what I had always known, and what made me either abandon everything else or make it incomprehensible to myself.

The entire name, the one wherein you can, all at once, touch hear and see everything.

The Goatskin?

The journey is long, from me to the Goatskin, and that's why I had to really toil to catch sight once again of all the cracks that ran through or destroyed every instant and every life in the town.

I couldn't believe there was nothing out beyond, I couldn't keep on living as if nothing had transpired, nothing definitive, or irrevocable, even though, at times, there's the feeling that nothing has ever happened, and you can just be content with inscribing on endless pages the branches of a country that kills, or that dies.

Yes: because ever since our history began, the one you can now read in the newspaper or in those tracts you see all over town, the country has felt terrible shocks.

Despite all that: there is the goatskin, the one I see swelling around us because there's not a single hope, murder, wish or independence that's not related to the goatskin as to its own place.

Place?

But: a weight, because the goatskin is inscribed in you, names you, calls out to you, creates your scares and your joys, even when the goatskin becomes invisible on your surface, even at that moment, when you think you have traversed who knows how many miles, and you think yourself somehow free of its weight, the goatskin comes back into you, in you, around you, and names you anew, or wounds you, for your greater harm but benefit as well.

I haven't forgotten this lesson because I'd had to learn something very much the opposite of *it* so that, later, in the most dire moment, the most naked moment when language and reason escaped me, it would come back to me, and set free the conditions of my craziness.

This is how I was saved from that kind of antecedence so revered in mankind's beliefs, and then, bound to fully understand a different kind of words, I was able to limit the dislocations caused by our wounds, and demand with all my strength that we exercise a judgment and reason liberated from all the false histories and accompanying curses.

Hamid would have trouble believing that I have, *in this way*, arrived at a point beyond many people and that, *despite the terrible pressure that sometimes grinds my limbs and above all my head*—sometimes: I can't see anymore; yes: my eyes are open, but I can't say what I'm seeing; the first time I told Hamid's brother that—it was some time after Jidda's death—he immediately replied, and curtly: *but you hear, right? you hear?* : and it was true because all the time that I couldn't see I was hearing something, something adequate to what I was feeling and thinking, as if my eyesight no longer had any purpose, and that I

Just as in that moment *then* I could perfectly well see Hamid seated *there* before me ten or twelve inches from me but: nothing: what I see is: *right? isn't that right?*—Hamid's brother came to my rescue because: one day when I was sitting on a chair in my room near the balcony, Hamid comes in, and I was there and, even though I wanted to, unable to say anything.

Yes: I'm still sitting on my chair, eyes turned toward Hamid's brother, then, after a long pause, a moment in which I saw a gigantic door opening before me, a door revealing a gigantic abyss before me, and I looked back to the balcony, the sea I guess or something like that.

Hamid's brother came into the room and I tracked his movements until they reached that bed where I spend hours trying to understand, in those moments when, abruptly or for a lingering while, a kind of attentive lucidity descended on me, along with a struggle to preserve this against any foreign intrusion, trying to clasp it within me like a precious toy, a fragile one that mustn't be dropped.

Several hours in the night, alone—because at those times Mother is no longer any help, with her tears and the way I can make out their sound, tears I'd rather not see or hear or suffer.

Of course: *I understand everything* in spite of the veil they've thrown over my face and eyes, *your* veil, I'm sure of it, gripping me. So that's how I'm alone

and understand everything, without being able to *say* I understand everything, and that's how, no matter what means I adopt, I will succeed one day in saying that: *I understand everything*.

Hamid—or his brother—

yes, why?

there are moments when you can touch every wall at the same time, find the entrance and the exit, the courtyard, the second floor, the cellar, and the surrounding areas;

certain times you guess at or recognize people, people going by, near or a bit farther off, whom you greet, name, or, also, ignore;

certain times that you have in your hands without knowing it, you think you hold nothing, which is wrong, absolutely false.

that's why many people thought we had nothing, that we were nothing, and all because of us ourselves, because of one simple thought, murderous and irreparable: that we had nothing, that we were nothing.

that's why I say Hamid, *or his brother;*

—Hamid

why does dad keep on making these genealogy lists when he knows the country is forever transformed, yes, *transformed* in a way no genealogy could ever show.

So?

How to understand my father's stubbornness? out beyond myself and everything else, and pursue this quest slowly as if nothing much were happening, while, at the same time, what's happening is a whole neglected and falsified world, altered so you can't believe your eyes and ears?

A minor thing, this thing that passes through me, and yet if there hadn't been that moment when father disappeared in the distance, I wouldn't have understood much, either, about the country, or Jidda.

As if the country had revolved within me, or might have turned around in me because we all are, in one degree or level or requirement or another the relay points in a territory and a landscape more ancient than ourselves. I tried to tell Dahmane well before the irreversible happened, well before the country was twisted beyond all repair, before my thoughts, desires and illusions might launch themselves like tracers over the flat pavement of the world. I tried to tell Dahmane that, but Dahmane is smoking, and through the smoke I see the smile on his lips.

Yes, Dahmane is smoking, his lips move and I can hear that voice, still distanced from all the warfare and waste, reaching out to me:

Did you know Malika before today?

Dahmane had always thought he might write something about Malika, a theater piece of sorts, to duly offer her her kingdom.

But the play got written in me, in me, against me: what I wouldn't know how to say but can still enunciate in this way, within my own trajectory beyond country-mother, toward those zones that might receive me brutally, I don't know, but that I'm going to know for the first time as I wait for my father.

Dahmane smokes, and I see, through the smoke, his smiling lips, speaking, telling me something, or maybe just: he must be thinking of our running there, in the dunes, among the spots where the summits of the dunes are covered with bushes and shrubs where... but Dahmane's smile bothers me because I don't like talking about these things that make your heart drift within you, like a cloud.

A girl from Batna: Dahmane says, and my hide cracks open: She's a Batna girl: with a stone's weight. A Batna girl.

On the inside I see several veins than run through the stone, blue
The intensity of blue that Jidda's eyes have.

The stone crumbles, on the surface, all around where it's cracked, so that my fingers gather not dust, but sand.

The same sand as that of the dunes when Malika stretched out on it, when I caressed her temple, when I kissed her.

No: Malika is silent.

Her hands rummage in my hair as in grass, slowly, as if trying to find something there, in my hair, or in those dunes that hide the beach and the sea but let the sky surge above us like a dream.

I know nothing about any of this, though I've heard much said about it, though, more than once, they've tried to drag me toward these things.

Yes. But.

Malika did everything everything and I'm not even sure I understood everything she did, especially when I think about that look Dahmane had, about everyone at the beach, about my desire to know everything and at the same time know nothing at all, because

Malika was already in the bus from The Redoubt when we got in, as if—yes—I...—Dahmane's smile bothers me and would bother anyone who might find himself there before him—she was waiting for us: that's right: Waiting for Us.

Dahmane introduced us, just enough to bring it off in a laughing way, our first sight. Clos-Salembier will be the first independent city in the country, even if there are still soldiers around.

"She's a Batna girl," Dahmane says, and she surveys whatever Clos-Salembier might look like from high on a bus: you see it all.

The trip toward Sidi-Ferruch—yet another marabout, even less competent than the others given that the shore should have remained unapproached or unapproachable, but now, with all the construction and the arriving and leaving: well we're still happy that you can occasionally get to Sidi-Ferruch[66]—is calm, as if I were Malika's body, her sand-body, laugh-body, languor-body seated between Dahmane and me, as if I were

Several people are staring at us, in the bus, and in a strange way, as if the trip to Sidi-Ferruch could be some kind of pilgrimage or ritual

---

66 This confusing passage is either ironic, suggesting that the marabout (the local headman) would typically make the beach inaccessible through incompetence, or it is a frank suggestion that a competent marabout would have impeded routes and access in the area to frustrate French troops.

procession, as if there weren't enough sad or dead people in this town and this country.

Several stare at us, in the bus, not in a curious way, no: hard.

Others look away, pretend to be looking far off, beyond the bus's route, but I know—and Malika knows too—and Dahmane too—that we're the ones they're looking at that way, as if we weren't a side of their own selves, the part they hide, the one they don't want to enjoy, while everywhere there already reigns, over the territories of this country about to be born, the dusty panting of death.

Malika looks at me

I think she understands what's going on in the bus better than anyone here, Dahmane and I, or those feigning indifference.

We are here

Yes We and the other Europeans or Muslims who stare at us and inwardly insult us

Not so nice, the inward insult, I'm thinking   I'm thinking!

Not so pretty; it makes your face out to be something in a newspaper, with, moreover, an evil caption on your forehead:

Malika asked me to stay silent

to not look insolently at everyone in the bus and to wait till we were far from everybody, near the beach, and the ground, the rocks where the ocean's white memory bursts, or the road, smelling of salt and broadening before us, like the sea.

Dahmane says nothing.

But I know he's already a thousand miles from here, and that nothing, not even the faces turned upon us in the bus, will cost him his joy, this calculated, fragile joy stolen out of the world's suffocation.

Malika shifted, so then I wrote on the drawing, on the flattest part of their heads:

"THE QUEEN OF THE AURĒS IS TRAVELLING IN THE SIDI-FERRUCH BUS,

the key city where they came ashore in 1830."[67]

---

67 Sidi-Ferruch is where the French landed, in a reprisal action, and began their colonization of Algeria, 1830. July 5 (mentioned next) is the date the town's fortress fell, after bombardment. "The Queen of the Aurès (Mountains)" is Kahéna (or Kahina), mentioned earlier.

then added:

"TWO ALGERIAN MEN AND A WOMAN ARE CAUGHT ON
THE SIDI-FERRUCH BUS,
            the police are making inquiries
     but they despair of getting a
     confession to the crime
     what crime? it doesn't matter
                what crime."

Malika laughs now, with every newspaper page or headline I read for
her.

> *Breaking news: "Every morning, around 1830, I dunk my buttered
> bread in my warm coffee, and I run off to be the watch dog of
> Public Health. The Algerians don't like me. I don't like the
> Algerians. One day, Algeria will be independent. And that day, I'll
> beat it out of here."*

At this point, Dahmane can't handle it anymore, he'll shatter the bus
windows with his laugh, the big jerk.

Pick a number.

This is Malika speaking.

Pick a number.

5.

Pick a month.

5 is a loser, in the whole territory

: July

One date yields another

Always the same one

Dug into our hearts like a fishhook

My skin is ripping afresh, like the tender flesh, pink or white or blue
or red of a fish *1830.*

We have been bitten in our most tender place and someday we'll have
to fix this, take the fish back to the ocean it came from, let salt have its way
on the wound and bury the fishhook in a hole, far off

1830.

It's useless circling around, you always come back to this point, at least for the moment, and that's in spite of

:Dahmane says we have to get off and run to the East end of the beach where he's supposed to meet someone

Who?

The ocean, my man!

The ocean, the one that hollows your stomach, reddens your eyes, envelopes your body, animates your arms and legs, colors your skin, bathes your head, lends you its aroma, its irresistible aroma, and leaves you flat on your back with happiness and being

Your skin.

Dahmane is already running ahead of us: a day of all the world's blue, and elsewhere, doubtless, someone very dear will have to die, die, for me to have so much happiness in one day.

Elsewhere?

Yes

In that space that's always there between souls, that narrow space, so finely drawn, that snips out the shapes of your dreams or pleasures, in that space where you learn to survive against alien laws, the laws that stab and endlessly lacerate your back, there must be a solution, so preciously buried away that nobody sees it nor desires it anymore, and that

Malika is really quite different from a stone

And yet

From her first day and first word play

My skin has been split open

in two

like a book.

I laid, pressed, my two hands on either side of the pages, I felt something within me; something that existed with me as a starting point, something hard, warm, much more alive than I was.

Yes: a long changing. And then.

Where is day's first moment found.

You're aware of this confusion of a white thread and a black thread in your vision and your hand But, this moment when your body opens itself, in two pieces, to the other body; when one mouth lives through the other;

when your lip seems to burst like an explosive shell in the world's sky; yes: I ask you: Where is day's first moment found, as if, with each new appearance of the light the world memorialized some sacrifice, the one decided between death and desire or, more feverishly, between body and body.

Yes : where you find that first moment that fills your throat and swells arms and legs, for the exhalted sacrifice of the special lamb; that suspends you in the farthest wellsprings of your self; frees you from the world's fear; and bears you up in the game of your life.

Where day's first instant is found because, at the very same time, Malika asked me my age, and I felt the planet topple strangely.

"We have to keep on loving love itself, otherwise they'll beat us down."

That's what she says, or what she thinks.

I feel a drop of sweat leave my temple and start down my cheek, while another drops from the nape of my neck straight down, along my vertebrae to the small of my back, and

Yelling. Yes, a shouting breaks out in me, shaping a kind of panic, but Malika, close in, laughs and her eyes are now unrecognizable up above mine.

A yelling: it must be wonderful in the water, now, because the day and the sun too are dropping into the sea and making it blush all over.

Malika is thinking something, in a murmur, that hits me violently, like a shattering of glass, or steel.

"Do you think I'm a slut, being here with you, in the dunes?"

Malika's eyes are unrecognizable, except for that wrinkle along the side of her nose, I know it's hers now from all the words, laughs, newspaper readings on the bus.

It's awful to no longer comprehend a face: not to know if it's laughing or dying, and I don't know what to say, or how to invent anything other than stupor.

Malika goes on living within her question, there, next to me, under me, and I don't know how to answer.

"Hey?"

Fingernails, in the small of my back.

An enormous desire:

"I don't know what a slut is."

Malika has just given me a full slap, but I

Me

What I heard her say was: "Me," and I sensed Malika searching for something deep in me; something at the level of love's pain or the pain of being; something deep in the roots of anger and love; something that became more fresh the more Malika uncovered it; something that must have, for a long time, been there, invisible, in my depths, reanimated by Malika's playfulness.

"I'm going to kill you,"

Malika says

"because you're too sweet."

I'm looking at Malika's eyes, black and gold, like seaweed.

Around us there's a sort of water tank where you can yield your desires over to getting wet; above that, at the place where you think you hear a prayer, is your forehead, the very place where a tiny squiggle of ink has inscribed your lineage and dependence; and in this brief instant of being you make out the sign of your burrowing away or your uncovering.

Malika! Malika! And it's no more than that prosaic name of the queen,[68] since legend and history, the old myth and its believers are already beyond us in death's unapproachable reaches, Malika, the girl who, deep in you, and in spite of you, reinvented the awesome phrases of the Narrator.[69]

"I would like to kill you."

Already I can almost grasp it all because

"As in the early times in the Aurès, among the cedars, thyme and olive trees. Yes: I'd like to kill you, as we kill the goat or the ram, and drop you into a vineyard basket, and offer you, only you, the song of the newborn."

Malika has put her right hand over my mouth and I, a throwaway scrap at this point, I have only her words in my head, her words, advancing, surrounding me, drowning me, bearing me up, striking me, devouring my

---

68 The Arabic word for "queen." Kahéna (al-Kahina), the Berber warrior queen, is sometimes referred to this way (and the "Berber kingdom" is referred to on this page).

69 This translation uses "narrator, instead of "reciter." The latter, or the suggestive "chanter," would more clearly evoke the Koran than Farès normally chose to. And Farès is clearly setting up the protagonist's role as Narrator.

eyes and mouth, gazing at me the way Malika does, Malika who sees me with her eyes of death or seaweed, while her lips keep moving and moving and turning me all around.

"Yes. As in the early times in the Aurès, in the Berber kingdom, in the earth's warm red dusk, in the shade of the tall cedar, there where you pronounced the mother-speech, the speech that condemned this country to several centuries' wandering, the speech that split time open for the world in its long harsh mad rape by the Foreigner, Yes, there where I have to rediscover the role of the man who, in this part of the world, brought forth the word to the other: the Narrator, yes, the one who cast me as a being deep within your being, the woman many call, the way they do, a slut."

I : who no longer recognize Malika, and in my wild desire to shout out, but Malika, Malika's hand, is still on my mouth, and caresses it while pressing down, despite my desire: Dahmane?

But Malika's hand (that I'm kissing, softly, brushing with my lips, beyond the prison of my lips, softly, as if in the ultimate deliverance.

Yet I'm the one on top, I'm on her, legs against legs, yes, I'm squeezing her.

But Malika's hand is the stronger, especially in love or after love, when Malika is there talking, her speech everywhere in me, deep in me, and my strength wavers, like a branch of olive or cedar.

It's been so long since I left the country, its interior of trees, words and mysteries, and yet everything is already here, between my mouth and Malika's.

The Narrator? The one who leads the village as the shepherd his flock over the days and months of transhumance, who accompanies and organizes the ritual, who rebirths a locus in the world and relates the story of all the other histories told by their narrators.

Me: The Narrator?

He who was born in the places of springtime's antecedence : Me?

I would have to yell Dahmane's name a thousand times, into your face, against what's just come before my eyes, shadow or Falcon, while your mouth presses against mine, and my body cries out, and I slap yes slap Hamid right there in the taxi and I cite in myself the moment of mastery of Violence.

Malika? I would have to

But Malika is once again stretched out under me, her hands gripping my shoulders, and I have to fight against this stifling that points toward the towering sun.

This I know, because of the light that still hovers around me, hot and white, filtering through the grass and bushes that cling to the dunes.

Near us, as a slight wind starts up, there's shade and the cool of hiding away, and we must have travelled far, very far, fallen in some well or gulley hidden there in the dunes.

We hadn't swum much but Malika still had a taste of salt on her skin, a taste I'm convinced is the taste of a knife.

So hard to open my eyes, to pull away from the spell Malika has cast on me.

What will I tell Dahmane?

Malika forces me to take her mouth, laugh, breasts and the joy of being on the verge of tears.

Yes.

Malika weeps, softly, like a salt rain brushing my cheeks, wetting them, overturning me.

As before, I don't know what to do, except prolong this pressure of my lips on hers, and try to say these unpardonable words:

Malika don't cry

I love you Malika

Like speech newly embraced, like the distance of nights out beyond the valleys of despair and a life blocked by a terrible defensiveness.

The sea-salt in me, along with the wind, the wind that detaches the sun and carries it, here, into the belly of your tears.

Don't cry Malika

I understand.

Yes: I understand: your violence and your body, the inadequacy of my kisses, of language's soothing, my heart is open, inside, like your heart, because now I can see through bodies.

That's how I can see this fleeing—our flight—beyond this world, as an unfathomable flight, a personal one.

Yes: they always tell that old tale of travelling on the back of the Eagle of the Seven Seas,[70] and I would never want to hover in mid-speech—without you.

Malika nibbled at Abdenouar's mouth and the landscape became all stony, the road dusty, on which a man walks—his precarious orientation hurled across the humble fertility of stones—with his head wrapped in blue cloth.

His footstep eliminates distance, his voice strikes like a sword. Below and behind him the plains stretch and play, around contours of water, and bear strange trees with roots showing, designs of roots on the open ground: the eye can behold its own gaze.

Here, at least, something imposes a kind of silence around the man, around his footstep that inaugurates other distances and other places.

Can you dwell out of range of the healer?

Can a country survive with no shepherd? Without the person who drives the word deep into the dark parts of space and the body, and who interrogates history the way the Narrator does?

Can a country live without True-Psalmers? Who spread that other knowledge in spite of these times and their lack of depth, space or dimension?

The narrator is several, they are dispersed in the alternating and in the trace of their propositions, but the actual narration is unique, unique in its breath and its depth.

Listen, in this brusque era

Listen to this glory destined for the lands of vagabond intensity

And glory to language, which causes movement

in the strata of adultery, for:

: what is the sage saying, on his elbow, by his book?

He preaches the worshipping of manuals and textbooks.

But what is a manual?

Just a lonely word launched toward the sphere

of the Narrator

and the manual tumbles

---

70 Related tales exist in several folklores, including Berber. The "Seven Seas" is a common phrase in Arab tales.

into the opus of the Narrator.

Listen in this brusque era
And come running
Women and old men
Young ones or children
Villages or Hills
The first dance
is going to open the
place of dance
the first step
of the first dance.

Come running
Virgins with a taste
for violence,
your bodies buried
under rocks.

The place of sand
where love
of the land
and the place
the country
bares the footstep
her new step
of primal dance.

The Country?

Yes.
The country is discovering
its first step
in primal dance.

The Country?

Come running,
Men or Women
Exiled from that place
that first step
is your dance
inaugurating
the new dance
of your world.

Come running,
Valleys or Beings
who hang back
insisting.
The country
has opened the veins
of everything
that composes
its dance step.

Run,
Young bodies
aimed for the men
beyond the acidic bedding
of death.
Run,
the country
has opened its veins
to the living
words
of the Narrator.

VII

"The way they tell it, Kahéna fell victim to a betrayal. Those who wanted to divide the land or the immense country bounded by the two seas did not want to know the foreigner…

Verily, it was so…" says the Narrator.

"Those who, until then, had linked their fate to Kahéna's, withdrew in one night all their troops, soldiers who had stepped forth frankly from every corner of the country…

Verily, it was so..." says the Narrator, once again.

The Narrator looks out there, above the trees, toward the mountains and hills where the man with the blue headdress is trekking.

A vast opening in this silence!

This man is of awesome weight among his brothers. The land must fill out his movements and

thoughts, for none other than he can, in his way, tell us about the land.

This is how it is, with the Narrator.

He who cannot hold forth open speech must learn to do battle. The world is not ours without a

word spoken. Such is the truth (the opus) of the Narrator. And this, in spite of his warrior's heart.

Men are not born this way, in a void of world. Each must espouse a place. His own direction. His being. Movement. Disorder. And magnificence. Every being enjoys some share of glory in this world. For such is the way of man and the world.

Terrible is the Alien place

For a being loses his or her foundations, in a place where being is not possible. Where one must not be.

Lose the foundation and you encounter fear.

The fear of the world. Shut out of the world.

Behold the fruit fallen from the tree. The fish out of water. Is the fish useless to the water? The fruit to the tree? See how beings mix and mingle. Do you think water would have these splashes of light if the fish Yes the fish didn't with each leap make a gift of those scales dangling from the light? Do you think so? And the tree?

Man, and his world?

A single muscle stretched above the ages

Yes:

Such is the Narrator's site.

Kahéna is intangible; and speech must take a bite out of silence to rediscover the Narrator. He whose power is not limited to this world. Rather it is deployed. And brews. And animates. And opens kills operates produces invents hurls the world's words

That is how it is.

The Narrator is bound by no restrictions in his speech; he is the Narrator.

A work. Praises. Or ravings.

Such is the space of the Narrator. Who confounds prudence. And the century. False oratory. He who manages the left-hand gate of desire. The lips' trembling. Or the new channel of our talk.

He who struggles against the disappearances in this world. Who raises up the Mother-word in the heat of being or of death. Who intensifies the gaze and binds the fibers of distant times.

Here the day must brush against shadow like a grass blade in its season

say

and why

should we say?

This is the moment when an audience must be born. On the harried tracks of exile and return. Near a kind of ground where oratory can grow.

Among the audience, several men tremble because they left, a few years earlier, for Indochina.[71] Skirmishers of that other war, before coming here and taking their place among the members of this audience.

> *"What*
> *Did you learn*
> *Men of*
> *The other war?*

---

71 A reference to the French colonial effort in Viet Nam, and the military campaign which ended in 1954.

The game
of the Tiger
or
the falcon?"

   The women point out these silent men, mute, rendered mute by the other war.

   His words spurt, like a stone exploding, there in the middle of the audience.

 ...is there more to say, the narrator thinks.

To labor. As a narrator labors
or the scribe,
 the old scribe
of ancient eras...

One man stands, already, in the audience.

He crosses the short distance to the center of the group. He pushes a woman before him, *Kahéna, Kahéna in her red tunic.*

The gift of an old dream to the audience! Because this group must bend these words toward the other place, place of dividing, the place the earth knew as the Great Movement drew near.

"They say the Tribes of Hijaz were halted by *Kahéna's* war."

   Such is the truth, says the Narrator.

 "Oh Resistance
 Ancient Kingdom
 spread
 over the
 harsh stones
 of the Aurès
 Mountains."

• •

 Oh Listeners
 Have you
 ever seen
 the Wild
 Land
 the Land that

I burned
from Olive tree
to Olive tree
from Cedar
to Cedar,
from Fig
to Fig."

• •

"Have you
seen
The Wild Land?"

• •

Her voice rises, as the narrator lowers his gaze to the ground.

Kahéna.

The one they accuse of having burned the land.

A Young Woman who rends the husband

Exiles the son

Slits the ram's throat

or

Assassinates the lover.

(Now we must learn to close the body's eyes; open that other gaze, like a celebration sung out from a funereal realm.)

Kahéna is visible. In her tunic of red wool

Two breaths like the flight of two birds brought up short.

A stony breath from the

Earth

Stony like language;

This language that I place here, before you, venerable Assembly; too many shadows blend into my trek; the stone must become Eagle; the day, Vulture; the night, Falcon. You belong to the place of no Return; vigilant Stalkers of a fathomless anger.

(Thus your movement drags on

256

Like so much bark wrapped around the sap; life is
extracted, through you, like the desert's alcohol.

Men drink

Today

Of your death

But the blood is not the same.

The woman singing

Or speaking

Among us

Is headless.)

The narrator is no longer the same, before this
assembly...

His body is no longer the same.

He is dressed in the garb of

The Shepherd, the one encompassing

every stretch of land,

stars brilliant

against a shadow sky.

He says...

"I am

the guardian

of   And he points to...

this woman.

My name is

Ameksa, [72]

the Shepherd.

He who

opened

his heart

before the

defeat or

the peril

of my master.

He points again...

---

72 Not a proper noun, *ameksa* is Berber (Amazigh) for "shepherd."

"Ameksa,
He who
opened his heart
Before The Defeat."

He says…

"He who
accompanied
the first master
Then,
The Lover
The woman
Whose throat
the Bedouins
wanted to cut
on the plains."

• • • • • • • • • • •

"Ameksa,
yes, Ameksa
watcher over
shadows
among
the stones."

… He says…

The Narrator is still sitting before the group. His arms are stretched out toward Kahéna. His hands rest on two stones, lying there amid the dry grass, dry like the bunches of grass women put on tombstones forty days after the advent of death.

Death is already there, among the stones, drifting and certain, nearing Kahéna who is going mad before It.

What Death?
The one men drink in
Nowadays
among Ameksa's
stones,
the Shepherd

He who

opened

the chorus[73]

of the World

with a saber slash

under the orchards?

What death?

The one that possesses

the chorus

of the world;

which man sings

when he

has reached

the site of his

downfall;

which man sings

when he

attains his

time of agon; and says:

"Here is my back; here is my heart; here my legs; here my hands; here my eyes; here my mouth; my head; my blood; I've had everything I needed to make it here to you, Vigilant Woman, Guardian of This Place.

What do we have to be? To see everything at once;
Isn't there anything out beyond the dead?

Nothing smooth, warm and liquid? What do you have to say, to be beyond the Place?"

and, at these words, the man can only reply with other words from beyond the place; other words; (sharp ones); which construct a world beyond this place; other words... he says... (Ameksa, the Shepherd)... (The one they call the Shepherd)... (the one who explodes among the stones)... (Who can reach several hilltops at the same time) (yes) (Ameksa) (The one who opens up the hill) and says...

• • • • • • • • • •

---

73   In the original it is "choeur," a homophone of the earlier "coeur."

"Here
is my arm
and my
every gesture
Vigilant
Guardian
of the hills.
· · · · · · ·
They say
· · · · · · ·"

Daughter of grass or of wind; daughter of sand or air; of the word or the stone; the Vigilant Guardian of the Hills has now entered Ameksa's body.

She is woman. As womanly as Kahéna. The Vigilant Guardian of the Hills has now entered the body of Ameksa.

... (Ameklsa) ... (He whom they named Ameksa: the Shepherd)... (The being who explodes among the stones) ... (Who can reach several hills at the same time)... (Ameksa)... (He who opens up the hill)... and who says...

"They say," the Narrator goes on, "that it was Ameksa who, in those early times, relieved Kahéna, that night at Chetma[74]..."

"...Yes... the one they all thought was already too old... Yes... The one they thought already under the sod..."

"... Yes... Ameksa

The Shepherd..."

Amid the buzz of the crowd, a few words are made out; they drift toward that center where sits the person they call, here in this country of trees, hills and death, the Narrator.

"As in a death-game suddenly in our midst, the Narrator searches for his tongue; perhaps it is stretched out in some shadow; the shadow that hobbles the voice, deep in the throat...?

Game of death now among us! What can the Narrator teach us that we didn't know before? We ourselves were born in the wounding and treachery of the dividing up, since we marched beside Kahéna, escorting

---

74   In more recent times Chetma was the site of skirmishes with the French.

delirium and dream, into exile. Yes. We marched in the full caress of sand and the earth's skin. We marched. For the Foreigner had penetrated to our heart or our praises in the person of Khaled,[75] Kahéna's lover.

This is how the enemy shook our unity; like a mere bundle of rags."

Kahéna is before the crowd. Standing, she gazes at her audience. But the men are talking. Love-words tossed at the feet, ankles, the dance, of the woman who was their Queen so long ago.

"Unity! Unity! Oh Unity of cedar and fig tree! The Man of the South was there. The one with the shadow veil. Black, or blue. In war-speak.

Unity! Oh Unity of saber-speak. The wind allied with the sands; the mountain with the rocks.

Unity!

The woman took the man beyond the land, into the country of the Foreigner.

Unity!

Like a rending of the alliances; a long lament; men roamed in the night like flames around the bed of the adored.

Woman,"

The assembly asks Kahéna in front of the Narrator. "Woman, why did you sleep with the Foreigner?

The crowd repeats:

"Woman, why did you desert the olive tree, for the rough skin of that Bedouin?

Woman, Koceila's[76] love cannot survive the teeth of the Foreigner.

Woman, why put out the fire of our unity? Or, is the Bedouin a better lover than the Olive Tree; You are no longer fit to be among the people of this audience. You will walk around the circle; around the site; around pleasure without ever finding the center; outside and around, like us... Yes... Like us... Pain the equal of burning thirst on the endless plains of the Great Desert...

Woman, You will stay on the trek, dragging along many men who wave their arms like Olive Trees.

---

75 According to legend, an Arab (other spellings exist) whom she had adopted—and who betrayed and killed her.

76 Also spelled Kusaila, 7th century Berber (and Christian) king and militant against the Muslim invasion.

Men, like You, will turn around the site, arms stretched toward You, as if imprisoned in dream.

Men will turn around the site, Kahéna, without much hope, infinitely, but in fact they had come to you, Kahéna, to bring about unity, and not to see, Kahéna, love between a woman and a Bedouin."

The crowd's voice fell silent as the narrator tried to pick up his speech again where it had been interrupted by the Bedouin.

From now on the country is wide open, dispersed in multiple territories.

The Narrator hesitates because his speech must now inscribe, in the audience's shifting, the long agony and death of the oldest Berber kingdom.

This is how it was: the work of the Bedouin: the woman is dead, she who briefly, like a falcon, held the kingdom in her hands.

The work of the Bedouin.

"Woman
whose love
I see stretched
out on the dazzled
surface of the sun,
happy, your two
hands joined around
the lover's body,
infinitely happy
and alone.
Alone, in the
impossible site of love
the embrace of
Wild One
and Woman. What
can I say to the audience
who tries to imagine
your story: a reflection
of the soul up above
the Dead Hills and Villages
the soul alive, and Queen
of the rights that
elect Narrators."

the land had encountered a new meaning That of Khaled the Son of the Bedouin the Captive He whom the Woman fell in love with and whose breath she believes she can own He whose anger hovers like a wind over the sands He whose body hardly moves on Kahéna's He whose head they cry out for, here, in this group of men come from all over the field: the territory multiple again Oh unity The woman Guardian of this place she slipped the Gods' watchfulness: Kahéna makes love with the Foreigner: Kahéna Oh Unity Kahéna makes love with the Foreigner: the territory is again multiple, all at once, in Kahéna's love.

The land has encountered a new meaning.

Here's how it happened: Among the Audience several people rose.

The shadow drew away from the group, and fled toward the flank of the hill whose eye opens on the plain.

A warm love-stirring abides on the flank of the hill, while anger or despair seizes the men, in their bodies and clothes, standing before the Narrator.

The Narrator tries to find his voice; a voice of air shadow and wind; like an opening upon the land, this ground that opens its plains, flanks, hills and villages to the shock of the Bedouin.

The Narrator tries to find his voice; a reef, a reef against his speech, a speech promoted to a raving degree beyond the ruptures of history: the Narrator must bear his voice against his own body and hurl his chant against the anger or despair of those men standing before Kahéna.

The Narrator presses his fingers on his eyelids; he turns his head three times to the left, three times to the right, picks up some dirt in his right hand, dry crumbly dirt that he lets sift to the ground before him as he talks.

> *"What can I say*
> *Woman of sudden*
> *movements, you who are*
> *broken upon the various*
> *rivalries of our soul*
> *or misfortune—confusion Yes*
> confusion *has invaded*
> *this audience."*
> • • • • • • • • • •

The Narrator looks over at those who have gotten up; no glance more humid than this, more humid than Autumn prayer; no being more anxious and desperate, because everyone in the Audience knows: what Kahéna's destiny is.

• • • • • • • • • •

"The men are leaving,
Woman,
this wild place.
The place
where you launched
toward Us,
Oh Kahéna,
deaths and offenses
over all
the Aurès.

• • • • • • • • • •

men are leaving,
Woman,
this wild place.
The one
where you
cried out
to Us,
Oh Kahéna
a presence and forces
over all
the Aurès."

• • • • • • • • • •

Confusion settles now over the audience, for the Narrator has reached the death-place beneath the trees.

His voice cannot go on beneath the trees, in the obscure temptation of bodies or lost souls in search of their bodies.

Who can go beyond the body?

The Narrator?

But Kahéna's breathing is slow, held by the supple belly of the Bedouin.

· · · · · · · · · · ·

"Khaled,
the son of the Bedouin,
is in the shadow
of the Audience,
and love
has let the captive
triumph,
in spite of Kahéna's
strength
and her Audience,
free woman
of the Aurès
Mountains."

· · · · · · · · · · ·

The Narrator sits, an equal distance from several of the men standing before him, His hands before his eyes, open, before him and toward him like a book.

Kahéna stands, eyes reddened with tears.

Under the wool of her tunic two birds, captive, blind; Kahéna in her red tunic.

Kahéna's breathing is slow, slow, like a June day, like one of those June days when twilight seems to brush (already) the brow of the dawn.

Just one sound from the crowd, the sound of lips moving and murmuring a chant or some memory of ancient struggles.

Kahéna's tunic is cut wide around her neck, right where the sword must hit home for the kingdom of the Bedouins.

This is how it is, Kahéna will have to die at the brow of the dawn, at the instant the day is chosen, after destroying the House of Love.

That is how it is, Kahéna must die, as evening slips into the House of Love.

> *"Place of being*
> *on this side of*
> *age or*
> *strength,*
> *love for a Bedouin*
> *triumphed over*
> *the cycle*
> *of ancient lands."*
>
> • • • • • • • • • •
>
> *"What does it matter*
> *since,*
> *in our shadow*
> *domicile,*
> *time wanders*
> *through us*
> *like a breath*
> *fire*
> *amid*
> *ash.*
>
> • • • • • • • • • •
>
> *Is it true*
> *Kahéna,*
> *that the dark*
> *warriors*
> *listen still*
> *to the sand*
> *or wind*
> *that gives life*
> *to earth?*
>
> • • • • • • • • • •
>
> *Is it true*
> *Kahéna?"*
>
> • • • • • • • • • •

The sky is red and gold above the audience.

Voices rise, caught up in their last breaths.

Already, Osmane comes forward, taking his place next to the Narrator, Osmane, Ameksa's companion, Ameksa the Shepherd, the one who bore witness to the speech of the audience.

> *"... We must*
>> *animate our senses*
>> *beyond meaning*
>> *or war,*
>> *speech*
>> *is*   *(the shadow,*
>> *a prey*   *its*
>> *and its place*   *deliverance)*
>> *vast,*
>> *vast as the world."*

Kahéna stands before Osmane and the man of the desert He who came from the southern country to uphold the Aurès. Strange strength in this woman, who makes the blue Man chase over the sands, against the advance of the Bedouins.

> *"Could you*
> *say,*
> *you, the man*
> *who wears a veil*
> *Who*
> *in the*
> *world*
> *conquered*
> *the land*
> *of the singing*
> *stone?*
> • • • • • • • • • •
> *Could*
> *you, Man,*
> *tell me this?"*

Kahéna's hands are caught in the thongs that bind her wrists, one against the other, as when you bind up the folds and legs of the goatskin.

She says:

> *"Could you*
> *tell me,*
> *you, the man*
> *who confronts*
> *the world*
> *with gaze*
> *lowered*
> *like*
> *a pious*
> *old man,*
> *could you*
> *tell me*
> *Who*
> *ravished*
> *that blue gaze of yours*
> *in which are*
> *reflected*
> *the shadow's*
> *footsteps?"*
>
> • • • • • • • • • •

On Kahéna's bare arms, above the wrists, blue veins can be seen, sketching out her former bravery, under her skin.

The Narrator now dwells in Kahéna's speech, his eyes fixed on that breast—still, for a little while longer, swollen with love.

> *"I have scorched*
> *the land*
> *of proud*
> *Kairouan,*[77]
> *as you would*

---

77 A city in Tunisia, attacked by Berbers under both Kahéna and Kusaila.

burn
the right side
of your
own heart.
But the man
did not
believe
in the woman's
cause,
and,
with the treachery
of the blind,
he ran
to pay tribute
to the Bedouin's
strength."

• • • • • • • • • •

Kahéna looks at the Narrator, then at the assembly, with a stirring at her wrists, like a prayer or supplication addressed to the movement of the stars and the earth, Kahéna now far from divine faith but love, love is there, trying to find the cause of despair or death, love that is beaten, torn like the still young and lively body and tunic of Kahéna.

The Narrator lowered his head, and hands, toward the ground, this ground where shadow continues its creeping or burrowing, ground going gold and somber at the same time, this ground that carries the knight arrived from the far desert, who makes Kahéna's son drink of his pride or his history.

Sobs shake Kahéna's chest.

"and
the son
defeated me
he who rallied
the Bedouin's
strength."

A gesture from the Narrator who brushes away the end of the kingdom and this suffocating: the crowd is silent, while those who, at Kahéna's arrival, had wanted to flee the cursed trysting place, sit down again, at another gesture from the Narrator.

> *"You,*
> *Men*
> *of the Assembly,*
> *I have*
> *opened*
> *(yes, opened)*
> *the plains,*
> *mountains,*
> *and rivers of*
> *this country*
> *like a goatskin,*
> *and*
> *I've spread*
> *my turbulent*
> *words and thoughts*
> *to the deepest*
> *reach*
> *of the Desert.*
> *Everyone came*
> *Men*
> *of the Assembly,*
> *except the son,*
> *he who rallied*
> *the Bedouin's*
> *ranks.*
>
> • • • • • • • • • •
>
> *Everyone came,*
> *Men*
> *of the Assembly,*
> *from the different*
> *corners*

of the Kingdom of
Ancient Lands,
All came,
except
the son.
Who will come
and untie
the thongs
that burn
the stilled talons
of the Falcon?"
• • • • • • • • • •

Kahéna tries to free her wrists; Osmane has come near, and kneels, Osmane the freed slave of the Narrator; he looks at Kahéna's wrists as she turns away from him to address the Narrator, who sits a few yards from the crowd, with head and hands lowered.

"Rise
Man
of a land   .
too ancient
I would have liked
to behold
you younger
in that struggle
with the Bedouin.
That is why
I chose
the Bedouin
he whose
seed
had more vigor.
• • • • • • • • • •
Rise
Men
of the Audience

and Bear
your murmuring
up to the
mother-word.

• • • • • • • • • •

The Mother-Word
The Word that
Subsumes
your Climax.

• • • • • • • • • •

Kill
The Slave
He who
dissembles
his heart's speech
deserves not
to survive."

• • • • • • • • • •

Osmane now stands near Kahéna, his right hand reaching toward the Narrator's neck, as if he (Osmane) he held, in his right hand, the Narrator's head.

"Woman
who's come
from the Mother-Word
Here
is the other
being of
my being.
I am
Osmane,
The Narrator."

• • • • • • • • • •

The Audience is no longer under any illusion, because, as if under the sword, the head has really dropped to Osmane's right hand, the Narrator's head.

"Who
might I be?
Woman,
I, a man
of diffused light
sometimes living
sometimes dead,
sometimes a young buck
sometimes old,
and Slave of the day
of the light
or of a gaze.
• • • • • • • • • •
Who
Might I be?
Woman promoted
to the chorus
of this Audience.
What
might I be, far
from the night
or night's
dark torment,
closer
to that other place
of prestige
what am I
but the one signaled
by what Abd-Nouar spoke
against me, Osmane,
become Narrator!
As in ancient times
today I would like to leave
the stronghold

of Téhouda;[78]
and so it is,
Woman promoted
to the chorus
of the Audience,
I am Osmane,
the slave
Osmane,
become..
The Narrator."
• • • • • • • • • •

At the word *Téhouda*, Kahéna is overcome with trembling, as if, suddenly, new breath had entered her, given to her despite her bound wrists.

"Koceila!
Koceila!
My more gallant
Master. He who
remained the captive
of Arab
vigor,
and whom I
freed.
• • • • • • • • • •
Koceila!
A name
sings out
like the
south-wind
in the olive trees.
• • • • • • • • • •
Koceila

---

78   Also Thouda—a town south-east of Algiers

my first
master,
is it true?"

• • • • • • • • • • •

It is Osmane who takes up Kahéna's question, as she throws herself on
the ground, before the Audience.

"Is it true
Kahéna?
As the
falcon
in its chains
or in the hands
that hold it firm
Is it   True
Kahéna
That men
live
in a kind of
mad shadow
attentive
to
end-of-history
words.

• • • • • • • • • • •

The country will
die,
Kahéna.
is it   so?

• • • • • • • • • • •

Like a
desert
sepulcher,
the sky has become
sand.

• • • • • • • • • • •

Is it true
Kahéna,
That
without countries
men,
women,
or children
remain empty
like trees
hollow
under bark.

• • • • • • • • • •

Is it
true, Kahena?"

• • • • • • • • • •

Kahéna started walking from the group, Osmane, the Narrator, and the Assembly. Her disappearance, and the disappearance of Kahéna's country has to happen out on the plain: where the Bedouin forces lie.

Ever since that era the country has become several, and the Maghreb has become the history of an impossible Berber kingdom.

The spirit of the inhabitants is still attached to the hills and rocks that don't dare give their names, but the world and all its wars

the world and all its wars the World? To whom will it offer its wars, and their terrifying names?

The Narrator

Woman
whose love
I see stretched
out on the dazzled
surface of the sun,
happy, your two
hands joined around
the lover's body,
infinitely happy
and alone.
Alone, in the
impossible site of love
the embrace of
Wild One
and Woman. What
can I say to the audience
who tries to imagine
your story: a reflection
of the soul up above
the Dead Hills and Villages
the soul alive, and Queen
of the rights that
elect Narrators.

the land had encountered a
new meaning That of Khaled
the Son of the Bedouin the
Captive He whom the Woman
fell in love with and whose
breath she believes she can
own He whose anger hovers
like a wind over the sands He
whose body hardly moves on
Kahéna's He whose head they
cry out for, here, in this group
of men come from all over the
field: But Kahéna is in love
with the foreign captive This
woman Guardian of the place
slipped through the guards of
the place because men leave
the territory wounded in their
pride by the love of their
woman for a Bedouin. That at
least was how it was told in the
land come down from Khaled
and Kahéna.

VIII

*"They say Kahéna was the victim
of betrayal; those who wanted
to divide up the land or the
immense country by the two seas
had no desire to know the Foreigner...*
and this is the truth," *says the Narrator.*

PART THREE

The Narrator

IX

The sea's salt is in me now. The wind as well. The breeze that detaches the sun and bears it along, here, into the belly of your tears.

Don't cry, Malika.

Don't cry.

I understand.

Yes. I understood your violence and your body. The inadequacy of my kisses. Of the sweetness of words. My heart has stayed open, inside, like your heart, for I can now see through bodies.

That's how I see this fleeing—our fleeing—beyond and within this world, like an inexhaustible and personal flight.

Yes. Malika. We have been born in the House of Love, the one the Narrator built around our bodies and limbs.

There are times when I am (violently) (I can be) in contact with the Narrator and his world of vagabond words. The shock is real. As much as a man can bear, reasonably or in his folly.

This is the way it is, Malika, I can transcribe or translate a good many of the words the Narrator scatters before us or upon us. There are times when I am The Narrator. Because there must exist, some place somewhere where we can be—in words, acts, voyages—sheltered from all destruction.

May this moment, my penetrating in you, last. In the liveliness of your lips and your anxiety. When your voice begins to breathe the other's voice—my story. When your body carries mine away. And your mouth pushes against mine. Hurling my name. Far. In the dark slavery of my being. Offering your name. The name that leads me to you. In pleasure. Rivalry. Killing off this world.

The taxi swings around the square still, always, as if through it the diffuse and consonant circles of that rumor could be fulfilled—the rumor that, for two years, was always dampening that survival instinct in which (for two years) I persisted in the thought of my father's return.

I liked laughing, yes, there, in love's first games, in the game of that day when, through you, I was able to see a faint glory in living, as if, suddenly, the warmth of being and of life woke up in me, after being completely unconscious.

Yes, we had left the city, not to get to the other town, or another region altogether, but just to be at the marriage of the island (El-Djazaïr),[79] and Malika was there, yes, there, sitting, on the flank of the dunes, sitting, while I didn't yet know that Malika was there, sitting, in this center of life's warmth, where Malika's presence awaited me.

Malika

I'll get it all out

Absolutely everything because that day I learned what our war really was, yes, I learned it that day, conquering love or happiness, while the frameworks within which the whole country, we and our parents, had lived were exploding on every side, in front of us, in us, behind us.

Yes, I learned it that very day: as a first offering to the terrorism that bore our hopes, the town was to split open, in two halves, like a head.

The high school was integrated, and that way we learned, every day, to appreciate the void we were living in. Very few "Muslims," some "Europeans," and us, behind the Europeans, between the school walls and the two proctors. That pernicious apprenticeship had begun in seven- (*but really earlier, in your case, and elsewhere*) -th grade, until tenth grade when, abruptly, all masks suggesting equality and fraternity fell away: that was the moment to really get the meaning of 1830's Landing.

The Mallet-Isaac[80] spoke of a debt and the wave of a fan; a history teacher whose subject was pre-established necessity, as the European society of the time knew it, and we—astounded or acerbic—accepted alien propositions so that one day, we could say we'd always thought just the opposite.

How did all that happen?

Very simply. At that point we had to settle scores, despite our shortcomings, despite the various disadvantages to be revealed in due course.

Spring was already upon us: Pentecost the holiday for some; for us, the end of our classes. The last assembly of students and *Muslim* students (this bit of vocabulary inscribed the exclusion in which colonial society had kept us since 1830 and the different decrees that had pronounced the decrepitude we were supposed to be kept in: *Muslim-French, some said,*

---

79 Arabic for Algeria, and Algiers. The place name, ever since Phoenician times, has connoted "island" or "rocky island."

80 A *manual*—typical French textbook format—of history.

simply Muslim said others, while neither of these two terms could ever offer us the illusion of some kind of judicial viability) had decided on *The General Colonial High School and University Strike*: we had to carry out the strike with no let-up, leave the high school the morning of the Pentecost holiday, at eight o'clock, and take all our suitcases, for good.

As far as ending school, or starting school vacation, I think (I can be completely sure in fact) I've never since done anything as beautiful as that.

Because, despite the precautions of those who called themselves (and they were) our *delegates*, there was a real mess—a panic, more like—when, after the first half hour of surprise and wildness, terrible news reached us, along all the different routes we were taking (students of all ages) to get to the Algiers train station and then to the interior of the country: *"They're sending the CRS[81] wagons toward Ben Aknoun."*

I was living in Algiers, in Clos-Salembier, a quarter built up high in the Nadhor section, where People had come from the interior and were piled up in their montagnard ways with all their wounds, dirt and despair, come in search of some work, far from the insecurity of the interior, bodies beset with cycles of tuberculosis and malaria, foggy memories of tribal migrations: Clos-Salembier, the edge of the city and of communal contact: you could count the Europeans who lived in this island of misery on one hand.

Clos-Salembier was our taking-off point and our point of return; the City was our twilight or *cinematographic* crossing; we could get back to Clos-Salembier on foot from the center, or from the High School, which we did that day, since, on the shaded road that leads around several bends to the El-Biar hill (avoiding checkpoints or preventive detentions), Yellow-Teeth was already waiting for us, to take us to his house, the house he and his father lived in, six or seven hundred yards from the gates of the High School.

That was how we spent one of the most intense afternoons of our pre-war years, shut out in this way from the school, and from our city's parasitic life.

This house belonged to a very rich man we never saw, who was said to live in the South. It was an isle of tenderness, a peaceful spot hidden under trees (we had transformed the pool in the inner courtyard into an

---

81   The Corps of French riot police, still in existence today in France.

aquatic mirror where, among the pine needles and the leafy reflections, scattered sketches of the sky jiggled) where, because it was so near school, we had learned to spend the free time between classes, or the baking mid-afternoons, before descending or fleeing to Algiers. We liked that house, and its garden, especially the water sounds, sensitive ones, like the shadows' own joy, our own desires.

We liked the old gardener too; us, the actors in and of two worlds, or of several *intercepting* worlds, who in this way made the discovery (or discoveries) of a few new words mixed now into our beings and becomings, aged fifteen and sixteen,[82] at the edge of a world, a world if not *Shadowy* at least poorly timed to welcome us in.

But, scores had to be settled: the *delegates* were on the lookout, down at the Algiers Station, to try to pay for the train tickets of the youngest and poorest students, the ones who spent the whole year at the school except summer and the end of each trimester.

This situation was at the root of the dust-up, because the Strike was a total success: there was not a soul left at the school after 9:30.

The *delegates* had a lot to do, because the bolt from school had been like lightning, and the various police forces had quickly been alerted.

We had crossed (Wild-Ahmed and I) the school gates in the first group: quarter of eight, content, *happy*, to be thus following the day-students' path this time in reverse, more and more proud of a decision that restored distance to us, and irony, over an existence that seemed to be shrinking.

This is what we believed in:

(Independence

is

our love

story)

A novelty of our lives and of that place. You could easily see it in the way we carried ourselves, and in the growing fear in the proctors and day students—the end of our humiliation.

Sentences went over our heads, without reaching or finally meeting us. "But you," said the *Hyena*, "you've always been a good student. You can't just leave like that…"

"It's a rebellion, Monsieur, a rebellion…"

---

82   Farès was fifteen at the time of the great student strike (noted earlier: 1956)

The kind of response hurled about in those new times when Ahmed didn't bother with mincing words or convolutions, yelling: "We're screwing on out of here, Monsieur,

We're screwing..." and the proctors, and day students, burst out laughing, right in front of me.

A few more yards, and we were beyond the gates, at the bottom of the road lined with mulberry trees, in the clear May air. A few more meters, and now the vision of the gates, open, held open by two *Muslim* dorm masters, now brothers in this strike, in bus tickets, in instructions of all kinds.

> (*To tell the truth*
> *Independence*
> *is not an absolute*
> *fact*
> *but a construct*
> *of loving*
> *living and being.*)

A few more yards, and the high school would belong only to a time of first wanderings, the erring of our first social and legal see-sawing, a first wandering since the one we were about to experience would lash us everywhere like a whip, like a constant reminder of the historical denials we had been subjected to forever.

Yes, the world was opening up, earthy, like that road of yellow dust under the mulberry trees

Our job was to set off again toward ourselves, toward the people we had left

(*hastily*

innocently)

and who were waiting for us on the lower slopes of the city, ready to set fires, flames nervous as dry twigs.

We were to set off toward ourselves, or toward someone we could name with that word, since, undoubtedly, we didn't *yet know* who we were, how to reach back to some silent or repressed antecedent and become *what we were supposed to become*: beings, so to speak, that would be real, whole, and yet not entirely free.

Therefore it was not without harshness that the gardener spoke to us about our future beings, which held us in his thrall, next to him, several half hours.

His son Yellow-Teeth (because of all the dates he'd eaten in the South, and the mark they'd left on him) was exceptionally casual toward him, which seemed to us as marvelous as it was shameless.

Yellow-Teeth was in the habit of calling his father by one simple name, "*Chaïb*," which meant "Old One" to which we added his first name "*Djelloul*," out of respect.

We all had first and last names; mine, aside from Abdenouar, was Abdel-The-Tomb, because I hardly ever spoke, so seldom that after first calling me *Abdel Sekket*, meaning Abdel-Silence, they decided on that other one: Abdel-Tomb. Which turned out to be very helpful to me.

There was also Left-Foot, and above all Wild-Ahmed, because of that fight he'd had one night with a proctor he mistook for an older student, a proctor who had a terrible nickname, loaded as it was with all the curses and calamities of the animal, The Hyena, because of the way he seemed to be everywhere at once, in the school hallways at any hour, night and day, dry weather or foul, on free days or holidays.

There were also two Europeans, François The Ladykiller, on account of his constant hair combing, and Nut-Chops, who was always chewing something, peanuts or gum, everywhere and no matter to him if it were grilled or raw, menthol gum or fruit flavored.

The Strike put an end to all our arrangements, and the world began to crack. We had to take up our respective destinies again; nicknames dropped away and the war galloped up to the school gates.

Ben Aknoun High School became hostile territory, alien to our prowling. Faces and glances shied away. In sum, we had to learn to live: this way, in this dying, or this killing.

Despite several attempts
or efforts
I have never
been able
to learn
to
kill.

...this house belonged to a very
rich man we never saw, who was
said to live in the South...
we liked that house, and its garden,
especially the water sounds,
sensitive ones, like the shadows'
own joy, our own desires.

It started like a prayer, yes, a prayer thrown out ahead of us, in the direction we thought we should advance since, after all, we'd just quit school, or, more exactly, high school.

"S-Salem A'Leikum"

"S-Salem A'Leikum"

Said Old Djelloul

A simple greeting delivered as an ironic welcome, one that surprised our bubbly and "revolutionary" youth: we were leaving school territory to enter the House of Love.

Our first work.

Yes. First opus!

What was that place, where we should have stayed, forever, sheltered from any wreckage? The city pulled away. Or rather, we forgot about the city to let ourselves get caught up in Old Djelloul's magnificent detour. Weaving his own distance, he drove us toward the strangest part of ourselves, to later abandon us like old newspapers blowing on city sidewalks.

Old Djelloul had no special feeling for us. For him we were—and this is said without animosity but equally without warmth—strictly speaking, strangers. Yes. As odd as that might sound, strangers.

Going to school, having napkins or books, to him that only meant being subject to someone's money and authority, something he knew all about, besides, because he had worked for sixty-two years in the same house for the same master, and because his son, Yellow-Teeth, due to all this work, service and the master's recommendation, could in turn go to the high school.

That is why he acted toward us (a thing I only understood later, when I started asking myself what Old Djelloul had wanted to become) with so much prudence and circumspection—all of which revealed, in his reticence about any violence, what he thought was the error of our ways.

This judgment carried weight—weight in the ways of injustice and negligence—because we weren't in fact the artisans of our own error, rather we were the plaything of that place our history was passing through, that history we only possessed as a heritage of disagreements and violations, a history we had somehow to peruse backward, rewinding it.

Yes. Old Djelloul kept his distance, an attitude or distance that surely allowed both father and son (Yellow-Teeth and *Chaïb Djelloul*) to be so familiar with each other, or rather, required that familiarity, while we couldn't, or *I couldn't* (not that I had any wish or thirst to) be so familiar (at least this is what I imagine, for Ahmed and Left-Foot) with the old man. One of them (the father) was no doubt a limit for the other (the son). The son had to go beyond the father, exceed his history.

At least that was one way you could picture our futures, in the negativity of first relations with a father, since, up until those explosive Strike days in town and country, all I had understood was the negative of the relationship: the father didn't express the son,

Very much the opposite, he excluded him.

The father's story had to be transformed, not reinvented but radically transformed, we had to transform the absconding and imprisonment into vivacity, that is, liberate both fathers and ourselves from all the alienations we'd undergone. Of course, in this world, everyone wishes he had gone to war: his own war, or his father's. Which means that: unfortunately for those waging this war (us among them): you're always fighting the last war.

"We have to do something." My father was telling me to help him straighten up the room down below; the place where he had worked for the many years we lived in Clos-Salembier, working late and alone, as if unknown to the city and the world around us.

"Do not ask me any questions," my father had said. "But listen carefully. Right? You're going to listen."

I had to listen to my father for a long time without understanding.

Yes: *do you know?*

how to listen to father?

And understand what he might say to me without asking questions?

Very rarely, besides, had I ever been able to ask my father questions!
Yes. Very rarely! A few times, because of a moment of life-anguish, forming
on my lips, a shuddering of question-forming, but; yes, but no chance
of actually reaching my father because of two things, two difficulties,
stretching above and within the two of us—my closeness and his pulling
away.

My closeness?

Who can understand this impossible interrogation of the father: who?

His pulling away, or his silence, this exclusion of a part that was near
me, critically so, but closed off.

The silence of my being, where the liveliness of my surroundings
vacillates; the law governing my life, a life in search of its own movement:
father: equals strong and stony speech, the speech of my childhood;

Mother weeps, here, next to me, in the shadows of the taxi, among
glints from the windows, from the avenue that keeps surging toward us,
keeps burying us under arcades of many and soft lights.

Hamid is still smiling, pointing out, his left hand hanging out the
window, some dark corner only he knows how to gain entry to, whose
night, games, kickbacks or explosions only he knows, whose varied
fragments are revived by Hamid's smiles, because I still, from time to
time, have to wipe away the anguish, this old rag that I drag behind me as
much as I do years and nonsense in the invasion and losses of this world.

Lost,

Oh;

Yes;

Lost

Oh; yes, lost

here,

my life is

lost

Oh; yes,

like the moment that blossoms in some place or other and dazzles,
brightens, dwells slowly in that place, then, slowly, descends, flows, sinks
in

conjoins with other moments dead and gone, and travels in this way, from a few places to a few other places, irreversibly, caught, caught up in Hamid's face,

lost, Oh; yes; lost

in this city that gashes the faces of men and of night in order to better kill

Yes; kill better

For this is the way the city kills

or the path leading to the city

because the route that leads to the city's exaltation is not simple, not adorned with..

because the city is a conquest that dispossesses; yes, strips a man of his route; you have to be born outside the city to know that the city dispossesses you despite the way it dazzles whoever is not from the city, already done in, by the city.

Lost,

Oh;

yes, because the trajectories are permanently crossed, muddled, and because the river runs near me, against me, and the taxi rolls amid sidewalks and streets I know nothing about, and someone is calling, yes calling: it's Hamid who's saying: it's 10:40, it's Hamid, yes, sitting there, next to the driver, and saying: I got your telegram this morning, a good thing I'd stayed at the hotel, otherwise, otherwise, and Hamid speaks to my mother who, in her corner of the taxi, weeps, and I say, or hear someone saying, or say: and to think I wanted to come here—or rather, since I should have said something different:

I'm eighteen

and that's enough. That's enough for me to know that I didn't come to this city like Mérad or Aziz to spend maybe eight months but: I know our country is far away and it would be hard to get back there after that harrowing departure and my father's being sent from Paul Cazelles

Yes: I'm eighteen, and that's enough for me to know that I have no time to lose, and that, as soon as my father gets back I

Hamid points sharply with finger and face and I see Mérad and Aziz, the hubcaps, as Dahmane called them, hubcaps, blue jeans and light blue cotton sweater; Mérad's get-up in the middle of summer; also, a swimsuit, sky blue, a blue to chase the clouds around, or to drown yourself in; headed my way: Sidi-Ferruch, the middle of July or August or maybe September 10.

The same get-up for Aziz, but different colors, and most important, most important: a pair of tennis shoes kept white as teeth: white, with red laces.

Those laces had been painted in the courtyard, Aziz soaked them in vermillion red, held them up from the can, "colored," with two fingers, before his face, his mouth, like strands of spaghetti.

Lovely.

Lovely.

Hamid is still vigorously pointing, face and finger, his eyes smile, the square is beautiful, very beautiful, full of lights, magnificent, really magnificent And it guides us along its white bollards, among multiple lines of cars and people whose faces shine and shy away in the many luminosities of the night.

"Concorde," says Hamid.

"The Place de La Concorde."

The cars roll, they have their own moves, lively, colorful, fleeting, shifting, the cars roll, slide and laugh yes laugh there on our left because all three are up front they laugh (mother is crying) and I see all this, and I draw my gaze back to the range of my arms only, my arms that want to squeeze the lights the happiness and the laughter, hold on, and all at once be capable of killing everyone.

This is how it is: you finally understand the motives, the *real* motives of certain acts, and still, the truth remains: crimes exist, yes, crimes that's how it is: crimes exist.

Hamid leans toward me to give me a light, a cigarette, and some complicity beyond death, I glance, I take in Everything: his smile, his lighter, his cigarette, his gaze. I will learn, like you, Hamid, to live up above the city sheltered like you like Malika or the Narrator: I will learn, like Ameksa, or Dahmane, to live sheltered from all manner of destruction, Hamid, like you, in the city, sheltered from all destruction.

Hamid drew near to offer his lighter, and I thought—never, never again—will the little man in my head enter there, in the silence of my nights, my desertions, and that I could say anything now to father when: Hamid drew near, and I was able to distance the fear that arose in me, and place, right there, near Mother's shoulder, what was left of my feelings and emotions, there, near her, and watch the thousand riches of the glowing city revolve around us, I could hold tight some movement in me, and utter the first lines and wanderings of the country of Ameksa.

X

Ameksa's country, the Shepherd, the country they say is still open to the Mother-word. The one in which the game of the grass, or of my footsteps—my discourse—dwells still.

The one where you enter, softly, and signifying; yes, far from the rumor of the world, the deaf and murderous rumor That stifles man and child, throws him down, deep in the depths of the river

I can't understand how certain things among those that make me run to you while the water rises, rises Oh the risk I've known My sweet love stretched over the new and vast plains of my kingdom: new and vast

I run Yes Beyond the river Beyond the city My sweet kingdom beyond the Day

And I catch sight of the first place and

there H'Midouche his shoulders hunched H'Midouche's shoulders sparkling with life

A kind of rain over his shoulders: streams, lengthening in the movement of his body.

Swimming

Swimming They open the river and

Surge toward me.

So much time is needed, to understand Oh My kingdom stretched over the vast world: you need so much time to understand and sate its Hatred. To take hold of the place and arrive like plainsong in the place of the world That is, the place of your speech, Oh Ameksa

I wish I were several people, to express abundance and love at the same time: for I see Dahmane who's laughing at the sight of me caught up in the folds of his coat, or the river.

Dahmane?

These two years since I left Clos-Salembier And our city In order to see, on the other side, what happened to my father

A sad gaze: my father became almost mute, at least the first few months, because he was at death's door, yes, almost dead in his thoughts as if all his attention were frozen on one thing then Father came alive again, but this time totally indulgent, so totally that

Dahmane? Dahmane? I think they got to the father and I think the sons, the sons

All the same, I saw my father undone and almost dead because he'd seen so much horror And, as for me, Dahmane, I never stopped wanting to leave, yes, leave that other side of our history, Dahmane, and not get caught in the waters of the River.

There's a sort of prescience in love for the world. In hate. A prescience of the next day. After the night of the River.

And H'Midouche does not drift. Not him.

I see his glinting shoulders. And his body. Swimming. Opening toward me. Ameksa's country. Yes. The country of our distant childhood. The one where the word unknots the enigma deep in me, in my color. Enigma that blurs, because there are several people, some seated, some standing, who seem to be waiting

For what?

You can always ask questions and answer in this way, perhaps: for the day to end. Yes perhaps the day's end, so they can stream on again, in the River.

A great silence surrounds or protects their movements, not that we can say: exactly: that these people we see seated or standing are making any movements. Thus.

A reflection that reaches from the other world.

I penetrate into the place without knowing, precisely, what I can do, desire caught on the banks while the river continues to rise around me—as I'm passing now, cross-river.

My body has become as fluid as the numbered days of: against the current of a life killed before it was even a life.

I'm amazed at the way we don't pay enough attention to life. Or, that, sometimes, we spit on it, as on an unpleasant feeling.

Because: on the other side of our impossible there exists the great kingdom of the living-on

What is it?

A reflection reaching from the other world: It masks the absurd murder of those men used to stalking another living movement in order to snuff it out Or: our being's unconscious effort toward its own expression and secular veil

Man is not brother to another man;

he is his mask, his mask of lying absurdity.

So, what does man matter: But… the place.

A place built beyond all wandering Because so many lives must be wasted to finally reach a place

History or Being, Meaning or memory so much waste is needed for men to produce: the evidence.

Thus: *the slave is beyond the river*

It would be too simple to believe we're open. Like two halves. Or several. After these last few years.

Way too simple.

You have to go further much further in our childhood or histories You'd have to understand the sense of place, of the man who turns a weapon upon Ameksa's heart.

Yes: *I would have run toward you to block that weapon and to have you tell me something of the Narrator's words And to see there before me Kahéna in her red tunic Yes*

> *To see Ameksa and Hear all*
> *Because that is how I understand the world*
> *Or the Venerable Assembly*
> *Yes she whom you call* Daughter of the sand or the wind;

the word, or the rock:

> *Vigilant Guardian of the Hills*

Yes: *I would have run toward you, and I would have waited for the world to open over H'Midouche's shoulders* Yes I would have crossed the ten thousand cubits of the world to get to you, the instant I saw yes where you were plunging the knife, there, amid the chorus, in the forest of great cedars Yes Ameksa, I would have crossed the ten thousand cubits that separate the two worlds, making them one, so our beings would no longer be disoriented in this primal gulf of world.

I would have crossed the ten thousand cubits that separate our lacks or graspings And would have come to you Yes to take away that weapon, before the soft target of your heart and turn it Immediately upon the other He who abandoned us in this gulf of world

Which requires some time, to know, what everyone knows in the different sites of body and soul, or gender or sex, or love or irruption.

It's no secret: not anywhere—because the place is the evidence Histories running over the brow of the world So many histories pouring forth from the same evidence and running toward meaning itself before turning the world inside out. There

Before you, like a glove.

One day, it will be

Because

The slave is beyond the River From now on

But the *Goatskin?*

You don't come into the world like a stone

and yet?

Isn't it inscribed in you, the old delirium, like a man's name, or the earth's? His history name or love name. Or hate name and violence name? Indwelling in you, like that other place in the mother-country?

So, *yes,* This is the way I can understand the design. The one you left to linger in me or behind me, wide open, and showing, *yes In that way,* the different surfaces of the place that link my body to the river's movement. Because it's very important that I understand something, though my limbs are caught up this way, in the river's cold.

Ameksa?

I would have turned the weapon away from your heart so that song would never die on this earth, so that from nights to nights, spaces to spaces, places to places, the soft trace of Ameksa's Country would be transmitted.

But? Am I far enough away from the other world? To admit this belief in the place, beyond any sight of it?

Ameksa? From that moment when your name was pronounced, through love's gesture, or your speech arrived, along with others, in my empire's awareness. In that way the land-beyond-death became open to my body and I can make out the violent shapes of the mother-country.

One isn't born without violence, but why did H'Midouche leave without saying anything, to go beyond the river? Since it is now February 27, 1955, H'Midouche's birthday, his nineteenth.

But H'Midouche rings the bell at the gate though he could perfectly well come in without ringing because the gate is open But he makes himself known and says

"Hi, everybody"

Yes, it's H'Midouche who says this, without looking at Dahmane, or me, sitting near the door, a few yards from the room below.

Take the Goatskin
and turn the river
around? Nothing.

And now?
   talk   Tell me

For no man or child can travel back over the mother-country, but only this other: the one who interrogates meaning and situates it in his ravings, dreams or childhoods.

Our skin is laid open, split, two or several times, and our bodies are washed by the river's water; the breeze flows too, hardly more muddled than clouds of moon or of presence: in the insoluble conquest of the place.

But far off

A night worked over, in the service of other murders: I am, quite certainly I mean to say, far, permanently far from the first days when, wending toward something else, you made me think of the place-before, before the first engagement.

But history

The abrupt irruption of the city and the military

I know that times have come and gone since my murder, in that other country, in the transfer, the one that brought to bear on us and against us the world's power and new will. But

Yes *But*

Where did I learn all these things?

There? Maybe it was There? Because, hurled into the river, I was able—quickly—to seize the fell urgency of the law cancelling the country and the other war, is that it?

The shadow of my days or words might have thus named all these things, the goatskin? and the river?

But you? Yes: *you?*

I didn't *invent you*

since, from the beginning

you'd been living there

and *you*

splattered my body with the many meanings and veins of a primally recognized and intimate countryside,

and

Yes Where did I learn these words that keep me alive suspended above death, in those places where I can move forward without light, not without difficulty, still seeing nothing and

because my eyes are fixed on the texture of the river, because that other day demands (in order to see) some beyond-death power?

But

You're not born without violence, and isn't H'Midouche here, before me, and hasn't he left before me, over beyond the river?

This is how, at any rate, I understand this long detour, across the river.

"Hi there, gang,"

H'Midouche says, as Dahmane asks me, "What's that on your brother's back?"

H'Midouche has on a green backpack. A military one. A complete set of gear. Dahmane looks at me, and I understand that:

"H'Midouche is coming with us." Someone spoke, starting from me yes moving toward H'Midouche who had already reached the top of the stairs, but who turns:

"Hi there, gang." Turns and looks at us, doesn't put the backpack down, or rather just looks at us;

"Hi there, gang; today," and he cuts off his sentence—how? Today, yes: February 27, 1955, meanwhile Dahmane, already, knows because he, Dahmane, was able to delay his departure because of the old woman, and his sister, and an officer from The Redoubt.

Certainly Dahmane knows, while I, I just listen or try to understand because everything, here, is happening so fast that every second you risk losing an eternity of time.

"Hi there, gang," Dahmane has understood, while as for me, I haven't even understood the greeting yet because

H'Midouche comes in and says: Hello or Good Evening. Or, says nothing most of the time; he asks for any news, just like that, without a greeting, or he shows what he's brought with him but

Here, none of that: Hi, gang, with a pack slung over his shoulders, like a soldier.

One question:

"Dad is here?"

"No," someone says emanating from me As Dahmane understands: "Come with me," Dahmane says, not daring to say too much to H'Midouche because

We're in the room below, Dahmane is sitting on the bed, near me H'Midouche is in the armchair near father's work table: Dahmane has stopped questioning H'Midouche since he seems to know things I don't know, and I see his whole body moving before me, as if he were dancing in one place, before me H'Midouche doesn't stretch it out H'Midouche is there, saying, just like that, "Hi, gang," which means: Dahmane speaks

"You went up to the barracks?"

H'Midouche knows he can speak Yes; choose, now, and quickly: the departure is in five days, five days for "How many days, till departure, Five days."

And, I look at H'Midouche.

The dog's paws rest against the door of the room below. Shut. Because of the cold and wind off the ocean. Cold, like your whole understanding being slapped.

Yes: I understand without understanding

as if, inside me,

Where? someone was preventing me from understanding.

I've never told anyone about this because

How can you express: *listen, there's someone there, inside my body, inside my head, who doesn't want me to understand:* Yes, do you think that

No one would understand you, no one, because they'd say: don't act like.. or like.., there's no one in your head: which is false: absolutely false. There is always someone in your head, and I've thought that since: But I don't even need to think about Jidda:

No   Because the person in my head

    is?

Every time a catastrophe is in the making I understand nothing, and the little man in my head makes his gift of incomprehension right there, in my hands, legs, so that I stay stupid, really stupid, seeking whatever greater understanding there might be but unable to speak, only wait, wait for pain to penetrate and toss me its undesired willpower: In five days.

I know everything now Yes, everything, while not understanding it all.

Dahmane doesn't ask what H'Midouche is going to do, the dog's paws scratch at the door as in certain stories Jidda tells, the dog is saying something with its paws and

but father enters, and the dog with him, bringing in the night and an odor of cold coming off the sea down in the town and the other side of the world: the dog is wild with cold and prowls by everyone's legs looking for a warm, comforting spot, something animal: a strong desire sweeps through me, to be like him, in some warm spot where I can listen to everything without trying to understand or to say certain things I can't—so obviously can't—say.

Father is now in the room below, calm before us, a few feet from the door looking then crossing the room by the table the bed and taking a seat on a bench near the bookshelves, and he opens his jacket as if he were going to open himself up before you suddenly the way a lamb is butchered.

Is this really your day?

But father hadn't asked he had just looked at H'Midouche then Dahmane not right in the eye but at their foreheads as if he already knew something as if he'd always known that this moment would come always and fairly soon and that when this moment came he would only be able to look at his son and wait to hear him say: here's Dad, the time has come. That moment when the son leaves the father.

But

This is the father's violent wish Or the sweetest desire The most intimate The furthest from any formulation since the father can't say: this is your day, H'Midouche, isn't it? And wait for the son's response Or, simply leave the room Yes since it's all been said.

Leave the room because finally it has all been said.

But the father is immobilized, and H'Midouche doesn't know what to say, because "Hi, gang" no longer has any meaning for the father: but: "Father, they…"

"It's OK," the father says before me as I look on

"It's OK."

Here it is: Try to understand something like this, because I'm looking at Dahmane and I say: "Hi, gang."

Yes Try to understand as Dahmane elbows me, while father isn't even looking at me and says to H'Midouche: so you're leaving in two days;

I could sense the dog's life among us, in the room, as if: the sea is strong all the way up here the wind is violent over the town as if the town and the dog had always lived together understood the whole world's movements together as if the town and the dog had always run together before the sea before the wind to get far away from me or H'Midouche because here, in the room, no one wants to understand anything anymore; and the only thing left is the departure time.

> In two days
> My hands are open on a
> Landscape? Maybe Dahmane's
> Or H'Midouche's?
> My forearms are open
> Upon a landscape My body this
> Birth-Landscape where through
> Blue veins my terrible feelings
> Steer My violence interrupted
> Like this tireless

Trekking through life looking for life; I could get to the other side of the room with just a movement of my head: and, through windows, see your eyes yes *blue* and believe that the veins' color is made from your *eyes*; but elsewhere I see the fictional and irreversible space of the other world that can do without our loves up above our lives and I glue my gaze to the paws of the dog so *Alive*

That's the way it is: father doesn't have much to say to H'Midouche. Each one stays on the other side of the other. Receiving not the slightest opening despite the fact that:

Wednesday, February 2, 1955[83]

---

83 It is not clear that this date has significance outside of the fiction. It is the date of a French government decree on Algeria, of an address to the legislature by François

The world is foreshortened because I've always known that H'Midouche was there somewhere in the world and the intensity of my thought shrank the distance as if we weren't in the room below but in the café in town, at the Tangier, near the two movie theaters, smoking with: Yellow-Teeth, who's there, who laughs and says: "Come with me tonight, we're having a party in the neighborhood: Europeans, guys 'n girls both, are coming. Nothing to worry about: everyone knows, even the police in El-Biar, and the soldiers, the ones at the Ben-Aknoun barracks."

H'Midouche laughs: touches Yellow-Teeth's temple with his index finger: "You're nuts."

Yellow-Teeth looks my way, out of friendship for me he does nothing about H'Midouche: H'Midouche who's shorter than Yellow-Teeth but wider in the shoulders and with hands that look—and hit—like boxing gloves: Yellow-Teeth asks "What's the matter with your brother?"

These are the moments you've got to just make something up, quick, before everyone understands and H'Midouche takes off but H'Midouche explains, saying: "Over near Ben-Aknoun, they found two guys with their throats slit, near the high school."

Yellow-Teeth interrupts, "That's not from around here, we can't worry about everything, that kind of stuff, and besides…" and besides, Yellow-Teeth doesn't care.

Where'd you get that?

What?

Nothing. Yellow-Teeth has already put the cigarettes in his pockets and is starting to light one as long as two cigarettes end to end.

H'Midouche clearly H'Midouche is talking to me but what can you say; I don't give a shit about Yellow-Teeth's cigarettes, or about what you might think H'Midouche: what I like is to feel or see, you understand: Seeing: and here Yellow-Teeth is much stronger than you or Dahmane because this guy, when he lies, he really lies and you see his eyes get wider; yes, I want to feel, and then, above all, I'm so different—already— from the others: just look at my red hair and my eyes and my white skin,

---

Mitterrand, and of an important Red Cross visit to Algerian prisoners (of the French military).

skin so white it's—in effect—black, blacker than a black person's skin. You understand?

"You, albino, shut up." Because H'Midouche's eyes and head are full of what's happened; so much that it shows.

"A blow-out," Yellow-Teeth says. "You know what that's about, a party?"

H'Midouche shows no interest: "You'll get shot at when you come out, or before."

"It's very simple," says Yellow-Teeth, "I know everyone. There won't be any trouble, or else we'll do the shooting. I've got the two rifles ready. Nothing to worry about," Yellow-Teeth says.

H'Midouche's head wags, carelessly, as a group of young guys, lost, like us, come through the Tangier's entrance and head for the pin-ball machines.

H'Midouche turned toward Yellow-Teeth, and

"At who, you're going to shoot. At who?"

H'Midouche was speaking in a strange way, and Yellow-Teeth understood, while I, I was looking at H'Midouche's hands because H'Midouche is a bit of a goer, and I was afraid of seeing the razor, suddenly in his hand But Yellow-Teeth said: I don't want to fight Why did you bring your brother?"

H'Midouche turned toward me

Tell your buddy you're not going to his place. You have no desire to shoot at anyone and that

So?

How to answer: Yellow-Teeth isn't going to fire at anyone because Yellow-Teeth is a talker and I can't go to his house without you and H'Midouche smiles wide at us, unexpectedly, a smile crazy like this afternoon devoured by sun and rain and cold What time is that?

H'Midouche giggles as if, now, he were really one of us, aimless, thoughtless, just a friend, that's all: maybe that's what mashed the smile wide as rain on H'Midouche's lips

Hey, Red: Dahmane

Hey, Blue, I find myself saying You think you're good-looking with your Blue guy's head. This is yellow-Teeth, from Ben-Aknoun.

Hi, says Dahmane Maybe someday I'll be able to leave The Redoubt and head toward Maison Blanche with the old woman and my sister Are you drinking? I'm buying It's five-thirty, and Algiers is the very city of my hidden desires Adieu life and long live death in this country of injustice thirty-six thousand times over Hey there, gang it's H'Midouche who's leaving for the front never to come back and it's impossible for me to go any further because we have only too impartially reached the lands of radiant happiness because around ten o'clock the police came knocking on all the doors by the park and the Vieux Djelloul, not an alley they didn't block off not a room they didn't inspect not a word left uninterrogated Of course the effect was the opposite H'Midouche is with Mania. Mania? God what a name! I've never heard a first name as beautiful as that Not even Malika So? You'd have to have scoured the whole country to one day run into a name like that Mania? Don't you agree? Mania? One day I'll be able to tell the whole story of Mania But when? One day But when? And go get yourself killed somewhere else But not here You hear me? Somewhere else, beyond the riverbed just so I don't have to find you here smoking your despair-butts Elsewhere beyond the day's slope or the night's Elsewhere While I, Kahlouche or the Red, sink far without you into the country of Ameksa following thus the tracks of shadow and glimmers scattered, jumbled among the remains of the goatskin, primal language of a story resembling in every way the pain of a man or a child who first understands the impossible place of his birth Dahmane Dahmane? I can't free myself from these colors dimming my long descent into the river's depths, while at the same time I know the slave has finally fallen to the river's bottom,[84] and that H'Midouche Yes H'Midouche? Have I really made it beyond the river? In these varied voices and bodies? But, I can't reach out and touch anyone, no one, while I feel something warm and shifting that's getting my body accustomed to something other than this voyage beyond the river?

Nothing?

---

84   It is quite likely that "the river" in this volume reflects African-American slave culture and imagery in Southern Baptist song and sermon: the River Jordan, and baptism and salvation in general. Farès was familiar with American literature, particularly southern literature (he wanted to re-name his first novel, were it ever translated, Kabylia Boy, after Erskine Caldwell's *Georgia Boy*).

Nothing? Really nothing?

Would there really be nothing beyond the river?

Except this flood of light and shadows that reaches my lips and body?

Nothing? But this tissue of black light wrapping around my lips and body Nothing?

Nothing?

Hamid opened the rear door of the taxi and I suddenly understood that, despite my efforts and fitful moments, I had slept, there, behind Hamid, forced to take in a depth of black light from which the different angles of a trajectory emerged, as if it were possible that at a precise instant in your life you could know, understand, see everything you ought to know, understand, say and see.

Hamid opened the rear door of the taxi, always with this same smile on his lips, this smile as if to convince you that you descend from the gods, while you know for a fact that you left the city of Algiers, your city, like a thief.

Mother seems appalled by the lack of light in the street; there, about two hundred yards away, a lamppost and a café, the rest, all blackness, pierced here and there by lighted windows.

Mother has some trouble getting out of the taxi.

"You'll be able to get some rest."

This phrase wafted high, from the rear of the taxi, and I saw the space shifting between my feet and the sidewalk, a quick sharp recall of the place, while the suitcases came out of the back of the taxi, like goatskins.

The telegram must have gotten there because Hamid did indeed come to pick us up, and because I did indeed leave Yellow-Teeth sitting there, by the bus station at the Grande Poste.

"I think it won't be long before I split, too, 'cause I have no desire to crap out here, even if there's some use in it."

But I wasn't able to respond

Because the country had already closed behind me, far from the dark paths and arrivals of this world, my legs bound by the terrible speech of Yellow-Teeth.

XI

It's Malika

Yes Malika who brought me this far

If not *Who else?*

Yes: Who else?

If you think you can correctly weigh or connect certain questions that shoot through your body your limbs or your thoughts, you'll notice that you run into the same questions all through your life, and that what changes isn't the questions or the way you understand or answer these questions, but, categorically, the places and times these questions arise. Thus—with a little attention to yourself—you can end up realizing what you yourself, in body and consciousness, have gone through and done in your many years, all the way to and including the subterranean regions or territories of your existence.

You don't even need any longer—so to speak—to know yourself; you perceive *simply*, on the surface: *directly.*

Yes: Malika

I will tell all because *now* I can approach the two sides of my comprehension, I can *almost*

unveil the multiple and diverse networks of my helplessness and happiness since each part of my kingdom and voyage beyond the Seven Seas corresponds to the two sites of human happiness, the two moments of minimal hope, the one that, from its first cerebral or corporal incidence, brought me all the way back to the territory of birth, and got me to seize, *on the spot,*

that disparity in our world, those dissections that, one by one, obligated the indigenes of the mother-country.

The fact is that: I would have liked to know something before, not to shuck this territory that's abandoned to the various regimes glories irruptions of others but in order that—once the discovery was envisioned or better: *come upon*—I might be able to bear witness, not to an endless exploding, but to a capacity completely my own to accept this meeting and this discovery, subvert its strength, and, like a skilled seducer, vanquish it barehanded.

I've killed no one in this world despite my strong desire to kill lots of people but the brutality of the attack was such that all I could think about was keeping loss and disappearance hidden within a potent living shape.

Malika: the danger or peril is always there, of existing through the whims of others and of worlds that hate each other or that only exist in the daily wasting of their forces—the danger of being buried beneath the turbulent waters of the river is always there, of being buried and left behind under sand, in the dark bed of the current, while the surface of the river still matters and man can one day become the river's master.

Yes Malika: it could be just like that opening-up moment for the city, when the native people of the mother-land ran from street and hill toward the center of the city, as if to a new center of the earth.

Yes Malika: never again will it be possible to burn souls bodies and fields the way they did a few times during the scorched-earth wars.

Yes, you can kill lots of people, but you can't kill a whole world, no, you can't kill off a whole world because, despite the empty spots the spaces the distancings wars and exiles, this world surges back, at first we don't know where from, yes; then, more precisely, this world designates itself as its own world, creates its hopes, sons, desires, behaviors—its haltings, soarings, breaths, moods, territories, loves, truths, and masters; this world can then say or rediscover what it is, *is*, itself, this world can then say that you have to deal with *its world*, or *existence*, that you have to *recognize* it—that's the word—recognize it for what it is and will have to be, for what it presupposes, for what it accepts about itself and demands for itself; yes, you can kill off lots of people, or act as if this world didn't exist, and attempt not negation but burial; yes, you can try not recognizing this world but you won't hurt the essential part of it, because all you've touched is the outside, the immediate exterior, and not its intimate place—a being taking shape.

That's why you can kill or imprison lots of people without harming *being*, the being that advances the interior and exterior, that nourishes tongue and dream, light and shadow; that's why the city was suddenly full of the Mother-Land's children, because, that day, the shadow had left the city to show only the other side of the city, the side burning with light, Clos-Salembier, *The Redoubt, Hussein-Dey, El-Biar, Ben Aknoun,* and, downtown, where everyone expected the worst, *Bugeaud* and *the University.*

Malika: this day is *yours*

because, on this day, the whole country had understood, all at once, arching over the surface and chest of men, that *Kahéna* was dead; yes, that *Kahéna* was dead For nothing is comprehensible in this land, without

the most distant densities of sand.

You think nothing is memory

traces or song in sand's shifting.

You think pulling away is the measure

of disappearance;

That time is a place where

the terrible attraction of the air

and of Nothingness

swirls endlessly.

You go on thinking and songs traces or memory

are found within Nothingness, active,

creating the world, that is, the work, your

act, and your incidence.

Yes, you arrive, or you are, like a place

and suddenly you understand that

everything is much farther on than You.

For there's no way out of the Circle of

Memory except the prolonging and o-

penings Toward

other prolongings and openings

alternating and linearities all deployed

within the motions and realities

of the Wheel that rolls over spaces and times

while never ceasing to be the same circle

or the same wheel. The taxi can always

roll on its wheels or stop in

a new spot, what does it matter: there exists

no other future but the one you

pull close, in spite of

so many people.

Malika: this is how I got the meaning of that day the gates of the city opened before us, and how, hardly advanced or reaching toward the New World, already we were bumping into its weapons and defenses.

The afternoon was barely winding down when the first police search hit me, down below, in the city.

That's when I discovered the true pallor of faces, what the pallor of a face signified because, suddenly, I sensed my face going dry, completely dry, and my stomach caving in so that I thought I'd been punched.

But the blow didn't matter.

Another key thing:

The end of a game.

Here: I had gone down to the street,

and the street gave me a sense of my place

and my murder.

Malika: since that moment—and despite the fact that, later on, in the years of father's absence, the world so drastically dislocated itself for me, in me—I'm never afraid anymore to be in the street: I've even desired the street: the street as site of our worshipful life.

That is how I came to understand the irruption: the joy that came over us as we left Ben-Aknoun.

What were we planning to do? Or say?

Nothing: or: just be everywhere at the same time.

The key thing about the student strike, and the country pulsing in me, its first moments of responsible life.

There it is, Malika: while the sayings of the place are already closing in on me, and while—in this space where my articulation was born—I can guess, through shadows and languages, the outlines and visibilities of Jidda's drawing.

Seize the shadow and make it speak its intention of light: seize the moment because, instead of the impossible void of its death, there come the lines, assemblages and tensions of our world.

If I could understand all the lines in the drawing

But there it is hurled deep within me like a rock in water, looking at
me, immobile, terrible, and childlike: Malika: Malika: I would tell all
    all the presence and risk

                                    of this drawing

    I look:

the slave is beyond the river.

EXILE AND HELPLESSNESS

VOLUME III OF THE TRILOGY: DISCOVERY OF THE
NEW WORLD

TRANSLATION OF *L'EXIL ET LE DÉSARROI.*

VOL. III, *LA DÉCOUVERTE DU NOUVEAU MONDE*

BY NABILE FARÈS, MASPERO, 1976

TRANSLATED AND ANNOTATED BY
PETER THOMPSON

the destructions caused by revolutionary bourgeoisisms and the current era's nationalists spare not a single one of the fields established and developed by human effort. This is the currency, and, as with any other, the true value of reality, and the work of writing does not escape the political conditions of this inhumanity.

PART ONE

Mokrane

Desgraciado aquél que come
el pan por manita ajena;
siempre mirando a la cara
si la ponen mala o buena.

—Copla Flamenca

I

Only after a few years could he understand what had happened, because, in the meantime, he had had to stay to one side of all involvement and tribulation right at the moment when the country—the *country? what convention would have us call it the country (?)*—was heading for a new ferment of lives and events.

Closed borders
Streets and
Villages
wizened—set atrembling

—

Silence and arrests
: you had, despite the political divisions of the moment, to advance.

Already the countryside was coming to life, and on fields of labor where, a few months earlier, colonials and their heritage had existed, new harvests were being announced, the fruit of decisions, transitions, prudent measures, which the politicians had hardly conceived.[85]

It was then we saw vast domains taken over on the spot by workers who, up till then, had no right but to work on Others'-Land, no right to a contented contemplation of the trees, the fields:

Cultures
Sky
Shade and Water
Opened this time to Limbs
Bodies Thoughts (not assassinated):
In two months,

---

85 Note that here we pick up the narration after the war of independence and after the establishment of a government (in which Farès's father was sidelined) that has greatly disappointed the author and countless other Algerians. With a change of publisher and a somewhat more conventional prose style the trilogy continues here with fewer historical references and less need for notes. But an intertextual reference is important: the trauma evoked in the first volumes is pursued here, with a feminist emphasis and new characters. This is relevant to the author's psychoanalytic practice in Paris and also links—most closely among all his works—to *Exile: Women's Turn* (poetry, Diálogos, 2017)

the fields of time's dwelling
and of the earth
of sadness
and of war
      of the   Conquest
         and of the Sea
            were plowed, turned back on their roots—properties
and Customs—drained of their inequalities,
   and,
   Offered,
      from October on,
to the first harvests of the year nineteen sixty-three.

Born this way, from the pain and joy of finally being alive, and free of itself like a river swelling with the many tributaries crossed along its way—*Rivers, desires, Loves, torrents, or Voices*—the movement of farm workers took over all the territory and its fields, destroying bondages and sequestrations: everywhere the process was the same: the Workers, independently from their parties, opposition groups or budding administrations, took up positions deep on the land and set up Management Committees. Such was this movement, born of itself, for working the land and for fallowing it, in no way directed from "above," but anchored, anchored in the sowing of August and September.

The movement was not simple because, after several years of a government's power, and the breaking of agreements, accords, readjustments, if there exist—*even till today, and, almost inadvertently or perhaps as witness to what once took place*—some self-governing Fields (open and spreading over thousands of acres), there nonetheless exist Fields closed to self-government, fields open and sprawling, guarded by their owners, the very ones who—

   being impostors
   and by embezzling—have the duty of spreading the word of justice,
   and, of revolution: the good word…

So there is that, and many things besides, which, beyond the declarations from the higher spheres of politics, show an amusing kind of gap between the words spoken by Power and the realities of the community.

A kind of ironic play between Powers and Realities which—with a certain negligence or flippancy regarding our principal beliefs—amuses itself by creating distances, conciliations, attempts, illusions.

"*Property is social, not of the state.*"

And, just as you've said this, you realize that Property is of the state, and not—social; you come to know this, at least here where words have suggestions that are often the reverse of what they designate or proclaim, as if, in the intervals of speech and its reception, words had become a camera obscura, and you now know that, in their dark legitimacy, they portray reality turned upside down, but accurate, the *true* reality, and, if you will: *the real.*

This is perhaps how we should view things and time, things and words: just perceptibly, reality inverts itself without any help; things and words reach degrees, and then impossibilities, of true recognition.

This is why:

Exiles and Uncoverings

Powers and Renouncements

Country and Turpitudes

All is thrown at Us

Pell-mell,

like tomorrowless

clothes,

and there we are Wandering

—*become Wanderers*—with miles of our road behind us, developing ideas, and reasons, to understand the break, the crumbling, the massacres and negations spilling from the many lacks of time's weight and of the lie.

Suspect

—*become Suspect*—

Drowned and rejected in the mud

as if

Our Bodies—*Souls and Hopes*—

      had never had that blaze

of

B

E

   I

    N

     G

Exiles

  and,

    Confinements

For there we are summoned to the precarious residences of the police and of confusions,

  Cloistered in the cells of

  Our half-truths

  of Our

  Falsifications

and Violences, Ready to be called all sorts of unfortunate names—

Exiles—Emigrants—Refugees—Petit   Bourgeois—Functionaries—Bureaucrats—

  all Issued from within us

  and,

against Us: Our Powers besiege us and annul us like vulgar words scribed on sand continually washed by tides.

  Poor words

  written down—

  what We

  Are—Ignorant of

  the sweetness,

  the Dream

  But

  Soon become

  —ourselves, in our misalliances—

  Soon Become

  Rapacious and Calculating

Greedy for money and honor, being long deprived of an outward and moneyed honorability, for which, these days, we are especially well known, with all our pomp and ceremonies.

Many hotels crowd the seas and the sands, eager for foreign occupations, generous of space, and, of Solitude.

The lobbies
are numerous,
visible, guarded not by people but by tiles, paintings, or tapestries, all in a line throughout the rooms, corridors, and lounges. This is very odd, because the breadth of the sea views, and the grounds, should allow for the deepest kind of sojourn, and regular customers.

But the country is so designed that it abandons the hotels to empty silhouettes, the habitués of hotel lobbies and bars, often to be found draped over the fourth or fifth whiskey of the afternoon, ready to melt into the landscape, or into the walls of a vulgar game room.

Among the tables, you can feel the lascivious draughts of ennui, annihilating any air or breath, hollowing your desire to live, with murders and derisions.

All around, this vast land exists, which the vastest and most digestive constructions cannot hide, this vast country where the sky traces aureoles of happiness, and of life, above the miraculous breath of the sea, of the wind.

Inequal relationships: from the land to the new constructions, a kind of immense distance. A Cecil B. De Mille décor where, according to their idleness or their persistence, silhouettes—of unemployed actresses, and actors, from films shot long ago—stroll about, in search of some laughable or insipid rowdiness. The merest appearance of a cat, or a dog lost among the backstairs, trays, machinery, among the false passageways, the large halls, creates the illusion of an action that is whole, and lived—an action envied by every glance because Nothingness's handiwork is here so noxious, invading, implacable.

Words gliding, among words, which accentuate the nullity, the lack of anything to do:
—Something else?
Something different?
—Yes. Something.

A strange interrogation, whose limits, or questions, define the very weights and servitudes of these new years. These new years ticked by in births, prolongings, works, post-war fevers.

—Something more real, true, than what we hear, or read, here, now, day in and day out.

Something that reconciles our hope—and, our life. That reconciles our desire to live out, fully, our new beliefs.

So it is.

But: the country waits.

Or, certain people of this country are waiting for what they call, on account of the lack of influences or rivalries: "democratization." The beginnings of "democratization," whose meaning, clearly, you have to try to understand, since those who proclaim this "democratization"—or, what they call around here "de-mo-cra-ti-za-tion"—are the various business milieux, who are driven by envies, obsessions, who want their concerns to be recognized forthwith and not cloaked by formidable and clandestine manoeuvres.

—Why don't you keep on working with us, in the Revolution.

—That's a question I'm anxious to respond to. And respond with all the force, and truth, of a new belief. But, it's as if the truth of the Revolution has pulled back: yes: pulled back, through social changes, certain social transformations, turned inward, toward money, prestige, self-satisfaction: narcissism. I would prefer to see something else: yes. Something else.

—Every country is nationalist. And there's no government, once "installed," that isn't predisposed to narcissism. So what?

—So what? So nothing. I don't know. First off, understanding what's happening to me, this way, so suddenly, ever since my return to the village. Understand: yes: understand: since now I'm ready to take off. Understand: since I don't want to hear people talk about anything anymore.

—Understand what?

—I don't know.

—Democracy?

—Which: democracy?

—My answer: the desire for "democratization," without really being against (it would seem) injustice, comes from clandestine financial practices.

And not far from there, beyond the glass bays of the lounge, and the bar, the caressing of water on the sand, its movement, suggests a silent proximity of death, of a stifling, for, at certain moments, there are within the water's movement, waves, in the current of the water's swell, shiftings, a far off cry, a spacious cry clinging to the ramparts of silences and expirations, a sort of primal cry, preceding all returnings of tears, of dreams, a stubborn cry, rending in its weakness and incongruity.

A cry: as if the immense pain gathered up in years' worth of wars, confrontations, had taken refuge here, at the water's bottom, between the walls of voids, burials; a fragile cry, barely identified, besieged from all sides

Poor

from its isolation

a vacuity: a cry-of-remaining

instead of eras

truths   last resource of

greatness, and, existence

affirmation   of a necessity

     another

      cry-of-remaining coming only from our values and heritage. Stuffed away there, beneath the various movements bold-striped with love and sun, the Cry of our misstep: the country—

this country which is ours—

today belongs to a few disseminated beings, or, rather—because this is one of the truths of the Territory—to several beings stationed in strategic spots ever Prompt to spy out political success as personal necessity, as urgency, being situated as they already are by the current powers in look-out posts, and, in their reconquest towers:

the country

a soft air falling down the hills, along the ravines, and, the paths. A Supple Sweet Air Which opens the World's Hands and places them there, On the Sky, to Draw it Away from the Earth Because the Earth needs to breathe—Deeply, Freshly Before Hurling Itself into the straits of Death and Birth.

For at Certain times Earth can show itself lascivious and lazy Can wait long moments for its desire for life. Because-Certain-times-Earth seems happy to arrange itself, its limbs, its gestures, its plowings and becomes Pregnant Open and Open Within.

But the world
Hesitates being not used to this offer
the World?
Clumsily it hesitates and then bows
the World?

Then it is that a God Howls in the arms of the Hills From out of those places where the roads go off in different Directions Toward the Villages and Towns A red-haired God—*and Godlike*—and, grimy With Hollow Stomach, stomach Empty Transparent As If the World had pulled out His guts An Abandoned Lonely God as well as Blind Deaf Dazed Who gnaws the Earth there—*Godlike*—In the arms of the hills Feverishly Nervously For no reason Against Nothingness.

A crazed God bays, howling against the Evening or Morning prayers Howling against the Silences and the supple delicate Movements: A crazed And lonely God Who Avidly scratches at the Earth and bites it As if from this Friction the sound of the World would rise up Or else that Powerful free speech Eager to bridge the long desire of the earth the lips the true thoughts of man.

A sweet air that comes from the hills and the pathways Comes Down along the ravines Runs in the new grasses and Softly Embraces all A sweet air that brings about in the god's invincible hand the Irreversible passing of the day Reveals Valleys, Villages, human Refuges in the seasonal Migrations The Villages of great aura and prestige Built in the Heart, Adventure of men Pulled from the Void from Misery against Imposture.

Trucks come and go quickly Penetrate the courtyards of crowded barracks—terribly crowded—with men and arms.

July 22 1962

Seventeen days ago the change happened, and, For seventeen days the Valleys and Roads have come to know this coming and going of trucks at the entries of Villages and Towns.

In the South

And on the Eastern front Combats have been many and Murderous Like those of 1957-58.

Sétif Constantine Philippeville Mostaganem Bone Souk-Ahras Alger Oran The Towns welcome the Troops and Display the territorial Reconquests like signals dotted on an immense mapping project.

The People

listen:

because the People do not understand these shocks coming from so many misunderstandings.

The People?

The Towns are Besieged Broken in their pretensions to rise up The New Pacification is gearing up Effective and Directly centered on the Taking of Power The Bridges The Radio Stations The Judges: the Ratification of Powers is always difficult Especially when their Passing is presented as the simple consecration of several years of fraternal life.

The People, themselves, Having struggled for Themselves and for Nobody Else, Lend an ear then begin to Question themselves Rise up They leave the neighborhoods on the outskirts Aim their marches Downtown—Alger, the Palace of the… People—bear down with warning cries Streamers Pickets which Suddenly they present Above the Gates of the Palace: the People shout their Disgust their Project their Disarray—the last wail before this long silence hollowing out the Future and Post-war History.

"*Long live the Revolution*

Down with the Bourgeoisie and Opportunists

Long live the Agrarian Revolution…"

Like the fragile silhouettes of futures and joys the Women pull off their veils Reject the various enslavements of Men and of the Earth Inscribe their Will to Live There Among The Men There Among the Streets the Boulevards, There!

Women Beyond Walls Outside of Prisons Outside of Voids Outside of Solitudes Women and Their Desires to Kill Off all Servitude.

"*Seb'a Snin… Baraket*

Seb'a Snin… Baraket"

The Women Shout the Women Speak the Women Demand the End of Fighting and Rivalries; the forces of Order are, for a time, maintained by the People, because the political factions, and the State, have not yet formed the territory's intervention Troops. The *Seb'a Snin Baraket* forces of order, The Ratifying of powers, has taken place and the Town is entirely risen like a lung struggling for air Then several months later the breathing slowed down—The Town—Like an ocean ebb on the Hidden face of the Moon This long cry of walled-up desire *Where are you going Wandering Star in the World's reaches in Exile's reaches This Mouth, Mouth of Childhood, overly widened by hunger These Countrysides These Valleys These Springs These Mountains These Villages where each person hastens to try to rediscover Something Other than Great Stands of Trees or of Wisdoms, Knocked Down beneath the Moon.*

Suddenly the sky has gone savage.

The Collection violently opened outward, Crowd of Voices Wills, Desires, Which Dart through the Bellies of Women and Towns.

The Night's Song is no longer the Same.

The Night's Song *We will live in the streets Among You The Celebrations The Splendors of a Staring Bright City*

The Parks Deep in the Squares surrounding Hills Memories of Men Women Girls And We will make Love Right There Without knowing each other There Without even having seen each other, and like a game—Yes: A Game—Game and Tenderness Through this Return and our Profusions

> *In the depths of the Days*
> *Sea Voyages*
> *Mouths Pressed on Mouths*
> *Hands joined*
> *In*
> *the World's greatest*
> *Desire.*
> *What*
> *do these people*
> *demand*
> *Peace*
> *and Revolution.*

In a word, Joy—that Joy which loosens Privations and tongues.

Joy: if the People are ready for their Independence the Politicians are not. Or. At Least. They demand a singular consecration, that of their talent, or (?) historic strategy, since, the very opposite takes place, July 5 1962 takes precedence over July 5 1930.

But: This People is definitely ready—As Well—for all disparagements, since—(Thus: in its demonstrations criticisms enthusiasms)—it does not strive against anyone in particular, lets anyone in, but, before anyone, itself: the People?

On the Hidden Face of the Moon there is a strange territory overrun by countless deer

always linked to each other by the desire to reach certain High Plateaus of the Levant.

But—it is no use—their dash is firmly reined in reduced drowned in the immensity of

the territory.

Everywhere—Round about them—the incomparable silence of the stars their sparkling

mad twinkling their disorder spinning in the profound illumination of the World.

Sometimes the Deer turn around or lift a hoof for a moment While their stare loses

itself in the nothingness of Shadow and of their far Run. Their Eyes are the color of

the most authentic valences of Love Anguish Nostalgias Only the stirring of day

drives Them further into the impossible vision of the Sea.

They stay This Way forever In the same places And If At Times Some Bold or Exotic

Traveler Sees Them He is immediately struck by this impression of a universal pawing on

a platform set up on the surface of a circle of Silence and Time.

The Deer bear within them the most lasting desires Those that persist in the development

or Expansion of the World.

That is why difference is immediately noticed among this multiplicity of desires ferried on the Moon Stones Dead Stars Sun Planets Streets that run through the Towns

Highways that cross Territories Villages Hills that hide a certain Progeny and always a

Virginal Ancestry.

One from Another—Desires from the Seas or Deer from Men—the Separations—trifling at

first—take over, progress, branch out: On the right Flank of the Moon a Doe has fallen

to its knees Its Eyes filled with an immense pain as with the shock and the fall its right

leg has snapped A Sort of Wail has invaded Space While the first glow of day has begun

its rolling above the Sea. Already, the Town rises from the waves Voluptuously reclining

against the lowest hills that surround the bay, the beaches, like a vast verdant sea shell, a

sculpted land-shell.

At the first tipping of the day the God of Foam leaps forth Runs on; alone, he disappears, dives, emerges, does it yet again, runs, fast, right there, over the surface of the water, to finally fold, die, there, on the sand, like a head thrown further than its body.

The God of Foam is wise: no protest escapes, for this landing beyond the Sea. Despite his urge to return deep below the waves, below the circled, but infinite, rocking of the bay.

The God of Foam…

—What they call "democracy" is power shared among fifteen people. A power which no one can grasp, and, which kills.

—?

—What kills me, is that everyone, here, says he is, and believes himself to be: "re-vo-lu-tio-nary."

—That's completely normal. Since. Here. In this country. What there is. Is: "Revolution."

—?

The voices go on with their day-in day-out of jokes, bringing responses that are as distant as two stars seen at the same time.

II

Mokrane picks up a paper napkin next to the hot-plate, protects the fingers of his right hand with it, and, after centering the strainer on the glass, slowly pours the coffee, which falls in fat drops, and, almost completely colors the glass.

An aroma darts here and there in search of a game that no longer exists, in search of coordinates, or existences, no longer there: Mokrane places the strainer next to the hot-plate, sinks two teaspoons of sugar into the glass, and takes a few deep breaths.

Already, after the first swallow has passed his lips, the fever beats a retreat, drifts away under the effects of the cure now broken off, a special cure for this type of calamity, this type of infection: Mokrane has spent the last week under the covers, a towel wrapped around his head, and triple-strength infusions within his reach.

Mokrane's body looks like a fine filament of pale moon, caught up in brown sleepwear, on which stir (or, seem to stir) scraps of cloth: the bathrobe is a few years old, but it is warm, supple in the way that it hides 132 pounds spread over a stature of five foot nine: thin on a tall frame. The coffee scalds each of Mokrane's thoughts and wishes, pours down through his arms, legs, burns, takes over the stomach, rolls, burns some more, slides and, vitally, takes up residence in Mokrane.

The coffee burns, opens Mokrane's eyes, wide, to something Mokrane wants to see, but which, by all evidence, and despite the sharp burn, he cannot see. All this, as if his attention had been focused by the burning liquid, the smell of the coffee, as if, before getting back to living, upright, far from his flu and his bed, he had to stop himself for a minute, or stop the idea in him, and settle himself, in some way, in place, and begin moving after the isolation of these last days.

The coffee goes even further down, as if it were reaching memory at the same time as the body, that memory contiguous to each of Mokrane's movements, but which Mokrane tries, in vain, to summon back with each step, or each new mood, fully back, to once again go forward in life.

A terrifying breaking forth of life, and Mokrane feels it advancing in him on the different trajectories of his thoughts, his muscles, because every time Mokrane feels this life beating in him he imputes strange plans to it—like the aim, among others, to firmly believe in him.

A terrifying overflowing of life, after the failures and the distancings, life is still there, bumping against the potentials or forms of new lives.

Life clings to life: this is the principle. In spite of every death. And Mokrane is able to think this because, out of the depths of that fever, after so many caring measures, something has arrived, emerged, that can shape all his hopes to live new lives.

Something very precise, which the evening's watch wants to repress, to push out of sight of daylight, of wakefulness: fear, or, some kind of drawing near, something alive in him, like a trembling.

Mokrane is afraid.

He lets the coffee burn his throat, slowly, while his eyes grope, there, beyond the window, among the gray-brown, gray-white movements of clouds and sky above Paris, while they seek out the passages of his being, his hopes, his life.

Mokrane is afraid.

He sets the glass of coffee down on his all-purpose table, his working, eating, sometimes sleeping table, table for cards, dominos, checkers. Mokrane is afraid, seems to observe his very interior, the immediate prospects of meetings, of health. He folds his arms on his bathrobe, over his belt, gazes at the wall opposite his bed, toward the shelves, seven or eight inches from his all-purpose table.

For the first time, these last days, an urge, the desire to smoke. He extends his left arm toward the table, takes a pack of Disques Bleus that is a week old—the week he spent in bed—raps its bottom, plucks out the cigarette that emerges from the rows of white filters.

He strikes a match on the edge of the bed, raises the flame, lights, draws on the cigarette, without inhaling the smoke.

At the third puff, he inhales, feels the smoke running over the same tracks in his body, almost visible ones, that were invaded a few minutes earlier by the coffee. Mokrane can no longer resist: he savors this first cigarette of his return to vertical life, and, already, he knows he has to get over to the café to get his last supply of the month. Facing him, on the wall, in big red letters, a phrase that dates the moment, the room, several years of constraints, desires: *Your being is not complete in mid-race*

   man is a frame of mind

   a migration through this world

Not far from this sentence, on the right end of the wall, a gigantic tree has been drawn, with roots showing: testifying to personal horizons sketched in the attentive bark of trees, of worlds; the various influences of joys barely glimpsed, and hurled forth into social functions; the Love of being, without destructive inequalities:

   the wombs   of things

              of events

              of people: Our lives

   imagined

   sensitive

   soft

   grasses

   conquered

   offered

   to the footsteps

   of loves

   of lives   Our lives

              heard

              penetrating

              veins

              alive

              animated

              warm

              from the vegetal

              journey

   the tree?

   How could it be destroyed

   or

   denounced

   in the Exile

of powers

and

things

The tree is shot through

with words, phrases, ideas that express several equivalences between
the wills to live, or to die, or, more basically just to keep quiet: to flee
language, and love, in the rivalry of time and space, to achieve nonsense,
or, when the crisis arrives, to pronounce the irreducible hope of holding on
to truth in the very meagerness of matter and the soil.

Mokrane pulls on his cigarette, while still looking at the phrase before
him, the phrase that calls out to him, or, names him, right there where: in
this way the land speaks or says a number of things, most often to your
complete stupefaction (that being part of its usages, or, efferve-
scence) so that you will be able to defer your anxiety, fear, or,
powerlessness, and so that once the future, and meaning, and the word
have been regained, you might understand what is being inscribed in you
in this way, almost independent of you.

July-August 1962: July-August 1972: Open doors, closed doors, of
villages. The world materializing: new fragile Interrogated from all sides:
contested.

The tree is shot through

with words, phrases, ideas that show the trajectories of the senses, the
thoughts open to the space where growing happens, the space of sap, of
multiplying truth-hopes, the tree's writing called forth by the land: writing
deployed, there, in the sky's nerves, in the community's vibrations.

The tree's writing, instructed by the desire to be present in the objects,
the realities, of day

or: articulated nomenclature of the spreading foliage

borne sculpted

in the wind which

delivers it.

Words given titles in their movement

The worry of lives challenged every day in their wound the definition
of worldly documents the undulation of leaves of plants bordering oblivion

the scrambled absurd manipulations of lands of existences mixed with the perceptible progress of the grass or the murmurs initiating dialogues.

The world opened up by worry, there, on the wall there are things, and, thoughts, visible signs of continuance.

Years, moments that define places, life-spaces of comings-home, in their various eras, adopted against the disorders of war, slavery, the many seizings of land, of souls, of farms: the returns from exile, dispersions, inscribed in written work, in the attempt at a new work, the one which will bring about not wealth, but justice, here, now, among the fields, women, children, territories, and, men.

Joy's return toward villages in mountains high and low: one question haunts his approaches, his discoveries: can he still exist—still, here—in all the valleys and trees that were slowly, scientifically, burned, assassinated?

One question haunts his joy. This new joy in living, and, in the world. A new joy borne by the world through the villages, and, the towns.

One question.

Inside it: an agony from long and accumulated sufferings. Silently, Mokrane whittles reeds for the game of five fingers.

His aunt is there, seated, on a bench,

in the courtyard.

All you do is rapidly throw the pieces of reed, like this, let them fall on the back of your right hand, or, maybe your left hand, and then, lay them, following a certain order, on the ground.

The rules are simple: you just observe them. His aunt looks at Mokrane, incredulous, as if Mokrane were not doing what he is actually doing, here, right in front of her, a couple of yards away.

How can you be *playing?*

And what are these desires (your desires) that I no longer understand? Your quick looks, but mild, and disoriented: my own head is stuck somewhere else, in an immense sand forest, where the sky is cold, empty, surrounded by water.

The years of shadow, air, acts of violence, years wandering among the various acts, limbs, and resting moments wherein each word is glorious with meaning, or, its own recitation: my head moves—yes, moves— right and left—yes—almost joyously, but, my body has become crazy, my thoughts crazy, not from separation, or terror, but in this way: the sweet return of faces, their faces, cuddling, every night, every day, every hour, against the left side of my body, of my life: Faces of Those—my Loves—my former joy in the world, in the garden, in the rooms, the courtyards, songs, words, sheltering the wind, cradling the wind: Their Faces Everywhere in Me Mild Swaying In Long Appeals drawn out by my Laughter my Visions, Long Appeals that I cannot say or Unveil this way, in front of You, Young Man—Old Man—of impossible returns.

I understand—Oh Yes I understand—the distances now rooted, and living, between life, and, death. The distances rooted, constructed, between the two times that you were here: my hands tremble with absence, or, dispossession (disappearance), with steps that lead—Them—close to Them: My Tireless searching ever since: but no more: since your arrival: no more: since your return.

Since:

My hands?

My memories.

Or: those of the body: Faces of Those who oversee my suffering, lifting the veils of visits: of the separation between visits: before me—a woman now abandoned to the shadows, to territories known-and-unknown, riparian lands of causes and births, who now see the sun's path and the stars' path begin to take flight, and liveliness, in the quickness and articulation of my hands.

Stars.

Or a Sun dispersed, blown up: I understand—Oh Yes I understand—the silences of the trees, of afternoons spent between four walls, among accents, partitions, shadow, air, violence. The afternoons:

Land Over There Breath withheld

in Space or Time

by Space or Time

Land scattered Stars

My hands?

Memories of Those

: their faces, in the rooms.

Her head moves, right, left, slowly, while *her* thoughts cross over the silences, or, the separations imposed by dreams. Solitude

Her solitude

That of a woman isolated by the: Solitude where time wanders, displaces things, images, the veils over events, things where time stirs—tirelessly—destiny visions instants bodies scattered like stars through the lands and memories of long migrations.

My hands? Souvenirs of Those People of the World of the Manufacturing of the World where their Wills exist Where my Hands touch their Births their Desires to live To Live Again there in my era my duration of a life prolonged beyond my body, in a painful and incomprehensible in-

sistence: their Gazes set, there, on my eyelids, my eyes: their Gazes scattered, with no connections, and, no words.

How then, going forward, to plan to keep on living my own continuance? This continuance inscribed in their Bodies, their Movements? A waiting for my life, in their Lives:

I have waited for their returns, or, regress, here, toward the village, and the courtyard: nothing.

Nothing except their Appeals—here, around me, in me—their Appeals—nothing more—than their prolonged Appeals.

Pro-long-ed

Do you understand Me?

III

I have questioned the neighboring houses: the color of their walls, pockmarks, holes, cracks, the splits left by different passages. I have even observed, here and there, a sinking of the soil, as if the ground was lowering itself, bending toward the valley that runs along the river.

I have questioned the village.

The village had two schools.

One was Koranic: on the hill Above.
The other European: on the square (in the village) down Below.

 No communication, between the two schools.

None.

Not even
: within me.

I went to the two schools,
and,
in the evening: in my grandfather's house
I would speak that other language
: the one I
no longer
know, which stirs up so much passion
in the villages,
and the towns.

Passion?

The two schools, and, that third one, unnamed, bare of books, which you bear with you, simply carry, out of concern for your being, and, for living.

That is the way of it: ever since the world was world: all beings are part of: civilization.

But: we must have The Book
Djamel said.
We must have the book.

Me:
I find that formula a bit
succinct.

We must have the book,
to be sure:
lots of books.
And, lots of other things
beforehand, and, after the books.

We must have: what they call
the land: and, all those comings together
that make the land come alive around us.

Man exists well before, and, after the book. So, why be "attached," and so clearly "tied" to the book?
Djamel said:
that our civilization is based on the book, one book, at the origin of all other books.
a book coming from the origins of books, of teachings.
Djamel.

This is why that school existed, built in the Village-Above. The one where they taught the book, the book of all books.

I have—however—searched for that first book, the one not yet become a book, but existing before books, the acute testimony of our world.

That is what we need, in addition to our lands, and, our daily toil.

But

:many things have passed, trampled by the hunters and the greyhounds.

Speech has become somehow other, after all the shots were fired, after the opening up of the hills, the fields, what we called, around here, the "regrouping" camps.

The long treks of those who went back to the mountains, and, the towns, the few cities that offered themselves, vibrant with new possessions.

That is when I saw the village, and, at the far end of the village,
beyond the Market square
: the House.
The one that had remained
alive.
deep
inside
me.
Alive.
Like
a
thought.

I made long detours, caught in the military marches, convoys.
Then
: the desire for a rest peopled with childhood happiness. *There were smiles, hand gestures. Smiles of young lives hidden in trees, and on the way, houses, shadow orchards lined up below the hills.*

I followed the wide road, the one that divides the village in two, from the mosque onward.

I saw the road, bordered by trees, and a tenderness surging up, flowing down from the hills, mountains, and forest—onto the belly of the world.

I ran into the hills, pointing with my finger at him, the one nobody, here, wants to hear about any more. The murderer

the murderer?

I ran: I encountered those who are building the world. Who open wide their gazes. Their hands. Who demand that (their!) Rights Power Works be clearly recognized. Who build. Walk. Advance. On the belly of the World.

I ran into the hills.

Like a river. On the surface. Warm.

Loud.

Like a God. Lively.

Tenderness. Of the hills.

Like a God.

I ran: into the hills.

Fast. On the surface. Of. God.

I ran.

Into the hills. And I met. Those who were no longer slaves. Or. Prey. Rather. The Living Guardians of the Place.

Those whose speeches blended with the roots. The Youth of the Moment. And I was surprised by this word, issuing from this place.

I ran into the hills. To reach the language of the earth. For: since July: my aunt's thoughts were all scrambled, and I, alive, visible, was someone who no longer understood anything.

anything.

as if suddenly the village had tried to completely disappear.

the village?

I wanted to speak

there, but my throat? syllables of welcome, of laughter? And I saw, a few meters away, July's light gnashing, whirling in the wind's heat.

I saw:

and, slowly I crossed the pathetic space of my return.

: crossed the courtyard

where not a blade of grass grows

where no word reaches

where no offering exists.

So: I pushed open the door of the place, and, I saw the lamb, dead. The one I could have been guardian for, shepherd of our happiness. Our innocence.

I pushed open the door of the place and, something in me broke. Like a tear. Or, a pleasure. Disheartened. I pushed the door of the place, and, I was able to arrive at the interior of my duration, because—the interior had just cracked.

That is when I began to hit out.

Yes: to strike.

The long neck of the ground. And its immediate insignificance. I struck it. To make the earth speak. Say something. Talk. Like us. In its own right. About hard times. Happiness. Truth. Our ignorances.

I struck

: and the ground's neck stretched forth

violently, like a bow:

: *there is no greater misfortune than that contained by your lips.*

the man who cannot speak

: cannot be.

I struck:

the man who cannot speak

cannot be.

So I threw aside the veil of caution.

I said:

Yes: I will speak.

I will speak more than any other. Until my voice is heard in all innocence.

I will speak:

each

has the right

to speak

on his

own ground.

That

is what

I think.

So I threw aside the veil of caution, there, far away, toward the big
city, the capital of decisions, Algiers, The Blue,
the green, The White
and, the exasperating.
Where men have decided
to keep quiet.
or: to offer
praises.

IV

: there were many arrests. Just as before 1962, people disappeared, after a summons, for three or four months, only to show up later on the other side of the big city, in the south.

And everyone kept quiet, because nobody understood any of it any more, except those who, once again, became part of the emigrant trail.

I was so afraid, there, deep in laughter and confusion. I was so afraid, so that my soul and my strength, the courage to be—that we call living—collapsed.

I was so afraid.

The terrible terrain of allegation. I live opposed to the misery of allegation, or its hate, or its wound. Some say the wise man prefers to bite his tongue on the idiom of the day.

The wise one? Or, the traitor: or the *jealous man,* he who keeps the day's silence for himself.

That is why—I buried the notebook. Written, in French, by the dead child, the child with a bullet in his forehead.

My soul has aged, all at once, like a leaf clinging to the fig tree's branch.

The nerve paths of speech, under the roots of the almond tree.

The fire stills burns today, despite incredulous thinking.

The incantation remains, for the country thirsts, thirsts. This is why I buried the notebook, and opened my love to those shadowed by exile and misfortune.

I even stayed in the village, near Rachida, the wisest of them, in my aunt's house, she who no longer spoke like us, she who stammered and hunted shadows faces nothings she thought were coming—right before her eyes—between her and us.

I took care to inform Ramdane, who has a position as military doctor in the region, but Ramdane told me right away that there was nothing more to be done, and that, very simply, you just had to entertain her once in a while in the courtyard.

I got what Ramdane was saying, but—as for me?

Rachida brought me into the room, offered me the house, since I was coming back from the front, no one else was. Rachida, whose hands were trembling like my lips.

A shivering, near the door, and I saw the aunt come in, her gaze upon me, like a sword.

—Why did you come back, why? There is nothing left alive here, why did you come back?

The voice is no longer the way it was—now cutting, and unmusical. The land is brought down, like a deer.

—Why?

I have no words to cross over the end of the world, only a gesture, to embrace my aunt, to die before her.

Her caresses are not simple signs of my coming back, but the body's memories, while her appeals come forth and the same old names crop up. To the earth she cries,

—Who are you, you whose body is made up of several? The mountain wind, or the prayer at the brick rampart, has fallen away from my lips, and I cannot even say what became of my heart. I lash out at returnings, in you, and the death of the first son, the death of his father. I want to live... to live... to learn all over again to live, against war. Here is my body: kill it; take it; or give it... I want to live...

I could clearly feel her hands letting go, on my back, and I felt her body suddenly relax. Rachida motioned to me to stretch her out on the bed, and took my hand to lead me from the room. "She'll sleep now, till night."

Outside it was still day, and hot.

Rachida took me towards the garden, across from the courtyard. I was feverish, and my mouth was unwilling to form words. So, no one came to the village any more, or, to this particular spot, for a long time. "No, no one," Rachida said, as if she understood what I could not come out with.

"And you, why are you here? Why isn't my aunt in Algiers, with all the relatives, or her brothers? Why is she so isolated, in her world of absence, her distress? I've seen the young partridge caught in terror in the gun-sights of men. I've seen her fine feet, like blades of grass, running around the grounds. And I've seen her head, maddened, darting in every direction. Why, alone, this way, with you?"

Rachida told me to wait there, a few minutes, in the garden invaded by rocks. As if the rocks... "Look," said Rachida. "Look."

My eyes search.

My head turns: it has been a long time since I saw that, so close, so mild, so quiet.

"Look, there, in among the rocks. Curious, isn't it? Completely odd that it would be there, this creature, under the rocks. You don't see it?"

My head swivels, for it is exactly as if someone has projected me several years back, several years, among the games and laughter of the animals.

This land is so full of games that at times it is frightening. There, among the rocks, while I am still reeling from my aunt's attitude. Rachida seems to have forgotten.

"I've been here eight months."

Look how it moves... Just as if someone were speaking inside its noggin. Someone extra-ordinarily alive, who thinks little of adversity, but instead digs his track with tenacity and joy, following his desire and his love.

Some people fear it, like a snake, or a jackal. "Yes... eight moths... Since... the fact is: she didn't want to stay in the village any longer, because they were beginning to say that the war's end was near... That's when she began to believe something completely impossible, as if by the sheer force of her belief anything might happen... Yes... It didn't happen overnight, but little by little, in alarming and baffling developments, depending on her moods and spells... She stayed on a chair, in the hall, listening for sounds... Then she would get up, and start walking the corridor, uttering a word here and there, or a murmur... Leila's kids started making fun of her... Yes, artlessly at first, then, directly and cruelly... Youcef and Zahir, the two youngest... So we had to do something, and Rachid asked me to leave with her, to Akbou... When..."

There, yes it has moved, slightly, off to her left. It is clearly very young, and still distrustful in its world of stones and short grass. "When we got here, she was no longer in any condition to handle noises... Her soul had become nervous, panicky in her waiting, for those returning... That's how she spent her days... waiting for something impossible... As if the returns could mean something new for her... entirely new and alive... as in those moments when the country assured its survival without weapons...I don't know how it was that she learned the name of the guy who denounced the men of the village to the soldiers... nor how she learned what day the people gave their verdict, but." This time, he gets more confident, comes out into the daylight. It is true times have changed, and that those beings still alive leave their holes, just to have a look, to breathe. Why didn't I think of that before? Why didn't I go to question him, him, first thing, before coming here, over the road.

However: words exist, along with the speech within words. "I will take you to him, on the narrow paths of the land and of life. He is on top of the hill in the village... And it appears that he remains there, day and night, wide awake."

Without a word, Rachida has taken Mokrane's left hand, has begun to count the cross-ways lines. She counts eight, which, without any doubt, means very little, but, there she goes starting to speak and to say, as if it could perfectly well be true, "Your suffering is over, because the number eight is the number of perpetual revolution... There are all sorts of resonances between what you can see, make up, think and say. Visible, perceptible correspondences... That is what is inscribed in this number... A real connection among all things... Which you have to find, and quietly follow, genuinely follow, without..."

A real connection among all things: Rachida's hand, among all things, the thing that leads and measures my return: "Don't believe that love is a kind of absence... On the contrary: it is a power, of being, and reunion... That's what it is... How does the world hold together, without some active element among things?"

Rachida does not speak, no longer speaks, but I know what she wants to say, because I was brought up in this prescience of unspoken words, speeches accumulated in the ancestral and arid mutism of our ancestors. That is why we have to understand women's silence, its unbelievable range beyond ourselves; while we judge ourselves to be rooted in another place, world, and universe.

love

the strange perfectibility of human separation: our worlds have opposing laws, violent ones impossible to break.

Our laws?

—But who are you?...

Yes... Tell me who you are... For it has been a long time that my body, and my voice, wander lost in the streets and cataclysm of the towns...

Who are you?

Or will I have to wait some more

here,

for the return

of my soul

or my body

astray in the wound of trees and men?... What remains of the other voice?... The one whose aim was to encircle the villages and the stones, the fountains and the springs...

Who are you?

For... this heading that leads me back to the village was not made to give me back my joy... the joy I would have liked to know and live...

That is when I felt her breathing, and her soft slow breath reaching my forehead, and my throat

as if we were no longer there,

seated

in the garden

but rather *lying* on the ground and the grass

as if our bodies and our mouths had exchanged their most intimate anguishes and silences,

as if we were no longer there *sitting*

but as if we had reached the limits of our deepest wanderings and disarrays.

what to call all this? "*I will tell you*

her story," said Rachida.

"*...I will tell you her story, so your hand no longer trembles... so your legs no longer tremble... I will tell you her story, so your desire no longer trembles... Do you know?...*

Do you know why..."

Rachida gently took my hand, and led me beside the tree, the one that sketches so much lightness and offering in the sky that, from spring on, its fruit are lively apparitions, about to yield up all their substance:

what I would like to know about (and even to know)—contrary to what I used to believe—is what happened, here, *in the village and in my aunt's youth because her head has shattered—*I know this now… I know it—*into several pieces and ideas*

: I would like it if, in your thoughts, there were only desires and memories of complete and uninterrupted enjoyment

like these: Rachida?

I'd like to ask you something Rachida?

ask you to grant me a returning

the true returning…

the one whose truth and pathway I have sought through years of study, years of exile, years of peace, and years of war…

yes: the true path,

the one that can lead my heart there, and my senses, there, before the door of my rest, and might instruct me in possessing it and the richness of its being, possessing its discourse and its innocence

yes: Rachida?

"…Tremble no more…

I will retell its progression for you,

and its trajectory.

Its dying in God's silence…

Tremble no more: the site of the world is now overturned, transformed, and there comes a playing

a play of air and wind

there, in the clay hills, for we must live with some belief… Very few understand these things; the most important ones, the most useful ones because it is in this game, yes, in the game… so I will tell you its story, and its dying in the silence of god… like a tree shifting and torn… a tree gone off in search of its roots and its shapes… a tree caught in all the meanings and silences of god… A tree shifting, free, and torn… a tree… in the dying and the silence of god…"

Rachida drew near again, and I realized that I was only a bursting among the world's many elements, I was opened up, strangely resembling the torn, exposed roots of a young and not yet fully identified tree; a wild bursting, and Rachida had no obligation to explain anything at all to me, to help me understand what might have happened, here, in this house where, after all, I had been so long absent.

"The first days must be like a long listening, because words flow for whoever knows how to hear and recognize them. There is no mystery, in these places where, after so many years, you come back to strengthen your vision and your heart—but instead gifts or offerings that the earth brings forth, expresses. Certain facts are not recognized, being of little use, just like certain ways of speaking, seeing, being; but that does not reduce their power and their reality, in the strength and youth of men."

Rachida drew near, and I realized that all would become clear to me, all, so to speak, in one moment:

"Now we have to wait until evening, that's when he comes back...
You'll see...

On his return he brings a few songs and a few sayings: you'll see... but... his manner has changed: he doesn't have the same tone of voice... the same simpleness... He says things about what happened and that we know must be true although no one can now say what really happened...

Long arguments with the aunt and the trees, that was the beginning of a vast bewitching... Yes, bewitching, because it was as if—and this has stayed with me to this day—he could get inside of us, not just with his thought, but with his body, yes, his body, and with many things besides; as if we had become nothing but his expression, his phrases, his face, his desires, and his spells...

As if... because he says things that take us far from ourselves, that kill us...

literally: that kill
us.

But it's better that he enter you, that he take you over, comfort you. That he name you, tell you what he has never told. That he..."

Rachida insisted I give up my hands to her. That my eyes fill with that incurable sweetness of the earth, as if the other voyage were then beginning. The voyage where, now barely back in the village, true destinies lived again. As if: And a kind of possession was already at work, violent and painful, spirited and vibrant, like an impossible reason inscribed in death, or in giving birth.

PART TWO

The Village

Primita,
llévame al huerto
que estoy
cayéndome
muerto.

—Copla Flamenca

V

The game on the clay hill: I remember his brow and his eyes on the hill of clay; his way of riding a horse, and wearing his light *burnous*, over his back. No one could restrain his desire to cleave the hill, the way you split a log, or a skull, for, back then, he addressed his prayer to the hill, to no one else.

His father wanted the game to end, because he thought it was nothing but a game, merely a child's game, or an adolescent's, on the verge of leaving childhood.

In this way certain separations hold true, between men and children, when it comes to games; and the separations become violent starting when the game feeds into a violent territory.

The father thought it was only a simple game, until the day when:

Here you are: the world torn open, like an animal whose wounds are being salted.

This is not a return to the past, for our past is nowhere, these days— hurled and spread in memories that have been falsified by too many centuries.

And how to exist beyond The Book? Out in the fields, in the richness of my desires and lights.

I have already wasted too much time, and I'm young, with the type of youth they describe as having known slavery.

You have to go beyond the limits set up on the inside of the territory. We cannot be free and, at the same time, stay cloistered in the word of The Book.

There you have it, what I call the "Renaissance" or *Nahda*. This reversal of The Book, in our hearts, to teach us to think.

Here it is, what I call the "Renaissance," this rediscovery of our freedom.

Father, I have been a disciple, in my master's *Zaouia*. But, today, The Book has changed its aim, and its readers.

I have questioned the hill, and the hill has told me more than The Book, and all its pages.

I have questioned the valley, and the valley has shown me more things than The Book, and all its pages.

I have questioned the mountain, and the mountain has demanded more of me than The Book, and all its pages.

I have questioned my brothers, and my brothers have had more answers than The Book, and all its pages.

And then I knew the following choice: to be a disciple of The Book, or a being in the world?

Father, I tell you these things even while my heart is still written down in the *Zaouia* of my master.

But, my

suffering, father?

(my suffering)

wishes to go beyond The Book.

I want

to be,

over there,

in

the free

play of the world.

Father, if there are words that came before my birth, those are the ones I want to understand; *yes,* the ones that lead back, *together,* man and the world, and, *not those which condemn* man and the world.

What I want, in the extreme, today, is god defeated, or god deceased, and thus the sharpest impact of human speech.

I will leave, for I have nothing more to do here, nothing. I feel as though I belong to another world, a world truly other. The Book is no longer enough for me, I have to somehow reach the world, beyond The Book.

I'm thirsty, father, thirsty for the delusions of stone and tree, the delusions of earth and river. Man cannot live on his knees, or seized with periodic genuflections, motivated by a desire for god.

I have listened to the words of The Book, and felt, within me, a sort of slavery; yes, exactly as if I were supposed to learn my bondage, carry slavery within me. There are already too many separations between beings, as if the world had been given to us to then be torn apart.

Please understand me, father: I want nothing, at this point, but to escape The Book, the one that had so many disciples and prophets in the Maghreb.

I want to understand the world, without The Book.

Yes, father.

There is where the land has led me, gently, voluptuously, within me, toward the words of tree and wind, as if tree and wind wanted to dwell in me, as if, gently, voluptuously, the land was in me, as if grass, stone, water and the far field and fountain were in me, running all through the insides of body and dream.

I'm going to leave the village, for the moment has come, to knock at the door of a restful stay. In spite of my youth, I know that is where man avoids mistaking himself.

Yesterday I led my platoon far around the police road-blocks. There is no doubt that he whose name has reached the very hills of light will come back tomorrow, in the afternoon. I'm sorry you can't come, father, the hills look so happy, right now. Why create trouble? As long as the game exists, the one that brings you to the edge of your irruption.

Why renew troubles?

Father, I no longer want to listen, but hear, yes: hear, without having to kneel. This is where the land has led me, gently, voluptuously, within me.

Its route is my resting place.

I would have liked to know other things, but, here, up till now, there's nothing else, just this land not yet deployed, and calling out.

I've visited the well of the guardian, the cave of meaning, the country of the founder. No offense to those weighed with sad and unsustainable reason, I have learned to name the place of a new abode.

A country's wealth is never apparent, because true richness is disguised, hidden, sneaks away from the surface glance to keep on living out of sight. That is how old Nouria came to talk to me about the land of the founder, the land that exists beyond other lands, about how it bears up above it, like a plateau of earth: fruit, and lies.

I saw Nouria in that house built in and under the rock, in the flank of the hill and its brush, Nouria who only rarely leaves her land to go down to the village. She was wearing a dress of blue cloth, very long, but torn in several places, just like her flesh and her heart. Nouria had me come in and sit near the fire, on a woodpile she had covered with old rags.

She spoke, yes, at great length, while I listened and watched the flames dancing before me, like horses gone mad, sparkling, and free. Nouria has a voice I know well; the same intonation as her mother, but a faster rhythm. Nouria never wanted to leave the hill, even when the war had seized it, and was lashing out on all sides with no decency, no respect.

Many from the village tried to bring Nouria back, but they would have had to watch her all the time, after that, cloister her, or… kill her, because she would have tried to run away, to run away…

Despite her age, Nouria is unusually strong, with a strength that comes from her treks and her labors among the rocks and hills.

She has a house that is sort of built into the earth, in the side of the hill, not far from the *Zaouia*, which you could call a cave. Nouria has lived there many long months, after moving toward the South of the country.

They say—but this was many years ago—that Nouria was very beautiful, but that, from early on, they kept her outside the village and away from men, and she had to come up with her own food and acquaintances.

Nouria was an illegitimate child, whose dark complexion occasioned violent arguments in the village, all the more because her mother was in fact the wife of the head of the village council.

Most of the villagers saw a warning in this birth. Something very ancient, and very new at the same time, was going to happen, sometime soon. The place or the time of this event mattered little: the main thing was knowing it was going to happen.

Songs were numerous, despite the recent destructions and violations of territory: the Occupier had smashed the last resistance of men and villages. There was no doubt—the child had to be removed from the village, and hidden in the hills, or sent South, near the earliest paths.

The years back then—people speak of the years before the actual occupation, starting in 1871 (Nouria's birth date is only approximate, but still somewhere between 1881 and 1892)—were the most terrible years of our lives, for, from that time on, we were defeated.

Until what era, what day, which year would this last?

The Elder made a point of our misfortune and our weakness: *"No one can live alone, such is the law of our land. We have to win, out in the world, in the reality of the world, in the face of this first war. That is the law of new lands."*

The Elder said many things, all of which touched our pride and our various ignorances. It was true, the country had not seen very far ahead, at the time of the first armed conflicts with the Occupier.

The country had even made one frightful error: not opening up all the land of the territory, but only one part, the part that was only an inconsistent reflection of its ego.

The people had always thought themselves sheltered, behind their mountains of rock and wind; ever distanced from the plains, the shooting, and politics. Men did not believe in their own encircling.

That fact is they themselves only lasted, or rather, crossed through their duration, following the old rhythms, misfortunes, words, and habits. Men did not want to change, but only to keep on being, this same way, as always, poor, almost naked, and proud.

People had no desire to change, trade their wool clothes for silk, or their silence, for blah-blah-blah.

People had no desire to change, but, the World? *Yes, the World?*

What did the World want?

Yes, that other World? The one that crushed everything as it went by, imposed everywhere the same forces, the same delirium, the same belief systems, and the same rites.

What did the other World want? The one that was now materializing, all the way up to the hills?

Men tried to resist, and, without taking up arms, made use of their indifference.

But what kind of power is there in indifference?

None: indifference leads to slavery; and the villages, men, hills—even those we thought beyond reach—became enslaved, because of a whole system of indifference.

The Elder denounced separation, and isolation: the country could only exist in the world, nowhere else.

That is why we had to fight.

Men, their words, their labors, and their fields, they too are part of the countryside, just like death, or time, or war, or the wind.

Myself?

Rather, which myself?

Here, in the uninterrupted tide of the land and the day, summoned toward a partial diction, of love and play: me?

All in all, death does not exist, because all is life, this is even true under torture, and in tears.

Death is life.

: *life.*

because everything is life, even unto death.

why not live?

Nouria threw another log on the fire, even though the cold was not very intense; maybe she wanted more light, there, at that spot where her eyes interrogate my coming, my forehead, my face, and my age.

Nouria sat down, facing me, on a blanket spread over a mat.

Nouria is poor, terribly poor, deprived of most of the things you see elsewhere, in other places and other houses, things that embellish life for the rich.

Nouria is poor, like a field of broom or heather, invaded by scorpions, and brambles.

A terrible locus of richness, and of murder: Nouria sits, facing me, her gaze burning with fever and courage.

I want no fallacious image of my own country, images that guarantee its hypocrisy or venality. I want absurd images, insolent ones, and old, equivalent to the origins of its presence.

Real images, those that challenge your vision and your person, like this one, in which, abruptly, I am caught.

Nouria's arm came to my neck, roughly, while her left hand went in search of something I prefer not to name.

Nouria is not angry, despite her arm's grip, on my neck, on the bones of my neck.

I feel her hair, supple on my left cheek, because Nouria wears her hair braided on the right side, in a long, soft tress, tied in a blue cloth, just a piece of her dress, torn in so many places.

Something cold runs across my throat, and everything is now humid, because, just here, tears have poured into my eyes.

Tears, red, and hot, that do not belong to me, still they…

In truth, my body is intimately linked to Nouria's pleasure, she who, in a slow, sweet caress, goes about dividing the skin that unites head and neck.

There are unfathomable passages among the surfaces of life, among their extensions in territories far from sight. In this way every birth could be grasped as a resurrection dependent on an act, whose origin is inscribed in the figure, the geometry, of a place.

What does the beginning, or the origin, of a place matter, for, what matters is the design, or architecture of a place.

For the village, Nouria is situated exactly at the crossroads of the *Zaouia* and ancient gods; and this, even though she was born late, and came forth like a *stranger*…

Only, after a few years off in the South, the *stranger* was back, old, and still in chains.

She was taken to the blacksmiths in the market, who, after some wrangling, decided to remove her chains, and to replace the steel links with bracelets of brass or silver. None should forget, seeing her, that she had once been chained.

Today every woman and girl wears these bracelets, and should remember that they bear witness to the first liberation, and to being enslaved.

The *stranger* quickly understood what lived within her adornment, in the bracelet, in the chains: a kind of explosive pairing, where the rivalries of war and the world appeared.

Thus was the soul constituted, a work of fire and steel, and the artisan had stepped in, this time, as a liberator of hidden forces.

At least that is what Nouria thought, since, without resorting to some violence or other, she left the village for good to live on that crossroad spot between a truth revealed by The Book, and the pure vitality of fire.

No one believed, at first, in any practical result of this retreat, but, day after day, year after year, anger took over the roots and the fields, eloquent witnesses to the wretchedness of lands.

In the eyes of every being, the sky burned the future—and the calm speech of the junebug, suddenly, achieved the blazing of the scorpion.

Every day, Nouria stirred the fire.

A fire of dry trees and thistles still wearing their mild, blue faces, like blades.

From time to time, but always at some distance from her dwelling, the inhabitants of the village climbed toward the hill and the fire, their eyes devoured by the flames that, night after night, danced deep in their eye-sockets, those cavities crowded with hallucinations, but which, for once, where aimed in one direction; every night, the territory was radiant with fury.

The hill flamed for three or four hours, while the circle of visionaries and voyeurs grew and grew.

Nouria, agitated, or perhaps hurried by all the past and future generations, addressed her supplications and praises to the Spirits of Revolt and Sacrifice, already alerted by the fire's feats.

The setting began to overflow the narrow, silent frame of the night, to reach, though shyly, some of the day's moments.

Between labors, the inhabitants of the surrounding hills and valleys learned how to shoot again: the smell of gunpowder mixed with the shadows fleeing over the rocks, the torrents, the new grass, the young sprouts, and the fields. Each spring, new celebrations broke out whenever the hunters gathered.

The proceedings took place in front of the Occupiers, who, all the while keeping their grip on the scene, considered these spring reunions as vague and utterly uncouth vestiges of practices or rites that were now dying off.

The people translated poems or prayers addressed by the hunters or their women to the gods of the mountains and springs.

(The rivers of snow
slide once again
over the frigid skin

of the Sun.)
(The mountain's life
                    is
all the newer
each year: the sky
            has opened its throat
                        the night
            which,
            like clay,
            flows
            on the earth.)
(Red is the color of the world's blood
like an eye, sad and lovely,
in the flow of clay.)
(Men are no longer afraid.)
(The mouth is no longer bitter
            but,
            the sweet,
            rough hide of a ram.)
(Man plays)
(his hand open
  on the world)
      (as if he
      were taking
      an Egg
      or his
      thought
      to create
      the next one).
(Man plays
his hand open
  on the world.)
(Red is the blood
of the world,
      luminous,

like a bull
blown up,
in the clay.)
(luminous,
    like a man,
blown up,
        in
        the clay.)

VI

A few stages, and praises too, are necessary, to interrupt the absurd rigor of crimes and murders.

To combat and shatter the foreignness of another man, for the greater collective peace. I will always live against that…

It is here that…

And I see the garden,

I am in the garden

as

the star

is in

the sky.

He

who speaks

is no

longer alone,

named as he is

in all

existing

words.

It is here that…

And the word

exists

knotted in the

tree

like

the almond's

tender flower.

The veil

is

now

lifted

since

the word's age
is inscribed
in the
reddish pages
of the notebook.
The very
body
is word
even
unto
its burning…

It is here that… Rachida did not interfere, rather a motion of the wind, there, in the branches of the almond tree, and that mildness I was able to read, there, in the eloquent visibility of matter.

You have to learn to read between the lines of the sky, and of the tree, in the gaps that overflow with light and possibility.

The landscape's offering, the day has a supple, humid breath, dropped on the grass, or its scattered sparseness over the surface of the world.

\A supple, humid breath, resembling man and woman's stay on the surface of the world.

A violent stay, and mild, linked to the peregrinations of words and actions: the world opened up that first time, in it, then the tree, and its luxuriant green, its olfactory overflowing.

The curve was born from the powerful immensity of love and sky, for, no portion of shadow or night is bare of union, or unity. The curve was born of this hope, held out towards unity.

If certain limits exist, all they are is the expression of man's wandering intensities, lost in the immensity of woman, and his desire.

Man is nothing, but he wants everything.

The tree exists in the countryside, and
also woman,
like a mirror
among
the stones,
Or the other unstable

Slope
of the world,
Avid and warm
in the amazement
of the Wellspring.
I am,
I exist,
like a complete bond
of this palpable and warm
surface
that we call The World,
my circle,
and my law.
I have no love
for the destroyers
of my joys,
the natural waves
of speech blooming
out of great dreams.

Here is the earth: a woman birthed by the sea, whom I have seen, tucking her hair in with each crash of the waves. The hill is her song.

Nouria did not let go, but sank her blade in the open speech of Death.

My fear grew, because

Nouria had become wild,

With a wildness that was intransigent, conscious of ruptures: in fact—*and this is what I have come to understand*—I have to flee the village where, *the orchard, sweet gathering of mother and neighborhood, is going to die of sorrow, like a donkey. I have a multiple kind of speech, in me, but the hill's song has become violent from its new course. A new risk, enlivened and carried by the song, beyond the hills, into the villages, to the very gates of the houses and the orchards, toward those places where hope stays alert like a hunting greyhound. The valleys open their arms where, more and more often, men from every direction arrive on forced marches*—yes, I must flee the village, these places where death strikes men down, and locks them deep in the courtyards, *like poultry. I had someone warn my father, because I find it impossible to tell him, straight out,* I'm leaving the village, to meet you *I don't have the heart for it, or the breath, I do not need to appear* disarmed *before him, once again, but, what I do want, is Si Moh's horse, the one whose hide is sleek, black, and shuddering, who obeys the slightest press of my hand, my foot, the ground. Further on, there lies the other country, opened up by the power of the horse's gallop, the land of necessary encounters, the place where the child loses his first body, to take on the world. I*

Nouria is bent over my head, and I see her smile, a smile blossoming before me, like a bush, or a bouquet. Her mouth is indeed young, her lips slightly parted, moist, so close to mine that some warmth travels through me, as when in the shade of the orchards, I use to have, now and again, Rachida's body.

Still, the blade is always there, in the word, deep in my throat, while Nouria's face shows a treachery or an immense imposture.

I am thirsty, for
my blood
flows
black and
red, in the sparkling light of the fire.
I am thirsty
and
warm.
I must lose my body
here,
truly,
yet again,
to transform
the space
of the hill.
My body?

Nouria is now on top of me, and her hands, thin and gliding, open up my skin, as if the lamb had not yet appeared,

or the ram...

I can see my skin,

on edge, as you say,

in the fire's hands.

Speech attained on the clay hill, grasped among the ravines and paths, the body is touched two times, the legs, then the forehead, and its face explodes, like a fury on the surface of the world.

A sweet face, and open, blasted by war, here, on the move, in the hill of clay.

Men run, chasing their being, or their luck, while the Archer points out new trajectories of strength.

The body stumbles, totters, and falls: my god, how stupid the world is, with an unbearable weakness and wretchedness, since, from time to helpless time men die or faint away like grains of wheat or millet, thrown for good into the river.

Between truth and faith, the passageway remains murky, even though the Archer is there, among the hopes and dreams, to show the paths.

This is how fire took hold in the hearts of men, since, from the first flames, and before the body was completely burnt, the Archer, out of the most profound métier, and alone, handed out the words, and the resting places.

The mother weeps

at

the death

of her son

while

the father

lives on

in the son's

strength.

Nouria is present, in the crazy action of the flames. Her hands have already nursed the body, and destroyed the burns.

Death flees

The vast space of a song urging human hopes, like men's arms over plowed land. The earth opens strange places in me, passionate ones, and savage. I will tell you its story, so that your hand no longer trembles, so that your desire no longer trembles...

I will tell you its story so that your lips no longer tremble, and you know how to answer the questions that will invade this world...

I will tell you the story of the real connection between things, its progression, in the tall grass... its dying in god's silence...

I will tell you

of its face But, cease your trembling... the site of the world is now toppled, changed, and sort of *turned around*...

Tremble no more,

because the game exists,

now,

the play of air

and wind,

on the clay hill...

Few understand these things, these most important things, on account of their murderous proximities and vivacities, while I know,

me,

that it is in the

game

that we live.

What does the beginning matter, or the origins, what matters is the design, or the architecture of a place, as with the bracelet first worn then abandoned, because, here is how it happened, each time I came back, to the village, towards him, who was supposed to be, later on, my husband, but who, it turned out, never was.

I'm the one who brought back the aunt, that is, his mother, to the village, after the uncle was taken away, and the six long months spent in Algiers.

And as for me, how did I not fall apart?

How did I resist, in the waiting for returns, for prayers, here, next to this woman whose gestures and words already belonged to a completely separate world.

How did I not run away? Didn't I run down to the river, or the spring, to drink every drop there was, and in that way slake my body with coolness, newness, and innocence.

We used to take leave, in the garden—this goes back quite a few years before the war—during the great heat, just when the village, the house, and the earth's and the day's breathing stopped, at the moment when everything seemed a prisoner of space, immobilized by the weight of the place, its heat, its insistence, the moment when every movement, gesture, or footstep, or laugh, caused a kind of fracture in the air or your breath, as if the air, or your breath, had become palpable, solid, vastly spread out around us and all the objects.

We spoke little then, but our mouths were alive, intensely alive, avid for touches, tastes, and surprises.

I had my first orgasm with him, and it tore my skin and my throat, in one move, and that liquid, beautiful and white, that rose in me, covered my belly and breasts: I actually saw different things, heard new things, as if the earth was really opening up, and I…; but, maybe you too want to hear something different, because, I can already see your embarrassment, that you're not opening up to me, because all you want is to know, and not to hear, or, understand, truly, from the bottom of your soul, what love of life is, or love of death.

Learn this, that I wept over his death,

yes, but, unlike her, I was not despairing, and I didn't weaken: the book was there, finally written on the world, the trees, the springs, the hills and the olive trees.

I thought, for a second, a short but cruel moment, that he would never come back, then, unlike her beliefs, that thought vanished, and I sensed something else, and I opened my eyes, touched the ground and the almond tree. No one believed me, but I, I saw him, there, embedded in the bark, in the wood, I saw him alive, and happy, the bullet had left no mark, and his brow was young and pale, in the wood.

Surely I ran towards him.

Surely I touched his mouth and his stomach, surely I grabbed his hands and his face. Nouria was there, leaning against an incandescent sun, while I was able to almost completely penetrate the tree, and lie down in it.

Really, I was alone, because she didn't come to the garden any more. Two months after we came back here, she was only living in a corner of the house, right where you came in, with a room, and the courtyard where, in clear, warm weather, she would spend her nights, sitting on a mat, her eyes turned to the sky and the stars.

This is her way of finding some relief, and of then being able to bear witness to the immense pain her madness holds.

My motions, she said—her hand snatching at thousands of insects and thoughts—have turned toward the pixies, the *djnouns*, the tiny ones.

Despite my attacks, it's hard to grab one, because these are really miniscule horsemen who live and project themselves through the light, that you see crossing through thousands of worlds every second.

I'd like it if one of them took me away, all at once, to those places where, surely, he is, yes him, lovely and alive, but, it's as if they refuse my appeal, to go off so far, into those limpid regions, so unknown to them.

Then, she falls silent, and invents silence, a silence where I understand everything, as in that moment when, there, among the stones, the hedgehog comes forth, here, among our words and caresses, towards the roots of the almond tree.

The world opens up
and I understand
everything *blue moon*
that walks
its alternating walk
on the firmly laid sky
Grass course
where the murderer
of the day
runs away, on the
Western Slope of
fear
men walk
in this way
their eyes cast
beyond the day.
It is cold... Cold...
the torrent of water is glacial... almost frozen... caught in the last
veins *of winter.*

We still have to climb the hills, all those hills that, in this land, are going to drink the first refrain of space...

This first refrain of space?

Will the grass tell it to me?

Or will the night?

blue moon, walking, like this, backwards, among the trees... The blue moon, this way, among the trees; the day's milk darkened, and our march, like the moon's, among the trees: I see the world swelling, like a head, among the trees; right now, as my eyes rest on the other's back, the: dozen men in the silence of the day. A marching step is a beat in the diction that spreads on the earth's surface. Man's violence, when he cannot defend his wound with one word.

Now the march is stretched out, since day ended, and the roadblock is six hours removed from all these hills, and it is lighted, now and again, like a shining river, running beneath the Western Slope of fear.

You could no longer get any sentence, in the village, but these two, united, like two sabres slashing the night: death, or expulsion, men chose death (or life) in the asperity of certain songs, those uttered by the women, against servitude...

Men of the hill Above
do you know the river?
Inscribed
like a word
in the villages
Below:
Do you know
the river?

PART THREE

The Changes

Cada vez que considero
que me tengo que morir
tiendo la capa en el suelo
y me harto de dormir.

—Copla Flamenca

VII

Words of the World of Hope and of the Universe   The stars are shown as a point dyed with henna. Written. At the center of the palm of their Hands.

The Women have put on their very best clothes. The ones that cover their shoulders. Their chests. Their legs. Like manifold flowers scattered over the hills. And. The fields. Their waists are bound. Squeezed in belts of gold and brass. On their brows the writing spells the offerings they give to the villages. To the fields. Daily they are stirred by the same gestures. The same breaths of air. The same hopes. The same tyrannies.

Their dream of freedom is immense. Stretched over the World like a wide net where men's words and actions will surely end up getting caught. For not a single woman exists in this land who does not want, today, to live the present and future of her own life.

And this: Independently of the tyranny of men, and their regressive legislations.

For: in their raiment of Sky and Stars, Women dream of transgressing, against their secular submissions. Of acting. According to their own boldness. Their profusions. Sensibilities.

Against men.

Or: their pretensions of strength.

The women echo in this way. The meaning of other Visions other Words. That name Insurrection. Independence. and. War. As if they have issued forth from their Wills. Desires. Liveliness.

 : *the sun's reach?*

Or, the night's silence? The thwarted loves of our bodies and thoughts, given up to the tastes and rigors of alliances and despotisms. We have not yet gotten out of our silences and constraints. Our language is not yet born. But our desire to break the laws set up against us is: immense.

And still today. Caught up in the inequality of laws and powers. We fall back on our old resources. And. In the glimmering of the Stars inscribed on the Sky. and. in our hands?—We point out to the men the very point of our attack. and. our drawing away.

Because: the two worlds that compose our existences are opposites. Opposed in their truths, and, effervescences. Our desires manifest themselves in silences, and, the darkness of nights, only to manifest themselves, in this way, in the rising of the day.

Our desires?

   (Youth touched)

    (Youth smashed)

Our cherished desires?

Because: We understand only with great difficulty man's pleasure, and, his quiet way of coming, while we, we are absent from this pleasure, face turned toward the other pleasure, the world.

We understand with great difficulty, and, during the feast, or, the ritual, we beg

  : the village

  or the valley

  the hills

  or the fields

because: We have no other way to speak our world, or, our abandonment, and its site, there, within man's desire, and, his preponderance.

We beg, then

  : the Tree, the Conqueror of the earth, and of the sky, the one we never underestimate, who fights for us, who speaks for us, bears witness for us.

The one whose body is not foulness, but truth of language, of land, and, of men, the one who listens to our abandonment, gives it

  Justice and Worth

  (Our young and sharp

  desires:

  our young women's

  pleasure

  destroyed, forbidden).

Man might have been our surest vestment, but, man has undressed our tenderness, as he undressed our bodies, brutally, hearing none of the cries, and, rendings.

  Man?

We have no other way of speaking our world, or, the site of our abandonment, there, within man's desire, and his preponderance.

So
   do you
      understand
   Me?
      woman isolated
        by the earth
      and
      the clay
        Do you
           understand
              Me?

Young Man
   killed
      in your
   Exile.
           Do you
                understand
                      Me?

The day, however, had arrived.
That day when.

After the Exiles
well known to us.

Young Women
of the hills
and of the men.

Many
are the Exiles
on the inside of our
souls
our villages
our fields.

The Exiles
of our bodies
and freedoms: the Exiles.
Vigilance
is
our lot: since we live
surrounded.

> *Young Women*
> *of the Hills*
> *and of the men.*

> by walls
> and by
> defenses.

THE EXILES

That day
when we were supposed to prepare
the meals
for their returns
and the
wedding vows

That day

Do you
       understand
             Me?

That

    dust

    streaming

    there

    powder

    of tears

    powder kept going

    by the puffs

    of wind

    or of

    light.

Do you   You

understand   would not have

Me?   recognized

                        the village

                        streaming

                          there

                          twisted

                      animated   vibrant

                      in

                      its every

                      street.

And

the mouths

of Women

who.

    Young Women

    of the Hills

    and of the Men.

        You

        would not have

        recognized

the village   *there*

           the gardens

that
day
newly
opened
and
set free.

the gardens?

the *smiles*
of the Young Women
powder
of
tears
kept going
by
the
war.

You
would not
have: recognized
the
village
but: the men,
and, that woman, *old,*
with horribly widened eyes
who, also, ran, *there*
in the streets, where the feet of the villagers, and the peasants escaped
from the mountains, and the plains, also streamed: likewise, arrived not to
be present at the bustle of buying and of selling, but,
that day, at the exchange of gifts (promises of lives lived beyond
exile, and, beyond deaths)
of meals
: the day for

Lehbia
had come.
: the day
for *Farida*
or for *Louiza.*
the day
when
your *body*
gets lost
there (or your
return) *here*
in the
intensity
of my wound
and my vow.
…………………..
How many nights
spent in
the distant peregrinations
of my memory-acts.
……………………
How many Shadows
painful vigils
peopled by
the worries of those beings
abandoned
by the world.
How many
days
?

  Do you
  understand
  Me?

    Do you
    understand

Me?

. . . .

A murder

has taken

place

(Oh Young Man

attentive

to the other spaces

of the land

and the world.)

(a murder)

that

robs me of

the love

of your return

and

your

playing.

Do you

    understand

      Me

        ?

I

    desired *you*

ardently

the way one

wants to understand

one day

the world's truth,

our thirst

for being and for freedom.

I

    imagined

nothing

but: I thought

that
freedom
is not
death—within
or out beyond
us—rather
existence affirmed
by the day's speech
and life's,
existence all one with
the jealousy and the
simplicity of our relations,
our lives,
relationships laboriously built,
constructed,
built up *undefined*
against the absurdity
and cynicism
of the Postwar's
evil spells.
....
Oh *Joy*
of returns
and of plains
mountains
and springs
my *mouth*
waited for *you*
my lips
needed *you*
because I had acquired a taste
and a life—
lightness and
heaviness too—for this
thought

of seeing *you*
finally appear
and *liberate* me.

....

Oh *Joy*
Young Women
of the hills
and of men
: Here I am
grown old
with eyes
horribly wide
and
: spinning.

....

Oh *Joy*

: I learned, in that circled space we call youth, the words of sacrifice, and of dishonor, and all I got from that was the squalid widowhood of the land, and, of the world, both centered on my old woman's pain, a disabled old woman at that, me, and stricken, by the shock, the violence of my loves, and their prohibitions.

A youth thrown away in sacrifice, and opposing dishonor: when they came to take me to the village Below, no man had touched my arms, nor my legs. I lived in one of the last houses, out past the square, happy, used to coming and going, far beyond the house and the courtyard, way out to the first family-owned fields, the fountains, and wells—and, happy.

Autumns and winters found us settled around fires, almost immobilized by the snow, the cold, and the mud, toiling at each new apparition of the sun and the day: our fingers wove wools, and grasses, to make clothes, baskets or mats. Every day, sitting by the fire, we renewed its attraction, and the old necessity, of deep and revived warmth.

We let the fires—their sharp movements, gaudy, wild, untamed—take over our hair, our will, our imaginings: we let them spread over our reveries of violent enjoyments, because, during that time, we were all hoping for the festivals of spring, real horseback rides through the fields—real desires, real inexperience.

For

: we were

by all evidence

: inexperienced.

Inexperienced in our choices, our possibilities.

Inexperienced, and, jealous.

: in spite of all common sense, our fingers wove, quickly, and we caused springtime to rise up, and summers too, woven against the wishes of our brothers, and our parents.

Young, and alive, lost, in the prison of men, there was little we could do deep in those villages and fields. We had to be alert for the night, for the silences, because, sooner or later, the man would come, here, into the courtyard, to take what was his, and—his pleasure.

We could never escape the privileges, and orders, of the adults. Those who had a voice in the village assembly: and the adults let those who *should* have chosen us go away—those who could have taken us far from our future sorrows, and miseries. Despite what we wanted, we could not escape the privileges, the orders, of the adults. So that we might live a life far from constraint and the ancient and precise rites that grounded our present and future, as much as plowing, as much as harvest.

: men know, in the depth of their solitude, and selfishness, that we belong to them, as much as their clothes do, or, their strength, as much as their suffering, or their good fortune.

Privileges of unawareness, and of strength. They made laws that multiplied their advantages, all the while suspecting that, here and there, grew secret revolts, and that you had to head them off, or defeat them.

They brought in survival experts, legislation too, decided that the harvests, and women's revolts, were the most dangerous things, for these things endangered the walling off, and the foundations, of the lands.

They announced edicts meant to contain women in their apparent submissions.

From that moment on, every being had to invent his own defenses: the law's reach was long, touching not only customs, but the enduring of families, and of fields. So, women put on their finest clothes, those that covered their shoulders, chests and legs; their waists were squeezed in belts of gold and brass. On their brows were written the offerings they brought for the villages, for the men, the fields. Every day urged on, by the same gestures, the same breaths, the same submissions.

On the palm of their hand the stars were represented by a miniscule dot, colored in henna.

Young Women of the Hills and Fields: become, someday, that free and nervous speech that breaks laws, favoritisms, injustices: a speech emerging from iron, from tree, from grass, from livelihood: worthy pursuit of the elements: do not invent new wounds, but new depths in your smiles, and in your joys: the world is there, hanging in your gesture, like the star shown in the heavenly body in your hand.

VIII

To each thought there is a corresponding act: an act arising from matter, or, the senses, an act justifying, or irremediably condemning, life and its events. In truth, of all the deaths that took place in Uncle Saddek's house—a house to be sold now, by his inheritors, brothers, sisters, themselves now older, pressured to sell by their own sons and descendants—of all these deaths, none could really be known, that is, real-ly observed, not just by those present, right then, at the moment of death, but even by those who had lived and worked in the village for a long time.

Such events were bound to happen, not only because of life's requirements, and the changes, the inexorable unspooling of lives, of ages, but such events were also bound to happen, for, despite the fact that Aunt Aloula never left the one place in the whole world that was hers, the house she had entered one spring afternoon, never to leave it, after many disappointments, joys, torments, despite the fact that, as a widow, and also in death, finally condemned by years (and this is how it was, since her husband, Uncle Saddek, never having been declared: dead : officially, nobody had been able to deprive her of her rights—she had stayed there, in her home, in the same house, against her relatives' advice, relatives who, after the war and migrations toward the interior, had their eyes on selling, at an excellent price), everyone knew what she had suffered, what she had endured to stay alive, until the first days after the war, not in order to give free rein to her hatred, or craziness, but only to finally understand that certain returns were not to be, that she was going to remain alone forever, and crazy, despite her concerted, and impossible, attempts to change herself into frail rays of light, or simple veils stirred by the winds.

Of all the nights passed, all the days spent by her in this quest, in this incurable waiting, one question alone remained, swirled, travelled in her, like the heart and breath of a tornado, spreading images, ideas, through all the spaces and vicissitudes of her life, startling her last bit of strength, constructing, day after day, the illusion, and the advantage, of some further survival.

The fact is, after all the memories and isolation, this woman expected nothing more from people, for she had gone off into other zones, and places—other than those that make up the concerns, hopes, of the new generations, people down from the mountains to inhabit roomier, less uncertain, places than those they had known. That is why such events were bound to happen, it was not that this woman had arrived, somehow, at the end, the dying out, of her strength, rather that just as all those dear to her had already gone off before her, she had to go off herself, and catch up to them in some realm or other of time, or, of dream.

And the only problem this woman needed to solve was that of the *passage* inherent in this question, a passage she knew very little about, as she devoted almost a year to finding a way to answer the sole, and indelible, question: *"How will I find my children?"*

That is why such events were bound to happen, inexorably according to what people thought in the village, and became, according to what is now revealed, after many years of waiting, hopes, and survival: a threshold, beyond which life, for her, would never again be life.

"How will I find my children?" She had come thus to speak of her *"children"* including, in this plural list, so full of love and blessings, not only her son Ali-Saïd, but, above all, the one she had, so to speak, linked her life to, ever since that moment when, following custom and ritual, he had appeared in the courtyard to take them, her (then only seventeen) and her youth, the youth of a girl of the hills and the fields, down there, off to the village Below, to that house where two of the upper walls were still missing—those that extended the house and yard beyond the stable and courtyard—walls he built by himself, as soon as he knew of the coming of what would turn out to be his only son, a child who, many years later, rose up against his philosophy, or was it his patience, and broke down the barriers that he himself, Uncle Saddek, thought *he* had broken, in his own youth. And what Mokrane did, having understood that the irreparable had happened, and that, according to certain attitudes, a certain smallmindedness, they could (the people of the village and the area) forbid any burial of that woman's body, was to restrict Rachida to the inside of the house, to take off alone, to Oulderman's, to tell him what

had happened, and, most important, to ask for a death certificate—banal, and finally of no real use.

In the end, it seems, after several attempts, she had found the passage, the one which must lead to her dear *"children"*: Rachida, at that moment when the stars seem to swing a bit in the sky, as in the palm of your hand: Rachida had found her, in clean clothes, and happy, hanging from one of the lower branches of The Tree, or The Almond.

It was exactly as if she thought the ground was going to open up, there, all at once, for her, between the very branches of The Tree, and, just as she had imagined ten years earlier, for her son, it, The Tree, or The Almond, would keep her safe from all anguish, all loss. No doubt this is why Rachida, then Mokrane, then Rouïchède, understood this act—which, according to the guidelines accepted by societies, the various justices, the administrations of the era, could only be due to a chronic illness, one favorable to an act of despair and terrible malediction.

A short time later, the house was sold, caught up, like the village, or the thoughts of the village, in accelerated change.

IX

The City extends, with some affectation, over fifteen kilometers, proud, and at the same time narrow, after the countrysides, villages, seasides. It is full of strange whisperings, anecdotes about the political Office Holders, it can be violent, in some places, vain, apt to devour the spaces that still separate it from more modern, aggressive capitals; it acts newly-reconquered, newly-inhabited, dangerous, and, alive—both poor and rich, depending on the neighborhood, the zones, the degree of state administration—it also seems extinguished, and not a place you would frequent after nine in the evening. Not a single spot: You will not find one place, in your travels through the City, that has not borne witness, right there, in the moment, as of several decades, to those upheavals that gave birth to the City, kept up even today by embezzlings, thefts, and politics. You will not find one spot, apartment block, dead-end or street that does not reveal multiple disintegrations, power-losses, crossings-over, miseries, reefs against upward mobility, those utterly recent (and most importantly: limited) promotions. Most of the inhabitants of the City watch this soaring without being part of it, for, according to unofficial but rigorously precise statistics, only three per cent of the inhabitants have the right to make unsparing use of all the riches, job openings, fads and marvels of the City: certain key members of the Party, or the Administration, have heated swimming pools—despite the mildness of the climate that reigns (except for January and February) over the City. The remaining ninety-seven per cent divide up the inhuman and unjustifiable hierarchy of wretchedness that surrounds the City, from the hills right to the center, where a new access to royalty is somewhat curiously represented by a bronze horse, on which a knight, profoundly respected here, strikes a "noble pose."[86]

Considering all the recent history, something stronger would have been better, something more "with it" than this attempt, cast too soon, resembling (if you ignore the clothes) any old knight of the Empire, or from the last century—a European, foreign and highly signifying mixture of unalloyed nationalism with an esthetic revealing poor taste. On Sundays,

---

86   The statue of the Emir Abdelkader, in Algiers (note by Farès)

for those given over to the objects and attitudes of modernity, the return to the City takes place along the seaside corniches, in streams of cars, their lights, by ordinance, always on. Coming home takes place with the languor of day's end in the countryside, and to the whistle of policemen at established corners: now and again, depending on rumors that grip the neighborhoods, regions and politics generally, identity-checks slow your passage, so that, after two or three hours in a car, you are glad to think back on your movements over beach, woods and dunes.

Far from true, however, that these pastimes, or customs, utterly modern rites let's call them, are taken up by all the inhabitants. That fact is that the city-dwellers, these new landlords of human transformation, are the ones enjoying this type of distraction: the villagers, for their part, still distanced from the trickle-down of money, and from gentrification, stick to their ancient passions, their treks, silences, labors, confinements, even though, owing to all this obligatory transmutation, they are subjected to every one of the changes.

This is how Rouïchède, starting as a simple and solitary shepherd from the mountains, crossed over to mechanic's work, mechanisms and drive engines of all types. Now an employee, his new profession consisted of verifying the combustion, carburation, and overall functioning of the cars parked just outside, and in the entry, of the garage—no public garage, this, but a private one. The garage belonged to a family from the area, they had gotten rich abroad—not spectacularly, but methodically—and they had come back here after the war years, to the village of Akbou.

Before working there Rouïchède, on the advice of his father and a few other relatives, had also left for the City, to learn a trade, and to experience all the upheavals. His father's intentions were quite clear: if the country really adopted this new way of life (our thinking "garage" instead of "grocery" was a kind of revolution in ideas and morals), if the country got industrialized, mechanized, we had to think about how, from then on, people would more likely go to cities, instead of the villages of the plains and mountains. That is why he had made the decision that, according to him, he was going to change his life and that of his offspring: all during that time, his thoughts bustled back and forth, just as he did among the counters of his stall, the back of the shop, and the walls of his house.

When Independence came, he had raised a sort of flag over his roof, meant to show his alliance with the new order. But, faced with the general indifference that greeted this cloth fluttering above such a modest grocery store, he had taken the flag down, and, ever since, had constantly mulled the destinies likely to preside over this country's development.

While many things were said, or simply blurted out, during the war years, there, in Si Moh's grocery, he picked up a certain indifference to his post-independence patriotism, like a warning about his business's future, his financial future. So he started studying catalogs, and, through them, the chances of his productivity matching the mood of the times. Old Si Moh, always attuned to what was on the wind, to the spurs of what was sure to be, had still asked for his son's blessing, a request which, in the traditional verities and hidebound ways of that entourage, had been a formality pure and simple: Rouïchède had divined that it was all over for him, no more daily wanderings beyond the villages, on the dusty roads, out toward the hills and the fields.

Very cleverly, but just as hypocritically, his father had given him to understand that, since—according to most people, and recent politics— something fundamental had happened in the country, something fundamental had to take place in him, too, and that he should show, through his existence, his bearing, his work, that he was keeping up with this fundamental change.

There was no chance of Rouïchède continuing with his old ways: the country, the village, the people had changed and no one could gainsay these changes. He had not so much to choose as to *understand*, that the hikes, the walks through the hills, were now for someone else to enjoy. Si Moh well knew that his son would not last long under these rules, and, like his other sons, would ask to leave the village, to learn new things, and grow up.

This happened a year later, after the Death of Aloula, and after Mokrane's departure, one winter evening, in December, 1964.

Rouïchède decided to leave the village, not to live elsewhere the same things he had been living here, rather to understand, close up, or, in a different sense, from farther *off*, what, in fact, was being asked of him, and what he, Rouïchède, really wanted.

The fact is, he wanted nothing, except perhaps to come back, afterwards, towards the places where he had learned so much, from his youngest days. He felt this departure as an abandoning of the world, the true world, the one that you finally get to seize, to identify, through so much patience, love, and curiosity—the one you finally know, the way you know sounds, the murmuring of the trees on those hot days, or in those moments of vast repose.

Whatever he had known that was most intimate, most comforting in all adversities, and in all solitude, had come from this aspect of the village, its hills and fields, through the daily (yet frugal) rapport that he had kept up, day after day, with the shadows, lives, stones, animals, springs, caves and all the surrounding fields.

No one could measure the sediment and its depth, left by the years of hard childhoods, and the war too; the sum of all the murders and disappearances the war had brought us, here, had not changed the awareness, and, we could almost say, the preciousness of this rapport: even the war had disappeared, now only referred to by its traces, its memories, the Young Ali-Saïd's memoir.

For a while Rouïchède thought he would be able to reconstitute phrases, fragments, give some kind of order, and happiness, to the Notebook's pages, but he also understood that the country was not yet ready to read these pages, and, above all, to admit the existence of its language, now spoken here and there—even outside the country—written as well, as much as possible, given the problem of communication and distances. He had shared his discoveries with Rachida, then with Mokrane, while Mokrane lived in the village, the first two years after Independence. He also told Party members about the Notebook, he told the local Administration, too, but those types all instantly let him know that nobody was interested, or rather, from what Rouïchède could gather, this kind of thing upset a lot of people, as if the simple discovery of a Notebook of life, love, laughter, and folktales could threaten a whole way of envisioning history, or life: the New World.

Naively, but painfully, Rouïchède chalked up this neglect, these reactions of the political Authorities, to the general uniformity that was starting to affect the country: its morals, its inhabitants, its desires, its insignificances. The last kid of a family on the path to disappearance and transformation: Rouïchède spent a year minding the grocery, with no feeling for it, nor even interest. His desires remained fastened on the dustings of gold, of wheat, spread from the early hours on, over the hills: the mere thought that, right then, while he was at the store, shadows, or beings, were stalking, up above, through the brush and the grasses, caused him strong, painful emotions. So he used to go out, in the street, and look for a long time toward the sun, as if he hoped to discover some revelation, promise, or face, then he would slowly go back and sit on a chair behind the counter. Gaudy weaves, cloth, spices, tobacco, shoes, seeds, grains, all was accounted for, laid out on long, high shelves: the grains and seeds were stored in enormous, rough sacks, which made the grocery like a warehouse, where people came to load their mules, the way it had always been, for most of Si Mouhand's life. But now, the villages Above no longer existed in the same way, men did their errands at a faster pace, and with less care: they came through the village, asked for their goods, paid, went off again, saying nothing, telling no tales. Nobody hung around in the streets, except for the denizens of the main square, who, not necessarily paying for anything, lingered at tables, prisoners of their silence, or their despair. The village was evolving, but towards what, and what place? Nobody knew, except those who, from the beginning, had set themselves to making money. The differences between families grew sharper, gravitated toward their truths, in concentration or absence of wealth or of power. Their outward signs tended, as well, toward clothes, toward ways of going shopping, toward the use—less and less spectacular—of cars, and buses. The dreams, emotions, solitudes that arose from dwelling, like that, in a shop, condemned by the years, persuaded Rouïchède to leave the place as fast as he could, and, even though any act of confiding is not taken as a mark of esteem in this part of the country, or a sign of real understanding, he did not hesitate to express his desire: "I think now it is time to leave the village, learn a trade. Or else—" (and he said this less to formulate a real wish than to clarify how this kind of life could never again be his, situated as he already was at the intersection of worlds, and of various enslavements)—"or else: I go back, up to the mountains, to Khali's." If the term *Khali*, in its colloquial use, means the Maternal

Uncle, as distinct from Paternal Uncle (that is, *Ammi*), Rouïchède did not use the term because he was motivated by a real intention of visiting his Maternal Uncle, but instead through the flavor, the sense of intimacy, in the relations Rouïchède still kept up with the village's outer self, or the surrounding mountains. The father understood perfectly what his son was getting at, but let his own thoughts bump against the narrowness, the whole reality of the store, after they too had wandered toward the hills, and the fields. "Yes," he said, "this village will be just a pile of scrap, if no one takes charge, a pile of scrap." Clearly, these words were not uttered as an insult to the village, to inhabitants perfectly willing to swap their souls for nothing, for metallic coachwork, rather he meant them as the signal of a real development, if a certain number of measures were not grasped, taken right away. In his mental space, a kind of calculator for him at the moment, or predictor, these measures needed to be grasped by his own family: Rouïchède, in the event, twenty-two years old, close to expiring from displeasure all day, but living—like a robber of mountains, of moons—by night. It was as if, despite the irreversibility of all the changes, he wanted to preserve a bit of the distant foundation: most of the families who had lived in the Villages Above had moved out, over the last sixty years, toward the Villages Below, or else, under threat of death, of slaughter, they had attempted some kind of survival—and one of the reasons the Villages Above experienced new and profound migrations was that once Peace and Independence returned, the families wanted to forget the young dead, those of the most recent years, and to learn, this way, a way of living, far from memories, painful reminiscences, and the origins of their past, and their story. It was as if, beyond his own pleasure at being once again close to the earth, in his nearest, simplest desires, or the ones that were most aware, he wanted to find all over again what constituted the true limitations of his powers, his reflections. Starting with the end of day, knowing perfectly all those places his steps set out for, he took the path toward the hills, and, the fields.

X

On the other side of the village:
Darkness
Night:
Immense lands, crossed with Shadows, Flashes,
Quickly shifting
Like the
Back
Of a
Lamb.

Here and there, on the paths, the fields, grass bursts forth, like newborn insects with supple, fragile bodies. The paths, like great, bared veins, shining white, trace different accesses to the villages, the hills, the huge drops into the Valley, the lights, roads, Cities.

Rouïchède, in this way, spends most of his night coming and going around these Shadows, Bushes, feverish from having rediscovered space, and wind. His treks and runs lead him to the outskirts of the Village Above, near the living quarters that formerly made up the real village.

Once arrived there, he looks around: now barriers lie there, between him and the inhabitants, whose shapes, and silences, he begins to make out. Invisible, yet uncrossable, barriers: Rouïchède looks: all their efforts are fervent, focused untiringly on falcons and places stained with hare's blood.

Rouïchède looks: attentive, as much to his relations with the living as to the landscapes reserved for those borne off by death or by the disappearance of former times.

Rouïchède looks: motionless, as if he had wanted to distance the spirits that his presence might stir up, there in the intersections, the equivalences, that enliven and unite villages with their immemorial founding place.

Stars, moons, moving according to the displacements and articulations of various forces. A mimetic force, or, the poignant reciprocity of Things and the Universe: at the same instant, children, twelve, maybe fourteen years old, transformed one of their group: his name covers vast territories, where every political, or administrative, or religious being is marked with an isolating sign: one of the children wears a maroon *djellaba*, enveloping his body, right to his ankles, wrists, neck: his feet and hands are wrapped in maroon, or is it black, cloth, attached with little cords at the calves and forearms. The hood of the *djellaba* has been cut to let his ears show— pointed, alert, organs straining toward words, mystifications, Political Representatives, or perhaps Religion. With his usual hypocrisy—this is what we call the perspicacity of this speaking animal, yelping against anything that threatens his nature as a forgotten individualist, (in the villages you will never see any of those people we call adults representing the jackal; very much the opposite, here each adult is the guarantor of usages, of the permanence of the existing order; it is only the kids, the kids alone, who can represent that being, for they themselves, at that age, are not yet guarantors of the existing powers)—, the Jackal says:

"So, Father Village, how are we going to live now?"

Father Village questions the night, pointing out, with hardly a word, the streets, names, family origins. Father Village does not really answer, and the Jackal asks a second time:

"So, Father Village, how are we to live, now?"

Father Village points to the boy, who mimes, and thus sketches, the village:

"So, Father Village, are you trying to fool us?"

Father Village does not answer, but raises his arm toward the Jackal, who, abruptly, jumps to one side, getting to the left of the boy who is laying out the true village. Father Village does not answer, but looks, all around, observes, listens to this night where animals, and stones, animals and plants, animals and men communicate their struggles, their languages, their lives. Father Village listens, and takes in the soft, warm breathing of the night, as if this listening to the night were the auscultation of his own breathing, as if listening to the night were the confirmation, the unshakeable evidence of his persistence, his life, there, at the edge of an abyss, at the edge of vast changes. Father Village is strangely dressed, in a way that contrasts with the solemnity, the importance, of his role: he wears a cloak, unsewn in places, torn, letting his exquisitely thin body show through, where his limbs, and bones, in an absurd and unexpected way, look like branches, ramifications of trees, limbs not fully grown.

Father Village waves, or just shifts, his arms, and, at the same time, the torn or unraveled cloth moves, with the lightness, the shivering, of leaves caught by a sudden puff of wind.

The village, and its people?

Father Village listens to the warm, soft breathing of the night, thronging with the lively, thrilling scrapings of cicadas, and crickets.

THE EXILES

XI

The oldest of us say that, infallibly, the questions arises in the depths of Exile, at the limits of the Field, because the Sons of the land, or the underground rivers of the Field, continue their unfolding among the wanderings, nights, lightning passages and landscapes of memory. This is how the landscape can change, the territory expand, while the Field, not the one we can see, but the Other, within, without any regulation of property, the one which lets us see the layers and stratifications of the earth, whose time elapses with that of the Field, which causes appearances and competence to cave in, which:

Mokrane hesitates for a moment, then gets up, and, after spinning the cold water faucet, plunges his head in the basin.

Nothing to be done: dream, or the impossible denouement, has reclaimed its rights, after a few detours: fatality does not exist, only intense, unbearable solitude.

Rouïchède tries to wash off the grease, the oil, that clings, to his hands and forearms: the Country?

A mild air, tumbling down from the hills, and the paths. A supple, mild air: on the hidden side of the moon there is a strange territory, dotted with innumerable deer. One of them has fallen on her right side, her eyes show immense pain, because, in the fall, her right leg was broken. A kind of cry has filled out into space, and the first glimmers of day have begun their progress over the sea.

The God of Sea-Foam springs up, runs ahead alone, dives, disappears, comes up a second time, trips along the shifting surface of the water, dives, disappears: the God of Sea-Foam, and with him our cry, violent and warm, violent in the depths of space, and time:

> Men
> of the hill
> Below
> do you know
> the river
> inscribed

       like
       a word
       in the
Village
Below
do you know
this river?

Made in the USA
Middletown, DE
15 January 2021